GINA GIORDANO

COLOR OF FIRE

Content warnings for *Color of Fire*:
Contains instances and references of graphic violence, sexual assault, period-typical racism and slavery, and drug use

PBK: ISBN- 979-8-9869834-4-8
EBK: ISBN- 979-8-9869834-5-5

Cover design by Coverkitchen Pte. Ltd.
Author headshot by Nakita Gonzalez
Illustrations by Lindsey Carr
Cartography created by Lark Sloan of Fantasy Cartography

KÄFERHAUS
PRESS

ALSO BY GINA GIORDANO

Strange Eden

The Island King

For Michael
My soul, my director, my conscience…

Lady Eliza Sharpe

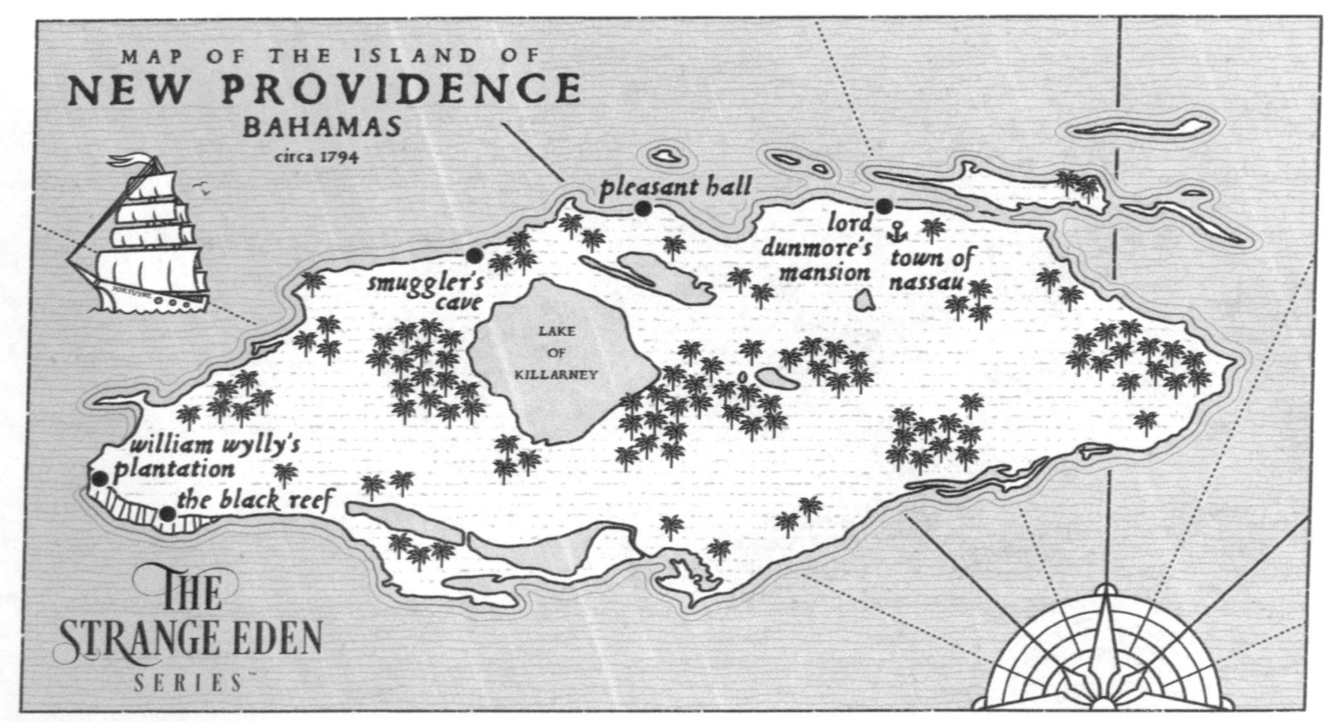

MAP OF THE ISLAND OF
NEW PROVIDENCE
BAHAMAS
circa 1794
pleasant hall
lord dunmore's mansion
town of nassau
smuggler's cave
LAKE OF KILLARNEY
william wylly's plantation
the black reef
THE STRANGE EDEN SERIES

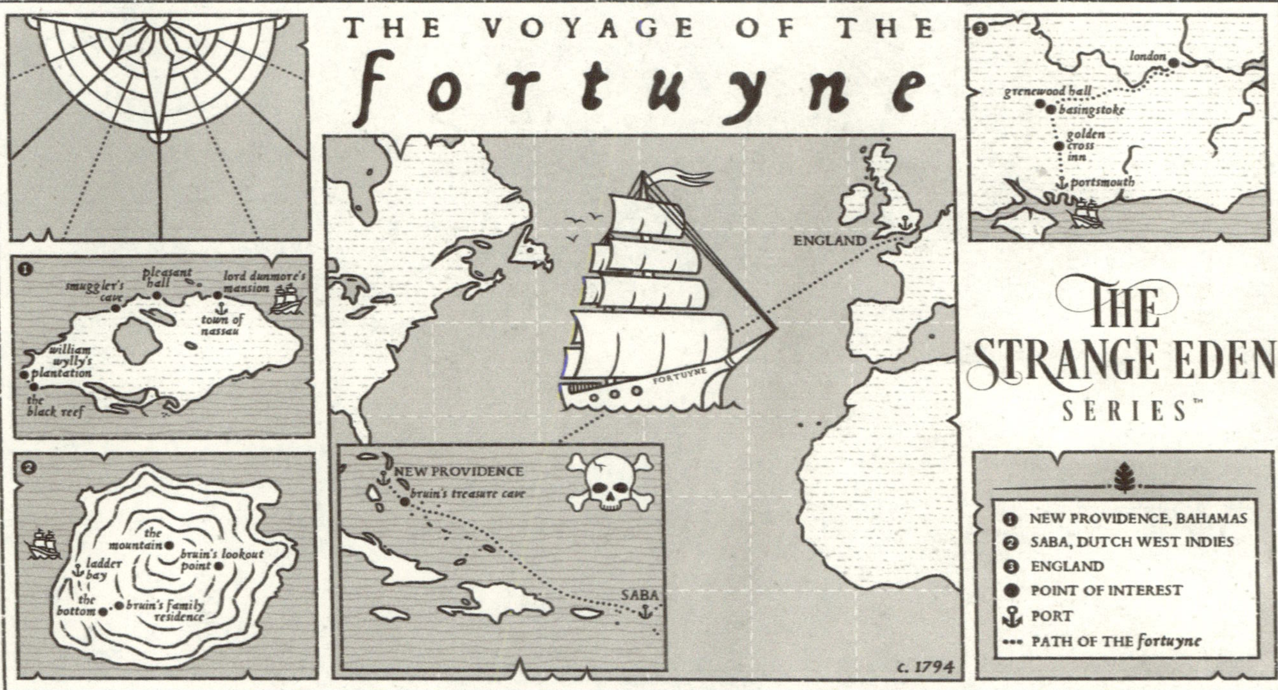

THE VOYAGE OF THE
Fortuyne
THE STRANGE EDEN
SERIES™
ENGLAND
FORTUYNE
london
grenewood hall
basingstoke
golden cross inn
portsmouth
smuggler's cave
pleasant hall
lord dunmore's mansion
town of nassau
william wylly's plantation
the black reef
the mountain
bruin's lookout point
ladder bay
the bottom
bruin's family residence
NEW PROVIDENCE
bruin's treasure cave
SABA
c. 1794
1 NEW PROVIDENCE, BAHAMAS
2 SABA, DUTCH WEST INDIES
3 ENGLAND
POINT OF INTEREST
PORT
PATH OF THE fortuyne

CHAPTER I.

March 16ᵗʰ, 1794—Nassau, Bahamas

" Your husband is dead, Lady Sharpe."

The creditor's voice was flat and toneless. Eliza's hand gripped the porch finial. She focused her gaze on the wavering palm trees that surrounded the front yard. But the rattling green distraction they offered was not enough to stop the turmoil his words had conjured.

It sent her reeling back to that violent afternoon.

Alastor's eyes projected drama; the animal's instincts well understood that disaster had struck. His tail whipped, his chest heaved with the strain of carrying Eliza from danger.

Eliza's eyes burned from crying, and she could feel tears coming anew.

Do not show weakness in front of him. Do not cry. He won't understand.

Perhaps her eyes were so rimmed with red it did not matter. Her appearance was the same; her face so flushed and reddened it was obvious she had just shed more tears before coming out to the porch. The thought of looking strong and unaffected was a pointless venture. Her tolerance of these men and their probing questions had stretched to the thinnest of strings. The chaos that had unfurled that day had not stopped spinning, and she stood a broken woman before a new enemy.

"Lady Sharpe, your husband is dead," the man repeated. He was with another man, presumably for additional support or coercion, but she saw past them to a different afternoon, back to when it had happened. Her narrow escape plagued her mind, burning a hole deep within herself, a wound that only cut deeper because the man who had saved her had not been able to save himself. Charles had given his life to save hers. Flashes of that afternoon played on a cruel loop before her eyes. She had escaped on his horse and left him behind, outnumbered and surrounded.

Massive puddles from unexpected floods made the dark soil murky and had blocked her path on the trail that harrowing day. She had driven the horse around them and the piles of damp, fiery orange petals recently fallen from the Royal Ponciana trees. She raced back to the relative safety of Pleasant Hall with the horse breathing madly, his back hot against her trembling thighs.

"Water, water for the horse!" she had shouted as she half-fell off his back. Julius came running. "Where is my child? Where is he? Show me?" she raged between breaths.

Julius was helpless to her onslaught of commands. Captain Johnson, standing on the porch, had run down to them, so she directed her panic to the captain.

"Go to him! You must stop them! Charles has been taken! They have taken him!"

His eyes were widened with concern.

"Who, Lady Sharpe? Who took him?"

"Pirates, a band of men, I know not who. They attacked the town; they fired on the fort. You must go and help him!" she pleaded, holding on to him with shaking hands.

Captain Johnson took a long, grave look towards the direction she had come from, and the way his face paled only increased her fear.

"Please! Go!" she yelled from her gut, as if it would spur his feet into action.

She took a deep gulp of air and fell onto her knees. The men scrambled to lift her back to a stand, but she resisted them.

"Where is my son …" she muttered in between sobs.

"He safe, Lady Sharpe. Celia watchin' over him now. Just like she suppose to."

Eliza bowed her head down into her skirts, her body wracked with wailing.

"Why won't you go to him? Why do you not move?" she cried.

Captain Johnson crouched down to her level and placed a wide hand on her sweaty back.

"I only one man, Lady Sharpe. I must stay here, protectin' you."

"I am safe!" she screeched. Her dark eyes searched his. "I do not need protection!"

"Lady Sharpe, I think they makin' their way here next. If Dunmore has his hands in any of this, you best believe they ain't done yet. They be comin' here next. I have to stay and protect you and the boy."

A group of slaves had gathered around her now, watching her unravel with mute expressions. All eyes were on her, and they waited for her direction.

"Arm the slaves; arm them. And set up a lookup on the road. Send two boys down the beach to watch from there," Eliza said, talking faster than they could comprehend.

Captain Johnson looked at her incredulously.

"Arm the slaves? Slaves ain't allowed to handle firearms. For good reason, too. Lady Sharpe, I don't think Colonel Sharpe would be wantin' that. Maybe you can—"

"Arm them," she replied through gritted teeth. "Josiah, Brutus, the ones who are strong and will take direction. Give them weapons and orders to defend this house."

Captain Johnson seemed to hover between trying to console her and thinking of what to say to the small crowd that had gathered.

"Maybe it best to discuss this inside, Lady Sharpe; maybe you can …"

Eliza stood up now, but her balance wavered like the tears streaming down her cheeks. Julius and Captain Johnson followed her, ready to catch her if she stumbled.

"He saved me. They captured him because of me. I should be dead. And now he is gone …" She cried so hard she began to heave, choking on her tears. "He cannot be dead. He is not. He isn't dead." She had spoken it as a mantra, repeating it endlessly.

Eliza repeated the same now, only in the present.

It did not impress the official in front of her today. He sighed, clearly irritated, and handed her a letter.

She took it slowly and opened it with trembling hands.

"This is … a petition to have Charles declared legally dead?" Her voice cracked.

The man stood erect and bounced on his heels, eager to conclude their discussion.

"It is a matter of the property involved here, Lady Sharpe. My men have visited you several times in the past week …"

A series of men paraded before her tortured memory.

The first time she had received a visitor, Eliza had not sensed danger. She had opened the door and stepped out into the heavy heat, desperate for news. She trusted his navy jacket and gleaming brass buttons. The boys posted on the beach had not signaled any warning.

"Have you news of my husband?" she had foolishly inquired.

The young clerk had looked confused at first, but his face hardened at once. "Surely, you have been informed, Lady Sharpe. That is not my task here today."

"Informed? Of what?"

"He is dead, ma'am." The man had immediately tightened his face, as if this alone could ward off any feminine hysterics. But he was met with defiance.

"He is not dead. You have no proof!" Eliza insisted. "There is no body!" The words sounded ugly on her tongue. She hated them. They did have the effect of stalling his response, though, so she continued.

"He was captured, and must be found!" She spoke to the young man as if he alone was in charge of this daunting task.

"Lady Sharpe, the colony under the governor's orders

has declared Charles Sharpe dead. There will be no searches."

"You lie," she said, her voice full of venom.

"However," he continued, "I am an agent employed by Barret & Company. Lord Sharpe had a number of loans with us, and we must unfortunately call them in. I understand that you are unschooled in these matters, as you are a woman. We can provide estimates of what you have on the property."

He was no clerk sent by government officials. He was a creditor from a banking firm that extended capital to plantation owners. The man made an inquiring look at Lucy, who was sweeping the porch behind Eliza. Eliza looked at her with confusion, then she paled with disgust. This man was here inquiring about Charles' property, but his greedy eyes did not focus on the stately white house. They locked on the moving, toiling bodies of his slaves.

"We can make due with what's available. We'll make sure to follow his will and leave you what is allotted, but we must take what we are owed first. Surely, you understand." His words were laced with false cordiality.

"He is not dead," Eliza said stiffly. "He has not been legally declared dead."

Now his face had turned red. He was losing his patience.

"Are you in want of hearing? I understand you are very upset, but I will send my man tomorrow to assist you."

"If you send anyone here tomorrow, they will not leave," she threatened.

But her threat had been empty. More creditors continued to come, some from different companies, harassing her when her nerves were already frayed.

"I am sorry it is so close to your husband's death, but his affairs must be put into order. He was killed by cannon fire …"

"He was shot …"

"He was taken by pirates and presumed dead, along with many others. Have you seen the town? It is lawlessness. They took my goods, even from our offices! Nassau is ablaze!" This man's theatrics fell flat for her. She scanned the horizon, looking for any telltale sign of smoke or malevolent fire.

"Get off my land," she hissed, crossing her arms.

"But that is the very thing, my dear; it is your land no longer. It once belonged to your husband, and now it belongs to his creditors."

Then came an unwanted visit from Mr. Rivett, the pompous owner of a store on Bay Street that she had last encountered during the political meeting.

"Creditors? My, that is a serious problem, Lady Sharpe. You must be desperate indeed," he had said with a leer as he leaned towards her. "I advise you to let them take what they want. Men are more schooled in these matters. I can help. I would be willing to buy back many goods. You have a lovely rosewood cabinet somewhere in there I believe, purchased in '87. As long as the furniture is in proper condition, of course …"

"Lady Sharpe? Lady Sharpe!"

The present agent's voice was demanding, interrupting her wild flurry of thoughts.

She looked back down at the paper. *Missing or Presumed*

Dead … This was wrong. This was all terribly wrong. She knew from discussions with her father that courts were not generally in a hurry to have gentlemen declared dead. She recalled one case of a man who had returned to his home fourteen years after he was declared missing. The courts in England had refused to declare him legally deceased, and he had resumed his former life without losing his property.

What was behind the impetus to have Charles declared dead so fast? What necessitated this mad legal dash? She knew the answer lay in the pudgy hands of Lord Dunmore, the island's governor. That man's wicked ways knew no end. Eliza once foolishly thought her terrors couldn't grow any worse after that disastrous afternoon. Now she understood they had only just begun. She was caught in the center of a web of deceit and bloodshed, tangled in the lies of conniving men.

"Dead people can return …" Eliza mumbled aloud, reading the offensive paper.

"Beg pardon, Lady Sharpe?"

"Dead people can return. The courts never initiate anything this fast. It is common knowledge!"

"That dead people can return? They are dead, my dear. Do you hear yourself?"

"He is not dead," she repeated, an endless loop. It circled over and over in her mind and was as easy to utter as breathing. The difficulty was in convincing others of the same. Especially when they had cause to disregard the truth.

"The Lieutenant Colonel has defaulted on loans totaling over £7,000. You are his next of kin, and the law may interpret you as his guarantor. Your husband has absconded and either has no intention of repaying his creditors or cannot possibly do so. You may face arrest, Lady Sharpe. You could be sent to debtor's jail."

"You are highly misinformed, sir," she said stiffly. "No wrong has been committed here."

"A debtor has not broken any laws; they simply have debts that they cannot pay. You will be in a terrible way if you find yourself in prison for it. Once there, your debts will only increase. You can request for us, as the creditors, to release you, but we do not have to comply. I beg you to not force us to try that route."

The fool who had joined him smiled a disingenuous smile. Eliza looked off to the side, tears of frustration welling in her eyes. The first man then tried a softer approach.

"Lady Sharpe, I myself have bills that are due, and this matter is more pressing than the whereabouts of your husband, fallen as he may be. That is the price of war," he said in a more gentle voice. "His affairs are much disordered. I advise you to secure the services of a barrister to sell all the goods and furniture, as well as any books or jewelry in the house." He readjusted his stance, peering behind her shoulder, attempting to look inside the open front door. "Or we can purchase it from you now. Perhaps the quickest way to settle this and your position in society is to sell these slaves."

Her face turned ashen. The way this man brought up one of her fears so blithely unsettled her.

He continued. "I believe you have abolitionist tendencies. Let me take them off your hands, then you may need never consider them again. You must pay what is owed. We, of course, will make a consideration to set aside a small sum so you can purchase the necessary mourning rings and perhaps a widow's dress."

The only response she could manage was, "My husband is not dead; I do not need to don black."

"Please, Lady Sharpe. We understand that grief wracks the mind in a terrible way and that women are weak in times like this," the second man added unhelpfully. "It is only natural."

"You know nothing of my grief …" she growled. "You waste your time."

"We have read his will and are only following through with the clearest legal methods."

The will. That was the one document that had eluded her thus far. After the first creditor had called, she had torn through Charles' papers in his study but uncovered nothing to serve in her defense. No will, no proof that these debts even existed, and yet, at the same time, she had nothing to disprove these men.

"I admit I have not been able to find a will amongst his papers. And no inventory has yet been made."

"We can easily take care of that, Lady Sharpe."

"But that matters not since he is alive! And I doubt he would allow for no annuity to be made for his wife and child." She was exasperated and was quickly losing patience.

"We have a copy in our offices, and we assure you he made no such allowances. Your marriage was fairly recent, was it not? This happens more often than you may realize.

Either way, the sums of his debt are greater and must needs be paid first."

Eliza said nothing in response to his last words. She knew they were lying to her. If they truly possessed a copy of Charles' actual will, and not some forged deception, she would be entitled to review it. These men could have brought it with them in hand, proving their dubious claims. The first man lost his patience and stamped his foot on the porch step above him.

"We are here to take immediate possession of the remainder of the Negroes to satisfy the Lieutenant Colonel's debt."

"His affairs are in order. They are—"

"No, woman, your husband's debts were most certainly not in order!" the man snapped.

Eliza glared at him. "What is your name? Who are you to speak to me in such a manner?"

"My name does not concern you. I work for Lord Dun—Barret & Company."

"Ah, you speak the truth even as you lie through your teeth," she said, stepping down to be closer to the corrupt man. "I will play your deceitful game. I am a widow of a soldier who died in defense of this colony. I will be awarded a certificate for a pension. And your petition to declare this *soldier* dead has no standing!"

They treated her like a foolish girl. They couldn't even afford her the respect of a woman. She refused to tolerate this treatment a second longer.

"You will receive no such pension as a widow. Your husband was a rebel, and you are therefore not entitled to that honor. He has sullied the name of His Majesty's Royal Army."

Eliza's boldness deflated when she realized the depths of their dishonor. She was forced to not only accept the cruel reality of her husband's capture but also the malevolence of these corrupt men who sought to taint his character even further. Even in this false death, this realm of unknowing and in-between, greed drove them to seize what was not theirs to take.

Eliza knew better. Charles was incapable of betraying his country. But she did know of one man who lacked the moral fortitude to withstand temptations, and he, unfortunately, sat in the most powerful seat in this colony. In her heart, she cursed the name of John Murray, 4th Earl of Dunmore.

"If you truly believe my husband guilty of these offenses, as his wife, I ask whether it is fair to punish his only child," she quipped.

"Children are often the misfortunes of war, Lady Sharpe."

"You know nothing of the costs of war. Men like you create it without nary a second thought."

He sneered at her. "I am no simple soldier. You confuse me for your husband."

"I could never be confused. My husband was a good man, unlike you."

"There is the issue of him breaking the law in several instances. Need I remind you of his recent attempts to incite insurrection on this island? He was an outlaw."

She was shaking her head with refusal, and this only

aggravated him further.

"If you do as you're told, there may be a consideration to set you up for some maintenance for the rest of your years … or else you will be forced to declare bankruptcy. The only home you will know is a debtor's prison, and your child will have no parents. You have been living in a style of profusion far beyond your fortune and, to the detriment of your child, spending money belonging to another!"

"Get off of my property, *now*," she seethed.

"Mr. Jones, start seizing the assets," the first man ordered.

The second man alighted the steps and marched straight up to Lucy and pulled her by the arm. As his associate did that, the agent started to make his way inside the house.

"I cannot admit you inside. I do not have my husband's permission," Eliza said, as she blocked the doorway with her body.

"He is deceased; no permission is necessary," he said, trying to push past her.

Eliza turned and saw Lucy screaming.

"This slave is in the process of manumission; take your hands off her!"

"Manumission? You mean the recent manumission deed that was found to be forged?" the first man answered swiftly.

"Forged? It was not, I assure you—" she began.

"Then there is the issue of failure to deliver the final papers to the court …"

It was the very reason Charles and she had even

ventured into town that accursed afternoon. It was freedom announced but not delivered, and their grueling task in manumitting all the slaves was far from over. It was cruel that the one who had come closest to freedom was the first to be seized.

"Charles was captured!" she spat.

The second man continued to drag poor Lucy down the stairs. Eliza knew she had no other recourse. She whistled, and Captain Johnson and a handful of other slaves walked out from their cover in the bushes surrounding the house.

The two men wheeled around in horror. Eliza quickly regained the porch as the first man stepped away from her. They raised their pale hands in half-submission.

"He is not present on this island, Lady Sharpe, and, therefore, no manumission has occurred." Now the man's voice sounded less confident as he stared down the barrel of the musket closest to him.

"You probably helped orchestrate it," she said coldly.

The man gasped. "You would accuse *me* of such a capital evil?"

Eliza did not answer and stood, firm and tall, as the armed slaves encircled the two men more closely. Eliza motioned for Lucy to rejoin her on the top of the steps.

"She is my property," Eliza said, the words distasteful on her tongue. She had to speak a language these greedy men would understand. They did not care for the manumission that had been started. She would need to be more forceful.

The men's fear gave way to arrogance.

"You are arming your slaves now? What is this

madness?"

"He is a captain in His Majesty's army," she said, pointing to Captain Johnson, who stood as the leader of the men.

"Ah, is this the nefarious missing captain, the Black Guard?"

The way he spoke made Eliza nervous. She was playing more than one dangerous game. In all of the turmoil, she had nearly forgotten that Captain Johnson would likewise be deemed an enemy of the governor for helping save Charles from a near assassination. She would have to be careful with their new arrangement. He would need to stay well hidden, more so than the others.

"You can't be left alone with them! You are a woman!" the man said, clearly incredulous at the sight before him. She knew what men like them thought of enslaved men, and it only enraged her further. His shallow attempt of feigning any sympathy for Eliza's plight was poorly received.

"I am safer in their company than I ever would be in yours."

"You insult me and my character, woman. Lord Dunmore was right. You are nothing but a —"

The situation had escalated far out of control, and Eliza was tired of pretending to behave. She would be no pawn in their mercenary ruse.

"I listened to you prattle on for long enough. Leave now, or I will have them blow your heads off," she declared, her anger emboldening her.

Captain Johnson adjusted his aim squarely on the first

man's head for emphasis.

The men understood this threat at once. The sight of a slave holding a musket was a living nightmare to them. They slowly backed down the steps and out of the yard and mounted their horses. But in the true nature of foolish men, the first man had to have the last word.

"You are breaking the law, Lady Sharpe! You are forbidden to leave this house until these matters are settled. We will return, and we will be armed! I warn you now!" He spit with disgust into the dusty, bone-colored ground.

They furiously kicked their horses into a reckless gallop. Eliza clutched the railing of the porch stairs, her heart hammering wildly.

"I ain't never takin' this off," Captain Johnson said, his voice flustered. He was talking about the red uniform he wore so proudly. The captain acted as if the red color alone was a surety of his freedom. But he had a second, more important one. He cursed, furiously checked his pocket for his own manumission paper, now creased with age, and returned it to a safe pocket.

"We must be ready for when they return," Eliza said breathlessly.

CHAPTER II.

The bell in the front yard rang, a welcome signal. The boys she had posted out on the beach had strict orders to blow a conch shell if they spotted any unwelcome trespassers. So far two days had passed, and the creditors had not yet returned. They would come again, this time with the reinforcements they had threatened, but the metallic clarity of the bell assured her of some newly sprung hope. Eliza had recently sent a letter to Mr. Wylly and knew her answer had arrived.

"I am gladdened to see you," she said, managing a smile.

The men in the yard nodded, holding their hats to their chests. But she did not see the one person she had hoped to encounter.

"I bear unfortunate news, Lady Sharpe," a ruddy-faced man said.

She steeled herself; she did not know how much more ill fortune she could manage. Cicadas sang their shrill song high in the treetops, increasing her anxiety by the second.

"Mr. Wylly is abroad. He went to London. I do know

he plans on sending a report by the next packet boat, but he is unable to help you at this time," he said in a conciliatory tone.

Eliza's heart sank. She had been elated when she thought of asking for help from a political ally who was also a skilled attorney. The plan had seemed perfect up until now, when reality destroyed her newfound hopes.

"I see," Eliza said quietly, trying to mask her disappointment.

Still, this group of men, Charles' political allies, had visited her. Surely one of them could offer aid.

"We must organize a meeting. We can write a petition to the Council of Trade and Plantations to consider what the government should do about the affairs on this island. We can petition the king again! We have now been attacked and plundered by pirates, and what has Lord Dunmore done for us? This colony has suffered severe losses by their hands, and more to come. We must restore order!" Her voice was bright, echoing across the yard.

The men retained their sullen demeanors.

"We are now at his mercy, Lady Sharpe," an elderly man said.

"To our utter ruin," a disgruntled man uttered. His northern accent was heavy. "I thought there was a wee chance. Bless Lord Sharpe, aye, bless your husband's memory, Lady Sharpe. He was a braw man."

She ignored that last comment and continued with her speech. She had to make them see what they could do; she had to inspire them with her words. Surely a woman speaking in such a manner would spur them on to action if nothing else. When else had they been addressed so by someone of the fairer sex?

"Think of your trade! The king must be reminded of the importance of the commerce Nassau offers!" she continued, her passion getting the better of her.

At first, she was met by an awkward silence, then by contempt. A man sneered. She recognized immediately that he was the same gentleman who had sprawled himself in one of their chairs a few months ago and nearly cracked it. "I do not take kindly to a lecture by a woman, Lady Sharpe. With all due respect, I handle my affairs to the best of my ability."

The men were taking what she said personally. As if her utterance of their inability to act was only true when spoken across the sticky air.

"But something *is* overshadowing it. Why does Lord Dunmore spend such ludicrous amounts of money to build forts if he allows pirates to come and loot at will? Someone must stop him!"

"Maybe *you* can, Lady Sharpe. I do wonder where you studied law and economy," the man rudely retorted. A few of the other men snickered. Her optimism deflated like a sheet fallen from the laundry line.

"Lady Sharpe, this is a lawless and dangerous island. You must be careful," the elderly man said, coming forward to touch her shoulder.

"It doesn't have to be. Especially when men like you say something. Will you truly do nothing?" she asked, unable to stop the horror from leaking into her voice.

The ruddy-faced man shook his head. "The fear of

being murdered is a strong enough caution. Watch your-self, Lady Sharpe. I can send some of my slaves to help guard you."

She shook her head. "I have protection enough, thank you." She did not seek manpower; she sought legal might. Only these men could help her. She, as a woman, had no voice.

"Do you not want this colony to succeed? The gover-nor is a plague to these islands. This government is most irregular and illegal in its administration. Did you not sit there with my husband nigh three months ago and discuss your plans to have the governor recalled?"

"That was different. That was before Charles was killed," a timid-faced man spoke up.

"He is not dead, gentlemen. He lives," she said, urging them to believe it with the inflection of her voice.

The group of men was not convinced.

"He was our leader, and he is gone. And now Wylly has left," someone added.

"For shame!" she retorted. "How easily you abandon your cause in its hour of most desperate need! The king will take our misfortune into consideration. We are not abandoned yet, we need only ask …"

"Should we scream for it? They are deaf to our entreat-ies. We have tried that, time and again, Lady Sharpe."

"Scream louder. They *will* make some allowance for our losses."

"No one is coming to save this island, Lady Sharpe. I think it best to cut short your losses. I would take the next boat to England," the ruddy-faced man said with sadness in his voice.

"I cannot do that. There is unfinished business to attend to here that requires my presence."

As she said that, she looked at a slave raking browned palm leaves from the ground. The man speaking to her immediately inferred where her concerns lay.

"Lady Sharpe, now listen here. I think I know of what business you speak, but no good will come from it. Lord Sharpe had a fanciful idea, nothing more. It can't be brought to fruition. You are at risk for your life here! Think of your child!"

"That is business between my husband and me," she snapped.

"Yes, yes, of course, Lady Sharpe, I did not mean to intrude." The man took a step back, surprised by her sudden ferocity on the subject. He turned behind him. "Here! We gathered a small gift to show our condolences for the late Lord Sharpe. We wanted to bring you our goodwill and prayers, Lady Sharpe. We had a brotherhood with your late husband, and we shan't soon forget it."

A younger man, whom she assumed was one of his sons, came from the back, and a basket of pineapples and fruit was passed to the front of the group. She accepted it reluctantly.

"Your goodwill … and prayers?" she repeated slowly, gazing down at the freshly picked produce. "You expect this to help me?"

A burst of rage overtook her, and she threw the fruit down to the ground.

"Leave!" She cried and picked up her skirts, storming

back to the sanctuary of her porch.

She heard their judgmental tones behind her and could almost see them shaking their heads. One man muttered something about how women were ruled only by their emotions. She did not care. They could help. They *should* help. It was for their livelihood as well as hers. But they were cowards. She stopped, clenching her fists.

"Cowards! You are worthless cowards all! Don't you dare return to Pleasant Hall! I will not receive you," she shouted from the steps of the porch.

She heard someone running after her, despite the fact that the group had now dispersed.

"Lady Sharpe, Lady Sharpe!" a voice called.

She turned, hastily wiping away a tear from her eye. It was the young man who had stood at the back of the group. "What is it?" she asked.

"My name is Thomas Cullen. My family owns the apothecary on the east end of Bay Street. I know we have never spoke, but I can help you." He steeled himself as he said his next words. "You need a husband, Lady Sharpe. I know I am younger than you, but I am still a man."

Eliza's eyes nearly popped from her face.

"A husband?" she repeated, dumbfounded.

"Aye, a husband. I am capable, and strong in my wits …"

She wanted to cut him down with her words, but he was so young, so seemingly innocent. There weren't many women who chose to live on this island; the number of men was always greater, and a wife was hard to come by.

There was almost something endearing about his

proposal. The poor fool had no idea who he was talking to.

"Go back home and never speak of this again," she said, her tone grave.

Her words seemed to frighten him. His face paled, and he turned and ran, returning to the other men before anyone noticed his fatal blunder.

Eliza needed to stop what had been set in motion, but she didn't know how. She rushed inside towards the stairs, stopping to look at the grandfather clock in her desperation. She could sell it and gather some money to pay the creditors. Maybe they would pause their relentless visits until another solution appeared.

As if in response to her thoughts, the clock gonged for the hour. No, she could not. This had been with the Sharpe family for decades. She couldn't sell it just to appease men who could not be satisfied. And she knew in her bones that Charles was still alive.

Her weary steps took her past her bedroom and to Charles' room. Now when she passed by his empty chamber, it struck her chest, a kind of twisting heaviness. She pictured him lying there recovering from the first attempt on his life, and her eyes welled up. She cursed herself that she was ever once excited for his absence. That time had passed by long ago. Now she mourned him.

His chamber seemed so small now, as if he had never really occupied it. She had come here often and looked for something, some clue that would reveal more of what had happened. But like her search in the study, she found nothing that could explain what had occurred.

She went to the drawer and pulled out a shirt he

had worn, the one she had told Lucy to not wash. Eliza squeezed it to her face, inhaling the scent of him, the sole connection she still had to him. But this time it did not console her. It only made her feel worse; it reopened the giant hole that gnawed at her insides when she was alone. She lost herself in sobs, swallowed by guilt and irrational thoughts.

She could have hidden better when he ordered her to flee; she shouldn't have accompanied him that day; he was gone because of her. These small details played on a limitless loop, driving her to madness. She despaired of when deliverance would come, and for the preservation of her family, and of herself.

"I love you, Eliza. Please, let me show you."

He stepped back from her, slowly taking her forearm and studying her injured hand.

"You are my soul, my director, my conscience," he said, his eyes connecting with hers.

He pressed his lips against the pale inner skin of her arm, kissing her slowly until he reached the soot-covered fabric near her elbow.

She would give anything to wake up next to him again. To open her eyes in a light-filled room, his warm hand entwined with hers. He had been her guiding star, and his absence left her drowning in darkness and a despair unlike anything she had yet encountered. To have her husband by her side, to hear his voice, and in another instant know he was gone, taken away from her without warning, made the weight of each waking day heavier than the last. She carried him like a stone in her chest and untangled his name from her endless worries. Eliza could discern the shape of his absence in every room, the way the echoes against the walls magnified her grief, how the new silence of the house constricted every humid breath of air she inhaled.

How stupid she had been to celebrate the lack of his presence before. Now it was all she wanted.

Time was no longer measured in minutes but with the rise and fall of the tides and the weight of each heavy sunset. Now when the sun dipped below the line of blue horizon, she feared what the next day would bring. Eliza's company was an empty bed, a dust-filled study, with one less voice to maintain order, to protect, to lead, to father her child. She missed Charles' form, the way he had to stoop and duck under certain doorways, the march of his boots against the hard floor.

Each of her senses felt his loss keenly; habit had made his tall, imposing figure necessary to her, and tragedy had torn it all away. Their short time together, once seemingly unbearable, frayed away, the power of time threatening to diminish it all. To wash its hard-won meaning and significance like scattered sand underneath a wave.

When Eliza looked in the mirror now, she did not recognize the hollowness of her collarbones, the red-rimmed eyes that stared back at her, or the indomitable tightness of her jaw. Tension ruled her body, and even the warm waves could not dissolve the pressure that pressed her from every angle. She took slow, deliberate steps, crossing the churning, powdery white tidal line in an effort to release herself with the suction and pull of the water. But there was no true relief to be found. The acrid smoke of decaying brush Josiah burned, the mindless motions of scattered chickens, the idle palms swaying—it all passed over her like a darkening cloud shifting closer to land, threatening rain but only casting the land into darkness.

Eliza's sky would never break. She would never feel the cool rush of descending raindrops bouncing off her skin. She was suspended, driven to act but powerless at the same time.

She feared grief would win, that it would smother her from ever feeling hope again. She didn't want to know a world without Charles, understanding this now even as past thoughts resurfaced of when she would pray for deliverance from him. Those old feelings sickened her. She had found love where it wasn't supposed to be, laying right in front of her, a possibility she had actively shunned. And when their signals no longer crossed, when the progress of sense had finally won against all odds, life threatened her with the chilling idea that good things could not last, would not last, in a cruel world that moved faster than a bullet shot from a gun.

What had driven her to the cliff's edge last summer waited for her, but she refused to let those demons in again. On some nights, she would open a bottle of wine for herself, then push it away in disgust, letting the lazy black flies swoon over the red pool in her glass.

And on the days when she faded into a haze of despair, Philippe was there, reminding her to go on. The one reason to press forward, to keep moving, to not lose herself in drink again. The boy was nearly one year old now, and he could walk with her guiding hand. He made sport of finding abandoned snail shells, collecting the hollow brown swirls as if they were coins, waddling back to Eliza to show her his treasure. Lucy would take them and toss them when he was put to bed, so the thrill of discovery could begin anew the next day. In the afternoons, Eliza would hold him, murmuring to him as he stared outward at the flat expanse of glowing blue as if he could absorb the possibility the horizon offered, the water signaling something to the child that had long grown dim in his mother's eyes.

She feared heaven had taken the boy's newfound father from him, the only source of hope she had managed to find after Jean's untimely death. But she bravely fought on for him—for the boy's missing father, her fated husband, and for things to come. For Philippe's sake alone, Eliza imitated what she believed Charles would do in her stead and, like a good soldier, keep marching on.

But her enemy was the greed and corruption of men. It weighed against Eliza, and she feared the condition of her soul was eroding. The brilliant purple princess flowers Lucy had gathered and set on the table did not attract her notice, and soon they too wilted and grew overwhelmed with a steady trail of ants, an infinitesimal army that swept from the vase down to the floor. She saw the beauty of the island less and less. It was merely a haunted spit of sand and limestone floating in the vast sea.

Who was a friend and who was a foe? Were there any men on this island left to be trusted? Since the time of Charles' capture two weeks ago, Eliza was met with apathy and indifference from the men in this colony and a painful silence from those in England who continued to turn a blind eye to Lord Dunmore's corruption. She felt increasingly isolated; it was maddening, oppressive like the heat of the midday sun. The faces of the various creditors and the group of men she had just told to leave moved through her thoughts in a troubling procession.

The creditors, Lord Dunmore's men, were hungry for conquest and only she stood in the way of stopping another crime from happening to this family. The shaky peace she had been granted in the past two days would not last. She alone would have to account for her husband's debts, if such debts existed at all. She swept through her memories of conversations past and even of their heated arguments.

"I fear I will run out of money. This plantation oftentimes seems a burden. My wealth is the land itself and the slaves that occupy it. I have very little profit coming in. It is no easy task to conjure funds in order to free them. I must deliberate my next steps very carefully." His words that afternoon on a gold-swept beach, the sun descending in its slow track, reminded her of the pain of a future torn away from them.

The gold coins weighed heavily on her. She had just moved them to a new hiding spot, away from the porch stairs and the crevices beneath the conch shells on her shelves. Two bags remained in the cellar, but the rest she had buried behind Cleo's freshly erected gravestone. She knew no man on this island would dare to presume that a slave's grave contained any wealth; the idea reassured her that they were safe.

She imagined Cleo's spirit still keeping a watchful eye over the grounds. Revelations from a fistful of bones, when

Cleo had once given Eliza a reading, reminded her that she and Charles were bound together by some ancient thread. But now, the one person who had told her their union was meant to be was also gone. If Charles was not meant for her, why was Eliza still here? Was that moment of panic in town the last time she would ever see him alive? The suffocating madness of believing something so necessary to her survival, a thought all others disregarded and sought to stamp out like a wavering flame from a candle, overwhelmed her.

Cleo would know what to say. Cleo would know what to do. Cleo understood that there was more to living than met the human eye. But Eliza was bound by the rules of men. She needed Charles here to fend off the devious creditors, to prove their wrongdoing and send them packing, their heads downcast in shame. And she needed him here to free the remaining slaves.

Eliza, as a woman, had no legal rights to defend herself. She could not act as the power of attorney in order to finish the deed of freeing the rest of them. She had a hoard of gold stored away, but lacked the powers to use it for any good. Its utility existed in its sense of promise. Promise that once Charles returned, they could collectively use it to buy the slaves' freedom and to win their legal battle in the court, or, and her heart stilled at the idea, of a last minute means of escape if no rescue ever came. Gold could prove useful for desperate bribes or a journey by ship, but she balked at the idea of handing it over to the creditors when their cause was not true. It was her family's to keep.

Charles had been captured in the middle of the process

of manumitting Lucy and the others, preventing their gambit from being carried out in full. She had uncovered petitions that Charles had started for a handful of other slaves, carefully choosing those whose years were numbered or who had suffered an injury to be selected first. But the petitions were meaningless pieces of paper now. It was only a matter of time before Dunmore's men would confiscate everything on the property, including the human beings.

Eliza could plead for financial relief, but it would take too long. Any bank would say the answer lay right in front of her—the sweating, moving limbs of the enslaved workers of Pleasant Hall. But that did not constitute a solution to her. She could not borrow money from any wealthy merchant. She would run up considerable debts without Charles' oversight monitoring the activities of the plantation. She needed something to absolve her husband's so-called debts, something to change their doomed fortune.

Pleasant Hall was much more than a white house to her now. It consisted of more than just sorrow, of more than its aching hulk of sturdy, unrelenting wood that stood in contest with nature, that battled the salt and wind. It stood for possibility. A small whisper that things could change. A change that others on the island feared, and she would defend every inch of its frame.

She understood the scarcity of cash when running a plantation, but Charles had never mentioned any debts. When she had encouraged Celia to run, he had been upset with her. She'd feared he would strike her that night. Now she saw the events of that evening in a different light.

Eliza recalled when he had to sell Lucy and how she had hated him for his decision. She had been reckless, defiant, judgmental. His cutting words were true. Before, she had truly not known the ways this colony worked. Now she understood the wickedness of men in more ways than one. The creditors knew that plantations were wealthy but only because of the land they stood on and the enslaved people who worked there. If corrupt bankers wanted to call in any loan, they well understood the plantation owners had very little cash on hand. But in the tropics, money did not exchange hands—human lives did, and it was this weakness they sought to exploit.

A human being who could live for decades and toil the land was always more valuable than a purse of coin that could be spent and forgotten. A slave could work and break their bodies until they collapsed. A slave could create more enslaved, and the cruel cycle would continue like the steady march of a goatskin drum. It was clear to Eliza now that more than one nefarious actor had orchestrated Charles' capture. So many on this island stood to profit from it, hoping to catch a handful of wealth that poured from Lord Dunmore's cup.

She thought of the famed Woodes Rogers, the brave conqueror of wicked pirates and a true governor of the island. He too had been used by the Crown and then cast aside without gratitude. He had even served time in a debtor's prison, and she found herself contemplating his life's story again and again. The colony sorely needed a man like him now, not one driven by greed and corruption. Lord Dunmore openly consorted with the likes of men

Rogers would hang without a second thought.

She had seen a portrait of Rogers once in England with a motto she had never forgotten. It was a curious thing to be so affected by a cracked oil painting created before she was even born. The careful strokes of a castle wall bore a cartouche reading *"Dum spiro, spero." While I breathe, I hope.* She needed those words now more than ever. She was breathing. She was still alive. And she would fight until that changed.

Woodes Rogers' story inspired her. He had circumnavigated the world in a daring venture, cementing his place as more myth than man. He had been shot through his left cheek in the heat of battle fighting for England and left with an enduring scar on his face. In another naval engagement, a splinter of wood had knocked out a part of his heel bone, and still he continued to command his men. He had rid the Bahamas of pirates when no one else could. He alone had restored law and order. And like him, she too would die on this forgotten island.

It saddened her that ghosts of the past brought her more comfort than living men, but the depravity of the men around her sickened her. She used Charles as a focal point so she would not lose sight of the possibilities of the ways men could serve and protect. Of the ways they could change for the better. Eliza wore her wedding ring now, putting it on as some token of luck, a guarantee cast in gold that he could return to her after all. The fierce way he had loved her had changed who she was. She regretted her past refusal to commission a wedding portrait. It made her cling to her ring all the more dearly, for without it she now had no proof of their union.

Her old thoughts, her past sins, they weighed heavily on her. Their shared misunderstandings were so clear to her now in this new fractured, painful light. And with the strange synchronicity of life, one day a token of her turbulent past was uncovered.

A small slave boy had come running up to her, excited by discovery, just as Philippe was moved when he found his snail shells. He gingerly placed the prized object in her cupped hands, and she was left without words. It was something she once thought invaluable—Jean's amulet. She studied the purple pearl from the Orient, tied elaborately with a red string. Its luster had faded from the heat and the roughness of sand. It still remained here, though, even though the man who had once possessed it was gone. He lived on through the burgeoning steps of Philippe, whose facial expressions and mannerisms matched a man he would never meet. But she also thought of all the pain this talisman resurfaced and saw nothing but ill tidings when she rubbed its smoothness.

"You have broken that contract. You have disgraced this house. You are not fit to be my wife. To carry my name!" Charles had shouted, the pain of her betrayal driving him to fury.

"That name means nothing to me. I want freedom, Charles—freedom!" The past echoed in her mind.

Now the Sharpe family name meant everything to her. It meant hope, a vision for the future, and it meant love. An impossible love.

Eliza thanked the boy, whose confusion at her silence made her feel sorry for him. She gave him a guinea in return, and he ran back towards the slave dwellings full of the hopefulness of youth. Then after one sleepless night, she returned outside with it and buried it, praying she could bury her past regrets alongside it. It was a new day, and she was no longer the same woman. She willed to leave it all behind.

CHAPTER III.

Sleep had not come willingly the last few nights. Whenever Eliza felt herself slipping away into nothingness, her mind raged on, shaping her dreams into sharpened nightmares. But one night offered a different vision.

Eliza stands at a crossroads, barefoot against the dry, parched dirt. She looks up and sees an elderly colored man, but his attire marks him as different. She begins to think he is a free man, like she once did before, and then recalls where she has seen him. It is the man she encountered on the porch at Lord Dunmore's mansion so long ago, the old charming man who had once spoken to her in a riddle. He turns to face her, a smile full of white teeth, and tips his tall hat with the yellow band towards her. In the nature of dreams, he feels the same as in waking life, and she speaks to him as if this can make a difference. As if he was not an ancient ghost, an orisha *from Cleo's world of spirits.*

"You! You started all of this!" she says as she confronts him one last time.

He says nothing, and Eliza jumps as something touches her

left foot. There are two slave children groveling on the ground, pushing empty bowls waiting to be filled with rice towards her. One clings to the hem of her dress. They say nothing, but their eyes speak for them. They are emaciated, nothing like the way the enslaved children look at Pleasant Hall. But then she realizes this is what lays in store for them if she cannot stop the greed of men. She steps away in horror. How can she, one woman, stop all of this?

The old man stamps his cane down into the ground, then raises it up towards the sky. But it is a fine silver cane no longer. Now it is nothing but a broom-less broomstick. Wealth is a deception, like beauty, it is in the eye of the beholder. And like beauty, it too will fade. Eliza looks back down as a shift in the air envelops her. The starving children are gone. The old man peers up to the blistering sun, shielding his eyes with an elegant swipe of his hand.

"They have him. They have my husband; is he truly dead?" she asks.

He says nothing and only points in the direction of town, balancing himself on his cane once again.

"I cannot go into town. I have no news. I have no one to help me. Please …"

A faint thumping of drums, emanating from the depths of the earth bounces off her legs, banging madly until it blends with the beats of her heart. There is another source of help. There is always another source of help from the world of spirit. She need only ask.

"Please help me!" Eliza demands, impatient and desperate.

They stand now in the church yard, in the cemetery filled with mounds and graves like crooked teeth. The old man steps to the side, his every move like a silent step in the dance of life, and a grave is revealed. Eliza stares at it with disbelief. Beneath the skull and crossbones, under the carefully carved hourglass, it reads "In memory of Jean Charles de Longchamp, late of Nassau, who died July 22nd, 1792. Aged 33." She steps forward, reading it with uncertain eyes.

"The father of my child has no grave. There is no grave at the church ..." she says slowly, disagreeing with the sight.

She beholds a new scene, but it has already transpired. It is stale with the smell of the past. In the shadowy coolness of Cleo's dwelling, she and Charles held a secret meeting. How often had Charles sought her advice, unbeknownst to Eliza? She watches the memory unfold in the way a hibiscus, damp with dew, unfurls for the morning sun.

"Show her the grave. Show her Jean's grave," Cleo added.

Charles' face paled.

"You spent enough money on it; you might as well tell her what you have done."

"She will think my intentions are suspect. She does not need to know. There is time enough for that. Her heart is so attached to his memory, I fear she will sleep alongside his tombstone," Charles said. "I am not a perfect man. I fear she will never understand me."

"This will help her see. To see the man you truly are."

"But ... I did not know, I never knew ..." Eliza says with disbelief.

The old man smiles and waves a finger.

A second scene begins to play, of Charles and her as they stood in the heat, sweating, waiting for Lord Dunmore to arrive for Sunday service in front of Christ Church. Of how

Charles had suggested she take a stroll among the graves. How she had arrogantly claimed that the decaying ruins of past islanders held no interest for her.

"This was here the entire time?" she asks now, pointing at it, full of regret and sadness.

The words of the past echo and wrap themselves around her like the coils of a slow-moving snake. The weight of what she did not yet know is heavy like a chain. But the old man is not done with her. He points to another grave. A thunderous single drum beat silences all other noise. She reads it and her heart stops.

"Charles, husband of Eliza Sharpe, who departed this life ______ "

The date is blank, for the date has not yet come.

Relief floods Eliza. "Thank you, thank you!" she says, hands folded in prayer. "But how will he return to me? What must I do?"

He finally speaks, his voice strange yet comfortably familiar to her ears. "Born of the sea and of a brutal dream, detached from human society, without a home or a cemetery." The old man's cane taps on Charles' tombstone, and he continues, "One hand carries death, the other a key …"

"Another riddle? I beg of you, I know not what you mean. Please help me!"

"Then ask, child."

He smiles and bows, and she fears the dream will end, receiving confirmation as the edges of her vision curl inward and disintegrate like paper aflame. Before it burns away to nothingness, she looks up and sees the figure of Reverend James standing in the doorway of the open church, watching her with hatred fixed in his small eyes. There is no doubt he has her destined for Hell in his mind.

Eliza awoke to bed sheets wet and sticky with perspiration. A solitary rooster crowed, and she looked around her room in a haze. When sleep did come, it always came for an hour or two after the sun rose, as if the presence of its warming light signaled the safety to rest. But it was far from restful. She was just as tired as she had been before her vivid dream. It was a peculiar sensation because while it disturbed her, it also reassured her. Charles' grave had had no date of death inscribed in it. He still lived.

She watched with disinterest as a small red centipede inched its way slowly across her wrinkled sheet. She idly wondered how many times it had taken that route without her notice. Or maybe Cleo had carefully eliminated them all, and after her sudden death they had returned. When she spotted one by her pillow, where her face had only recently lain, she left the bed in disgust.

After readying herself for another day of bated breath, Eliza sat on the porch listening to the chatter of the palm trees surrounding the house, as if they were deep in conversation each time the breeze swung by. The smell of horse dung wafted by her, and when she saw Julius, the groom, she approached him.

"Julius, do you still tend the stables regularly?"

"Yes, Lady Sharpe. I do it every morning, first thing."

She cast a disapproving look towards where the horses were kept. The smell was one of manure and sweating animals.

"I believe Charles would do it more often. I want it

done as he would do it."

"But now the horses aren't being used as often, so I thought—"

"He is returning. He wouldn't want it in such a state," she said, irritation sharpening her voice.

She looked at him, and took a deep breath. She prayed Julius understood that her agitation wasn't necessarily caused by anything that he had done or failed to do.

"Yes, Lady Sharpe. Of course, Lady Sharpe. I'll keep it proper for when Lord Sharpe returns."

"Thank you," she said in a softer tone.

When she saw Celia walking towards the house, she excused herself and ran over to her.

"Celia, I must ask for your help," Eliza said, as she walked in step with her.

Celia didn't even suffer her a glance.

"What help do you need, Lady Sharpe?"

"Teach me how to pray. To your gods."

Celia stopped, placing the basket of folded laundry down. Her hands sat on her hips, and she narrowed her strange amber-colored eyes.

"Did you see Papa Legba again?"

Her voice was cold and tired of the conversation.

"Who is that?" Eliza asked.

"Did he sing and dance for you, Lady Sharpe?"

Celia was mocking her, but Eliza finally understood her meaning.

"Yes, yes, he did. He gave me a new riddle. I confess I do not understand it, but it reminded me that there is still something I can do to bring Charles home."

Celia looked her up and down, but true to her fashion, she changed the subject.

"Why you want to bring that man home? You cried every time he lay with you," Celia said with a sneer.

Eliza colored and looked out towards the beach.

"That is in the past and, frankly, does not concern you."

"Your request does not concern me, either. Laundry, dusting, sweeping, that is what my job is. Not this."

She bent down and picked up her basket, continuing up the porch to the house.

"Your job is what I tell you to do," Eliza said, starting to lose patience. "Please, Celia. Please help me. I know you saw something that day shortly before Cleo died. When I screamed because I saw the house in disarray. There was a presence in the house, and I know you felt it too."

Celia stopped in her tracks and slowly turned.

"And what do you think I can do?" she questioned Eliza.

"Teach me how to pray. Teach me what to do."

"I don't know what you're talking about."

"Yes, you do. I've seen them. I know it's real. And you know it is too."

Her answer was not forthcoming.

"Tell me what to do. I beg of you. I have nowhere else to turn."

Celia was dismissive and impatient. "You were confused with dreams. Nothing more than that," she said in a low tone.

"The one I saw at Dunmore's mansion, that Legba, he was no dream. Neither was the king I encountered on the beach. He touched me. The warrior king …" Eliza protested.

But she struggled to remember his name.

"Shango," Celia finally said quietly. "He has a voice like thunder, and a mouth that spews fire when he speaks. He is both a creator and a destroyer. But most of all, he protects his people. He delivers justice."

"Yes! That one! Tell me what I need to do. Cleo is not here. Otherwise, I would ask her and not bother you. I swear, Celia. When Lucy was sold before and all the women prayed for her return, what was that?"

"You mean the slaves?" Her disgust was palpable.

"Celia, please. I promise you I will help you. I will …"

Celia's anger rose, her nostrils flaring.

"You cannot help me. The one who could help any of us, who could free us, is gone. Why should I help you?"

"To bring him back. Help me bring Charles back. Tell me what to do. Tell me what words to say. It was for the one called Oya, wasn't it?"

"Oya is not for you," she snapped. "You want your soldier husband returned? Ask the king of all warriors."

But she spoke too rashly and revealed the answer Eliza sought. Her eyes lit up. Celia seemed to capitulate. She sighed and walked Eliza over to the dormant fireplace.

"You have to pray to him. Ask him to intercede."

"In front of the fireplace?"

"Yes, but place an offering inside it."

"An offering of what?"

Celia rolled her eyes, and looked around them, ensuring no one else could hear.

"Give him a drink, offer him some green bananas, six red apples. Six is his number, and red is his color. He has a day, but it don't matter. You are not his daughter. It works stronger with a blood offering, but you asking him ain't gonna do nothing anyway."

"Cleo said I am a daughter of Yemaya."

"I don't know about that," she muttered.

"Are you saying Cleo was wrong?"

Her honey-colored eyes became slits of internal rage.

"Yemaya is his mother. Close enough."

She bent down and began drawing a strange symbol with chalk on the bricks of the fireplace, white lines clashing with black soot. The shape of gallows and crisscrossing "Ts" up and down its frame appeared. Then she drew a curving snake to its right, with two stars on the bottom and a line.

"What are you doing?"

Celia was rapidly losing patience.

"Never mind what I'm doing. Go get the things we need and come back here."

When Eliza returned, a small glass of water, an empty glass, and two lit candles were arranged in the fireplace. There was a simplistic elegance to the display, and Eliza carefully placed the apples and green bananas she had gathered. Then she poured some whiskey in the empty glass.

A door closed at the end of the hallway. Eliza paused, unsure if she should continue.

"I sent Lucy away to the kitchen. She doesn't like this. It scares her," Celia explained.

It was ironic that Cleo's daughter was afraid of the very thing Cleo embodied. But the thought that what they were about to do terrified Lucy, unsettled Eliza in turn.

"What are the prayers?" Eliza asked, nervously staring at the decorated fireplace.

"You can say *Oba koso … Baba Shango … Omo Shango* …" Celia said, her tone more reverent now.

"That is all? Surely there must be more words."

Both women kneeled before the fireplace, and Eliza began to feel awkward next to her new teacher.

"Shango does not want you to pray to him like a god. He wants to show you your power. To remind you what you are capable of."

Eliza watched in awe as something softened in Celia as she gazed down at the offering and wavering candles. Something told Eliza she had often prayed to him like this, and she wondered if she had surreptitiously done it while cleaning.

Eliza lowered her head and began to pray to God and to Shango for help. It felt strange to pray to Shango.

"But you may not like the answer you receive. Don't start anything with him that you can't finish," Celia added ominously.

Eliza's eyes widened. "What do you mean?"

"Just pray and be done with it, so I can clear this away."

Despite the harsh words, Eliza felt a shared sense of communion with Celia as they knelt in silence. For once, this was not about housework, and there was no bitter arguing.

"But I feel nothing. It doesn't feel like the other times.

Something is wrong," Eliza said, wariness in her voice.

Without warning, the glass filled with whiskey toppled over, slamming to the ground. But what terrified Eliza was the shape of a man's wet handprint stamped into the dirty brick. Both women gasped and backed away from the fireplace. And then a rumbling noise grew louder.

"Celia, do you hear that too?" Eliza whispered.

Celia nodded, her eyes huge. "The sun is out; it cannot possibly be thunder."

It gave Eliza comfort to know that there was something else on the other side of this pained world. But the way she had received this confirmation was also frightening.

"You called him in. He is here," Celia said, after they listened to the cacophony of banging sounds around them. Then a rare smile crossed her face. "But Shango does not hear you. He will not serve you. He does not like whiskey; he favors rum. Dark rum."

Eliza cursed.

"Why did you not tell me?"

"Because you won't know the difference!"

Celia laughed as Eliza grabbed the empty glass with a shaking hand. She ran to get a damp rag and the rum, and returned, nervously blotting out the otherworldly stain. Her ears burned. What if Celia was telling her the wrong things on purpose?

"Here. *Obom kassa.* No, that's not it ... *Oba koso! Oba koso!* Return my husband to me. He is a soldier like you, Shango."

But her entreaties fell flat. In truth, she did not know what she expected. But they had already received a chilling spectacle.

"It's no use. I am not like you or Cleo. I cannot pray to Shango or Yemaya or Oya like you can." Eliza spoke to the fireplace now, an unevenly shaped apple shifting to its side. "Can you hear me? Can any of you hear me? God!" Eliza said, her voice breaking.

Celia sighed. "You can say something like, 'There is no reason to fear, you will be with me, and you will help me in all of my needs. Thank you,'" she said, as she closed her eyes with reverence.

"What?"

"You must thank him!" Celia said, annoyed with Eliza's lack of comprehension.

Chills descended Eliza's back. Just as she repeated what Celia had said, the candles' flames seemed to expand in recognition. A calmness swept over Eliza, and she felt oddly comforted. It was the kind of reassurance she had only ever felt from her father, in the many conversations they had shared about the workings of the world. It began to stir up feelings she had long refused to allow herself to feel, the very first wave of grief she had experienced after arriving in Nassau when she had learnt of her parents' deaths. Despite not wanting to feel more emotional pain, it served as an unusual form of proof. This was indeed real. Eliza knew Celia had not tricked her any further.

"I think he has heard you now," Celia confirmed.

Eliza said a few extra prayers to herself, and blew out the candles. Both women stood up. Eliza looked out the windows, making sure they were still alone.

"Remember, when you pray to the *orishas*, you will

receive an answer. But it may not be the answer you prefer," Celia said, watching her.

"I want any answer. I need an answer. I cannot go on like this."

Celia looked at her with a new expression, as if she only now recognized her sincerity. "I hope you do not regret it."

"How long have you been doing this?" Eliza asked out of curiosity.

"My mother was an Obeah woman. It's the only way for me to feel any power. Any control. When your mother is killed and her body is thrown away like garbage … it is my only comfort."

Answers came flooding to Eliza's mind. Celia was Tabitha's daughter. Tabitha, the one constant spirit who resided in Pleasant Hall. The woman whose invisible spirit electrified the air in Eliza's room when she fell asleep and who awakened her with the slam of a random door with unseen hands. The quiet, knowing presence who sat on the edge of her bed, as solid as a living person. Someone who looked like an older, wiser version of Celia. How had she never realized this before? They were indeed mirror images of each other.

Words Cleo had spoken once resurfaced in her mind.

"Tabitha had a beautiful girl, strong-minded like her, and Charles and her would play in the yard sometimes. That is why this world is cruel, Miss Ellie. We let the children be free to see the world with innocent eyes. Black children and white children playing. They do not see a difference."

"I know why you are so angry, Celia. Forgive me, I did not see it before. You are Tabitha's daughter. That is why you can read. You were able to find Jean's letter the night before he was executed. You found my letter that I left for Cleo the day I tried to take my life. Tabitha could read, and she taught you, too. The old Master Sharpe caught Charles' mother teaching Tabitha with the Bible. And then he killed her too … because your mother knew what the old Master Sharpe had done. He had killed his wife, Jane. Charles' mother. He killed both women in this house."

Eliza expected her defiance. "I ain't never said none of that."

"You don't need to. I saw it. I saw it in my dreams. You once played with Charles in the yard. You were raised as equals until one day you were suddenly not. I am so sorry, Celia. And then Charles gave you to me as a wedding present. I understand your hatred, Celia, truly I do."

"You don't understand a thing," Celia spat. "I liked you better when you hated that man. Hated him like I do. I should have never shown you shit."

The urge to tell Celia everything burned inside Eliza until she could not stand it for a moment longer.

"We must get Charles back. Alive. He plans on freeing you, freeing all of you."

Celia stopped; the shock of Eliza's words clearly rattling her. "You speaking nonsense. Now you just playing a game to trick me."

"No, Celia, I swear to you. He was nearly halfway done with freeing Lucy. That was our business in town the very day he was taken."

Celia clicked her tongue. "Freeing Lucy, whatever for? That girl wouldn't know what to do with freedom if it fell in her lap."

"It was one of Cleo's last requests. But he means to free all of you, you included, Celia. The creditors keep visiting, desperate to start taking the slaves away. I am fighting to stop it, and the only way I can do that is if Charles returns!"

Celia looked down, squeezing her hands into fists. Then she grasped the molding of the doorway to steady herself. She took a deep breath.

"I see," she said quietly. "I won't clear away the shrine. I will leave it. We need it."

Eliza sighed, feeling relief for finally sharing what she had long kept inside herself. That something good had already happened after the intense scene by the fireplace only reassured her further. Matters were changing.

"Thank you, Celia. Please do not tell the others. I share this with you in confidence," Eliza added.

Celia nodded, and they walked back out to the porch.

Eliza headed towards the water side, when she stopped midway and let out a small shriek. There, perched high on the siding in the corner, was a huge brown moth, the very same kind she had chased that fateful afternoon back at her childhood home in England. The day she had met Charles, when she had agreed to come to this island as his wife. The *Antheraea polyphemus* moth. Its two huge, dark spots on its velvety wings stared back at her, giving her more peace than she had felt in days.

Celia wasn't far behind her, and she cursed. She came back with a broom, wielding it like a weapon.

"Want me to kill it, Lady Sharpe?"

Eliza wheeled around in horror.

"No! No! Don't you see? It's the moth! It's the same moth I saw years ago!"

"You saw that same moth before? How you know?"

"No, not the same exact one. The same species. Don't you see? It's a sign! From Shango! Charles will return!"

"It's a bug …" Celia said, clearly not moved by the natural miracle perched on the wall.

Eliza watched the unmoving creature with her hands cupped to her face. Celia studied her for a second and then shook her head, walking back to the other side of the porch.

"These white women, they all mad," she muttered to herself as she carried on with her list of tasks. And when she was fully out of ear shot, crossed herself and added, "Baba Shango, please help us. *Asé.*"

CHAPTER IV.

The precise notes of the string quartet wafted into the gentleman's parlor, stirring Charles to attention.

"It is a shame the Frenchman is not here. He is a better liar than you," Captain Bruin said.

Charles was engaged in a card game of écarté with the privateer. It was late at night, and the festivities of the ball were winding down. Many of the guests had already left, and those few who remained were drunk beyond measure. Only Bruin and he retained their sobriety.

Bruin now pointed at the stack of cards. "I propose …"

Charles nodded, accepting his proposal. Bruin flashed the number two with a slight wave of his hand and exchanged two of the cards from his deck. Then it was Charles' turn. He studied his cards, his mind overwhelmed with thoughts of what would occur tomorrow morning. Jean's public execution. His once-childhood friend had betrayed everything they believed in.

Charles clenched his jaw. Women with tall feathers in their hair stumbled into a side table in the hallway, giggling madly as they clutched each other for balance. He thought of how he had left Eliza tied up to the banister in Pleasant Hall. He felt uneasy about the entire venture. He wanted to return home.

"I told the governor to give the Frenchman to me to throw from the cliffs. Sharks do wonders on a body," Bruin continued, his tone light and casual. As if they were discussing anything but a man's life.

Charles must have revealed his true thoughts on the matter because he heard Bruin scoff.

"Do I upset you?" the captain asked, his tone mocking.

Charles looked up at him, trying his best to mask his feelings.

"I think you aim to make me lose my concentration," he quipped.

He studied his cards. He had a King, a Queen, an Ace, and 10 in his hand. He was confident in what he already had and did not exchange any of his cards from the deck. Charles already possessed the highest card: the King.

Bruin tarried for a moment and then began the play. Cards flashed down on the table as Charles won one trick after another. When they reached the fifth and final trick, Charles laid down his last card. He looked up to see Bruin smiling wickedly. He slammed down his card, 2 Spades, the trump card, winning the trick and the game itself.

"You would have scored an extra point had you stated your possession earlier," Charles said,

"I never like to reveal my hand," Bruin retorted, twisting a garnet ring on his finger. "Why accept my proposal but exchange none of your own cards? Foolish. You have allowed your opponent the chance at a better hand."

But cards were not in the forefront of Charles' thoughts. Bruin reached over and moved a pile of chips to his side of the green, velvet-covered table. Charles slugged his whiskey down, rubbing his hands through his hair.

"I see ... you have a history with de Longchamp. That is why you are so melancholy tonight." Bruin gathered all the cards on the table and began shuffling them. "But do we not all have a history?" He smirked slyly.

"I am simply tired. That is all. Sometimes the heat still affects me."

"You have spent too much time away from the island. One could say you have neglected the estate belonging to your family."

"Sometimes I think you mean to rob me of my home," Charles remarked with a dry laugh.

"I would not mind, if it is for the taking."

Bruin gestured at starting a new game, but Charles declined.

"One more round. Perhaps you will win this time."

"No, Bruin. I am done for the evening."

Bruin clicked his tongue. "I do not think you enjoy the game when I am your opponent."

"One might say it has more to do with the company than the game itself."

Bruin leaned back in his chair and sighed. "Your mood is sour tonight," he said. "But tomorrow is a new day. He made for a poor spy anyway. Good men are easy to compromise. When you need something important done, it is always wise to ask those better suited to shadowy intrigues. It is all too easy for the wrong papers to slip into the possession of a gentleman and for the right papers to slip out."

For effect, he tossed the 2 of Spades card at Charles. He looked down at it, his head full of tension and worrying *thoughts. He was about to question Bruin further when a door slammed and screams erupted from the top floor.*

"You whore! I knew you had designs on His Lordship! You conniving . . ." Charlotte's voice, the governor's mistress, echoed throughout the house.

A few seconds later, Charles heard another voice he recognized. A voice belonging to someone whom he had left behind, hours ago, securely tied up back in the house.

"On the contrary, I am the only one here who is not a paid whore, Mistress Charlotte. You can find one in his bed right now, and the other I am presently speaking to," Eliza said. "You may share a name with his wife, but you will never attain her status, no matter how wide you open your legs."

Charles shot up off his chair. Bruin's eyes grew huge, and he threw his head back with laughter.

"Get out. Get out of this house! I am calling the guards!" Charlotte shouted.

Footsteps rumbled on the floor above the men. He had gambled tonight, choosing his wife's emotional devastation in order to protect her life. But his plan had failed; she had somehow untied herself and made an appearance regardless. This was a political game she had no experience in, and these men had little regard for life. Charles dashed to the hallway, climbing the stairs to the second floor. He found a sniveling, tear-stained Charlotte surrounded by three guards. She looked up at him, her eyes narrowing.

"Have you come to collect your whore?" she sneered, wiping her nose with her sleeve.

Embarrassment flooded his cheeks. He said nothing to her, but followed the trail of chaos, stopping at a servant's stairway.

The door was left ajar, and he had no doubt Eliza had used that as her escape route. She was already gone.

"What have I done?" he asked himself.

A force knocked into him and then hit him again.

"You, are you alive?" a gruff man asked.

Charles opened his eyes and tried to shield himself from the sudden brightness. But his wrists were weighed down with iron fetters.

"The General is still alive, Captain," the man now shouted back above deck.

The hatch slammed shut. Charles looked around him, trying to hold his breath. The stench of dried blood was sickening.

Yes, still alive … but at what cost?

A dark and airless cavern in the lower deck of a ship had become his new home. He had awoken to this horrible reality after the pirates had knocked him out cold. Irons on his ankles and wrists chafed against his raw skin, pushing against his bones with a force that no longer resembled pain but a permanent fixture against his flesh. His head throbbed, and his throat ached with thirst. As he watched a multitude of flies buzz about in the stagnant, putrid, air he had no doubts that this was a former slave ship. He could tell by the stench alone. The eleven men who were shackled alongside him were simply not capable of producing an odor this offensive.

Charles marked his days by watching the slats of light from the grating of the hatch. The deck they occupied was below the waterline and stunk of feces and bilge water. Deprived of sunlight and fresh air, breathing in nothing but excrement and the sweat of their own bodies, almost made him forget he was a man. That the resplendent scarlet officer's coat he wore ever truly belonged on his shoulders. That he had ever had a life before this.

The unsettling glare of the others' vacant eyes gazed outward at him. It was a look without connection, without meaning. No one spoke except in muffled groans or fits of coughing. He would idly watch the lice jump from one man's shoulders to the next. The rats came at night, scampering through puddles of water or urine, he could no longer tell which, and sometimes bit an arm or leg, inspecting a new source of potential food.

But what was worse than the lack of ventilation or the disease was the realization of why he was there. He had failed. The first time he had woken up and found himself in that floating hell, surrounded by the miasma of human misery, he retched on himself. It was like an act of initiation, for only once he had dirtied himself in such a manner did it mark him as a new man. No longer was he the Lieutenant Colonel of the 47th Regiment in the West Indies. Now he was a prisoner, with the same fate as the other wretches around him. The only things he owned were the bloodstained clothes on his back and his place on the rough wooden floor.

Charles thought of the family he would never see again. He was full of fear for his wife. He could feel it like a darkness covering his soul, more tangible than the filthy shadows that surrounded him on the rocking ship. The separation from her was most unbearable of all. He would wake up in a cold sweat, after nightmares of her first appearing safe, healthy, and glowing in her youth and boundless hope, then seeing Eliza on her back, her dress ripped, a trickle of dried blood in the corner of her lips.

His dreams always ended with her dead. He would see her swimming in the ocean, only for men to be waiting in the bush on the beach, ready to grab her, to violate her and slit her throat. He could see the pirates chasing after her, preventing her flight home, grabbing hold of Alastor's reins and shooting his beloved horse. He saw Pleasant Hall engulfed in flames, Philippe crying in his bassinet, his mother gone, the heat reaching his delicate skin.

Charles knew he was stuck here on this ship, not because he had manumitted Cleo, an act of freedom for an elderly slave most islanders cared little for, but because he had dared to set in motion something much grander. He alone threatened to challenge the island's economy. Freeing a slave was a convenient cover for crooked men, the kind who worked for the governor. It enticed weak men to hatred and a willingness to help the ruler of the island.

Charles' fear rose again. Because above all things, he understood this about his miserable turn of fate: he was a threat to Lord Dunmore.

"I declare that Lord Sharpe be our governor!" a young man had shouted during one of his many political meetings on the island. The words seemed a fever dream now. Charles had survived a knife attack at the fort, but his enemies had come for him a second time. And he feared they would not be satisfied with his capture alone.

Charles had a long time to think about things. He

thought of Eliza's vulnerability the most. Now she was left alone on the island to defend herself from men of such character. He had left her disastrously short of funds. Surely she would not know how to manage the plantation, and she would run out of money. How would she survive? If, indeed, Alastor had even carried her to safety after the attack on the town. She would have to work manual labor, selling some goods or wares. He prayed she would not resort to selling herself.

These thoughts horrified him. Eliza had a noble mind; she was not destined for such devastating ventures. He felt helpless and hated his lack of power. He hated imagining the terror she was surely enduring. Charles was well accustomed to danger, but she was not. And what of the boy? The child he had agreed to father out of honor, out of a debt owed to his natural father.

He prayed to hear the voice of God.

"Protect them. Bless my wife, bless my child," he would repeat endlessly.

He had promised to protect her for the rest of her life, and how miserably he had failed. His mind roved through the last two years with her. Their terrible start, the many mistakes he had made, how even while he had poured his hope into her, she had busied herself reading a book or staring at the sea—anything to keep her company apart from him. Yet before he had been captured, there had been a shift between them. Charles had felt it deep within him, and the words she had spoken to him had only confirmed it.

She reached for his hand and squeezed it. "You make me

forget that I am not ready for love. For the sweeter things to return to my life," she had said softly.

He wanted to return to her, to walk on that beach, carrying Philippe so her back did not have to tolerate the burden. To be covered in the golden light of a descending sun with her at his side. He had done the unthinkable and broken through her barriers. He had breached her defenses, not by force or power of will, but with a softness and patience he long thought himself incapable of. Her image, her dark hair full of waves like the sea itself, her large brown eyes questioning the world around them, her burgeoning curiosity, her appreciation of natural wonders … his wife was indelibly fixed in his heart.

For one brief, unguarded instant, he had finally felt love from her on that beach. Only for it all to be taken away. Charles lowered his head and wept openly, thinking only of her.

Violence was a thread running through his life, like the red string that held his officer's jacket together. He had been brutalized over and over again, losing his mother at the hands of his father and his father from the power of drink. He had grown up on a plantation, playing with young black boys and girls he would later own. Assets inherited from his father, security for his uncertain future.

Charles had chosen a different path, but violence ruled the only employment he could seek. He was compelled to become a soldier to avoid the cruelty of his father. The British army served as his escape. He was forced to kill other men in the most brutal of ways, bloodshed made justified because of king and country until even this was revealed to be nothing but a facade, a ruse used to urge men to commit unthinkable acts.

Yet Charles was undeniably good at serving, at leading others into the heat of battle, of rushing a trusted steed straight into danger. He could think of no other task he would be so well suited for. The army had given him salvation; it had brought him away from the Bahamas.

He remembered his first victory. When he was a young man, barely twenty, he had captured a notorious pirate captain from the small island of St. Eustatius. It instantly set him up for success within the army, and he proved his merit throughout the rebellion in the American colonies. It was ironic that the same power that had changed his career for the better was the very thing to cause his undoing. As he looked around at the filth he was mired in, there was no doubt he was still in the hands of pirates.

These islands in the Caribbean only knew of an unending war. Not the kind between countries and kings, but the kind that stemmed from the greed of men, that pitted them one against the other. When kings *did* have cause for war, when treaties were broken, these same islanders only saw a chance at more profit. Now everything he held dear dangled into the hands of death.

He worked himself into a fury, unable to think through his rage. Charles could do nothing; the chains he wore around his ankles day and night delivered the cruel reminder. He drifted into abstraction, swayed by the tilts of the current.

But the words of his dream, of his past memory, began to swirl around him again.

"I do not think you enjoy the game when I am your opponent."

Charles' green eyes grew wide.

"I am your opponent," the man said boldly.

He suddenly placed those rings he had seen that terrible afternoon. He recognized that masked voice; he had spent hours listening to it at the gambling table. He knew the man who had done this to him. His masked enemy had a clear face. And despite his shackles, Charles knew that he would stop at nothing to destroy him.

CHAPTER V.

From the stifling heat of the parlor, Eliza heard a solitary gunshot. Its singularity was unsettling, and its noise disturbingly too close to their land. She sat up on the hard sofa and looked over at Captain Johnson. Without exchanging words, the small party filed out to the porch.

The dry rustling of hundreds of palm fronds collided with the shrill, metallic choir of invisible insects. It almost made for a repetitive, soothing lullaby, but Eliza could not quiet the anxiety coursing through her. This period of waiting was one of the worst parts of her life, and yet she simultaneously feared its end. It meant that her enemies were coming. They wanted to take the house. The land. The slaves. Her small corner of this island was poised to be swallowed up by an even worse fate.

A hidden rooster crowed, a blaring warning. The air was moist outside, and the heat made her damp with sweat as they waited in agonizing stillness. The creditors had stopped coming to Pleasant Hall. Three agonizing days had passed since she had last received a visit from them.

There could only be one reason for the sudden silence.

They would no longer ask. They would seize with violence the property and all it contained.

Two cicadas trilled loudly in the trees above them, straining Eliza's nerves even more. She looked at Josiah and Celia. Men on this island would say she had armed them out of foolishness, but their steadfast presence brought her some degree of comfort. Brutus and a few other slaves had run away from the land, choosing freedom on their own terms the minute they realized Pleasant Hall had truly fallen. She did not blame them; she only hoped they found lasting liberation. Because of her, they were armed, and Eliza feared the other colonists would realize she was guilty of playing with fire.

Further out in the distance, she saw the bushes quivering and knew that Captain Johnson had settled in his usual spot. It was to her advantage that the enemy would not realize Eliza had even more hidden aid.

The sweat welled up in the crease of her eyelids, blinding her drop by salty drop as it rolled behind her ears, down her neck, and into the space between her breasts. Her breaths were labored and heavy, but she made sure to keep an even, steady rhythm. Then she heard the pounding of hooves. A conch shell horn sounded from further up the beach, and she knew the boys she had posted there to monitor the dusty road had seen whatever was hurtling its way towards her now.

New Providence was twenty-one miles long and seven miles wide, and it felt as if the entirety of the island and its blood-soaked past was pressing against her now. That fear that Eliza had so often failed to keep buried rose up in the back of her throat. Nassau was a different place without Charles there. She had always relied on him more than she ever cared to admit, and now she felt his absence like a knife in her side. Danger was driving its way straight into Pleasant Hall.

The burden of not knowing who approached was almost too much to bear. It burned her stomach, and she watched in tense silence with the others, the palms growing darker with each moment as sunlight withdrew from the land. Even the mosquitoes no longer bothered her. They landed on her skin like an unseen whisper she could only feel, but even they could not break her determined gaze on the front yard. Her fingers tightened against the metal barrel of the musket, her arms strained by the tight hold she retained. She thought she heard a horse neigh in the distance. Now Captain Johnson's attention was sharpened, shifting in his crouched stance, fixated on the dark lane edged with silk cotton trees before them.

A party of nearly thirty horses appeared now, their riders charging the beasts forward in a frenzy. Eliza moved off to the side, right outside the open parlor door where Celia stood, armed in the shadows of the house. She was grateful she had told the slaves to let the plants grow wild over the porch. It afforded them cover, and she savored every minute it enshrouded her.

Through the veil of leaves she saw a partial view of the intruders and the rough sort of men they were. Pink bougainvillea petals tumbled down the dirt yard in the breeze, rolling between trotting horse hooves. Josiah was to her left, and as the group of men rode up to the house and began to dismount, he rushed forward and discharged his pistol. Whatever he had seen left no room for hesitation. The response of two shots in return was swift and knocked him down the steps. Eliza cried out and went to move forward when she heard someone thunder up the wooden stairs.

The privateer, Captain Hiram Bruin, turned the corner, his eyes wide as he realized Eliza was standing there alone. In his arrogance he strode right up to her as if she wasn't armed. As if she wasn't fixing the barrel straight at his face, aiming for the thin lips that curved upwards the closer he got to her. When he was within a few feet, she fired, and the explosion rocked her arm, reeling her backward. But when she saw Bruin's hands gripping the smoking barrel, her heart sank. He was the force that had moved her body. He had slammed it upright at the last moment, causing her to misfire. He looked at her now with all the confidence of knowing she had never truly posed a threat to him. She had sorely missed, her mark striking the ceiling of the porch, Bruin's sneering face still intact.

With a burst of strength, he slammed her into the house wall, crooked musket and all. Her resistance ended with a faint whimper. She was amazed by the brawniness of his arm, hidden under his black leather jacket. He was as tall as Charles but much leaner, and his power was not immediately apparent. She quickly remembered that he was someone to fear in this colony.

"Did you truly aim to kill me?" The first words to leave his lips were mingled with misplaced admiration and dark amusement. "I believe you did." He smiled as his hand latched on to her sweating throat. He leaned forward. "You missed," he hissed into her ear.

He relished her defeat and would not ease the pressure of his body against hers. The smell of gunpowder hung in the hot, still air.

All Eliza could hear was the sound of her pulse pounding madly in her ears as she struggled to swallow. He loosened his grip around her neck and stared at her unabashedly.

"You are not very confident with your firearms. At least you fired, but if you were his teacher, no wonder he faltered." He was talking about Josiah, who lay on the porch steps, blood pooling from his still body. "That is one of the many reasons it is a waste of time to teach them things. Slavery is not just their state; it is a way of thinking. You cannot undo that. If someone put you in chains, what would *you* do?" His hips drove into her.

The encounter seemed to excite him, as if he had long awaited this moment. He looked at her as if truly seeing her for the first time.

Eliza was trapped. She finally released her weapon, and the pain seared up her arm to her shoulder. Bruin kicked it away from them with his boot, and then another man came and retrieved it.

"And what is this?" he growled as his other hand patted down the length of her skirt too freely. He inspected the smaller pistol he pulled out of it. "You already fired this one. I doubt you know how to reload, even if you possessed spare shot and powder. It is a paperweight."

There was no time for mortification; she only saw the threat of him before her. He laughed to himself, but then something off to the side erased the mirth from his features.

"Tell your Negro to lower her gun. Unlike you, I do not need to face my target," he said, in a raspy voice as he raised his pistol off toward the side.

Eliza twisted painfully in that direction to find a defiant Celia holding her pistol at him. She was fierce enough to take Eliza's breath away, but he only scoffed.

"Celia, put it down," she said, choking.

Bruin squeezed her throat harder, his impatience thick like the humid air.

"Celia!" Eliza managed to utter one more time.

She heard Celia's pistol clatter to the floor as she dropped it with reluctance. Now more men filed up onto the porch, but Bruin still kept Eliza pinned against the siding of the house. His attention was only fixed on her, and it lingered there.

"An old firearm in the shaky hands of a woman … events on this island have taken a pitiful turn. I have never had a woman fire a musket at me before."

His eyes roamed over her face, and she found it hard to look anywhere else. He studied her with a painfully close scrutiny. And then he took a long, slow breath. "Tell your slaves to prepare a meal for my men."

"Why would I do that?" she replied, managing to inflict venom in her tone.

"Because I am in charge now, and unlike Lord Dunmore, I like to play with my food."

She felt his thumb graze the center of her throat. He wasn't trying to strangle her. He seemed to know the exact amount of pressure necessary to keep her contained and uncomfortable but breathing.

"I want you to beg me to save your life," his wet lips urged near her ear.

She stiffened up.

"And maybe I will."

He suddenly released her, and she slid away from him, rushing into the house as a terrified Lucy ran to another room screaming. She heard Bruin stalking behind her, laughing. Eliza knew Captain Johnson was still hiding in the woods. He was probably waiting for the perfect opportunity, but what could one man truly do against so many?

She was alone. She was alone with death.

The angle of the setting sun was nearly parallel with the hallway, filling it with a blinding gold light that was disorientating. She hesitated, taking a step back, and then all she could see was Bruin's eyes. Eliza didn't like the emotion she detected beneath that snarky gaze. He brandished his musket and cutlass, forcing her towards the end of the glowing hallway. She side-stepped into the dining room, and her heart sank when he followed her. Now she was no longer merely trapped inside a house with this man, but inside a room with only one door.

He moved with smooth strides, holding her glance for several seconds until she found the courage to speak. Eliza tried to keep her voice from shaking with fear, but the words tumbled out of her mouth, weak and unsteady.

"What is the news?" she asked. "How many in Nassau

have died now?"

She was engaging in conversation to distract him as she used the table and chairs to gain space between them.

"No one," he replied with confusion.

His answer surprised her. Was the attack on the town truly over? What had happened?

"But surely other men were taken prisoner?"

They circled each other around the table.

"Only one."

She knew he spoke of her husband. "I fail to understand."

"Your flag still flies above the fort, Lady Sharpe."

To her dismay, the outside was too quiet. The men remained in the yard, some still on their horses. They were waiting for something, for Bruin's orders.

"I would like to offer an apology for that late, unhappy affair," he said, stopping by a chair near the middle of the table.

"What is your meaning?"

"For this unwelcome mission that I have been dispatched, of course."

Had the governor sent him to take her husband's assets? The days of mere conversation with creditors were at an end. Now it would be seized by pirates. He had brought enough men with him to do the job.

"Do you speak of Lord Dunmore's wicked orders to take this house? Lord Sharpe does not owe these debts!" She felt the anger return to her voice.

"No, madame. I am here to take your life. Those are my orders."

The truth was obvious and hung in the air. When she

heard those words leave his lips, she believed him. Driven by the instinct to survive, she made a move to flee from the dining room, but he caught her by her hair. She screamed in pain.

"Please! Please, just let me see my son," she begged as he yanked her and dragged her back towards the table.

Bruin pulled out a chair and savagely sat her in it.

"Now to the matter of food. My men are hungry. What would you like to eat for your final meal?"

She felt tears welling up in her eyes despite her best efforts. "Hunger doesn't concern me."

He ignored her. "What would you like to eat?" he asked, folding his hands on the table. "I have a certain method of doing things."

She cast a worried look at the doorway, spying Lucy lingering in the hallway, wringing her skirt. She motioned her to join them.

"Please tell the kitchen to prepare food for the captain's men," she said in a trembling voice.

"My pleasure," replied Lucy, her voice sad. Lucy had clearly passed through several stages of fright and was left with quiet dejection.

"And for yourself, madame, do not weaken yourself in this heat," Bruin added with a detached informality.

Eliza cast a troubled look at him. She swallowed, trying to steady her voice.

"Rice, Lucy. Rice for myself. Rice to steady my stomach." For some reason her answer had emerged more honest than she was willing to share with this unwanted guest. She hated displaying any vulnerability in front of him.

"The rice should be a remedy," Bruin said.

For the first time, she detected a noticeable accent when he spoke. His Dutch accent rolled the "r"s , and she wondered why she had never heard it before. But if these were to be her last few moments alive, she would listen to every word he spoke more carefully than she had ever done before. It could be the key to making it out of this house with her life.

"Lady Sharpe, fish for the men is all right?" Lucy asked nervously.

Eliza nodded, but Bruin seemed to dislike the idea.

"Fish? Fish on an island? Do you not have any beef? I saw some chickens running around the yard when we arrived. My men could kill some for you and deliver them to the kitchen. Perhaps you can make use of those ..."

"Fish, Lucy. If you could," Eliza said, cutting him off. Such light conversation at a time like this nauseated her. She refused to give him full control.

"It is still your house. And I find myself a guest, unless the creditors take it from you. But I sorely doubt they would show up here now with all of my men in the yard."

For the first time, it occurred to Eliza that she had cast one set of troubles off for another, and for something much, much worse. She would give anything to argue with crafty, devious creditors. Anything was preferable to the torture she now endured.

Bruin walked behind her so she could no longer see what he was doing. Her hands were shaking, and her heartbeats raged against her chest. She waited for some inevitable strike against her head or a swift lunge at her side, but moments passed and no attack came. She heard a metallic click and started in her seat. As she turned, she saw Bruin had opened the cabinet behind her and taken glasses out. He poured them drinks from an already opened bottle of wine, moving around the room with the air of someone very familiar with the house.

Then, he reached over her shoulder and handed her a crystal glass.

"Let us sweeten this difficult task," he said, close to her face. "Drink this for the fear."

She let him place it before her, but she didn't touch it. He took a seat next to her.

He scoffed and then changed the subject. "I have survived every single effort intended to destroy me. Including yours."

His words reminded Eliza that she had done the unthinkable. She had decided to shoot a man, and she had failed.

"I wonder what will become of you," he said with a lightness in his voice. But his narrow blue eyes were on her, like a snake watching a mouse.

She realized he was trapping her in some cruel game. Her death would not come quickly.

I am in charge now, and unlike Lord Dunmore, I like to play with my food.

If he was involving her in this dark sport, then she would engage in trickery too.

"I think I will check on the food. The slaves oftentimes make mistakes," she said quickly.

"No."

"It will only take a moment."

He grabbed her arm and with his free hand, took out his pistol and cocked it. He slammed it on the table, scratching the dark mahogany surface.

Eliza shrank back.

"You will do no such thing. Your kind has never stepped foot in a kitchen. Do not lie to me now," he said. He released her arm as if satisfied with the amount of fear he had caused. "You can either deal with me or with my men outside. I think we both know which you would prefer. My men have wandering hands …"

Lucy returned with some bread and began setting out the crockery. Eliza took a sip of her wine to steel her nerves. If Bruin was going to kill her, why was he waiting to do it?

She could think of only one reason. He enjoyed causing her terror. It enlivened him.

"It is pleasant to see this house so occupied," he continued.

In the background, a slave screamed, and from the windows she watched one of Bruin's men chase a chicken in the front yard. The way he moved revealed his drunkenness. She wondered how many of his men were inebriated.

"We seldom have guests," she said through gritted teeth.

A pained yelp erupted from the hallway, and Eliza shot up from her seat. Bruin extended a hand over her in a silent command, and he strode over to the doorway to inspect the source of the disruption. It was clear someone had grabbed Lucy on her way out of the room.

"This is her house. You must respect it," Bruin muttered in a low tone.

The other man sounded upset.

"Well, can I? There's no harm."

"Absolutely not," Bruin ordered. He returned to the room just as Eliza tried getting back up. She froze and pretended to not have moved.

But then he added a hasty "yet" under his breath.

The two men laughed. Eliza clenched her shoulders until they were taut with stiffness. Bruin sat down, replacing his napkin on his lap as if he was a proper gentleman, and continued with his business.

"I was sent to seize a quantity of military stores and the bodies of you and your husband, but now I am missing one. So I have moved on to the next task," he said, pointing to Eliza. "My orders were to put you to death, destroy your home, and plunder its effects. We were promised four pounds for every sailor who participated, bribed to descend upon Pleasant Hall this very night and pose as ruffians all." He ripped the bread apart and ate his fill.

"You are mistaken, Captain Bruin. You *are* a ruffian. The very worst sort," Eliza spoke with an edge to her voice.

She kept her gaze on the firearm on the table, but the threat to extinguish her life could very well come from some other hidden source. It could even come from his bare hands. She watched him tear apart a new roll with particular interest. She downed more wine, praying it would ease her nerves.

"Call me, Hiram," he said.

"I do not presume to keep such confidence in your

society."

A flash of annoyance crossed his features, but the awkward pause was cut in half with the shrill cry of Philippe upstairs.

Eliza pushed back her chair, but Hiram waved his hand in warning. She heard someone rush up the stairs and soothe him with hushed caresses. Celia must have gone to him.

"Where is the babe?" he asked Eliza. When she did not answer, he sighed. "Bring him here!" Bruin shouted out towards the hall.

After a few moments of stillness, he repeated his command. A somber Celia appeared at the doorway, clutching Philippe in her arms.

He struggled to leave Celia's grasp when he saw his mother. Celia lowered him to the ground and guided him in a waddle towards Eliza, as if the greatest threat to all of them was not occupying the chair beside her. Despite the tension in the room, Eliza bent down and picked him up, clutching him to her chest. He was safe. He was in her arms. She kissed the dark twists of his hair and took a deep breath.

"Keep him here," Bruin said as he motioned to the table top. Eliza balked at the suggestion, but she could tell by his mannerisms that he would not repeat himself. He reached for the pistol, and Eliza sat the baby down on the table, her eyes watering with fear.

Something clicked deep within her core, moving her from the depths of trauma to a sharpened instinct for survival. She had reached a turning point and a place that had less tolerance for fear. Whatever Bruin did to Eliza was one matter, but she would not let him harm her son.

"Now I have your full attention," he said, brimming with self-satisfaction.

She gripped the chair arms until it pained her. Eliza released her hands, but the tension coursed elsewhere in her body, making a line of tight knots in her stomach.

"Ah … here he is. So he is to be the new master of Pleasant Hall," Bruin said, studying the child.

"My husband is not dead," Eliza replied. She would repeat that statement until the end of her days, until she had the proof standing in front of her.

Lucy returned with hot food, and Bruin began eating without a care. Eliza did not even so much as look at her plate.

"He is lucky to have secured an heir. It would be terrible if anything befell the little boy."

"That's enough. Celia, please take him," Eliza snapped, reaching for her son. "Come, Philippe …"

But Bruin blocked her and instead took the child on his knee and started to bounce him.

"My rules tonight," Bruin warned her with a sly look. Then he turned to face Philippe, even as the child tried to edge away from him. "Your mother must learn. She is in sore need of teaching."

The baby bit his small hand and looked down, uncomfortable in his presence.

"You, my boy, have eyes like another man I once knew." When Bruin looked up, his penetrating gaze locked on Eliza. Then he smiled his customary twisted smile. His skin was tanned and taut from days in the sun, and his face was framed by a mass of dark blonde curls. And now he held her entire world.

"I see why you chose the second name of Jean. Philippe. I truly thought that was his given name when we worked in the caves. The boy is his child after all."

He let the words slip from his mouth as if they had no consequence to Eliza whatsoever. Her stomach dropped. This man, her soon-to-be killer, had more information about her than she cared to admit. He simply knew too many things. No one had ever connected the reason for her son's name back to the illegal smuggling operation in the caves before.

But Bruin was a criminal, after all. That shadowy underworld was his territory. Still, she felt the need to defend the child's father.

"And you were fooled the entire time. You assumed Jean was a thief like you," she heard herself say out of spite.

"Oh, I do not know about that. We all worked for the governor, did we not? Even your unfortunate husband. He too once reported to Lord Dunmore."

Bruin continued to bump Philippe on his knee and smiled at him like a benevolent uncle. The baby stiffened up and squealed, looking for Eliza. Once he saw her, he let out a piercing wail.

"Give him to me," Eliza said quietly.

Philippe continued to cry.

Bruin got disgusted and shoved the boy back to his mother. "I cannot stand the sound of a baby crying. Make him stop."

Eliza tried soothing him, but she could not blame the child. She could barely mask her own fear. The way Bruin was eyeing him as he leaned on his hand made her nervous. Eliza called Celia back to the table and handed her the child. She wanted Philippe far away from him. He needed to be taken to safety, whatever that looked like now. When Bruin did kill her, at least the child would have a fighting chance.

Celia looked down at Philippe and muttered something to herself.

"He lost one of his shoes again."

"Search for it and put him to bed, please," Eliza said. Then she lowered her voice and added, "And do not leave the room."

"Why is that?" Bruin interjected, stabbing his food, reminding both women of his awful presence. He constituted a strange blend of taking pleasure by causing others fear while also taking insult that he was indeed the source of their terror.

Philippe started to cry again, as if he could sense he would be parted from his mother forever.

"But if I cannot find it, what would you like me to do? He already lost one last week. Maybe it's in the yard. He kicks them off."

Eliza grew irritated; she wanted Philippe out of that room. The shoes did not concern her. Philippe continued to cry, his shrill voice echoing against the walls.

"It's no matter, it's —" Eliza started to say.

Bruin stamped his foot. "Take the child and go. Search for the stupid shoe and then come back here. I will keep watch. Ten minutes," he said, raising his voice. "At least for that long, I will have peace." He took out a brass pocket watch to monitor the time.

Eliza looked at him incredulously. Celia backed away with the baby like Bruin was a madman, but Eliza did not need to hear his order a second time. Both women rushed out of the room and through Charles' deserted study to the back porch.

Eliza wheeled around.

"Give me Philippe. Go summon Captain Johnson. Meet me in Cleo's house," she said wildly.

Celia understood, disappearing into the darkness to find Captain Johnson, and Eliza took off running towards the back of the plantation and the thick, overgrown banana trees. She passed the scullery where the dishes were washed and heard the noises of furious scrubbing. Pleasant Hall had guests once again, unwelcome as they were. She stopped by Cleo's grave for a few moments, then made her way past her vegetable patch to her old house.

As she waited in the shadows in what was once Cleo's dwelling, she swayed and rocked Philippe while tears gathered in her eyes. If only Cleo's spirit could watch over their enterprise now. Just a few weeks ago, she had been inside this same dirt-covered floor, alive, humming a nameless tune. As Eliza wandered through her empty house with only the dried raffia hanging from the roof making any kind of noise, a deep emptiness carved its way into her core, bringing a fresh wave of melancholy with it.

It was all too much. Her life had swayed violently out of control in a matter of weeks. Charles had been captured by pirates, Dunmore and his crew of greedy men sought to take the house and everything from them, and now, Josiah was dead. Josiah, the slave who introduced her to Shango, the quiet, gentle man who had tended to the gardens and plants around Pleasant Hall.

Eliza had somehow managed to rein in her emotions for this long, but now she released them. Hiram Bruin was not the type of man who would understand tears shed for a fallen slave. Josiah was still lying on the porch steps, his death the most ignominious of all. He had tried to defend her and the house until the very end. He, of all people, who had no reason to want to stay. He had ended up paying with his life. He could have simply run away, like Brutus and a handful of other men had done. But he had stayed, against all reason.

As she wiped her wet face, Eliza felt her fingers crush a small insect. She was no doubt getting ravaged by bugs standing here in the dark, but she had other concerns now. The pouch of gold she had uncovered from Cleo's fresh grave pulled her pocket down. She was covered in dirt now, and Bruin would surely ask questions. But she was also acutely aware that none of this would matter in a few moments.

She heard footsteps approaching, and the captain and Celia ducked into the dwelling. There was a moment of silence, and then the captain spoke.

"Lady Sharpe, there too many o' them. They watchin' the other men, I can't even rally them. And you in that house with that crooked man, he a crooked man, Lady Sharpe. I know him and his ilk, they bad men, Lady

Sharpe. You gonna run?"

His question surprised her. No, she would not run. She would fight. She would stand down and fight for everything that she and Charles had dreamt of accomplishing. If she ran now, the fate of all those enslaved at Pleasant Hall would be sealed. She couldn't run. But she could ensure her only child was safe.

"Captain … Celia … I want you to take this child and guard him with your lives. Row out to the far side of the beach and do not return until it is safe here, do you understand? I will not let this monster use my child as a wager against me. I will not let him harm a single hair on his head."

It was dark, but she could still discern their incredulous faces.

"And if Nassau is not safe, you must leave this island. Sail for London. I will prepare a note for you that no one will question."

There was an uncomfortable pause, and Eliza was on the verge of repeating herself.

"People will stare. They will see two slaves with a white child …" Celia said.

"The note will explain what has occurred here. There is a military headquarters you can go to; the captain will know. Do not stop for any reason." Eliza turned to the captain's towering figure. "I am giving you this pouch of gold. I want you to buy Celia's freedom as soon as you make landfall in London. Pretend you are husband and wife if necessary. And —"

"Are you mad? You gone mad, Lady Sharpe." The

captain sounded horrified. He had accepted the weighted pouch, but he did not retract his hand. He remained
holding it, waiting for Eliza to take it back.

"I have no other choice. Consider it a reward for saving
Charles' life and that of his son."

Now Celia spoke up.

"But Lucy is better suited for this."

Past memories of Celia and Eliza's strained relationship seemed to surface in the shadows between them. She
was aware she was not asking for her input and simply
ordering her to do this, but her reward would be freedom.

"No, her kindness is a weakness. I want *you*." Eliza
recognized that same defiance in Celia that she herself
carried. It was an asset in times like these. "Do you understand? Do not return to that house. Go towards the
beach, through the bush, and take the boat. The one the
men use to catch lobsters."

"White men will look at us and see that baby, take that
gold, and say we stole it," Celia said.

"Captain Johnson will protect both of you. In the note,
I'll leave the addresses for my sisters. I have two of them.
They are in England … how did I not think of this be-
fore? You may not even have to purchase Celia's freedom.
Slavery is not recognized by English common law."

"So he's not going to free me after all …" Eliza could
already hear the anger in her voice.

"Celia, if you set foot on English soil, you *are* free. No
man can compel you to return to the West Indies!" Eliza
exclaimed.

She could tell the two of them were still hesitant, but

ten minutes had passed. Several gunshots erupted in the yard, a warning and reminder that her time was at an end.

"I have to leave," she said as she handed Philippe back to Celia.

In the darkness, she hugged him for one last time and kissed his cheek. She felt her hands pull away from the warmth of his body, his giant eyes watching her, and she turned and left, praying the entire way back to the house. She would have to hurry; Bruin had to suspect something. Fear and adrenaline coursed through her, and something else as well. Hope.

She could not control everything, but she had saved her son. And that was worth everything.

CHAPTER VI

She picked up her skirts, ran back to the lights of the house and up the back porch and inside. With heaving breaths, she returned to the dining room.

"You are late," Bruin drawled. "Eleven minutes. You must have completed a diligent search. Was the lost shoe found?"

"Yes, we located the shoe," Eliza lied, taking her seat once again.

She could tell he was staring at her skirt and her dirt-stained fingernails.

"I took the liberty of refilling your glass," he said.

Eliza was in no mood for pleasantries. She wanted this over with.

"Have you decided how you will kill me?"

This made him laugh. He ran a hand through his hair. "Why would I tell you that?"

His reaction only emboldened her.

"It seems to me that it is rather peculiar that I am still breathing. You arrived over an hour ago."

"My men and I were hungry."

"Perhaps you don't intend to kill me at all."

"It is true. I could find other uses for you before I carry out my orders."

His answer was sickening to hear, but she ignored the lewd remark. An idea had come to her.

"It is rather conflicting. You have orders to kill me, yet I am in possession of something you own. If you were to take my life, I fear you'd never recover it."

She looked down at her dirty fingernails and clenched her hand. It was a risk to bring up the coins when he hadn't mentioned a word about them. After Charles had revealed his father would regale his sons with tales of coins he had buried in the sea just outside the house, she was even less sure that they belonged to Bruin. But she did know one thing: he was ruled by his avarice.

Bruin readjusted his position in the chair, smiling to himself, no doubt entertained by dark thoughts of what he wanted to do to her before he killed her. The coins were evidently the last thing on his mind. Had she calculated poorly?

"There is time enough for that," he answered.

He surveyed the room around them and the crystal chandelier that hung over the table.

"It must be pleasant to have this grand house, away from the stink of town, on the water. With a charming son and wife who looks like you. I envy Charles. It is true. I know you believe me in possession of a black heart, but it is a terrible calamity that has befallen him. After all he has gone through on this island. And now what troubles will be brought to you, his poor wife? You are in a most weak and helpless position. The woman he loves should not have to suffer so."

Eliza's eyes grew wide. He used the present tense. He did not speak like all the other men she had encountered since this disaster had struck. He spoke as if he knew Charles was indeed still living.

"You speak as if he's still alive. He is, isn't he?" she asserted. "You know something. Tell me!"

Bruin relished this sudden onslaught of attention. He played with his gold rings, the red and blue gemstones in them catching the shifting light from the candles.

"Indeed, I know all of the dark elements that frequent this island," he said slowly. He looked up at her with a narrowed gaze. "But why should I tell you a thing?"

Bruin used a peculiar breed of truth telling, a raw mix of honesty and lies that she would do well to keep at the forefront of her mind.

"Please, Captain. If you know anything, anything at all, please tell me. I am in need of help."

She could no longer contain herself. She kneeled before his seat, holding the arm of his chair because she dared not touch the man.

"There is no need for formality. Call me Hiram," he reminded her.

"Hiram," she said, pleading with him.

Something had shifted in the room. She understood that she was playing with fire, but a burn seemed more than worthwhile if she could finally attain the answers she sought.

He reached down and stroked the side of her face. "The way you say my name sounds like a prayer."

Eliza felt her ears grow hot. She looked down.

"Although, one matter puzzles me. I have heard the rumors. Why do you want him back?"

Now her blush deepened. "He is my husband. The rest is not your concern."

"But if you want my help, I think it is."

He tipped her chin up so she faced him again.

"I am still here. My husband has been accused of betrayal by treasonous men. I will be successful in clearing his name and bringing him back to Pleasant Hall, even if I have to risk my life."

She stopped herself short of telling him the entire truth. That Charles had planned to slowly manumit his slaves. It was as if by speaking this shared dream of theirs aloud, she might cause it to disintegrate into the ether. Especially in front of a man like Hiram Bruin.

"Lofty ambitions, Lady Sharpe. But no doubt very noble of you."

Bruin reached for something near his knee, and she heard a blade unsheathed. He held her still before she could move away, and danced the edge of the blade across her neck.

"The question is, how badly do you want your husband back? He clearly was not a good enough husband to guard his most precious jewel. It also seems to me that he caused enough distress for you to seek ... *help* elsewhere." The trail of the blade began to move lower, near the swell of her breasts. "Unless the rumors are true, and you are insatiable in appetite. Tell me, Lady Sharpe … no, that will not do. Eliza. But that name does not suit you, either … no."

Eliza exhaled sharply, louder than she intended.

"Liza. I much prefer that name. It is shorter, more sudden. More urgent. *Liza* …"

She closed her eyes, immediately thinking of one thing he would agree to. Eliza feared the key to her survival lay between her legs. The act would bring him a few moments of satisfaction and her a lifetime of pain. She refused to suffer the thought any further.

"I beg you to remember your place, Captain. You are a guest." She used the title as a boundary, placing more space between him and her.

"I am a guest no longer. Would you speak to a guest using his first name? I believe we are on more intimate terms now, Liza." His tone was annoyed, but he was still entertained by the spectacle of her on her knees before him.

"Hiram, please … tell me what you know."

Her insistence about Charles further frustrated him. He put his knife away and motioned for her to return back to her seat. The increased distance between them was a blessing. She took her glass of wine and drank it, savoring the way it settled her. She would take any relief she could get.

Bruin was still infinitely pleased by her display of weakness. He refilled her glass.

"You, Liza, are as weak as water."

She shot a glare at him,

"You must forget the sight of the sea in a storm."

Bruin raised his glass in the air as acknowledgment of her sharp wit. "I am here on orders to kill you, and you think I can help you …" He shook his head.

"Yes." She was unflinching in her answer. "I am still alive, just as Charles was not killed on the street that day. We both know it. If Dunmore truly wanted him dead, I would have his body. I have no answers. I know in my heart that he still lives. And you just confirmed the same."

"You are forgetting one important part. Why would I help someone like you?"

"I think you intend to use me. That's why we are still here, at this table, talking."

That made him smile again. He was always grinning, plotting, scheming. It made her sick, but she could survive this if she convinced him to keep her alive.

He did not hide the way he looked at her. "I do intend to use you in all sorts of ways you cannot possibly imagine."

A second warning, but she blundered past it. "Hiram, help me," she begged.

"And what do I get in return?"

"I will return your gold coins. And I am adding interest. I have held on to them for two years. Why shouldn't there be interest? Your payment will be doubled."

But she did not receive the reception she wanted. The coins appeared to hold less significance for him now, money not having the same sway over him as it once did. Her thoughts circled back to his pardon with the governor. What had Bruin promised the governor, Lord Dunmore, in exchange? What had made his fortunes so vastly improved?

"I am hardly the only sinner here in Nassau. I know the man who did it," Bruin finally said.

"What is his name? What is the name of his ship? I can seek passage on an armed merchantman and bring him back."

"There is war looming now, Liza. The waters are not the same as when you first arrived."

"I am aware. I will hire help. I only need a name. A starting point. I will give you the coins this very moment."

Bruin grinned and looked away. "I am looking at something of higher value."

She ignored him and pressed on with her mission. "Where do I need to sail? Who do I need to look for?"

"Why pay passage to sail with an armed ship? I am all the protection you would need," he said with a cunning smile. "No one knows the world of shadows better than I."

She recoiled at his suggestion, but she couldn't deny the truth of what he had said. "Or you can simply tell me where to look …"

"I cannot do that. My world is governed by a certain set of rules, but they are rules just the same. Perhaps you need to be reacquainted with them."

He moved his chair closer to her, so that their knees were almost touching. He was eyeing her like a prize, but she would not stop until she had answers.

"And I have something else to offer you," she said quietly. "For your cooperation. For a gentleman's decency …"

"I am redeemed a gentleman in your eyes now?" he said, his voice edged with sarcasm. "Although I do recall your words from before. At least you have given me the benefit of possessing more decency than the governor. And that I am honest in my thievery. I believe those were your words that afternoon."

She knew that he might have overheard her tirade the last time she had stepped foot in Lord Dunmore's mansion. But that he would remember her words after all this time surprised her.

She had more currency with him than she realized. Bruin was an older man, nearly eleven years older than Charles. Why would he be any less susceptible to a woman's charms?

"Even if I retrieve my husband, none of us are safe on this island with that man." She wanted him turned against his employer. A man like Bruin had shallow loyalty at best. Perhaps this angle would work stronger in her favor.

"You forget I have a pardon," he countered.

"You trust your security, your future, to a piece of paper?"

"Yes," he scoffed. "It is from the governor himself."

Bruin was taking offense again. She would have to tread carefully.

"Yet it seems to me … which paper would carry more weight? A moldy paper from a corrupt tyrant, or one from an anointed king?" It was a bold assertion, but she would say anything to get what she wanted.

That familiar crooked smile crossed his lips again.

"Now you have my interest. What is your womanly mind plotting now?"

"Only what serves your highest interest, Hiram," she replied as she touched his knee. She could feel his body warmth through the fabric. She swallowed her disgust away.

"My, have matters taken a turn here tonight …" he said as he watched her hand remain on him. His voice trailed off into breathlessness.

"I do wonder what you did in order to secure such a mercy from Lord Dunmore."

"We all do things out of desperation, as you are well aware, Lady Sharpe."

He leaned closer to her, and although she stiffened up, she did not retreat.

"One day you will have to face condemnation in an Admiralty Court," she said, "to prove that you sailed under British colors and not false ones. You have a questionable past, and these islands are riddled with pirates. Do you truly think Lord Dunmore's pardon will see you through? Men are planning on denouncing him to the king, with stronger evidence to support him being recalled. It would be foolish to rely solely on him. Dunmore's promise will count for nothing. What if Whitehall decides that the pardon Lord Dunmore granted you did not give him the authority to brand you an innocent man?"

The contempt had faded from his eyes, and he almost softened.

"Why do you suddenly care for my future?"

"Because you hold the key to mine."

A sudden wave of fatigue hit her. She hadn't slept in days. It was a mistake to drain those glasses of wine, especially when she couldn't afford to let her guard down in front of him.

"It is true. How will you maintain your table? Your manner of living? You cannot hide from the creditors forever. Everything will soon belong to them. You risk starvation and homelessness." He placed his hand on top of hers. "Let me spare you from the creditors. I hear they are particularly bloodthirsty on these small islands … you will lose all of this."

Now he was offering a solution to stop Dunmore's men from foreclosing on the property's debts. Bruin was far from a good man, but he was acting more open and franker than any other man she had sought help from. However, he appeared to be more concerned than their situation warranted, as if he suddenly had some personal stake in her nightmare. They had entered the room as a killer and his victim, and now they spoke as co-conspirators.

"Have they any proof that such debts even exist?" he continued.

She perked up. In her grief and the chaos that had ensued, she had let fear take over. When the first creditors had appeared, it seemed a dim possibility. It was all a ruse. They were Dunmore's men. But then more and more of them came, and when Charles' once staunch allies from the political meetings also abandoned her, the possibility was extinguished. But Bruin had just uttered it once again. He knew how these men worked; he understood these terrible things. He was telling the truth.

While she was repulsed by him, there was a certain allure to the words he spoke. He was the only man who had offered her hope. A real solution to a seemingly un-solvable dilemma. His timely aid and advice might prove to be the means of rescuing her from her dire lot. This problem was caused by darkness, and perhaps it could only be resolved with it.

She thought of Shango and the prayers she had uttered. Celia had said her prayers would be answered, but not in a way she would necessarily want. What transpired before her and the privateer seemed divinely orchestrated. She had called this in. It was violent, it was dark, and Bruin was a breathing version of such traits. If Lord Dunmore fancied himself the Island King, Captain Bruin was the King of the Shadow World. She had survived impossible odds, and now she had turned this pirate to have sympathy for her cause. It was the opportunity she'd prayed for, and it was brilliant in its danger.

A small part of her was attracted to the power this man held, for power was the only language the men of these islands spoke and understood. She could rail and scream all day at passing men, and they would only sit in judgment of her. They already called her a madwoman, and perhaps this venture was another sign that Eliza had indeed lost herself to some heat-induced madness. But these men would listen to Bruin. They feared him. And if they feared him, she needed him on her side.

"I saw my whole world fall apart before my eyes that day," she said quietly. "I am part of the forsaken now. I dread that Lord Dunmore will never be recalled."

"Leave this island." His tone was firm.

She couldn't do that. She needed to stay and defend this house.

"I fear that there will be no justice against him." She

gazed forlornly out the window.

"You have been deserted in your adversity. I want to help you. I have a ship, laden with men, with treasures, you will want for nothing."

Except for my husband.

His newfound willingness to help did not entirely bury his sinister intentions. Eliza was now engaging in a delicate dance with death itself. She knew instinctively that she would not leave this room tonight the same woman as before. But she also knew that she needed Bruin to take her to the underworld. To deliver her from this sphere of heartache and conspiring humanity. She would need to fight wickedness with wickedness, and here he was, already disobeying Lord Dunmore's orders. She still breathed. She repeated the thought again and again.

"Dum spiro, spero …" While I breathe, I hope …

"Leave with me and my men on my ship tomorrow morning, and I will bring you to your husband," Bruin said, urgency in his voice.

An answer to all her dilemmas sat before her. It was beyond tempting, but she hesitated. There was finally a light, a crack in the doorway that promised an end to her present misery. But still, she did not trust this new opportunity.

"You must do your utmost to deliver him to safety," she said.

"At the moment, I do not know what that may look like. But there is no safety to be found in this house or on this island," he replied.

It wasn't a lie. She wasn't even safe with him, and yet

she was about to trust him with her life and that of her husband. What other choice did she have?

"The creditors told me I am forbidden to leave," she added.

"If you are dead, does it matter?"

It was a clever play on words. Now, for the first time, she smiled. Her limbs were heavy with wine and lack of sleep.

"And you can hold me as surety that you will have your gold returned to you."

"With interest. And a pardon from the king himself," he confirmed.

She nodded, and the room began to turn.

"You should retire; you need to rest."

His accent was prominent again. The way he stressed every other syllable danced in her ears. She stood up, but her knees buckled. He was there to steady her. She excused herself. She had expended all of her energy, but she was one step closer in knowing what had happened to Charles.

"If you intend to stay the night, there is a room down the hall that you can make use of. Lucy will prepare it for you."

"I know where it is. Thank you. Good evening, Liza."

She was so exhausted the strangeness of that statement did not register with her. She saw him watch her leave from the corner of her eye. Her weary feet took her up the stairs and to the safety of her room. She put her trusted chair against the door, blockading herself in for the night. She doubted she would be able to sleep throughout the evening. She hadn't been able to any other night, but this wave of drowsiness was a welcome gift. She would rest for a few hours and then rise to make the note for Celia that she had promised. The slaves usually rose by four in the morning, so someone would be able to deliver the note to her and Captain Johnson. Perhaps by then, Captain Johnson would construe a better plan to deal with these pirates.

As she went to close the curtains by her window, she saw a handful of Bruin's men gathered by a bonfire they had erected. Their hearty laughter echoed throughout the otherwise still yard. They were commiserating and waiting for something.

Her stomach turned. Dealing with him was one matter, but to sail on a ship with these rough men? She would be outnumbered. Perhaps there was another way to get the answers she sought. At least she had received confirmation of the singular most important fact: Charles was indeed alive. Eliza could make different decisions now. She could fight harder with this fact confirmed. And if Bruin was in possession of this knowledge, surely others on the island knew it as well. The truth could not remain hidden for long.

Now a shadowy figure chased down a chicken and wrestled with it. They did not appear to have appreciated their fish meal. She pitied the poor chickens. She struck the curtain closed and lay down. Events had moved so fast in the last few days. It felt like a blur of desperation and violence that clouded her mind. Her solitude emphasized the hollow feeling in the pit of her stomach, occupying a space in between, of terror, madness, and the desperation of wanting to preserve her life. She had been offered a solution to her problems, but she could still feel Bruin's thumb pressed into her throat.

How could she know he would stay true to his word? Her doubts began to consume whatever fleeting hope he had offered her downstairs.

A few moments ago, she had felt reassured that she had chosen right. It was foolish and it was deadly, but if she joined Bruin and let him recover her husband, then she and Charles could finish the legal process of slowly manumitting the slaves at Pleasant Hall. They would stand a chance against the evil excesses of a crooked government.

But she did not trust Bruin. He profited off of Lord Dunmore's vile schemes. Eliza couldn't accept that fate had driven her into the arms of a killer. She recoiled at the thought of her supplications downstairs, how she had begged on her knees, how she had so desperately touched him. She was playing a risky game she was not sure she could win. The longer she stood in the room by herself, the louder the blaring warning rang out in her mind.

And she most certainly did not trust his crew. There didn't seem to be a reason for Bruin to lie to her, to risk his own standing by not following the governor's orders, but he was a criminal. He had survived this long due to his cunning ways. It was clear that he wanted something from her, and she knew in the depths of her heart that she would refuse to willingly give it. She had made a daring performance in front of him tonight, but she feared the thought of being trapped on a ship with him, an oaken vault with no escape except the bottomless sea.

Other concerns gnawed at her. She agonized over what fate would befall Pleasant Hall if she was no longer present. The creditors would probably rejoice at the sight of her absence. They would seize all the slaves and steal what property Charles owned. She could not leave this island until their false claims of entitlement were destroyed once and for all.

There had to be another solution. She needed more time. She needed silence to think. And most of all, she needed rest.

Her bed was calling her. She needed to sleep, and after she slept, she would have the energy to deal with Bruin. Philippe was safe. His bassinet was empty, and she wanted to be with him. But he was alive, and that was all she cared about. Now when she refused the captain's offer tomorrow, she would have the reassurance that they could not hurt her only child.

Eliza felt she had crossed some bridge with the privateer. She feared he would be upset, but it was not a crime to change her mind. He could take his coins, whether they were rightfully his or not, and leave. Perhaps that was their hidden purpose after all. They would save her life. She sighed, laying her head down on the pillow. As her spine finally released all she had carried that day, chills raced along the contours of her body. In the darkness of her closed eyes, the room began to spin, and she surrendered to it.

It would all make sense tomorrow.

CHAPTER VII.

Eliza tossed and turned on the now damp, wet bed, stirring, tangled in the sheets. What the creditors had so candidly accused her of was indeed true. She had descended into madness. Sleep evaded her, and instead, she walked the line between blackness and flashes of nightmares.

Josiah lies on the porch steps—they should have buried him. Why does he lie there still? Why is there so much death on this land? It is coming for her next. Philippe will be an orphan. She has lost the battle.

Alastor pants in heaving breaths, his deep eyes full of terror. She escaped only to get caught in more danger. The palm trees arc and spin in the sky above her. The musket she holds fires nothing but smoke. The metal barrel grows hot and burns her skin, like the fire from the stables.

The shadow of a stranger moves along the wall when there is no one there. Lucy screams, but she is far from this room. The scream is distanced and pained. The window slams open; the breeze engulfing the white curtains. Bruin's face hovers above hers, with his smile conveying twisted delight, and a door slams in the hallway, signaling the ghostly presence of Tabitha.

His voice rings out in her ears, "I will take Pleasant Hall. It belongs to us, Liza. Then I will take you, too …" He watches her, stroking her sweaty cheek. No, she should be alone.

The chair, the chair is against the door. Did you place it by the door?

Yes. She is safe, but why does she not feel safe?

In a haze, she awakened without opening her eyes. She remembered locking herself in and knew that no one could bother her. She flipped to her side as another cascade of shadowy figures covered everything she saw.

She tries to scream, but no noise leaves her lips, and now she can no longer move. Something holds her down, pressing on her. She sees herself lying there on her bed, the sheets twisted, like the thoughts ravaging her mind without mercy. Her body tenses, preparing to defend against an invasion. The bed is rocking, rocking, an idle rocking that she recognizes deep in her bones.

The window is cracked open far more than she would ever allow it. The candles blow out, their spent smoke wafts in lazy circles up to the ceiling, sticky with humidity and decay.

These images filter through her head until she sees black pieces of charred guinea corn leaves filtering through the air. Pleasant Hall is on fire. She has to leave; she has to escape. This will only end in misery.

And then a pause, a cessation in torment. A voice she recognizes, one that she once craved, "Be careful who you trust, Eliza. The age of chivalry is gone …" A strained whisper from a lover, violently ripped away from this world.

Jean. He is dead. She will soon join him. But she sees Charles, his back covered in his red officer's jacket. Red like

Shango's preferred color. He turns and reaches out his hand …
"I will wait for you, Eliza …"

She fully awoke now with a gasp, her bed still rocking from one side to another. Her shoulder had collided with a wooden wall, and once she regained her senses, she recognized it. It was a bulwark on a ship.

Eliza was drenched in sweat, and there seemed to be a lack of air in the space where she lay. For a moment, her thoughts raced back to the ship that had delivered her to Nassau over two years ago. In the haziness of her mind, she momentarily feared she had never made it there, that everything she had experienced, the horrors and the beauty, constituted nothing but a fever dream.

But then the sound of two disjointed hammers sounded above her on the upper deck, followed by a strange, mournful whistle that further settled her into wakefulness. The whistle was a low and clear sound, like the call of a bird, but slightly out of key. It wavered with a slight change of pitch between notes. It was a beautiful noise, strangely out of place for the situation she found herself in, but it also carried a precise tone of sorrow. It mingled with the sounds of water sloshing against the sides of the boat as it moved through the turquoise sea.

She froze when she heard it. It was so clear, so near-sounding. Then she slowly raised herself up. Her legs felt heavy, and in her fretful sleep, she had disturbed her skirts. She saw deep bruises printed on her thighs, and she stared at them in confusion. Now she looked at her surroundings in horror, not recognizing anything except for a single trunk from her bedroom. Terror seeped deep into her. She had been kidnapped, taken against her will.

She ran to the door, and on finding it unlocked, she flung it open and raced out to the quarterdeck. The smell of salt air and freshly varnished wood roasting in the Caribbean heat wafted past her face. When she didn't see anyone on the quarterdeck, she descended to the main deck. Dozens of men were stationed here, some hauling ropes while others adjusted the rigging. Some sailors were balancing themselves high over the breeze-swept ship, standing on lines and shouting to each other. A few of them stared at her presence, but the rest were too engaged in their tasks. A burly man approached her, holding a piece of paper.

"Where is the captain? Captain Bruin. I must speak to him."

"Ye must sign yer name," the man gruffly said. He ignored her entreaties.

"I was forced on board against my will; a grave crime has occurred."

"Before I do anything with ye on board, ye must sign yer name."

"You're not the captain. You cannot give me orders!"

She shoved past him, not realizing what a mistake she had committed.

Eliza kept walking, searching all the moving parts of the ship for a familiar face. She had already noticed that she did not recognize the small islands that ambled past them as the ship cut a swift, hissing line through the clear water. They were moving fast. She tried to keep her panic at bay.

She heard cursing behind her just as she reached the steps leading to the forecastle at the front of the ship. A rough arm grabbed her and spun her around.

"Listen, sign yer name and be done with it, ye damned whore! I am the quartermaster here, and ye will do as I say!"

"Where is the captain?" she repeated, slowly as if he was incapable of speaking English.

"I'll make the damned woman sign it; she can sign it with her blood if she protests so."

A group of sailors who were gawking at the spectacle made way for a large shirtless man who reeked of body odor.

"Are you deaf? Or are you stupid? Don't insult the quartermaster. Sign it," he demanded, towering over her.

A chorus of angry voices erupted behind him. The men grew more rowdy the longer she protested.

"We didn't even want her here!"

"This was a terrible idea; what's gotten into that man's head—having a woman on board."

"Sign it!" The quartermaster shoved the paper at her.

"No! Take me to the captain!"

"Just kill her and be done with it!" the tall man roared.

She backed up into the steps leading to the deck above them.

"*Godverdomme!*" "Goddamit!" a familiar voice cursed.

Eliza twisted her head and saw Bruin perched by the railing of the forecastle, smiling as if he had enjoyed witnessing the entire scene.

"You! You monster! You fiend! You have taken me against my will!" she began to shout.

Eliza tried making her way up towards him, but the privateer stopped her and dragged her back down with him to the small mob of discontented men. He held on to her wrist like she was a disobedient child.

"Lady Sharpe, I advise you to not upset my quartermaster. He is older in his years, and such disturbances try his patience. He is only doing his job. These are our written articles. Every crew member is expected to sign. It is custom. Otherwise, you risk insulting him."

"I am not a member of your crew, you devil!" Eliza snarled.

Bruin sighed. "But you find yourself transplanted on the *Fortuyne*, do you not? You have to sign. It sets out the rules and punishments for those who break them."

He waved the paper so close to her face it hit her.

"I can't read that. It's not in English," she snapped.

"It is in Dutch. Most of my men cannot read. That matters not. Just sign it."

Eliza exhaled, her rage only growing the more these men ogled at her. They watched her like hungry dogs, animalistic in nature. A thin blonde man at the edge of the group said something in Dutch to Bruin, and they engaged in a conversation that ended in laughter. The other man walked off, bundling a pile of rope together. Heat flushed Eliza's chest.

"I would sign it, or my men will know you are being treated better than them. They are nearly impossible to control once they get started."

Eliza broke free of his grip and ran back towards the cabin she had awakened in. She refused to think of it as her room. Eliza would lock herself inside it, then find a way to leave this ship.

But she didn't make it very far. Bruin caught up to her and steered her towards a room past the one she was familiar with. It was a large, spacious cabin with a series of glass windows that overlooked the sea and the wake the ship was making. It was clearly his room. She spied a lengthy bed on the side and a large bookshelf filled with dusty books and maps. Large sea shells and pieces of sea fans dotted the other shelves. On the wall was a dark and bubbling oil painting of Jesus Christ, his stern face watching in judgment, one hand reaching out to the viewer while another held a large black globe. The way the artist had painted the pale face made it appear as though it was floating over the dark, scarred background.

It was strange to see a holy picture hung up in such a depraved man's chambers. Then she noticed the numerous weapons, swords, and pistols, all arranged in racks on the upper walls. This was no ordinary captain's cabin.

"Sign the damned paper and be done with it," he demanded.

Her body was tense with protest. "I have nothing to sign it with."

Bruin cursed and took a quill, dipping it in ink. He thrust it towards her.

She looked at the creased paper again, desperate to make sense of what she was about to sign, but she could not understand Dutch. At any rate, it seemed a small price to pay in order to get what she truly wanted. She signed it with a shaky hand and threw the quill.

"Eh, look, it is the prettiest signature there," he remarked, looking at it with pride.

"I find myself forced to be part of your crew. You brought me here against my will!"

"You want to find your husband, do you not?"

She threw her hands in the air, exasperated.

"I changed my mind. I was going to tell you in the morning, but you —"

"We delivered you unmolested, as you requested last night. Do you not remember? Or did you drink too much of that spoiled wine? I thought Pleasant Hall would offer finer claret."

"You did something to my drink. And I have bruises on my legs from you, you monster!"

"You were heavy to carry; I apologize for any damage that occurred."

"I did not agree to this!"

"I had to make you amenable. You would have surely protested my manner of transportation. I do not think highborn ladies like to have bags placed over their heads. There is a certain order in which we do things. One day you will understand."

"So you drugged me? You admit to your malfeasance!"

"You said you wanted to be on this ship, so why does it matter?"

"It matters greatly! Don't be such a fool! I demand to be taken off this cursed ship."

"Do you?" He smiled and looked down, shaking his head.

"Yes! This is unacceptable. And my poor son, who will

watch him?" She added this to prove her point. She did not want to reveal that he had secretly been carried to safety. But it was still a sore point. Children did not often make it past five years of age, and she was squandering that precious time away from him.

Then her heart sank as she realized she had never created the note for Celia. Now they were tasked with keeping the boy alive in a hostile world with no surety from her and no address for her sisters in England. In a moment of weakness, she had chosen to close her eyes and sleep while danger stalked in her home. Eliza had felt so sure of herself; she had believed she had outsmarted the conniving privateer. Only he had a failproof plan that he set into motion the minute she lost consciousness. He had waited so patiently, refilling her glass drop by drop, and when she had fallen asleep, he had made his move.

Eliza had outsmarted no one. She had failed. And now everything she cared for, including her son, was at risk. The creditors would descend on Pleasant Hall and haul away the slaves. And what would become of her child now?

The truth was debilitating. What if she had truly lost everything? She felt sick to her stomach. She took a seat in a chair in front of Bruin's desk. She felt like she was out of her body, that she was not herself, that she was floating in a void. Her hands began to shake.

"Are you feeling seasick, Liza?"

"Damn you. That is not my name."

"Yes, it is. I christened you last night."

The fingerprints on her legs, the heaviness of the wine, the fact that she had awakened in a place that was not her bed, the way this man spoke in whispers of threats, drove her into a burst of panic. Shock had transformed to urgent flight. She fled to the door, only for him to stop her.

"Shh, shh," he whispered softly to her.

She struggled to maintain control of her breaths. Her chest rose and fell in rapid succession, and she was disgusted to see that he had noticed as well.

"I do not have many rules, but I do have one. Never show these men your fear. My men are animals, and they will not hesitate to seek advantage," he murmured in her ear. "That is why I brought you in here. Alone."

She could feel his hot breath on her neck. She closed her eyes, taking an unsteady swallow.

"Shh, there we go … breathe, Liza." He spoke like the Devil in her ear.

Every time he said that name, the name he had given her, it was like a slap across her face. When he comforted her, it did not bring her comfort. When he spoke the truth, she could only discern new lies trapped in his teeth, waiting to be used on her.

"Would you like to lay down, Liza?" Bruin asked.

The suggestion was insidious. Tears began to blur her vision.

"Your son is safe. That slave is watching him like a hawk."

She didn't give a damn about his reassurances. "I want to leave this ship. I demand it," she managed to say.

His scheming hand gripped her shoulder. "Liza, we are in motion, and we are not stopping."

"I will leave!" she snarled.

"You can, over the side. It has not stopped you before."

His attempt at humor made her lose control. Angry, bitter tears spilled over her cheeks. The bright cabin disappeared in a shifting waver of defeat. She could feel a cold dampness in her armpits, brought on by fear.

Bruin sighed and continued, "But you also demanded that I help you recover your husband. You confuse me, Liza."

"You took me against my will," she said angrily.

"You knew we were to leave in the morning."

"I changed my mind, you bastard."

"I have reason to believe that once you set your mind to something, you very rarely change course. Like my ship, Liza," Bruin replied, his tone confident.

"I did not say goodbye to my son." A cry escaped her lips, and she covered her mouth with embarrassment.

"He will not even know you are gone. At his age, he will not know the difference."

"What have I done?" she whispered to herself.

"There was a terrible fire. Do you not recall anything? I had to carry you from the house in my arms."

"If there was a fire, then you set it; do not lie to me!"

"What a terrible thing to accuse me of."

He laughed. An innocent man would have surely taken offense at that. She focused on steadying her breaths when his mood suddenly switched and he slammed her into the door.

"I hope you never forget for one moment that the only reason you are alive right now is because of me," Bruin said, the venom unmistakable in his voice. "Your every breath is a gift—from me." He mocked her shallow breaths, then pushed into her again. "You should be thanking me."

Eliza's eyes narrowed. She hated him, and she cursed that she had missed hitting him with her bullet last night.

Bruin would not release her. "You are on my ship, you will abide by my rules. And I do not give a damn how you ended up on here with me now."

"I didn't agree to your proposal."

He studied her, his eyes roaming over every inch of her tear-sodden face. "Oh, you did not need to. See, sometimes I ask because I like to pretend to be a gentleman. But truly … I had no intention of ever giving you a choice. The choice was always mine, and I decided long ago."

His words were ominous. How long ago had he planned this? He continued, delighting in her breakdown. "I took you from that cursed house. That house of witchcraft. Who is Tabitha?"

Eliza froze, her eyes wide. "How did you come by that name?"

"You said it in your sleep. A door moved of its own accord, and you spoke as if in answer to some evil spirit. I took you then, and I rushed out."

Eliza dropped to the floor, sinking slowly in a pool of her skirts. He joined her, crouching low. To hear that some fragments of her nightmares last night were real chilled her.

"What I have now accomplished was not without some risk."

"I fear the true cost of your generosity. I fear you will require some breathtaking sum for this service," she said solemnly. She wanted to add that she feared him, but she did not want to give him the pleasure.

"It is true, no one sails on my ship for free."

"And what sum do you require?" Her voice was strained and resentful.

"Pleasant Hall."

"But you, you said there was a terrible fire …" Her confusion stopped her midsentence.

He stood up and laughed quietly, walking back to his desk. She savored the space between them. "Perhaps there was not. Did you see any smoke from the deck?"

She looked at him like he was a man disturbed. If he truly returned Charles to her, he could take the damn house. But he would receive a house only. Not the slaves.

"And how did you know what to prepare?" she asked. "I saw a trunk in my cabin." She detested calling that space hers.

"I made one of your slaves do it. We forced the pretty young one." He was organizing his papers as if he was an ordinary sea captain concerned with tidiness. He paused when he saw the look of concern on her face. "To pack your belongings, I mean. She put up quite the protest. Her eyes were huge like saucers. One of my associates had to clamp a hand over her tight little mouth while I carried you to the horses."

Eliza rose to a shaky stand and began to open the door. She could no longer tolerate him or his manner of speaking. Her stomach was twisted into a knot, and every word that left his mouth only made the knot tighter. He saw that she was about to leave and crossed the room in two strides.

"Liza, remember, you flew to me and implored my protection. You should really thank me."

His eyes read her face, as if he actually expected her gratitude and not her hatred. "And something else; you really should not let the mosquitos ravage your skin like that. You are far too pretty to be marked up so."

Eliza had no more words for him. She glared at him and made her way back to her stuffy cabin. She felt hopeless and lost, and she did not want to unravel any further. He would only take delight in it.

CHAPTER VIII.

“You must dine with me, or the men will be upset. They are not afforded the privilege. What is more, John is hearing every complaint, and, like a woman, he will leave from here and gossip. He will tell them how ungrateful you were to your host,” Bruin said, taking a sip of his wine.

Eliza did not touch her food or her drink. She only glared at him and took an occasional glance at the young boy who served them. John, as he was called, couldn’t be more than fourteen years old. He wore a single hoop earring and had a golden mess of curls. He possessed an almost feminine beauty, and he was throwing his future away with this lot.

Perhaps he didn’t view it that way. She wondered what had driven him to seek employment on this ship and if he was an orphan. Working for a man like Hiram Bruin offered no good advantage in life, and she pitied him.

“I started my life on a ship when I was near his age. It is an honor to serve a captain. He will do well in this life,” Bruin remarked as if in response to her silent thoughts.

He watched the boy walk around the room with muted interest.

Eliza had initially refused to return to his cabin after yesterday. Tonight, she was not afforded the luxury. It was difficult to keep her distance when their cabins bordered one another. She was angry, but Bruin seemed pleased to have her there regardless of her mood. She looked down at her plate, and her stomach growled with hunger. She had forgotten the last time she had actually eaten. The wine glass stood off to the side. She refused to touch that, but despite her stubbornness, she began to eat, ravenously filling her mouth.

"You have a certain steadiness under trial that is to be admired," Bruin said.

Eliza wiped her mouth with a napkin and looked up, sorely disappointed to be reminded of his presence.

"I await a miracle, Captain."

"How far will your determination lead you, I wonder." He leaned on his hand and watched her consume the food. "Do you know why you will be called Liza from now on?" he said, his voice filled with amusement. "Because I will make you a new woman."

"That is not my name, nor will I answer to it."

"Do you find your quarters more agreeable now?"

Eliza did not answer him. She was too occupied cutting her vegetables.

In truth, she detested her new living space. It was cramped and barren. A nearly blackened mirror hung on the wall above a small table and stool, and there was an uncomfortable bed. That was almost all of it. When she returned to her cabin yesterday, she had more time to notice its true state. She had found a hair ribbon and one used stocking, no doubt from a whore the men had entertained on the ship. The air even smelled like cheap perfume.

An older man had come by offering to clean it, although he grumbled to himself the entire time. To her dismay, he had only made everything wet, but she did not know what she truly expected from a group of men. The rest of the ship seemed immaculate, but she did not dare to venture belowdecks. That was a separate dominion from the quarterdeck and the illusion of safety.

"We do not have the luxury of many private quarters, Liza. This is not an English naval ship, outfitted with cabins for the officers. There is either my cabin or the one you currently have."

"The one I have suits me," she quickly said, through gritted teeth.

"Do you not find ease in my company?"

She gave up keeping her face down and sent him a look full of daggers.

"I confess I cannot. You have broken all manner of trust between us, if such a concept indeed ever existed. There is no longer any assurance in our dealings."

"You have no choice but to trust me, Liza." Bruin leaned forward over the table.

It was difficult to ascertain whether she was his guest or his prisoner. Both positions were undesirable. She regretted ever considering an alliance with the king of Nassau's underworld.

"I do not love fortune. But God has blessed me with it," Bruin said, observing the contents of his own cabin. She could envision him counting piles of Dutch guilders in her mind.

Eliza looked up to see the eyes of God staring down at her from the cracked oil painting. She busied herself with her food, but Bruin was in the mood for conversation.

"I overcame my humble beginnings with my skills as a seaman with the design of making my own fortune. Surely you understand that?"

"Nothing on earth is worth going to Hell for," she hissed.

She wondered what secrets he kept stashed in his sea chest; what foul misdeeds he kept hidden from the prying eyes of the world. Bruin bit his lower lip and grinned.

"I will have you know that Lord Dunmore told me I could not carry a ship unless I accepted the command of my own ship to be fitted out. And so I became a privateer. My crew is mixed. Whoever can help man a ship, I take.

"Men will do anything for coin. The seas are anarchy. I found myself surrounded by the lowest scoundrels, the sort of men who, for a farthing, would slit the throat of their master or violate his wife behind his back."

Eliza assumed he spoke with so little regard to get a rise out of her. She retained her stony composure.

"So you are proud of that which you should be ashamed."

"I protect the island from attack by the French and the Spanish; you surely know that. I helped rid your kingdom of a notorious spy."

The food stuck in her throat. He spoke of Jean now, and she would not tolerate it. And he was lying again. The colony used the British Navy for protection.

"You most likely helped find the executioner. That is all you are good for."

Bruin smiled a sickening smile. Eliza picked up her wine glass out of habit and immediately placed it down with disgust. She was thirsty, but she refused to touch alcohol in front of him again. She glared at the dark green bottle.

"Is there something wrong with my wine? I assure you, it is better stuff than what you served me at Pleasant Hall."

"You served yourself. I cannot accept fault for your mistake."

"Perhaps you would like rum. My rum will leave you in a rapture."

"No."

Bruin snapped his fingers, called for the boy, and asked for water. He promptly returned, placing a large glass of it by her hand. She took it, sniffing the surface. Eliza could not discern anything wrong with the water, and she took a careful sip. Once she confirmed it was suitable for drinking, she gulped down the entire glass.

He laughed a bleak, broken laugh. "You have a heart wonderfully hardened."

"I am still in disbelief that this happened. And that Dunmore would commit so foul a crime."

"I have a saying for times like this, and it is a simple one. 'Dead men tell no tales,'" Bruin said, spinning one of his rings, watching her carefully. "Lord Dunmore makes adequate use of the practice, and you will shortly find out that the worst pirates are the ones you have never heard of. They operate in the true shadow world. That is who has taken your husband."

In the shifting candlelight, she could see a figure of a falcon carved into the face of the red gem. He wore many rings on his tanned hands. They most likely doubled as weapons for when he had to keep his men in line with force.

Bruin noticed where her gaze had shifted. "Fancy a look?"

He reached across the table, handing her the unwanted ring. It was warm from the heat of his hands, and she wanted to drop it. It was clearly made with fine craftsmanship. She wondered who the signet ring truly belonged to. It was no doubt stolen, just like this ship. The *Fortuyne* was not the same pirate ship she had jumped from almost two years ago. That had been a much smaller ship. This vessel was their flagship, their main operating hub.

"I like falcons. They represent spiritual insight. You see, the role of a falcon as a predator is nothing but a reflection of provision and order in the natural world. Every creature has its place and purpose. God intended it that way."

Even villains … She returned the ring to him.

Bruin shifted his position in his chair. "You know, I remember you the very day you came to Lord Dunmore on that sultry afternoon. I remember it well. One of the very first things you asked him was about pirates on the island. And here we sit today."

Eliza looked away, coloring slightly. She had been so

overwhelmed that day, paraded in front of too many faces and told too many names. She had never realized that Bruin had been present. Why had he remembered her and her words? Eliza had always thought their first encounter was when she had caught him intruding into Pleasant Hall, no doubt about to pilfer that gold snuffbox he had held. She changed the subject.

"For what purpose does a man like *you* have a painting of Christ?"

"Ah, one of my prized possessions. It is an authoritative, vigorous portrayal of Christ."

Eliza made a face. "And what is the black globe he holds?"

"It is darkened by the sins of a fallen world. The light is there to remind us that He will return."

"I cannot lie; you are a man of contradictions. I did not take you for a believer in anything but your own greed."

Bruin looked amazed by her coldness. "Indeed, the only submission I ever allow myself to make is one of religion. In the fullness of time, who among us will be celebrating in heaven … and who will experience the weeping and gnashing of teeth?"

"You would be an ideal candidate for the latter."

He clicked his tongue in disbelief and then forcefully exhaled.

"It is not your fault you are Anglican. Anglicans do not understand the ways of the true God. It is not a contract you can break. Not because man is good, but because He is God. You English think too highly of your sacraments. Salvation is won through faith alone. God has already chosen who is to be saved." He was smug and self-satisfied.

Bruin was clearly Calvinist in his faith, like any true Dutchman. She thought it was a clever excuse for a criminal to make himself right with God. Everything was already predetermined; he clearly believed he deserved the fortune he had obtained, regardless of the method.

"Have a drink. It would enhance your lowness of spirit," he commanded.

Her response was savage. "Removal from your society would enhance my spirit."

"*Mijn god,*" he muttered. Whenever he said God in Dutch, it was with a throaty "haut." It was a useful reminder that he served a very different God than anyone else she knew. "Empires require funding, Liza. What I do is not quite so insidious. Is Lord Dunmore really so wicked?"

"He is a villain. There is a reason he was driven from the Virginia colony. He robs men of their characters and injures them more than if he had robbed them of their land."

"Well, he is certainly in the process of that misdeed as well," Bruin quipped. "That is why I rebel against authority. We are more alike than you would care to admit."

She shook her head. "You and I are nothing alike."

"Do you think the king is there to help people? Has he helped you?" Bruin scoffed. "And yet you think men like me are the criminals. Kings are simply there to rule you. Your heart and your mind. It is the same with these island governors. Do they rule tiny islands because they are better than other men? Smarter than other men?"

Now Eliza laughed. She smoothed over her skirts.

"Certainly not Dunmore."

Bruin smiled, encouraged by her change in mood.

"Precisely. You are a smart woman. Governors do the bidding of the king, not of the people. Governors simply mold men into the roles they need, and they will always take the men who make them richer. Like the Frenchman. Dunmore took him and controlled him, used his intelligence to line his pocket. That clever tongue, those flawless lies. But the minute he questioned his master, he hung from a rope."

The levity left Eliza's face, but Bruin was not finished.

"And your husband, called to defend Nassau, the place of his birth. Irreplaceable, yes? Not so. Easily replaceable the moment he too questioned the lofty island king. He then tries to raise other men to his cause. And worse, to free his slaves. Now he is a dangerous man to the governor. And so he is gone.

"As for me? I make the governor richer. And so, I am the perfect man. He will never get rid of someone like me."

Eliza crossed her arms, looking off to the side. "A criminal is no less a fiend because he uses a fine razor instead of a jagged knife," she retorted.

Bruin leaned over the table and spoke in a lower tone. "Only, I want to step away. Because my goal has always been to make *myself* richer. And the moment that door swung open wide for me, the quicker I stepped through. And now, there is no turning back. Now, you and I find ourselves in alignment, Liza."

The intensity of his interest in her was overpowering.

"I will retire for the night," she said, standing up.

She placed her napkin on the table. "Thank you for your hospitality."

He was on her in a second. "Be at ease. You are irritating to share a meal with. You are too tense." Bruin directed her back to her chair, pushing her shoulders down. In the wavering reflections of the long, rounded windows, she saw him bend closer to her, as if he wanted to smell her hair. She stiffened up.

"There," he said, taking his seat again. "You underestimate my determination to anticipate your every resistance, Liza. I so rarely enjoy the company of the fairer sex."

Bruin motioned for the boy to come and refill their glasses. In truth, she was grateful for the water. She was still thirsty.

"I could squander my days on whores and drinking in some dark tavern, but I am not like most men. I want more. I always have. And it seems to me that you are a woman confused about the time to which you belong. You too want more. Your life must be very difficult."

"At present, it is most difficult."

"Damn the governor. You should really focus your ire on him. He glories in the trappings of office. He has always disgusted me. He is in sore need of a lesson of frugality, but questioning authority forfeits your life. Speak and you will be dead. And so, I hold my tongue."

He took a swig of wine.

"It may risk your life, but you will have freedom."

"You seem to care an awful lot about the concept."

"It is no mere concept; it is a natural born right."

Bruin's lips curved upward. "My, I can imagine how

the dinner table was with your planter husband. I pity Charles. Who knew he has more patience than even I?"

Eliza's eyes were full of contempt. "It is common courtesy to make a guest feel welcome in your presence. You continue to offend me."

"As do you, dear Liza. You act as if I am the most evil man alive on the high seas. I know you consider me a pirate."

"And are you not?"

"Would you like me to be? I could be, for *you* …" He laughed.

She did not find humor in his jest.

Bruin sighed. "The life I have chosen gives me power. There is no such thing as true peace in the world. It is only a luxury of illusion for the wealthy. But yet you chose to step out of your gilded cage. Why would a lady leave England for that mosquito-infested rock?"

"I wanted to see the world," Eliza admitted glumly.

Bruin nodded. "I understand that more than you know. I am free from the laws and regulations that govern us. I answer to no one but the wind and my sails. The only side I am on is my own. But I see you too possess an untamed spirit, and perhaps a cruel past. Or did that only start once you chose Lord Sharpe for a husband?"

Bruin only spoke about Charles in grudging, resentful tones. It reassured Eliza that he was indeed alive. The possibility of recovering him was at her fingertips. If she had to endure this conversation in order to achieve it, she would.

"I do not wish to speak of my marriage to someone

like you."

"But before we retrieve him, perhaps you should consider this. Are you alive or are you merely existing? I often ask myself the same."

Eliza's eyes grew huge. She herself had uttered a similar statement once before.

"Madness? Madness is having to bear the thought that I am sidled to you for eternity! I am not living when I am with you. I exist in name only. This is not living; this is not marriage. This, this existence is torture!" she had once shouted at Charles.

"The old world is giving way. I wonder what awaits us in the new century," Bruin said.

The sweet, lilting notes of a fiddle drifted over the waves, some token of beauty in this watery hell. She could spare no thoughts for the coming century. She was trying to survive the current one.

He drummed his fingers on the table, staring off to the side. "Maybe I am a dangerous man. But perhaps you are a dangerous woman."

"I pose no danger to anyone. Unlike you."

"Oh, but I think you do. Your beauty could wreck kingdoms."

Something fluttered in her stomach. She could not tell if it was mortification or something else. A period of prolonged silence passed, and then he spoke again, but his tone completely changed.

"Philippe … I feel for the boy. I know what it is like to have a father captured. That pain is enduring. It never leaves you."

She feared this was some ruse to get her to speak, to

endure more of this forced interaction with him. But her curiosity had been roused.

"What happened to your father?" she asked.

She imagined a thousand horrors, fantastical tales that belonged in her cherished novels.

"He was hung by the British. They branded him a thief."

His voice was pained. He was revealing a side to himself that Eliza had not yet seen.

"What … what did he steal?" She was afraid to hear the answer.

"His only true crime was that he wanted to feed his family," he said bitterly.

The answer shocked her. She was caught off guard and looked down. The image she had conjured of jewels and coins was reduced to livestock. To steal was a capital crime, no matter whether the item was a handkerchief or a candlestick made of gold. The poor often hung on the gallows for stealing food—it was a sad tale she often heard from the villagers near Bleinhall Manor.

"And your mother?" she asked softly.

"She died of disease. I was orphaned at a young age, and I found work on a ship. I was a steward. Like my John here. I take good care of him, for I have been in his shoes.

"My captain was a good man. He taught me everything I know. In a sense, he became my father. We sailed to Amsterdam on many voyages. It was there that I met Anna Snyde. I was a boy; she was a woman. A married woman. How can I say this in front of you … she made me a man."

Eliza listened but could not help judging this Mrs. Snyde. How young was he when she first approached him? That a woman could be the predator, that a woman could have a voracious appetite for a boy. She had never countenanced the idea. It shocked her. He did not appear as disturbed as she. Perhaps it was different for men.

"So you have forsaken everything to impress this woman? Is she rich?"

"Wealthy beyond measure. I thought if I worked harder, I could find a way to be with her."

"But you said she was already married."

"You are no stranger to the vagaries of love," he said, his eyes narrowing slyly. "In a way, she humiliated me. It is true. But I considered it noble love. The kind the world would never understand."

"Sometimes a love that lasts for mere days can feel heavy like the weight of a lifetime," she said, in an attempt to comfort him.

She couldn't believe the way this forced conversation had turned. He seemed lost in thought now.

"Will you return to her when this is done?" she asked quietly. "Who knew this is what the daring, brash Captain Bruin quivered before?"

She pictured their strange love, an older woman and this ruthless man. Did she have greying hair? Did she view Bruin as her protector? Was her husband cruel to her? Her interest in his past was heightened now.

A smile was half raised across his face, and then it abruptly fell. He took a long, deep sigh.

"No. It is not possible. She killed our son." He lingered

before saying the next part. "And then she threw herself into the canal." His voice cracked. "I was born under an unlucky star."

Eliza's mouth dropped open. Everything she once knew about him, all of the comments he had uttered, suddenly took on new meaning. Who was this man behind the curtain he had so carefully constructed?

"I cannot stand the sound of a baby crying. Make him stop."

Eliza was silent at first, and Bruin looked vulnerable, as if he had shared too much.

"You've rendered me speechless, Hiram. I am so sorry." Eliza said.

He looked up at her briefly, his eyes moist with ancient emotion. Then he shook it off with a weak laugh.

"Now you better know the man you share a table with." But he was desperate to have her pity shift away from him. "And you? Do your parents live?"

"No. They died of smallpox shortly after I arrived in the Bahamas."

"You will see them again," he said warmly.

Just then, a crooked tail of orange lightning swept across a bruised cloud, setting the horizon a fiery hue. He turned to see what had caught her interest, and angled his chair so he could observe it too.

"I admit it is pleasant to share this view with someone."

She dragged her chair closer to him. She left an ample amount of space, unwilling to trust him completely, but after what he had shared, she felt horrible.

"Hiram, my words can be very sharp. Especially when I am upset. Regardless of what has already happened, thank you for helping me. No one else would."

He looked down towards her, biting his lower lip. He suddenly no longer seemed like a roguish fiend.

"Liza, I have not told many people this. I ask that it be kept in your strictest confidence. No one understands the pain I have endured. They only see what they wish to see."

"I understand," she said. She was guilty of the same.

The sky behind them lit up with sweeping arcs of fire.

"You bring out another side in me, it is true. But then again, I have not had many women in my life," he said, leaning back in his chair.

"You could use the softness."

Bruin laughed. "I did not realize you had any left in you to give." And then he added, "Thank you for staying with me."

He gently smiled, disarming her. It was very different than the usual one he flashed at her.

"It seems a good many men have been ensnared by Lord Dunmore. It was only too easy for me to assume you lacked virtue."

"If there is a side of me that is dark, it is but this. In my eyes, my father was murdered. The English proudly proclaim law and order, but there is no justice in hanging a man who was merely providing for his family. This life is tragic. I am older now than he ever was. I will kill those who have dared to cross me, and I will not stop until I have ruined them. I will relish when their time comes to an end, and I will make sure that in their last moments, they will remember their callous acts of injustice. When you are not fed love, you learn to lick it off knives, Liza."

"There is no society to be found in these regions. It is as if the heat drives men to madness. In the absence of virtue, people only destroy themselves," she said quietly.

The lightning outside the ship intensified, and the first rumble of thunder accompanied it. But Eliza felt secure on the ship. The hull was not rocking; the *Fortuyne's* movements were smooth. She was perched high above, gliding across the water, the perfect vista unfolding before them. But Bruin's gaze was locked on her.

"Forgive me if I speak beyond my place, but I fear Charles does not deserve you."

Eliza laughed, but the remark frightened her. Whether it was from the hidden, inappropriate implication or from the fact that, despite all she had gone through, there was still a small part of her that feared the same, she was unsure. She buried the thought deep within herself and focused on the spectacle of the night sky.

"I can only tell you that we are perfectly matched. If there was ever a man worthy of the task, it is he," she said. But Bruin did not look convinced. "Is it so unbelievable that I am capable of loving my husband, Captain?"

"No, but other women at least pretend better."

Eliza loved Charles. She loved him more than her fear of this man's company, of this journey, this voyage of an extraordinary nature. She prayed it was not ill-fated.

Bruin continued. "I am under great pressure from my crew. I alone control them, and it would be wise to seek protection from me. Women are never allowed on board, as we cannot risk the distraction. You are a different matter. My men will need to watch their behavior, but I always plan for contingencies."

He stood up and retrieved a fine rosewood box. Bruin opened the lid, revealing a knife. "Here, this will make you feel safe."

Eliza did not believe his sincerity. "The blade is probably not even sharp."

"No?" Bruin asked, his eyes flashing a challenge.

He turned and threw the knife towards the door, where it stuck in deep with a quick thwack, vibrating from the force. Eliza paled. If there was one thing she had learned about him, it was that this man was familiar with his blades. Charles favored his elegant saber, a formal and sanctioned weapon. Hiram Bruin spoke through his knives. There was a certain brutality and deadliness they embodied.

"I would say so. Would you not?" He strolled over to it and pried it free before dropping it in her lap. He dug in the box and tossed a sheath to her.

Eliza took the blade and nervously covered it with its leather case. "Thank you for this." She stood up. "And good evening, Hiram."

The way he looked at her set her on edge. He clearly did not want her to leave.

"Your eyes … you express too much. You should not care for my story," he said.

She colored and looked away. "I am glad you shared your past with me," she managed to say.

He took her hand and pressed his lips to it. "Do not take my restraint for granted."

With those chilling words, she was returned to the

porch. She felt the press of his thumbs against her neck again. How precise and controlled the grip had been. It seemed to her now that when Charles had choked her, he had done so because he had lost all control. Hiram Bruin, despite his other faults, was a master of it. She wondered what other dark emotions he kept in check. She understood him better but walked away that night feeling she did not know the man at all. For like the black waters that swirled in the ship's wake, Bruin was like a dark dream she could not reconcile herself to.

CHAPTER IX.

Eliza wandered to the main deck. The ship had stopped sailing, and she could not find Bruin. They had dropped anchor in a glittering section of electric blue water, but she feared they were no longer moving for some ill reason. Since yesterday they had entered the glowing patch of ocean in the Bahamas, known as the Exumas, a hundred-and-twenty-mile-long island chain. Here, the unspoilt and untouched sea was more vibrant than even Nassau's.

But the crew was not as moved as she. Today they were acting strangely, and the energy had decidedly shifted as she approached the men. Each time she wandered around the crew, she studied them, looking for any familiar faces from the time she had encountered them in Nassau Harbor, but she recognized no one. She feared what fate had befallen them. Perhaps it was better to interact with a fresh set of men.

"All we need to do is set sail. We have his papers. We have his manifest. The good Lord is handing us this opportunity, boys!" It was the same shirtless man who had threatened physical harm to her for not signing the ship's articles two days ago. He seemed to be leading some rebellious conference.

A second man agreed with his logic. "Parker is right. He's defrauded us. He's defrauded the company. Marooning is the punishment!"

"The captain waited too long to get in the water. He's distracted by his new companion."

"Hear, hear! We are not allowed to bring a woman on board, so why is he allowed to?"

"Because he's the captain, ye dotard!" the quartermaster snapped.

"There's never been an opportunity like this. We don't even have to beat him or set him ashore. We only have to sail away!" Parker exclaimed, his eyes wide.

"Parker, for fuck's sake shut yer mouth! That is mutiny!"

Eliza's heart dropped. She attempted to backtrack her steps, but someone already spotted her lingering at the edge of the crowd.

"Ah, here is the Queen of the Ship herself!"

"Excuse me, where is Captain Bruin?" she asked, quietly taking a step away from them.

"The fool went into the cave to retrieve his coins. We were supposed to be paid the first of the month. We tried telling him the timing was dangerous, but he didn't want to lose another minute. He's speeding to our destination, and that's final he said."

Eliza cast a worrying look at the mound of limestone sitting in the ocean. Bruin had gone in there? "How long ago did he leave?" she asked nervously.

"Nigh about an hour ago."

"The tide started rushing in; now you can hardly see the mouth of the cave."

"It's too fucking long. He's made his choice, now let's make ours," Parker growled. "Elect me as your captain and we can quit this useless voyage," he demanded of the group. Then he turned to Eliza. "And then we can deal with his bitch."

A few of the men hollered approval. She had suddenly become their objective, and the sailors advanced, cornering her.

"We can finally have some fun here, boys."

"Aye, it's bad luck to have a woman on board. There's only one possible benefit to such a situation, methinks."

"I myself only see an opportunity. Why pay for a whore in town when we have one on board here?"

They continued to press on her.

"It's his stinking fault. Poor judgment."

"Aye, he's letting his cock think for him."

"But he won't touch her; he said so himself."

"He's a liar. He had the spoils before we even set sail. What do you think he did in that house all night?"

Every comment increased her panic. Her mind raced to find a way out of there.

"It's no matter to me. I'm aching here," one disgusting man said, starting to touch himself.

"He'll be furious if he finds out."

"That won't stop me. He's in a predicament, isn't he? After all, how's he to know? You won't open your pretty mouth, now, will you? If you do, I'll cut your tongue off."

The leering man threatened her directly.

"I daresay he isn't returning to the ship. Look at how the tide is rolling in. He should have returned by now. I do not think he can swim back out. Look how it rages."

"Do we even have a captain?" a timid man voiced.

A hush descended upon the men.

"I know ye lot don't like him, but rules are rules. He's been voted captain, and that's final. Talk like that will get ye hanged from the yardarm," the quartermaster warned.

A man slammed his boot down on the deck and spat. "He's taking too long. It will be an hour soon!"

"Doesn't trust a one of us to go with him. Serves his greed right," the man named Parker said bitterly.

"Parker, none of us swim proper."

But the conspiring man was not finished. He was convinced his moment of glory was imminent.

"It's time. First, we start with her. Then we steal his other lady—this here ship," Parker said. "With your vote, I will lead us from this day forward!"

"You should go and help him. He is your captain!" Eliza urged, trying to serve as a voice of reason.

This made the group hesitate momentarily.

"*You* wanting to save the captain?"

"Aren't you his prisoner?" another laughed. The man next to him elbowed him in the ribs and told him to be quiet.

His question turned her stomach. "He's the only man here who knows how to find my husband," she said, desperation creeping into her voice. She managed to improve the distance between them and herself.

"Oi, me eyes have seen it all," one bearded man said as he waved his hand.

"No, James, she can swim. I seen 'er meself. Jumped clean off the ship in shark water, yet stands here before us now!"

"Captain never was a strong swimmer; he's only good on top of it. Riding the waves as it were. I knew this day would come," the quartermaster complained.

Eliza sighed with resignation, looking over the edge of the railing. She began to undress down to her stays and shift, her customary swimming attire. She had jumped ship last time with a heavy dress and had nearly paid an exacting price for the mistake.

The men assumed she was treating them to a crude show and began to whistle and cheer.

"Look, she's agreeable to it, boys!" another pirate said. He hooted and slapped his muscular thigh. "Maybe she's a Queen Street whore after all!"

Eliza gathered the bottom of her shift to the side and tied it in a knot. Two men crept up behind her and grabbed her abandoned dress as if it was a wild animal, about to move of its own accord. They fought over it like some valued talisman.

She would worry about retrieving it later. She had to bring Bruin back on board first.

"Oh, she's stripping down to the bone now!"

Her ears burned as she moved to the edge of the ship. She tried her best to focus and ignore their lewd comments. Otherwise, she might step wrong and break her neck.

Using a rope, she climbed atop the gunwales and perched herself there, wind rustling in her hair, and looked down. The fast-moving outline of a sea turtle darted by. She swallowed nervously. The *Fortuyne* was a much more formidable ship than the last she'd jumped from, and the distance down to the clear sea was a much higher height. She knew the water would hurt when she slammed into it, and from there, it had to be another thirty yards of swimming to the cave itself.

She had run out of time to deliberate. Bruin knew where her husband was. Bruin kept these animals at bay. She needed him to remain captain of the *Fortuyne*.

A handful of the men advanced on her. She took a deep breath and jumped outwards. She shot down into the water, seawater rushing into her ears as she twisted with the force. Eliza rushed up the surface, gasping for air.

Their voices drifted down to her.

"Hey now, woman, don't think we're hoisting your ass back up!" Ripples of bawdy laughter echoed in the warm breeze. "You're good as dead!" Cheering erupted from the main deck.

The water hurt her skin like a slap, a cold shock after enduring the unbearable still heat on the ship. It took her breath away with a powerful sweep every time a wave crossed her. Eliza inhaled and pushed her body forward towards the cave. The bracing cold felt like it was biting her chin and upper neck, but she knew if she kept swimming, she would soon turn numb and ease herself into it.

The closer she got to her destination, the more she feared she had made a deadly mistake. Stabbing pains spasmed across her back as she stroked furiously, over the rolling waves. As she pushed herself, she could feel her body tensing up even further.

Clear blobs of jellyfish drifted in rocking motions around her, and she tried her best to avoid them. With heaving breaths, she managed to kick her way to the outer face of the cave. Now that she had paused, she felt the coldness of the water again, like a dagger in every space between her ribs. In the depths below, Eliza could see silver fish shining like mirrors beneath her kicking feet, and turpin stalking shadows at the edge of the cave mouth. Even in front of it, she still could not determine exactly where the entrance was. The pirates had been correct. The tide had risen dramatically. She lingered for a moment longer, listening to the slapping noises of the sea knocking against the hollow, cream limestone rock.

Eliza took a gulp of air, then dove below the surface. The salt water assaulted her eyes with its customary burn, but then the pain settled. Now she could clearly see where the entrance had been, but she had to move quickly. There was quite a distance before the bottom opened up. Ahead she saw a dazzling display of sunlight flitting across the bottom, and she knew that had to be the heart of the cave.

A school of yellow snapper swam out of her way, their bright tails like anxious rudders, darting to avoid her furious strokes. It was not very deep, but it was still a depth that could cover a man whole and drown him. The sun wavered over the coral, growing brighter and brighter the more she swam. She passed by dozens of small sergeant major fish, and then spied a cluster of them grouped towards the middle of the cave. These black and white damselfish were small, with a dash of yellow across their dark stripes, and they watched her with curiosity. When her lungs began to burn and she was sure she was able to clear her head of the sharp rocks, she broke through the surface, raising her head and trying to orient herself.

Above her, pockmarked holes in the cave ceiling hung with long strings of dried brown vegetation. Beams of sun played on the sandy bottom in the middle, and from the craters of footprints in the disturbed sand, she assumed it was also perfect for concealing treasure.

At first, she feared Bruin wasn't even in the cave. She did not see him. Eliza dropped her head and swam forward, rounding a corner until she was in the middle of the pool. When she surfaced, she saw him, sitting on a coral ledge, soaked to the skin. His pistol was fixed on her, and he was shocked to see her. Bruin kept his gun on her with his unsteady grip even as she rose out of the water, but his barrel was clogged with seawater, and they both knew it. It clattered on the limestone when he finally dropped it.

She had rendered him speechless, but she could also feel his stare roaming over her body and the way her wet shift clung to her. She paused to regain her breath, crouching with a bent back, and then delivered the news.

"They are now at this very moment deciding who is fit to replace you as captain," she said, in between ragged breaths. "I need you to remain captain of the *Fortuyne*. I cannot do this without you."

Surprise colored his features, and he was acting strangely.

"What happened?" she demanded, her irritation rising. "Why are you still here?"

Only the slopping sounds of the water answered her.

"They intend on mutiny!" she cried, her voice echoing across the cavern.

The second time she said it made him finally react. He focused on her like a predator. "Who?"

"Parker?" she answered, a bit unsure of his name.

"*Godverdomme!*" "God damn …" He turned and spat. "I was diving and I saw a bad omen. I saw my death," he said slowly.

She put her hands on her hips. "Was it in this cave?"

"No."

"Good. We must leave. I saw an opening that we could use as an exit over there."

But Bruin was still consumed by his haunting vision. "I saw blue wallpaper. It felt so cold, but worse—I knew I was betrayed. I was terribly betrayed by someone I trusted. It looked like a certain house I know in Amsterdam, but I never planned on returning there. I started to choke on the water."

He did not want to fully admit his fear, but it was evident in his voice. Eliza was in no mood to listen to any more of his worries.

"Well, you *will* die—both of us will—if we don't leave now. They will maroon us!"

Pale horror turned to dark delight. "And you swam here to warn me of that? You *are* in sore need of a husband …"

"Please, return to the ship!" she pleaded.

"I need to bring my uncle his share of the money I owe

him." It was clear that pirates did not rely on lines of credit.

"I thought you needed to pay your crew."

"I do, but paying my uncle his share of our prize is why I stopped here. I have to dive one more time and pull another chest out. It is not enough."

He rose to a stand, steeling himself to reenter the water.

She grabbed his arm. "They are mutinying, Captain!"

But he brushed past her. "We can swim out when the tide eases," he called back.

"I wager that will be hours from now. We must go immediately!"

"Those rocks are too sharp. The tide is still coming in. Look at how the current is throwing even the fish around."

She looked behind him to the chest he had already retrieved from the depths.

"You have to make do with that one."

Bruin turned and cursed. He stalked over to it, throwing the lid open. Taking a handful of coarse canvas bags, he strode up to her, and without explanation, pulled her stays from her chest, shoving the heavy pouches down past her breasts before she could protest. He was so rough she felt his cold hands brush against her hard nipples through the thin fabric of her shift. She nearly stumbled backward from the force. Something told her that his touch was not merely accidental.

"How dare you!" she exclaimed, her voice echoing in the cavernous space. She looked down at her crooked stays with fury.

"I have made that damned garment useful. I cannot carry it all; it will weigh me down."

"And you expect me to swim with these two bags?"

"Would you like a third?"

She glared at him, tightening the laces on her stays.

"I take no responsibility if they fall out."

The captain was unfazed. "Then you better pray they do not."

Bruin took a few more bags, shoving them in his pockets and looping two through his belt. Eliza began to wade back in the water, and he followed suit. She dove forward, struggling harder to swim with the extra weight. Her eyes burned as she adjusted to the rush of salt water again.

Hundreds of sergeant major fish flew in with the rush of the tide. She took Bruin towards the exit she had spied on the other side. It was a wide, long blue space, and she could tell by its glowing light that this path would be quicker. But Bruin stopped, struggling to keep his head above the surface.

"The current rushes in from this side!"

She swam closer to him. "We cannot use the way we came in. We cannot hold our breaths long enough to reach the other side," she said, spitting sea water from her mouth. "We will drown trying."

True to what she had said, she saw the path where she had come from had filled up even more. She swam again, her feet dashing through strobes of sun dancing across the rippled coral, as fish darted in and out of the moving tunnels of light. A school of bar jack, their lifeless eyes seeing nothing, sat unmoving like the yellow growths of coral. The water grew rougher, and there was less visibility as kicked up sand filtered it.

A burst of his uneven breathing cut through the air. "This coral can tear a wooden hull apart, and yet you still came for me. This is madness. We should wait!"

"You have no choice. Follow me!" she shouted over her shoulder.

They both took a deep breath and continued to swim. The treachery of this exit was that it lay mostly below the water line, not above it. Every few minutes, the force of current rushed into the cave, sending even the fish tumbling further into the grotto. It was a dazzling display of glowing blue water on the top, the choppy surface acting as a mirror with tricks of lighting from above and below. It was disorientating, and Eliza kept her head down, actually grateful for the heavy coins. They kept her back from scraping against the limestone above the water. She was a few feet ahead of him when she saw that a strong push of limbs would be required to break past the cave's natural suction.

She was about to make her move when, from the corner of her eye, she saw Bruin rushing towards the top. He started to gasp, coughing out water. She raced back to him. He pressed himself in the narrowest crevice, desperate for air.

"Why have you stopped?" she panted, squeezing her face upward at an awkward angle.

"I cannot make it … my legs, the cramps … the coins are heavy …"

They both treaded the water, feet kicking each other.

"Leave them behind!" She tried to buoy herself by gripping the limestone by her face, but its surface was too slick.

Her hand slipped off, breaking a fingernail.

"No!" he growled.

"The current is strong here, but you only have to push forward for a few feet, then we will be outside the cave. Swim!"

She plunged forward, feeling him follow her lead. They reached the midpoint when he suddenly seized her, panicking. They both sank downwards in a flurry of bubbles. Eliza tried grabbing his arm and dragging him at an angle facing the exit. In a tangle of legs and mad strokes, they propelled themselves towards the natural light.

Eliza knew they had made it, but Bruin was still sinking. She summoned all of her strength and pushed his body upwards to the surface, gripping him with her legs and pulling with burning arms towards the sky. They splashed upwards, breaking past the water, both sputtering for a breath of fresh air as they bobbed in the waves. Bruin's face was red and strained, breathing far too heavy to keep going any further.

"The ship ... this way," she managed to say. She proceeded towards the boat in a broken paddling movement, trying to take turns with her aching limbs. The salt water sloshed up her nose and down her throat, but she would not stop for fear of him giving up. After what seemed an eternity of dodgy movements and desperate exertions, they reached the ship.

Eliza strained her neck, looking back up at it. Jumping off of it was one matter; climbing back aboard quite a different one. But then a rope was tossed over. This Bruin seized with all the fury of wanting to see another day, and he began climbing without hesitation, his legs made agile with urgency. Distant cheers sounded once he reached the top and stepped over. She continued floating, and then irrational fear whispered that no rope would be thrown down for her. Eliza had saved his life, but he retained all the power now. She regretted the way she had spoken to him, and prayed the coins stuffed down her stays would be enough to save her too.

"For fuck's sake, leave her!" a voice hollered across the air. "She's only good for one thing."

She recognized Parker immediately. A cacophony of voices broke out into argument, and then it was silent. She swallowed nervously, peering down her stays to make sure the coins were still safely wedged against her chest.

Finally, the rope descended again, slapping against the water as it fell. She grabbed it and raised herself into a crouch, her heels struggling for purchase against the hard ship. She began to climb, but her legs were too shaky, and she swung.

A new fear crossed her mind. They would leave her dangling. Next, pistols would be aimed at her, threatening that if she did not make it back up there with the gold, they would shoot her dead. Her thighs shook violently, driven by tremors she could not control. But then she felt the sensation of being lifted skyward, and heard the accompanying grunts of effort from atop the deck.

She saw Bruin at the edge, waiting with open arms. Eliza was hauled, wet and exhausted, onto the deck. She failed to steady her body and crumbled into him. He took her and leaned her against the gunwales, bowing his head with fatigue. He blew his nose over the side and then coughed. The men watched with dumb amazement, not fully believing the two of them had returned. She had done it. She had restored command of the ship to its rightful captain.

The way Bruin moved around her now shifted, as if after undergoing a saltwater baptism, they had come through the other side, newly born to one another. There was a group of sailors, and then there was the captain and her. There was now a distinct difference on the ship. She knew they had reached a new chapter in their partnership, but she prayed he didn't see anything other than the pure desperation and necessity that had driven her actions. She feared Bruin had pieced together some new conclusion about their strange voyage, this unwanted affair on the high seas.

Bruin huddled over her, water dripping from his hair onto her face. He closed his eyes, struggling to regain control of his breathing. Soon the panting subsided into more evenly drawn breaths, and he stood up straight, wiping his face with the side of his hand. But the moment he regained his senses, he was off again, slipping back into his leather boots. She could tell he had a plan by the way he moved.

Eliza slowly raised herself to a stand, legs still trembling and heavy. She watched him stride right up to Parker's back, the sole man who had not gathered to watch the spectacle of their rescue. He stood towards the opposite railing, busying himself with coiling a thick, heavy rope. Bruin stooped for a moment and then, in a flash of movement, struck the man's lower back. He was shorter than Parker, and of a slighter build, but it was enough for Parker to cry out.

And then Eliza saw the knife. Bruin pulled it out, then reached in front of the man in a wild half embrace, slashing him again and again. It was done and over with quicker than Eliza could release her breath. She screamed as the giant Parker wavered and then toppled to the deck, the front of his chest cut so badly all was laid open.

No one uttered a word. Parker gurgled, a rush of blood coming out of his mouth, oozing from his open throat and opened gut.

Bruin turned to the men, who stood hardened by the sight. "Is there anyone else here who wants to question my leadership?"

Only the wind rippling in the sails overhead answered.

Bruin spat on the man's body with vehemence. He had the power of life and death over all on the ship.

"Pak hem en gooi hem overboord! Verdomde klootzak!" he ordered in Dutch. "Take him and toss him overboard! Fucking bastard!"

Two muscular sailors approached, nervously waiting for Bruin to step away, as if they feared he would continue his rampage. He wiped his mouth, bending at the hip, still winded from last swim. It was as if he had managed a new burst of strength only so he could eliminate his enemy.

His words from last night rang in her mind. *"I will kill those who have dared to cross me. And I will not stop until I have ruined them …"*

Eliza watched it all unfold, and her fear of Bruin deepened with each quickened beat of her heart. Who had she saved? These men were vicious criminals, but the man who led them was undoubtedly worse. Bruin had taken down Parker as if the man had posed no challenge to him at all, and his confidence in his knives scared her. She made for her cabin, praying no one noticed her absence.

But Bruin noticed immediately. "And you!" he shouted.

She saw him from the corner of her eyes as he turned towards her pathetic escape, and she rushed up the quarterdeck stairs. But she had pushed herself to her limit; her limbs were useless and awkward out of the water. He pummeled her into a random bulwark, a carved wooden hook digging into her back. In one hand, he still clutched the dripping blade, its angle facing the side, but she feared he forgot he was holding it. She had seen how rapidly he could move with it, how devastatingly fast its sharp edge could slice soft flesh. What if her death came by accident?

"That was not your strength alone. That was unnatural. You are an unnatural woman. Are you a witch?" he accused her.

Eliza paled, not expecting his attack of words. She would be a fool to think he had chased her down to merely thank her. She looked down, his blood-covered hands were pinning her to the wall, staining her shift.

"How did we survive that?" he shouted in her face.

She closed her eyes, desperately trying to push away from him.

"Tell me! What is the spell I heard from your lips?"

"There was no spell! I saved your life!" Eliza whimpered, trying to free herself from him.

"You said a spell. What is Yemaya? You were muttering

it under your breath!"

Eliza sank in stature. She hadn't realized she had prayed aloud. When he had drifted towards the bottom and she had hauled him up, she had begun to pray. Desperate prayers to God, to Yemaya, the *orisha* of the sea, whose magic she had felt before beneath the waves. The invisible force of dancing rainbows that fluttered and blinked in the water whenever she swam.

"I cannot die in the water. I am protected …"

He pushed into her harder, a blood-slicked hand clawing its way around her neck.

Eliza's eyes watered. Why was he doing this to her? She had helped him. Was this to be her reward for playing this dangerous game?

"But you can die on this boat! By my hand! Your strength was not your own. I can snap your neck with my bare hands, and this is the one who saved me? Who carried me, with all the weight of these coins?"

"Should I have left you to die?" she sputtered, fear and confusion shaking her voice.

"You must admit that death and calamity follow you around, and now you have brought it to my ship!"

Eliza shook her head.

He added in a sinister tone. "How many people have already died, people that you once loved? You cannot touch their magic. It is real. It is dangerous!"

He spoke of the ancient religion the slaves practiced, the world of African spirits that beckoned her time and again.

He was relentless in his judgment. "I saw your fireplace

and what you placed there, the chalk markings and the candles. You left offerings with fruit. How could you?"

Eliza paled. She could not deny the offering to Shango.

"My slave placed that there. I did not have time to remove it. They are superstitious, and considering what has befallen Pleasant Hall, I cannot blame them!"

But her attempt at falsehood was on clear display to a natural-born liar.

"What kind of mistress allows their slaves to worship as they please?" Bruin demanded. "Do not lie to me! Who did they tell you to pray to?"

She studied his eyes and saw the depth of his religious mania that now gripped him. He was frenzied. She watched the knife move closer to her.

"That's between me and God," she managed to answer.

"*Godverdomme!* Do not consort with the Devil, Liza!"

His spit flecked her cheek, and he shook her ferociously. She screamed. It was clearly too late for that. She already had, and much worse. She had *saved* the Devil.

Bruin exhaled heavily, then pushed himself away from her. A dry, cracked laugh escaped his lips, and he rubbed his temples. Eliza remained where she was, pressed up against the bulwark, wishing she could pass through it and to the relative safety of her cabin.

"Was that the man who cried mutiny?" he asked, pointing down to the fallen Parker as a group of sailors heaved his body over the railing. A giant splash followed, and all that remained was a hot pool of blood.

The sight made her queasy. It was strange to only ask for confirmation now, once the killing had already happened. But perhaps the two men had had a long history, leaving no doubt in Bruin's mind. He was only toying with her, made more evident by the sly look that replaced the rage in his eye.

She nodded. That was all she could muster. She was beyond exhausted.

Bruin dropped his hands, and she saw the knife flash near her thigh. She released the smallest scream as Bruin took a handful of her skirt and used it to wipe his blade clean. He dropped the soiled fabric, and as the once white cloth hit her leg, she was overcome with disgust. Now that man's monstrous blood was all over her. Her eyes darted to her sleeves, made equally stained. The sight of blood had never bothered her before, but she had also never seen it so callously spilt. The smell was all around her, and it was nauseating.

"Now you have seen what I will do when someone tries to wrong me. When they try to take what is mine," he said, dark amusement brightening his mood. It was as if he was bent on impressing her.

She stayed silent, fearing the consequences of a single wrong word.

"I nearly forgot. You have a curious mind." His left hand wrapped around her lower back, and he squeezed. "If you puncture a man here, in the kidneys, he cannot live long. Only one strike. But then I thought better of it. I did not want to hear anything come from his mouth, so I sliced here and here." The blade cut the air in front of her with two strokes. "And if you ever reveal the contents of that cave, you will feel my blade in your back as well.

Let there be no illusions."

He stroked the side of her face. Eliza closed her eyes.

"Do not be frightened, I would never open you up like that," he said, leaning in closer. "I am told the pain comes from feeling air where it should never be felt. That is what burns and stuns men to silence." His blue eyes searched hers. "No, I would grant you a more fitting death. Parker was a dog, so I gutted him like one."

Eliza tried to take a step to the side, but he blocked her with his leg.

Shouts grew louder from the crew below.

"Ready about!"

"Weigh anchor! Make fast!"

The ship came around into the wind, slowly changing course.

"And I did not like the way he spoke about you. The way he leered at your figure when your back was turned." His voice was possessive, speaking as if he were an honorable man.

So he not only sought to impress her but to be thanked for his chivalry? What he had done had little to do with her virtue and everything to do with his pride. His face had regained an air of gravity.

"This, what you just saw," he said, turning slightly to the main deck. "It is all because of you. It is your fault."

"You lie!" she objected.

He laughed, and then sheathed his now clean blade back to its rightful place in his boot.

"Yes, it is because of you. There are no women allowed on board, and you have broken the rules." His lips curved into a wicked smile.

What had she set into motion? She watched the cave grow smaller as the sails caught the wind, driving into the open sea.

His sticky red hands reached for her stays, pulling the first laces apart wider than warranted, and he dug down to retrieve his coins. Eliza turned her head to the side, wincing from his rough touch, her hands clutching the wall. The warmth of his hands seemed to linger right near the under curves of her breasts despite already making contact with what he sought. He looked at her face, taking pleasure in her mortified expression.

"You should come to my cabin and wash up," he said, his voice low.

Eliza did not answer, hoping the fear in her eyes said enough.

Bruin kept her in this position, waiting for something, as if he was fighting some silent battle, some dark urge she had yet to experience from him. She finally felt his hands move, and he slowly brought the pouches out of her stays.

"Thank you for this," he said, in a near whisper, biting his lower lip.

Eliza knew he did not speak of the coins. She looked down, her face burning with shame. The heat of the sun on the deck penetrated down to her exposed chest. The thin fabric of her shift was translucent and useless for any modesty. She was covered in Parker's blood; Bruin had cleaned not only his knife, but his hands from his sins on her as well. She had never felt so degraded.

Furious tears came to her eyes. She would receive no

true gratitude from a man like him. A deck below her, the men tossed buckets of seawater, sloshing the blood away through the gun ports. When Bruin finally stalked away to his cabin to count his spoils, she lost control of her stomach and retched over the side.

CHAPTER X.

The *Fortuyne* ambled along under clear skies and smooth seas, a wooden world under a hot Caribbean sun. Awnings were spread to protect the crew from the heat. Eliza looked over the railing and clearly saw the sandy bottom beneath her. The calm blue sea was one of her few comforts, but from overhearing the crew, she knew they were bound for the open ocean, where the water would soon grow dark and menacing. At times, Eliza was amazed by this wind-powered vessel, this bridge across a vast ocean—a bridge back to him.

The sea was a blank expanse that held the answers to her future. And when the wind in the sails above propelled her forward, she wondered whether she could reunite with Charles or if she only pushed towards her doom with every crest of the waves. Looking outward, it was as if all the Earth had been submerged. Five days had passed since her last unfortunate encounter with Bruin after the cave. There was no way for her to call for help. The Caribbean Sea extended for nearly two thousand miles in each direction, and most days she only saw one ship in the distance. There had to be hundreds of ships plying the area, but they were hidden from her, reminding her how very alone she was. No one even knew where she could be found. This world was a vast place to hide her.

Whenever the surface of the sea was stirred, it stilled her breath. Was it disturbed by spawning fish, or was it broken by a treacherous reef? Some days they would pass by the sad, blackened hull of what was once a ship, drifting by tangible reminders of the danger she found herself surrounded by. Her fears would turn to the recent disaster near Grand Cayman, how a convoy of ten British ships had wrecked. The islanders had managed to save many of the sailors, but out here in the wide, wide sea, she knew no aid could ever come if the *Fortuyne* were to wreck.

When she saw the drunkenness of the sailors, she feared they lacked the sobriety to successfully navigate the ship. She was forced to place her trust in men who caroused and fought over rations of rum. Her days were governed by hoarse shouts and the tolling of bells every half hour, the sole reminder some form of order reigned on these decks. Eliza could not drive away the nagging feeling that her journey would end in death and destruction. The stays and shrouds vibrated in the wind, mimicking the tautness of her nerves every time the ship bucked wildly, or some loud crash sounded outside her cabin.

Still, thoughts of Charles, standing in the sun, sang in her head like a loud chorus of voices, beckoning her to hope. Just the mention of his name roused feelings in her. Her longing for him had not diminished, nor had the pain yet to dissolve. She yearned for him more than she ever had before. In the past, she had entertained thoughts of running away from Pleasant Hall. Now she ached for him so strongly she was willing to endure hell itself. To hear his voice, to feel his strong, reassuring touch, the way his green eyes looked like glass in the blazing sunlight, she craved such things from the moment she awoke, to when she closed her eyes at night. They had shared a dream once, and now it was impossible and meaningless without him. She did not belong to the underworld she had instinctively fled to, but she sensed that her days mired here were numbered.

Eliza grasped the gunwale.

Dear God, please don't let me go mad …

Eliza carried a part of Charles with her now. He lived inside her. She saw his face when blackness overpowered her at night. She would do whatever it took; she would survive the unwelcome advances, the suggestive language of the crew. It would all roll past her, like the ripples of water as the ship sliced through the sea. A reunion with her husband and child at times seemed unattainable, but she had to remind herself that the ship was only two days away from their mysterious destination. It would all end soon.

Eliza searched for a spot without wind and found a corner on the main deck where she could read a book. She had taken one by Virgil from Bruin's cabin. It was one of her few interactions with him these days. The men appeared occupied, some drying their clothes on the galley stove as a copious amount of choking smoke billowed up through the hatch from belowdecks, while others worked old cordage into swabs. She inhaled the scents of saline air and warm tar, closing her eyes momentarily, when she felt a presence intruding on her space.

It was one of the English sailors, she could tell from his Lincolnshire accent. He did not seem particularly threatening, and she did not protest when he joined her.

"Is it any good?"

"It's Virgil's rendition of the story of Orpheus and Eurydice."

"Who are they?"

His accent was thick and difficult to understand when he spoke fast.

"It's an old myth. It isn't quite about the story itself. It isn't a novel. It is more about what it inspires within you and what to choose to do with it. A myth is like another world we can turn to when this one is too harsh."

He took a moment, as if he needed the pause to digest what she had said. She feared he didn't quite understand her. "And what is it about?" he asked at last.

"Of loss and longing, a descent into darkness but with the purpose of recovering something, someone, his Eurydice. Orpheus, that is. He loved Eurydice. She was in Hell, and he went down there to rescue her."

"But why was she there? In Hell? Was she a whore?"

Eliza stifled a laugh, sensing his queries were made in earnest. She began to explain the entire story to him, and the man took a chair, sitting on it backwards.

"I thought the captain only kept sailing books."

"He has quite the assortment."

"Sounds like you know it well. Why read it again?"

"I've read it before, many times. But I suppose because it makes you ask what would you do if you lost what you value most?" she said quietly. "Orpheus urges us to overcome our suffering."

She began to read to him then, but her mind wandered over her own sufferings. It made Eliza question whether Orpheus mourned for someone he lost or something he never truly had. The similarities to the trial she currently endured were not lost on her. She found herself intruding in another world, one run by violent men, trying to recover her husband, to return to a sense of herself.

Charles had made her see how the world could be, and her time in this watery underworld served as a glimmer of salvation, but it was quickly fading. When she considered how Orpheus had failed to save Eurydice and how he had suffered death too, she questioned whether she was also too late. Orpheus' death was the birth of a god, a figure of a man that could never be. She feared that distance and her burning optimism had likewise fashioned Charles into someone unattainable, that, like a myth, she had reshaped him into something she secretly desired: a liberator of men. These pirates represented the cold reality of her world—violence, death, and greed. This was truth, the rough element she was destined to encounter daily.

The *Fortuyne* carried men of varying nationalities, but they were all united in their disaffection with the British Empire. Of everything Charles fought and bled for. Dirty and slippery decks, abominable smells, barefoot men— there was no glory to be found on this ship. Eliza tried to limit her wanderings to the quarterdeck or the very start of the main deck. But if she proceeded any further, she would find dead rats, piss and excrement, and unwashed livestock. To smell the pungent odor of human sweat mixing with rotten timber and wafts of foul bilge with every rock of the boat … To walk underneath moldy sails hauled by sweating men with tar-blackened fingers, waiting to catch her unaware, or for Bruin to suddenly cancel their arrangement, to dissolve the hastily constructed saltwater boundary he had created … the potential for disaster haunted her.

Amidst the perspiration and the sour stale smell of alcohol, she uncovered their hierarchy. At the top stood Captain Bruin, then the old quartermaster, responsible for discipline and order on board, the hunter who procured whatever food he could get his hands on, whether it be goat or turtle, the surgeon, the carpenters, and a handful of gunners. There was also John, the young cabin boy apprentice, a father and son duo who were Dutch like Bruin, and several dozen black sailors.

She noticed that the black sailors were only reserved for the most menial tasks: they worked the pumps, washed and cleaned, and acted more like servants, as if this cluster of men who had rebelled from society had never truly severed themselves completely from prejudice. The black sailors hailed from other seaports and were the only members of the crew who did not carry pistols. One older man had patches of white around his cheeks. She was told that the powder of cannons had burned his flesh. She wondered if they had any choice in their journey on the *Fortuyne*, or if, like bales of silk and spices, they too had been stolen off a prize ship. They were no doubt former slaves, and she questioned if they had truly attained freedom.

Overall, the crew was only a few years younger than she was, but the way they dressed, with their short-cut trousers to avoid getting tangled in the lines, and their suntanned and cracked, weathered skin, made them appear much older. They all walked with a rolling gait and were armed to the teeth, displaying scars and injuries from handling gear and sails in heavy weather. Most men carried two pistols in a silk sash that hung from their shoulders, or at least those were the weapons they had chosen not to conceal. Like Bruin's favored knife that he hid in his boot, she knew they too carried more tools to cut down any potential threats.

The *Fortuyne* was a complex ship, a small ecosystem that was constantly set in motion. It operated on its own hours, working with the capricious changes in wind and weather, and was governed by its own language. Eliza quickly learned that she did not sail *on* the *Fortuyne*; rather, she was *in* the *Fortuyne*. In the early hours of the morning, the boatswains, responsible for the operations of the ship, would pipe their whistles, shouting "All hands, all hands!" It would set into play a commotion of loosening sails, extinguishing candles, and lashing hammocks, a manic bustle, which changed and adapted throughout the day with new orders every half hour.

Eliza would find some quiet corner to read in the sun, her hair buffeted by the breezes that traveled up the decks, and then she would retire to her cabin. She had tried to keep interactions with Bruin at a minimum since the cave.

Moldering ship biscuits and salt pork were preferable to his company. The man who kindly brought her plate no doubt thought she was mad. She would pry the weevils from the hardtack biscuits and pretend that the bitter cracker soothed her hunger pains.

There was not much comfort to be found in this place. She certainly could not dine with the other men, nor did she want to. They ate like a kennel of hounds, snatching food from one another, drinking and carousing while they talked about the affairs of church and state and the vagaries of trade. When they were completely incapacitated by drink, which did not take long at all, she would hear shouts and swearing.

"Curse the King and all the Higher Powers and Damn the Governor! Damnation to King George!" In the breeze, it drifted past her cabin, and she would recheck if her door was secure. One night, a fight broke out, and as she listened to the thundering steps right below her, she readied the small knife Bruin had given her. But the quartermaster had put a swift end to it, and the rest of the evening passed by unremarkably.

Now the *Fortuyne* moved at fourteen knots, the wind pushing them to their hidden destination. Eliza could tell the crew was anxious to have this mission be done with. Both parties had nearly reached the end of their tolerance for the other, and Eliza did not want to test their willingness to listen to their captain's orders a day longer than necessary.

"Maybe they were both dead without realizing it ..." the Lincolnshire sailor said, staring out at the sea.

A second man who had joined their impromptu discussion scoffed.

"What, are you soft, James?"

"No! How does one step into the underworld without dying themselves? How do you escape it?" James asked.

A chill swept over Eliza. She hoped they did not expect her to answer. The new guest sat with them, picking apart oakum that the men used for caulking the ship. The charming smell, a strange sweetness she was unfamiliar with, drifted over to her. Now she could see Bruin standing vigilant, watching them, although he pretended to look outward, from his commanding perch on the quarterdeck. Yet another reason to avoid their more private deck.

"Christ. So this chap goes down to Hell, but what if she dunt love him back? And the fool is just laking-about, you know, wasting his time?"

"It's not about love, I suppose," Eliza said. "It's more about an impossible longing, that life would have no meaning if Eurydice was not recovered."

"I don't know, doesn't seem worth it to me," the oakum picker remarked.

Bruin took out a pistol and began cleaning his gun. The captain was skilled at listening to a change in the trade winds, and he did not appear to like what he witnessed below.

"Eurydice is Orpheus' guiding law; he cannot imagine life without her. She is his soul," Eliza said. She turned to a certain page to show them an engraving. "He's determined to recover her from the Lord of Death, see here?"

James looked amazed. "Aye, ain't that summats? The

captain's so rich he has pictures in his books. Look at that," he said. He puffed his chest out with bravado. "I would do the same for my Maggie."

"James, you cheat Maggie with every pair of legs that walks up to you. You wouldn't go down to Hell for her."

"Eigh, I would, you f—"

"Not in front of the lady!" he barked.

Eliza waited for them to settle down, and then she continued reading.

"Orpheus takes her by the hand, but he breaks the one rule he was bound to keep. He turns and looks back at her. 'What madness caused you to destroy us both?' she cries. She dies a second death." She turned the book towards them, showing them the next engraving.

"What a shan! And then what?" James said, his voice quiet.

Eliza sighed. "Orpheus loses his grip on reality. He sinks further into despair. Virgil tells us he had returned to the upper world but not to his social one. His body was there, but not his mind. For he thinks of nothing but his unbearable loss, and even as the Maenads kill him, he shouts, 'Eurydice! Eurydice!'"

"Perhaps he needed to accept her as dead and continue living," a smooth voice quipped near her back.

Eliza turned red and whipped around. It took everything in her to not glare at Bruin.

"She's reading to us about the Euphrates and how Virgil tried to rescue his wife from the bowels of Hell," James said, evidently very proud for incorrectly remembering their names.

"His death was a waste," the captain said, standing behind Eliza's chair. "His lesson was to move on."

Eliza felt his hand brush her shoulder. The energy in the group deflated like a fallen sail. The men weren't satisfied with his interpretation either.

"Aye, that's a terrible ending if ever I heard one," James said.

"Some writers tried to give them a happy ending. They wrote about their reunion in the underworld."

"In death?" the second man said grimly, revealing a score of missing teeth. He shook his head.

"It seems we are only pleased with happy, sweet endings, aren't we?" Eliza said.

"It's a myth. It's nothing but horse shit," the oakum picker declared.

"But that is the beauty of myths. We can each put our own meaning into it."

"The world is much larger than any Roman ever dreamt of. I do not understand why we still give them so much reverence. Virgil never knew this side of the world existed," Bruin said, evidently disgruntled with Eliza's lesson on ancient mythology.

"I too would prefer it if Orpheus saved Eurydice from Hades' grip," Eliza said to the two sailors in a low voice. She closed the book, smiling as she got up, and started walking back to the quarterdeck.

She heard Bruin following her.

"Perhaps you can come to my cabin and pick another story …"

Eliza turned to face him, the wind crackling against

canvas. She had tried to run from the tension between them, but he only chased her down.

"You would prefer to talk to my men and not their captain?" There was an edge to his voice, as if he was jealous of their innocent interaction. "You surprise me."

She looked at him, unsure of what to say. The soft rasping of timbers and the strain of the ropes filled the gap of silence.

"The weather is fair, we are gaining speed today," she finally said, as she moved to the railing.

She peered down, lost in the waves frothing at the hull. The dizziness of watching every curve of water flit by in succession, of the way the *Fortuyne* rocked upward and then down, numbed her to the persistent problem at her side.

"Light winds and calms are of no use to me. I need some kind of disturbance in order to sail my ship," Bruin said, studying her very carefully. "You will learn soon enough."

"I am just thankful for clear skies. I shudder to think what it would be like to be trapped in a storm."

They both leaned out, gazing at the horizon line. The sails of a ship much further out bobbed like roving clouds.

"Liza, I want to apologize for what I did that day," he said, "You expect better of me. I will try to deliver it."

There was something distressing about his apology. It only made her feel uneasy, as if he assumed something of her, and that by saying it, he was now granted access to her again. She did not want to voice acceptance of it.

Her lack of response tried his patience, and he took

her hand. "I mean it, Liza," he said.

"Do not concern yourself with it," she replied, pulling her hand away.

"I would be honored if you joined me for dinner tonight. We are nearing our destination and may not have another opportunity."

All she heard was that her trials were nearly at an end. A smile broke out across her face. She accepted without hesitation and walked away from him as if she was perched high in the shrouds, like the brave souls above her, floating freely in the wind.

It would all be over soon.

"Will you have no more?" Bruin asked as he motioned at her half-eaten plate.

"No," Eliza said with a sad smile. "You will assume it signals my acceptance of your society. You have masked your true intentions once before."

"I am sorry, the sea is a lonely place. You filled a space here in the last week. One I did not know I was lacking, and I was a greedy creature."

She wanted to avoid that topic at all costs. "I am also nervous. I will soon encounter an abrupt change of destiny," she added.

"That is in my hands. You do not have to do a thing. And a husband will be delivered to you." His voice was reassuring, reminding her that her time spent aboard the

Fortuyne had not been in vain.

Bruin smiled, drumming his fingers on the table. While Eliza did not entirely trust him in all things, she was impressed with what she had seen. Bruin saw language in the stars and the moon; he could detect the ebb and flow of the ceaseless tide. He fearlessly sailed from one ocean to the other. He was strong enough to handle physical labor, to conduct scores of unruly men, and to maintain order. Perhaps if Eliza had been born a man, her place would have been in a ship, like his was.

"What will you do when our time here is at an end?" he asked her now.

But he was also a ruthless killer. She would not forget it.

"Return to Nassau with my husband." She thought the question was strange. What else would she do? They sat poised on the eve of a new century, and she thought it fitting that she had not suffered so great a change in her fortune as to what she endured presently. It was a time of change for all mankind.

"Nassau is too small for a brilliant mind like yours."

Nothing he could say would charm her. The time for that had long since passed.

"And you, Captain? Do you intend to drift from port to port?"

"On the contrary, I wish to pursue a quiet life," he said. "I have a dream. It often repeats. There is a great blue parlor, and all of these riches coming to me, even more than I already have. But I do not care. I have my own place. My own land. Not just a stinking ship. A true home. The ceilings are gilded; there is old art on the walls.

Blue damask walls. Like a palace to call my own. And I will die there. It is sudden, a flash. But it is mine."

"Is it the same blue wallpaper you saw in the cave?"

A smirk crossed his lips.

"It must be mine; it is decorated handsomely."

"I am glad you have reconciled yourself to your deathly vision."

The porter boy began to clear their plates. He brought out two glasses of rum, and when Eliza waved it away, Bruin intervened.

"Let us toast to your husband and his recovery."

Despite her misgivings, there was a part of her that believed in superstitions. Perhaps she had spent too much time in the company of pirates. But she would take every ounce of good luck she could find, even if it was rum from Bruin's cask. Besides, he had not touched it. The boy had brought it.

"And for your aid, when no one else would help," she added.

They both took a sip. Eliza coughed. His rum was stronger than anything she had ever tasted. But then, like any good quality liquor, it settled in her gut, and she forgot about the initial burning.

"Does it suit you? It is from Barbados," Bruin explained, gazing into his glass.

"It is quite strong," she said, scrunching her face.

"Women do not usually drink it. Unless it is in the punch bowl."

"I am not like most women," Eliza declared proudly.

Bruin laughed and then grew quiet, his thoughts

consuming him.

"I have been practically everywhere but find I belong nowhere," he said quietly.

It was a thought she could find common sympathy with. "I confess I myself have felt the same at times. I stumbled upon a new world, but I knew nothing of its inner workings."

"I can show you what you lack," he spoke now, his voice bordering on bold flirtation.

Bruin was trying to convince her of something, but she was not asking for any more of his help. Her dark eyes roved over the Jesus painting, the look of it leaning nearly through the canvas itself, the strange black orb hovering over Christ's hand. There was an air of dread about Bruin tonight, a certain type of fatalism laced with melancholy, as if he knew this intimacy between them would never again occur.

He leaned forward now, some new idea livening his features.

"I could take you to the bottom of Africa. You would love Kaapstad. Or as you English call it, Cape Town. There Table Mountain looms over the bay, a blunt slab roiled in mist. Myrtles and oaks line the roads. Troops of baboons scrabble into the brush, making the most hideous noises. And every so often, you can hear the roar of a lion."

Eliza listened attentively, curious about the fantastical place he described.

"Arab and Chinese merchants sell their wares in ba-zaars. You can have the sweetest wines, succulent fruit, the finest beef. We have trouble stopping the lions from picking off the cattle. And then on the edge of the water is a granite bastion, crafted in the shape of a star, the Castle of Good Hope."

Eliza's eyes grew wider. "Does a king live there?"

Her imagination ran wild with images of a noble black king, covered in leopard fur, standing proudly with a spear. The kind of majesty she had seen from Shango when she encountered him on the beach. But then she reminded herself that Cape Town was no different than any other colony. The Dutch East India Trading Company ruled it. It was the product of human bondage and toil. The Dutch took their slaves from different places—Mozambique, Madagascar, Indonesia—but they engaged in the brutal trade just the same. Slaves and suffering had helped transform the African bush into a white-washed village reeking of Dutch simplicity and modesty, and from everything she had heard, the Dutch were very good at it. They could take the wilderness and force it into a shape more recognizable. The Calvinist attention to detail, their instinct for profit ever sharpened by hard work, frugality, self-discipline, and an unyielding conviction that God had delivered bounty straight into their grasping hands. The Dutch were a force to be reckoned with in the world of colonies and trade, but they were still no match for the naval prowess of the British.

"No, it protects our wares and secrets. Kapstaad is a middle point between Holland and the East Indies."

Bruin stood up and reached for something high on a bookshelf. He returned to the table with one of the most beautiful green sea shells Eliza had ever seen. He placed it gingerly in her hand.

"We make buttons for gentlemen with these. I think they are very pretty," he said, watching her gleeful reaction. "Large snails live in them. This is from the Indian Ocean."

She turned the shell around, the light catching the polished strokes of pearlescent and jade. It was nearly five inches in diameter. She reluctantly handed it back to him, but he refused.

"Consider it a gift," he said. "You should see the shells in Batavia. They have Gold Cone Shells, bigger than this even."

"I confess nothing impresses me more than what lies beneath the surface," she remarked, still turning the green turbo shell this way and that.

"We have made Batavia look like an Amsterdam of the East Indies. It is a sight to behold."

"I would rather see your Kapstaad," Eliza said. "Africa sounds like a dream. To hear a lion roar but live in safety, what a wonderous thing. Have you seen wild elephants?"

"Of course. They are everywhere on the outskirts of town. You need to be careful around the bulls. Nothing can stop a charging one. But I have been told the hippopotamuses are more dangerous."

She drank her rum, then stood up to look at a map he had tacked to the wall. Her finger started at some unknown spot in the Caribbean; their true location she could only hazard a guess, and she drew a sweeping line to the African land mass.

He stood behind her, and gently adjusting her hand, lowering it all the way to the bottom of the continent.

"It is here," he said. "We took a parched land and turned it into a garden at the cape."

"And you have travelled that far," she whispered.

She was oblivious to the fact that he had yet to release her wrist. The door opened as the porter returned, and Bruin returned to his seat.

Eliza looked at it for a moment longer and sat once again, still marveling at the shell. Bruin ordered more rum, and the boy left on his quest.

"How far is Kapstaad?"

"From where?"

"Nassau. If I were to sail to Africa …"

"It is the very bottom of Africa, as I have shown you. It is nearly seven thousand miles to reach. It could take three months. But it is well worth the journey. Every sailor dreams of docking at Kapstaad."

Eliza looked at the shell with a kind of wistfulness, knowing that she would probably never set foot there.

"That is so very far …" she said quietly.

"But three months would pass by with the right company."

Eliza was considering if she could ever get Charles to wander that long in a ship after this ordeal was over, but from Bruin's last comment, she sensed he was talking about their strange relationship. A journey across the world, it was all she ever wanted—to explore, to truly visit places most people only dreamt of. It all sounded so foreign, so exotic, so full of exhilarating danger. She felt she was halfway there, even though the entire Atlantic stood in the way. She wished travel was as simple as going to sleep and waking up in new, wondrous places.

"But that is still not the world I yearn to discover," Bruin said quietly. "Domestic bliss sounds better to my ears than any escapade. Perhaps it is my age."

Visions of home called to her too. She saw the palm-fringed white house that sat proudly on the hill on the beach. She saw Philippe and Charles. Eliza had changed. She was no longer the girl who chased after voyages. She had too much at stake. Now she knew what that yearning could bring her, the ways it could dramatically reshape her life. It only reminded her to be cautious. Her love of travel was like the flame of a candle—it brightened her world, but it could still burn her fingertips if she came too close to touching it. Now, nearly three years since she had left England, she understood this only too well.

They continued to talk, Bruin regaling her of all the places he had seen and places still yet to be conquered. The world had never seemed so vast yet accessible to her. He had more oceanic curiosities, engravings of exotic forts, and glimpses into strange cultures. He spoke of fish and animals she had never heard of. She listened with the eagerness of a pupil, unaware of how fast the time slipped away, and how light the night sky had grown.

Beneath the stars and billowing sails, the yellow moon was low, and Eliza could tell that dawn was not far off. She was fading, but she had so enjoyed learning about all the places Bruin had seen. She sipped her rum and spread her legs out into a stretch, oblivious to Bruin's focused stare. A lowered guard—that was the danger of fermented sugarcane.

He leaned forward now. "You forget yourself, Lady Sharpe."

His tone was nearly playful, and she still did not sense the imminent danger she was in. She laughed to herself, and fixed her dress. But Bruin did not want to move on.

"I felt your body against mine when we were in the water. I felt those legs wrapped around me, Liza. I felt something else, too. And I want to feel it again."

She heard him say that just as she drained her third glass. She set it down uneasily, looking at her now emptied mistake, already regretting it. Bruin eyed her current state like a snake coiled to strike. She took that as a sign to get up and head for the door. He blew the candles out on the table, signaling that events had taken a determined turn.

"I did not give you permission to leave," she heard him say.

Eliza turned, but it was too late. Bruin advanced on her with incoherent passion. He overpowered her, and there was nothing she could do.

Fear sobered her up. He wanted more than conversation. He had other ideas of how to while away the time before the sun rose. He pushed on her neck, using it as leverage as the ship rocked.

"I do not usually have to wait this long," he said, his cheek pressed against hers. A hand raised her skirt. "This was all planned by God." She heard him fumbling with his belt.

"You know nothing of God. You wear Christianity like a cloak," she said as she pushed his hand away. Eliza was surprised that he let her. Then she realized that he was in the mood for a prolonged intrigue; he wanted to play, to seduce her.

"The Frenchman and I made a wager on how soon he could get between your legs. I understand the challenge now. You are very trying."

Bruin had gone too far. Anger rose up within her. "Get off of me!" she shouted.

"You sound frightened, Liza. Sometimes sin leads to great rewards …"

Her hands flailed, struggling against him. He laughed, and she could feel his teeth brush against her cheek. His chest heaved against hers, and Bruin paused, considering his next words.

"This will make me sound like a rogue. I do remember him remarking on how very sweet your cunny tasted once he did have you. He said you were worth the wait."

Eliza's hand found the door handle, and she pulled it, but he forced it closed, slamming his hand over hers. He pried her grasp from the door handle and pulled it to his breeches. The swiftness of her hand retreating made him laugh.

"You are worse than a rogue!" she exclaimed.

"Did you think a gentleman is in control of those men out there? Do you want to see what kind of man I truly am?"

Eliza cursed the rum. She was up against a very different adversary than she had ever faced before. She had been tricked with well-wishes for her husband and glorious tales of travel. The wisps of smoke curled upwards in the shadows, the candles' flames now extinguished like the remnants of her hope that she could leave this ship unscathed.

"I beg of you to stop this …" she whispered, her voice pathetic.

"Let us have a moment of ecstasy in this unhappy business," he said, gripping her hair. A random wave pummeled the boat, and she nearly lost her footing. "Slide on me, I will steady you."

Bruin was a shadow covering her. She looked at the Jesus painting on the wall behind him, glowing even in the pale light, and found the help she so desperately needed.

"It is a sin, Bruin," she urged. "Control yourself."

He pulled away from her, studying her. "You no longer have to pretend that you are pure and whole. Not for me. I crave a sinner like you." He bowed his head against hers, forehead to forehead, struggling to control himself for much longer. A quivering hand trailed up her neck. "Charles does not deserve you. He will only return to his ways. He was never your lover." Bruin raked his fingers through her hair and tipped her face back, and kissed her as though he could convince her to become his with his lips alone. He paused, waiting for her to reciprocate. He was determined and relentless, a hand wandered to cup her bottom, and he began to moan with need.

"What do you wait for?" he breathed into her ear.

Her panic and rum-weakened senses collided. She was moved from the darkness of her shut eyes to the wisps of blue reflections that flitted across the cabin from the water's glare through the windows.

"I only do this with my husband," she stupidly said.

Eliza broke away from his mouth, but he found her lips again, the taste of him salty with sweat. He was more aggressive this time, biting her lower lip.

"You lie, that did not stop you before," he chided, allowing her a momentary break in his assault.

"I am married," she protested, pushing him away.

"I am aware, and it only excites me more. Charles does not need to know. Parting your legs will be my greatest secret."

A muscle jerked in his cheek, and he started to grind against her hips, rubbing his erection up and down her.

"I am prey to sudden, ungovernable impulses. I burn with longing for you, Liza. Let me have my fill," he said breathlessly.

Eliza dropped her body and slid sideways out of his arms, running deeper into his quarters.

He only followed her. "On the sea there is no church. Here, Hell is of no consequence. And *you* would tempt a saint to sin."

Eliza pulled out the knife he had given her, flashing it nervously. The grin he made when he saw it sickened her.

"How would you like me to use it on you? Should I press the cool metal to your skin, or should I make the smallest scratches up and down your thighs? I am yours."

"Do not take another step!" she hissed, fear weakening her voice to a whisper.

"Did you know the rhythm of the boat contributes greatly to the pleasure of the critical moment?" He stepped, cornering her by his bed. "I think you will enjoy this. I can tell by the way you move about on my deck, and I have finally figured out which words excite you."

He rushed forward and pushed her down, and she stumbled, falling backward on the bed. The knife was a terrible idea; it left her hand and was gripped in his own within minutes. All she carried now was pain and an aching wrist. She realized why he had given it to her so willingly. It was useless in her hands, but it was an extension of dark desires in his.

"I performed an astonishing act of restraint. I could have had you the very first night in my cabin." He kneeled over her, taking his leather jacket off and tossing it to the floor. His shirt came off next. "What will it take to bring you to submission?"

Eliza rushed to sit upright—she refused to lie down. Her core ached from fighting off his advances, from stopping him pulling her into his unwanted embrace.

"Do you quiver at the thought of that, or does some secret part of you delight in the very idea? I would have afforded you hellish pleasures … the kind that I know women secretly crave," he whispered in her ear, his hot breath sending chills down her back.

"This is some brief temptation. You cannot seduce me," she said defiantly.

"You let your passion get the better of you once before. Do you not feel it stirring again?"

"I am not the same woman I was before."

He was unrelenting. "Every woman has liaisons; it is only natural."

She struck him. He was surprised by her fury, but that awful smile returned to his features.

"I am not here to please you," she hissed.

"I want to hear all the little noises that will escape your lips, all the noises I am about to make you cry …"

He could not fool her. This was not about what Eliza wanted. It never was. By the look in his eyes, she could tell that he could unravel her life, and he would enjoy it.

His mouth captured hers, and he tried pulling her prone towards the mattress. She felt her control slipping away, her muscles not prepared for such an enduring fight, and she fell. Now he towered over her.

"It is a strange thing. You know only through sin can a man be saved. Perhaps it is true for women as well."

His voice sounded careless, but his hands were still on their determined course. She felt air on her legs as he hitched up her skirt.

"No!" she said, blocking him with a raised knee. "I made a marriage vow before God, one I am loathe to break again. We … we are here to be saved, to … to save each other. That is why God has placed us in each other's lives!"

The words that tumbled out of her mouth sounded ridiculous to her; her ruse surely too obvious to fully convince a man like him. But it did make him stop. She would seize her chance.

"But it is not to be through sin. Something like this is too beautiful to be a true sin. Do not spoil it with weakness, Hiram!" She knew he would be pleased she had used his name. "I have realized something tonight. You are no ordinary man."

Bruin's face shifted, and he finally backed away. She exhaled with relief, rushing to the opposite corner of the bed.

She waited for anger, for some furious reaction. But none came. She had truly stilled him.

"You are remarkable," he said.

Dread dropped in her stomach like a stone. She could not read him.

"You tried to take my life. And now you keep us chaste. In all things you correct my course, Liza …"

It was too early to tell, but she hoped beyond measure that she had tricked him.

"I will not make a mistake fueled by rum ever again," she said, speaking the truth, but albeit in a different way.

"You want to wait …" he said quietly.

"Yes, yes!" she cried, desperate to win the battle. "Hiram, we must wait!"

Bruin stood up, his stance completely changed. He paced about the room, deep in thought. Then he dropped to his knees, kneeling before the bed, clasping her hands.

"You know Lord Dunmore hired me to kill you. Do you not understand the manner of our friendship, Liza?"

"Yes, you happily told me so that night."

"But yet you never asked why I agreed."

"A man like you could never turn down money."

"You judge me so, Liza. Perhaps I deserve it." His voice sounded sad.

"Then why?"

"Because I knew if I refused, he would find someone else to do the job. And I cannot have that. I needed to keep you alive. So I agreed. To keep you safe."

His confession stunned her. The urgency in his voice could not be masked. But it made no sense to her. Bruin smiled and kissed her hand. She let him; it was a lesser evil. She needed to continue acting.

"*Hiram* ..." she softly said, imagining her tone alone could control him.

"I do not blame you for thinking differently of my true intentions, but I cannot hold it in any longer. I could not bear the thought of you dying."

"It beggars belief," she said, turning to face the windows. She needed to make this performance as real as possible. She felt him squeeze her hands.

"You will see soon enough. I have big plans in store for you and me. It will all make sense soon. We near our destination. Tomorrow we will be in sight of it. The Mountain will steal your breath away. We must not spoil the next few days."

Tomorrow ... her heart soared at the sound of that.

"Thank you, Hiram," she said, her voice full of gratitude and warmth. She knew thanking him would please him.

Eliza sighed. She was so close to saving Charles. Their reunion was imminent. It nearly erased this close brush with Bruin's unstoppable desire.

Soon, she would be with Charles, and none of this would matter. It could be forgotten. And she would never have to deal with Bruin or his devious designs for a second longer. Confident of her narrow victory, she rose from the bed and headed out the door. She did not hear his last words with the onslaught of wind that hit her face.

"It always tastes sweeter when you wait ..." he said, alone in the room once more.

CHAPTER XI

The light fell in long horizontal lines through the gun ports. Charles eyed them with increasing dread. The bars of light only accentuated his anxiety, lengthening his pathos every time the hull tilted and the shafts of sun swept across the men anew. Like the idle rocking of the ship, Charles thought the same thoughts, over and over. This time when his dreams came, he had felt her hand grasp his arm, and the pain when he awoke and discovered he had not moved from his wretched spot, hovelled on the floor, tore him apart. It reminded him of a deeper torment.

He had tried to protect Eliza. And he had failed.

He had lost track of time, the meager amount of daylight he was allotted blending in with the shadows of night. He never truly saw the sky, and he wondered if he ever would again. His discipline urged him to move past what had happened. To find some way out, to fight his unknown captors. But every creak and thunderous bootstep above him reminded him that he was unsure if he could make it. If he could survive. Despite his best attempts at self-control, he feared that he was going to die. He died five times a day in that watery prison. It was beginning to erode away at his mind, and there was little to nothing his shackled limbs could do to stop it.

"You! Are you a general?" a new voice asked across the shadows. He spoke in a grounded tone and a sense of confidence. Charles could not fathom where he had summoned such coolness of mind.

He did not answer, partially oblivious that the speaker truly wanted him.

"They say you are The General. Is it true?"

A swift kick landed on his shin, and he looked up at the man across from him. He was dark-skinned and covered in scarification on the right side of his face. Perfectly straight lines ran down his hairline to his brows, mimicking a sun's slanting burst.

He laughed, revealing a mouth of white teeth.

"Are you surprised I can speak your language? I have been on your ships long enough."

Charles' faculties were slow to react, he was so unused to being spoken to. For a moment, he feared he would not be able to properly speak.

"No," he said quietly, his voice hoarse. "I am not a general."

"No?" The man was amused. "But I see in you a leader. You can lead men. I can see it in your eyes."

"I am a British soldier, a lieutenant colonel."

The man slapped the grimy puddle next to him.

"Ah! I am right." Then he lowered his head with incredulity. "And the white man did not come for you? Why does your king not fight for you like you fight for him? You are in chains like me. Is this your punishment?"

Charles paused. He hesitated in voicing the truth of his betrayal.

"You can say that. I crossed the wrong man," he muttered with an edge to his voice.

"Then we are brothers. I am Chibueze, a noble warrior of Ọka Diedo, son of Chukwunonso. A mercenary from Abam captured me, but when he sold me, the white man saw my face and knew what I was. So here I am." He lifted his chin. "But I will never be a slave."

"Forgive me, but I am not partial to conversation, Chibu …"

"Chibueze," he corrected Charles, his pride foremost.

Charles bowed his head between his knees, praying the man would stop talking.

"This ship is nothing compared to what I have seen. Sometimes I think God has mistaken me for a fish and not a man. So I am to be chained on the waves, but never in it. Hearing the water but never feeling it against my skin. And no longer a man, never to be on land to walk again."

The water sloshed around them, and Chibueze shifted his position, animated by their conversation.

Charles spoke first, anticipating that the man was not through with him. "Why do you still speak to me?"

The man smiled. "Because you have not given up. You still carry the fire within you. These men are dead. They have given up." He cast a disparaging glance at the cramped space around them.

Charles looked around; indeed, most of the men did

appear lifeless in mind and body. Even the habitual groans had quietened that day. But then he realized that two men were missing.

As if on cue, the hatch violently flew open, and the two missing men were rudely thrown down, followed by a skinny guard. Charles watched him with narrowed eyes, thinking if not for his hunger and shackles, he could easily overpower a wretch like him. But he did not know how many others lay above topside.

The guard returned them to their heavy chains. The men were bloody and senseless and could not put up any resistance.

Charles could sense some of the other men beginning to stir, and he felt their fear. The thin man spat on the ground and then climbed back upwards to the main deck.

"I wish that man were in Heaven," another prisoner said, his voice tight and strained.

"No, not Heaven, for I wish to get there myself one day," Chibueze answered, his voice filling the heat box.

"Where are we?" Charles asked the men.

He dreaded the answer.

"This captain deals in men's bodies. He takes men and lines them up for bouts for well-paying clients," a sickly blonde man answered first. "The more violence he can muster out of us, the more coin he makes."

Charles scrutinized the two injured men. So, they had been forced to fight one another?

Now a second man joined their conversation. "Maalik is his name. I heard one of the crew curse him when his back was turned. Sounds like an Ottoman to me. A

Barbary pirate who lost his way."

"He's a Moor all right. Straight from Algiers," the blonde man said.

The men's conjectures discouraged Charles' spirit. There were no Barbary corsairs this far west. The Barbary pirates were the haunt of the Mediterranean. He had seen them in action during his time at Gibraltar when he had been called to help strengthen its defenses. The Crown feared a bombardment by Spanish artillery would return after The Great Siege, and the army constructed miles of tunnels deep into the limestone rock. The Barbary corsairs, meanwhile, were never bold enough to launch an attack on the British fort, but the soldiers could oftentimes see them pick off small merchant ships down below, like wooden toys drifting in the navy waters, covered in flames if they resisted.

"So we are to become prizefighters?" Charles asked, his voice weary. "Is that why they keep us alive?"

Barely alive.

The blonde man nodded, his cheeks so hollow he looked more skeleton than man. Charles looked down at his swollen, chafed wrists, browned with old blood. He clenched his fists, summoning a bout of phantom strength. A true gentleman would never fight in public for a prize, but now he would be forced to, and the prize would be the privilege of staying alive. It was a cruel game.

Then he thought of *her*. Eliza was in danger while he was stuck here, left to indulge the whims of some sadistic pirate.

"I fight for no other man but myself," he said angrily.

A man to his left sneered at him. "Then you will die first. You haven't been here long; we shan't miss you."

Chibueze spoke. "No, he may be the last among us. He is The General."

"You shut your mouth," a man snapped. "Curse whoever taught you the King's English."

But Chibueze was unaffected by their vitriol. He leaned towards Charles, eager to say more.

"We have a saying among my people. 'All you need to do in battle is trick your enemy.' We do not need to be more than them, we only need to trick them," he said, gesturing upwards with his face. "To my people, it is not wrong to trick others; cunning makes you survive. To survive, you need to be like *eke*."

"What is *eke*?" Charles asked. He did not know why he bothered. He feared the man was insane. Only a man in loss with his senses could speak with such hope here. But a part of Charles could admit there was something pleasant about speaking again. The more they talked, the more he could feel a small shred of his humanity returning.

They all sat huddled in a group of men, most showing no stamina, wasting away. It was a strange thing to feel alone in the presence of others, and until now, the isolation had been no small pressure. Chibueze was a reckoning force. He threatened the stagnant order of their cramped quarters.

"The *eke*, it is a serpent sacred to us. *Eke* is a messenger of the gods, *eke* is *Nne anyi* ... our mother." Chibueze's eyes lit up. "You need to be like *eke*. Lay in wait. Let them not see you. And when the time is right, you strike!"

Charles did not know why this man was talking to him about snakes and trickery. Loud bootsteps sounded above them, and the thin man returned, his ugly face peering down at them. He descended to their level for the second time and grabbed Charles, working quickly to undo his iron fetters. When the weight dropped from his limbs, he gasped. His legs tingled and felt foreign to him, and he stepped awkwardly as the feeling coursed through his legs.

"Like *eke*, General …" Chibueze said after him, as Charles was led topside.

The thin man's boot crushed a scuttling crab as he stepped on it. Then Charles realized it was a large roach. They both crunched the same. Who knew how many crawled down there in this prison?

The light above on the deck was blinding, and he felt chills cascade down his shoulders as he stood in it. Once his eyes adjusted, he scanned his surroundings to assess who controlled the vessel. His enemy had nearly every advantage, but now they would lose the element of surprise. Charles saw small signs that they cruised near land. There were birds in the air, and pieces of timber floating past the ship's track. They flew no flags, a sure indicator of piracy.

Then he saw a white skirt dance in the breeze. His heart almost stopped—in his delirium, he was sure that he had seen a glimpse of Eliza ducking behind a mast in her stays and shift she wore for swimming. But it was only a fallen sail, a mirage. When a person lived in your thoughts every waking minute of the day, it was only too easy to see them everywhere and in everything.

His fantasy was sorely interrupted by a man who

marched up to him.

"Any man can be broken. Is that not right, General?" he asked, studying him.

The man crossed his arms, his airs hostile. Charles assumed he was the dreaded captain.

"I am not a general," Charles said weakly.

The man strode up closer to him. Now he could clearly see his swarthy features. He had a broad, tanned forehead, his dark hair was slicked back, and he wore a thick beard. He was older than Charles by perhaps a decade, and now he glared down at Charles with simmering contempt.

"You are whatever I say you are. Prisoners. Mercenaries. Bargaining chips. A pet for some lustful man, some sodomite, I care not. I only care about what they pay me. So you will only be known as The General now. I would choose your actions carefully, General," he said, his accent heavy to Charles' ears. "I do not like the look in your eyes."

Charles did not know if this man was a Berber. If he didn't know any better, he would have assumed him to be Spanish. But maybe the men below in that squalid hovel were right. If this man was some pirate called Maalik who hailed from Algiers or maybe some corner of the Ottoman Empire, there was a possibility he was an outlaw of those lands, no longer welcome in their waters. Now he terrorized this side of the Atlantic.

Not all men knew the secrets of the sea. Piracy by its very nature was shrouded in mystery, and the nations of Europe did not know every captain that struck terror in the hearts of those living in faraway colonies. But perhaps this did not matter. Maybe Barbary pirates stood for nothing but Englishmen's unbridled fears that another race of man could capture them from their coastal homes and sell them into slavery. That somewhere else, in another ocean, the very tables of civilization were turned. This alone marked the Muslim pirates as distinct and placed them a peg higher on a scale of horror that all white men kept in their minds, in some shadowy corner where their darkest fears lived. And perhaps this man, whoever he was, knew this and used it to his full advantage.

Charles refused to let the unknown sharpen his despair. He already stood one step closer to freedom, as his chains had been unshackled. He might never receive such a chance again.

"Generals do not take orders," Charles said through gritted teeth.

The man's fist came flying out, striking Charles in his hollow stomach and knocking him down to the deck.

"If I wanted you dead, you already would be. No … I want to break you." The captain stalked over Charles, watching him weakly scramble back to a stand. "You are nothing now. Strip him," he ordered.

Two men that Charles would not want to walk alone down an alleyway with left their posts by the sides of the ship, and started tearing his filthy, stained shirt off. They made a move to remove his breeches, but Charles fought them until the captain signaled their assault to stop. The captain's comments about sodomites had not gone unnoticed.

"Ah, now I can better see what I am working with," the captain said. He tipped his chin up, eyes pouring over every inch of him, until Charles jerked his face away. The man laughed and began to walk around Charles. "The marks of insubordination! But they did not push you hard enough."

Charles knew he spoke of the numerous scars from his father's whip that he had received at Pleasant Hall. He clenched his jaw.

He heard his sinister voice in his ear. "I can tell you've never been tortured. And I do like to break people in," he whispered. "They call me *El Maldito*, for I assign destruction to men. Like a curse. And I will enjoy breaking you."

The Spanish pirate studied Charles now, looking for any signs of weakness. Charles steeled himself, displaying none. This pleased the captain. He walked over to a member of his crew, a ragtag assembly of men of varying nationalities.

"Bring another one up. I want to see what our General here can do before we drop anchor at Black River tonight."

Black River. Charles' mind raced to place the name. It was on the Mosquito Coast of Central America, close to British Honduras. Black River was a cursed settlement, plagued by tropical disease and the violence of the Miskito natives. The English had evacuated it eight years ago, leaving it in the hands of the Spanish, who now likewise suffered the same fate.

So this ship's course was headed due southwest, around the Spanish colony of Cuba, and south of the Honduras. He calculated the distance in his mind. He could not have been aboard this ship longer than five days. He scowled at the captain. Knowing his name and their location, he assumed he hailed from Cuba. Of course, this ruffian operated in one of the last wildernesses of the northern tropics. Charles listened desperately for anything else he might accidentally reveal; every word this insufferable fool uttered was a clue.

A rush of struggling footsteps brought Chibueze forward. Two men were needed to control him and force his way in front of Charles. The captain surveyed the two men and compared their bodies, deciding on who would win in this next bout.

"We have saved the best for last. Let us see who is the better warrior … an English General or the Dark *Bozal.*"

Fear quickened Charles' heart. Deprived of nutrition, of light, of fresh air, and without any kind of exercise, even to stretch his limbs, he knew he was too weakened to fight effectively. Chibueze had been kept a prisoner here for longer; he had had more time to adjust, to practice their unlawful fights on the open seas.

Chibueze crouched into a fighting stance and raised his fists. Even with the lack of food, Charles could see his muscles rippling, as if he was born for moments like this and no deprivation could dampen his spirit. He faced a warrior, and despite the confined conditions, Chibueze moved along the deck as if he had renewed his body at the smell of battle.

Charles barely had time to prepare before his dark fist arced towards him, but he managed to side step away unscathed. Prizefighting was illegal, but fights still occurred in the underbelly of sprawling, coal-stained cities in England. Rich men would throw money at the lower class, egging on the violence, excited by the forbidden sight of blood. He had been to a fight once, many, many years ago, and he struggled to remember something, some move, some plan of attack, that could help him now.

A true battle was not the same thing as fighting a perfectly matched opponent. Charles was only familiar with assaulting a weaker man, aided by an element of surprise and a trusted weapon. Now, he and Chibueze were truly balanced opponents, waiting for the other to strike, with only their fists and willpower to guide them. Charles and his rival moved side to side, trying to balance with the slow rocking of the ship.

"*¡Pelead!* Fight or I will shoot you both down!" the captain barked.

Charles lunged forward, throwing a jab towards Chibueze, uncertain of what distance and range he could control in his weakened state. When Chibueze likewise dodged him, Charles cringed from the sudden force on his muscles. This fight would be no easy feat; an exchange of blows like this would take some time. More punches were thrown, and more strikes were sidestepped until the captain finally lost patience.

"No man in his right mind would pay for this. You bore me!"

"They are both half the men they once were. I told you to increase their rations," one sailor said.

Another chimed in, sensing the captain's ire at having been spoken to like that. "Should I bring a sick one topside, Captain? That would be easy work."

But Chibueze did not care for their trifling conversation.

"They wanted this, they spoke of this for days,"

Chibueze muttered under his breath.

Charles' ears burned; he was afraid the captain had heard them.

"You know what you must do," he continued as they pretended to mirror each other's stances in a wandering, tight circle on the tilting, hot deck. "There is no glory in a grave."

Charles did not answer him and only focused on tracking his every move. The breeze Charles had first encountered had vanished. The heat of the sun beat down on his back like a red, angry sear.

"Ay, quit talking. Strike!" one of the sailors shouted.

Charles felt a sharp kick in his lower back that made him lose his balance. He propelled into Chibueze, and the match became one of wrestling. Now he could see the glint of sweat beading on his dark skin, and the rest of the onlooking crowd became a blur. But he could feel that Chibueze was not using his full strength on him.

"Like *eke*!" Chibueze said, releasing him and stepping back.

He prayed the roar of the sea had buried his voice. He did not need to receive more punishment because of his foolish snake story. Charles could think of nothing else to do but try to land another punch. He saw an opening and took a tremendous lunge, praying his reach would not be wasted this time. His punch was successful and knocked Chibueze's chin upright.

He heard the captain clap, clearly amused by the escalation. Charles had not hit Chibueze that hard. There was an undeniable comradery between them. It was them against the pirates, these wicked men, and he saw no reason to strike again, even though he could have easily bested him.

But Charles' restraint mattered little, his single blow was still too much for Chibueze. The combined tolls of fatigue and hunger had done their silent work, and the African warrior was clearly shaken by the strike. He stumbled backward, hitting his knee on the sweltering deck. He rose again, but wobbled.

"Get up, you dog! Show us what those scars are for!" the captain shouted, pushing him back in the invisible ring when his wavering footsteps carried him too far.

There was something sad to witness in the breakdown of a warrior. Charles did not understand his culture, but Chibueze had no doubt been a fierce fighter in his prime. He knew he had earned the scars carved into his skin.

"I crave violence. Throw them the sticks, let us have a fight to the death! This *bozal* has traveled with us for far too long. I bet on The General!"

Two sharpened sticks rolled over to his feet, and Charles felt a call of awakening. He was never rattled by chaos. On the contrary, he thought more clearly in it than he ever could languishing belowdecks in squalor. Charles had felt uncomfortable, wholly unfamiliar with this type of combat, but his focus was now sharpened and unshakeable.

Chibueze slowly rose to a stand, his wide eyes the last part of him to move. For a minute, Charles feared he had made a mistake in not hitting him more when he had the opportunity. But then he remembered his new state of weakness, knowing that vulnerability like that could not be easily overcome. Charles still had a chance.

There was a pause filled with undeniable tension, and then Chibueze screamed a terrifying war cry, rushing towards Charles and then past him. Shouts of confusion broke out on deck, and Charles turned to see Chibueze throw the sticks like spears, hurled with an accuracy honed over a lifetime, into two unsuspecting sailors.

Like eke ... he thought in amazement, repeating Chibueze's favorite phrase.

He had allowed Charles to strike him to convince the others of a feigned weakness. Chibueze had laid in wait, like a serpent, watching his surroundings, waiting for his true prey to lower their guard. And then he had seized the vulnerable moment with a perfection crafted by years of training. This was chaos and insanity, it was desperate and wild, but it was their only option. It would end in death, and Charles refused for it to be his.

A jolt of instinct surged through Charles, and he knew that the captain had to die next. He found him and rushed toward him.

"Mutiny! Mutiny!" a sailor cried. His voice had made him a target, and one of Chibueze's already bloodied spears impaled his back, and he dropped. Chibueze made quick work of him, his hands vicious and skilled with his makeshift weapon, and moved to his next target.

Charles ran into a hail of pistol fire from the starboard side, evading every brush with death, until he reached a speechless captain. These men were poor marksmen. He pushed the shocked man against the railing, smashing his body into the gunwale. The captain was surprisingly weaker than he assumed, but then again, men who found satisfaction in torturing other men generally lacked muscle themselves. They delighted in making their victims weak like themselves, invigorated by a false sense of vigor.

He thought of all the words the captain had spoken to him before the fight, all the ways he had insulted and threatened him, and it fueled his rage, shaping some other-worldly strength Charles had long thought impossible into existence. He shoved his two sticks up under his throat, unsure of whether he could suffocate him, break his neck, or, if he continued pushing, could topple him into the sea. It was taking too long, and Charles did not like how his back was exposed to further attack. He spied a pistol handle sticking out from his pocket, and he seized it as the captain flailed. Charles aimed it square in the man's forehead and pulled the trigger, eliminating him. He spun around, his face dripping with brain matter, and dropped the crude sticks, much more at ease with the sword he had unsheathed from the captain's lifeless form.

He searched for who he had to take down next, and saw that Chibueze had opened the hatch and gone down to free the other men. Bodies laid sprawled all over the deck, their hot blood running in thin rivulets one way, then stopping, and retreating with each tilt and lift of the boat. Charles was in awe of how much damage Chibueze could inflict with two sticks against a dozen or so men.

Then he saw a survivor, limping towards another hatch belowdecks. He heard a gunshot explode down there, and knew at once what his fatal plan was. The magazine room, no doubt filled with several cases of powder and explosives, was kept under lock and key, but many sailors carried orders to light the gunpowder stores in case of prisoner revolt. He looked down at the dead captain, his face missing, only a disfigured ball of flesh mounted on his shoulders. He wondered that this remaining sailor should choose to end his life as well, even though his captain had been killed.

But when he gazed at Chibueze's rampage again, the man clearly feared the retribution of the prisoners. Charles wondered how long Chibueze had been kept here against his will. When he had attended slave auctions, he had hardly seen men like him, with fierce markings on their faces. Now he understood why white men had avoided enslaving the likes of warriors like him. It was simply an exercise in futility.

"General! Are they dead?" His voice rang out as newly freed but weakened men slowly climbed up to the main deck. They shielded themselves from the brightness of the light and staggered about.

"A man ran down there!" Charles shouted.

Chibueze started to speed in that direction, but he made an abrupt turn and flung himself off the side of the ship. And when Charles saw what he had seen, the growing ball of orange flames creeping up the ladder, his heart sank.

Fire … what all men on the sea feared the most, more than any uprising. *He* ran now in the opposite direction towards the stern of the ship, as close to the edge as he could muster, powerless, and unsure of what to do. Panic gripped him, and he turned again to see a group of prisoners standing rigid with shock. They had achieved freedom, but at what cost? This last pirate had been resolved to defend the ship to the end, and he would selfishly bring all of them down to Hell with him.

Charles refused to join.

When the boom of the first explosion reached his ears, he held his breath and dove for the rippling expanse of blue, hurtling his body as far as he could manage from the rotten ship. Behind him, the flames reached the powder hold, and the ship exploded, rocketing upward in a cloud of fire towards the contrastingly calm sky. The heat burned his back, and he crashed into the water as something hard knocked the back of his head.

Then he felt nothing, no ache in his tired limbs nor pain from exertion, not even the gentle caress of the cold, moving current. Charles knew he had died.

CHAPTER XII.

April 14th, 1794—Island of Saba, Dutch Caribbean

Eliza follows a steep trail in a rainforest cloaked with rolling bouts of mist and cloud. Moss covers large round rocks, guiding her footsteps upward. Swinging ferns beaded with dew brush her ankles. In the mist, she can see orchids growing out of a cliff face, their long, thin yellow petals hanging down like hair. A large black hummingbird buzzes by her and dips into a white spider-lily up ahead on the trail, taking its fill of nectar.

Her surroundings speed up around her although, she does not move, and she is now deeper in the dark forest. An ancient statue is in front of her, but she is mesmerized by what covers it. A cluster of Cloudless Sulphur butterflies, their yellow silken wings beating neon green in the humid light, adorn the statue's face. Eliza reaches out a curious hand, and with instinct, one twitches away, setting the entire lot of them into flight.

Now she can see that it is a statue of a woman covered in liana vines and jungle moss. Then it transforms, and she recognizes Jane Ada Sharpe, Charles' mother. She stands before her breathing, made of stone no longer, and Eliza is at once afraid but also filled with love for this woman she has yet to meet, this woman whose grave she has visited many times.

Jane smiles at her, welcoming her to this vision. She is beautiful, but she is also battered, a bruise moving into place over her eye like a shadow. A few butterflies return, radiating in her light, for she is bright like the sun itself. "You make my son see the flowers again," she says, her voice unfamiliar to her but soothing at the same time.

Eliza sees a vision of the vibrant purple bougainvillea plant that creeps along the porch of Pleasant Hall. "Please," Eliza says, "I am searching for him. Where is he? Where has he gone?"

Jane takes Eliza's hands, a yellow butterfly lands on top of them. Eliza watches it with wonder. "My boy is alive," Jane says, her eyes wide and sparkling, green like the moving leaves that surround them.

Tears fill Eliza's eyes, and she looks off to the side, at the ground where, in a small puddle in the mud, the rest of the butterflies have congregated. They line up like small triangular soldiers, protecting the sacred rainforest. "I am going to save him," Eliza answers.

But then the butterflies are gone, and so is the light. Jane leans in, her voice deeper, darker like a shadow. "He will steal your happiness away. He is a thief."

A warning. Eliza feels cold creeping up her back. "Who?" she demands.

The answer is a wavering image of Hiram Bruin rippling like the surface of the water, his hair wet from when they es-caped the tides of the cave. Jane squeezes her hands. A breeze passes between them, and something trembles next to Eliza's face. A butterfly is stuck in a spider's web. But distance separates the women now, and she is far from her.

"He is a thief," she repeats as her voice echoes. The spider attacks the trapped butterfly, but it continues to struggle in vain.

Eliza awoke with a gasp. She had never had a dream with only Charles' mother and her before. It felt like a long overdue meeting, but she could only think of one thing. His mother had confirmed that Charles was indeed alive. All that was left was to free him, to recover him from the wicked men who had captured him.

She left the confines of her cabin half an hour later and began to stroll along the main deck. The ship had slowed considerably, and what she saw took her breath away. A massive mountain lay before her, covered in jungle and large enough for the fluffy clouds to touch its peaks. Velvet green slopes ran down its side, a vibrant color where the light hit, and filled with dark emerald shadows where it did not. Towards the top, dense jungles sprawled above the sea. The greenery stopped by steep, sheer bluffs that dropped almost straight down, hundreds of feet to the ocean's edge. At its bottom, no vegetation grew, and it was mostly rubble and rocky cliff face. The island's volcanic contours were sharp and jagged, and looked like the winds off the Atlantic whipped around it without mercy.

She imagined that this vast mountain seemed more reminiscent of land in Africa or Asia, as if no human could possibly live on the edge of such wilderness. It resembled nothing of the mostly flat limestone outcrop of Nassau she had left behind. She understood that Jamaica and Saint

Domingue had mountains, but they were not like this. Nothing was quite as dramatic as this. It was a combination of gentle curving beauty and craggy volcanic rock, and its silhouette stole her breath. These slopes offered no respite on their outer edges, and no palm-lined beaches graced their shores. It looked prehistoric, untouched by man.

It was teeming with life. Between the malachite green rainforests at its peaks and its deep bays teeming with fish, this jungle-covered mountain was a fertile place. Brown footed boobies flew over the ship's masts and around them, chasing unseen fish in the navy waters. They raced shipside, wheeling in circles, then dove in succession, slicing through the sea. Further ahead, sprightly porpoises broke the surface of the ocean. Behind her, she heard the men call out that a breaching whale had been spotted.

A whale foretold good luck, and Eliza savored the knowledge. She would take all the luck she could find. On the other side of the island, she saw more mountains, tinted blue in the early morning haze, and she wondered what they were.

"So what ye think?" the quartermaster's voice sounded next to her.

"It's beautiful. It's stunningly beautiful. It's massive," she said, her voice full of admiration.

"Aye, and it never seems to get any closer 'til yer right a top of it," he said, leaning over the railing. "Strange place to call home."

Home. So people did live here.

"What island is this?"

"'Tis the island Saba," he answered, as if it should have been obvious.

"Saba ..." Eliza repeated quietly.

A flying fish rocketed upwards from the waves, then dove back down again.

"Do many people live here?" she asked.

"Aye, they do. Not many, but there is a capital and isolated villages. The neighboring isles are home to more people. Ye will see many islands in your lifetime, but none like this."

"And mine is the prettiest one of them all," Bruin's smooth voice said as he approached them.

"This is where you're from?" Eliza asked incredulously.

"It is. It is a special place indeed."

A disturbance rippled across the water, and they both watched it.

"That is from the flying fish," Bruin pointed out.

A huge dark shadow emerged from the depths, and a chase ensued. Eliza was wholly engrossed in the spectacle, distracted as always by the wonder of nature. Bruin watched her face light up, studying her every reaction closely.

"And that is the dorado. It makes a good meal. *Dorado* means golden in Spanish."

Eliza could see why. The fish was made up of dazzling colors. Green, bright blue, and gold scales covered its sides. A handful of fish leapt out of the water, covering more ground in the air, and evading their predator. But then the brown footed boobies returned, swiping them mid-flight, and ending it all. She watched in amazement.

Bruin laughed. "You cannot escape death, no matter how crafty you are. Those flying fish can sail quite a distance, but it does not matter in the end."

"What kind of mountain is this? I have never seen such a one."

"That is a volcano. My home was formed by fire and lava."

"And above, near the top, are those jungles?"

"There are rainforests, filled with roving clouds. I will show you if you want."

Eliza was thrilled by his words. The dream she had been wrapped in not so long ago was real. She had somehow seen the secrets of this island before ever setting foot on it. And to know she could explore its wild beauty?

When she realized Bruin was staring at her and not at the fish, she calmed her excitement. She was there first and foremost for one thing: Charles.

The *Fortuyne* thrummed through the swells, and she was mesmerized by the strange sea that surrounded Saba. There was no crystal-clear water to be found here, nor white sand beaches. It was only land, leafy and dense, then brown rock, and the sapphire blue sea. This water here was deep, and she watched the lustrous center between every crest of wave, hoping to catch a glimpse of another creature. She had already been treated a few days ago to the sight of a flock of flamingos inhabiting a shallow sand bar, their bright pink feathers reflecting in the still blue water. What other wonders would mesmerize her here in Saba?

Between her burning curiosity and the glittering water they sailed over, she felt a surge in the tides of her emotions. How very large the world had felt to her now in the last week, alone on the edge of the world, with no one to trust. She began to feel lighter—her ordeal was nearing its end. As the island loomed closer, so did the start of the rest of her life. Every glistening wave of the rich jewel blue sea carried her closer to a reunion with Charles, and she felt an overpowering sense of joy. She would not only find answers in Saba, she would find *him*. The crew was smiling too, anxious to reach a familiar shore.

The sailors adjusted the *Fortuyne's* sails, and the ship reached a crawl. She heard the heavy anchor splash into the ocean, and the ship rode lightly now, moored well offshore in the dark water. But Eliza was confused; she saw no port, only a small beach tumbled with heavy rocks. Then she saw a winding, narrow staircase carved out of the volcanic stone, curving and twisting its way into the interior of the island. Her heart sank at the sight of it, but there was no time to question anything. A longboat was hoisted down to the water, and Eliza went over the side into Bruin's waiting arms and dropped into the rocking boat. It bobbed in the faint swells of the sea.

Bruin ordered the longboat to put off, and the cadence of stroking oars sounded, slicing through the water. Eliza's heart soared every time she heard the oars move: every stroke brought her closer to her husband. The men pulled strongly for shore as if not another minute could be lost. A conversation in Dutch started between Bruin and two blonde sailors. Bruin's laughter trailed into the wind.

They reached land and began the slow, tortuous climb upwards. There were over eight hundred steps, and soon

Eliza was heaving, her thighs burning. The heat and the wind only disoriented her more. Eventually, they reached the end, passing a small customs house where the guard inside was overjoyed to see Bruin. Beyond the customs house, there was a round clearing with several pack mules waiting for them. She learned that they had arrived from Ladder Bay, on the west side of the island, and now their intended destination was the capital, known as The Bottom.

Lush greenery gave way to reddish-brown rocks, and the terrain was dusty and dry. They traveled over a rocky trail, avoiding large boulders that had fallen in the path. The extreme topography made the construction of a true road impossible. The small group of men still dubbed their path a "road," but it was a very bad one. The mules were indifferent.

Hand-chopped volcanic stone walls lined their path, and the sun bore down on Eliza's back. Theirs was a slow ascent, but she still found it charming with its bursts of pink oleander flowers and giant aloe plants. The higher they climbed, a breeze accompanied them. The base of the island and those horrible stairs were much hotter than where they were headed.

Eliza's pack mule was cumbersome and its footing unstable. A man had offered to hand-lead her mule, but she had declined. She cast a weary look at the towering summit before them, fearing this dusty track wound all the way up.

"Do we have to continue until we reach the top?" she asked Bruin nervously.

He laughed. "No. I am taking you to The Bottom. To the house of my grandfather."

Eliza sighed with relief. The mule was slow, but the big black flies attacking its haunches and her legs were not. It took its own time, carrying her up the winding road at a lethargic pace. She wondered if she could walk faster. Then the path grew more treacherous, and each sharp curve on the trail began to make her feel dizzy as she glanced down at how very high they had already come. Eliza prayed that the animal did not lose its footing now.

She looked up at The Mountain. It was more than beautiful. It signified that she was one step closer to solving her dilemma. Bruin began to explain the land to her. There was a cloud forest located nearly three thousand feet up on the very top of The Mountain. She wondered what creatures lay hidden in its mossy mist-filled altitudes. Up there, mountain mahogany trees dwelled, and a layer below that in the underbrush were Sierran palms and a variety of tree ferns. He described rare orchids found nowhere else in the Caribbean, and wild raspberries and plantain trees. Below the cloud forest, redwood and mountain fuchsia trees grew wild, intermingling with cacti like the prickly pear, and Eliza's familiar seagrape trees.

Hillsides choked in forest and gripped by the snarls of tropical vines eventually gave way to smaller bush, then openings with dramatic viewpoints of fertile valleys the higher they ascended. The slopes here were covered with grassy meadows and scattered shrubs. From these heights, the sea no longer looked menacing. Instead, it was smooth and flat, like a painter's strokes, the clouds above appearing closer than she had ever seen, dappled and perfectly set apart. There were no palm trees on this island, but nature more than made up for it with its wild, savage beauty. They climbed higher and higher, the air sharp and crisp, the verdant jungle barely tamed.

The climb became less steep, and they headed towards the center of the island now. Small houses, crudely covered with crooked shingles, appeared. Slave children stood outside the house, drying round cassava bread on the roof and watching them with sad, hollowed eyes. A field of banana trees surrounded the dwelling, and men stooped and bent down low to place bushels of bananas in sackcloth bags. Further ahead, little white houses, barely perceptible in the wild greenery, nestled high on the slopes.

They continued until they reached a clearing filled with even more houses, whitewashed like bleached bone, simple and square but ornately trimmed with white geometric woodwork under the eaves of each roof. This architecture marked the presence of the industrious Dutch, with their stout, elegant houses, tidy villages, and narrow roads bordered with limestone walls. The Bottom looked like some portion of Europe had landed in the center of a tropical volcano. She wondered why Bruin chose to spend so much of his time away from these charming white houses and red shingled roofs. The Bottom was rugged, but beautiful, and Eliza was in awe of how truly removed they were from everything in this isolated valley.

They disembarked from their pack mules, and Bruin and Eliza separated from the rest of the party. He took her down a street, then another, until they stopped at one of the largest wooden homes she had yet to see on the island. It stood next to an old Anglican church whose walls were slathered in a blinding whitewash of lime and crushed shell. This home was a one-story dwelling, but it extended far back and enjoyed soaring views of the strange paradise. Two short, squat banana trees were planted in front of it, along with bursts of giant green elephant ear leaves and red and pink bougainvillea plants. Sash windows and a neat white picket fence hemmed in the tidy house. A small porch ran along its side facing The Mountain—a window into nature itself.

Everywhere on this island gave Eliza the sensation of being simultaneously on a mountaintop and at sea, for the blue expanse was still visible from almost every angle. It was hard to believe that the grandfather of a pirate lived here.

Bruin allowed Eliza to step through the gate first, and she immediately stopped, entranced by an extraordinary cluster of flowers. She reached out and grasped its beak-like structure, marveling at the three orange and three bruise-colored petals that grew out from it.

"Crane flowers," Bruin said with a sly grin. "My family brought seeds over from Kapstaad, and my grandfather has grown them for as long as I can remember."

The flower did resemble the profile of an exotic bird. Eliza knew it as a Bird of Paradise from her naturalist books. But she had never seen one in person, let alone several together. Saba was only sharpening her appetite for southern Africa. She lingered by the flowers, still touching their hard, beak-shaped form, in awe that such an unusual flower could even be real.

"Let us go inside," Bruin said, his hand at her lower back.

She pulled her hand away with reluctance and stepped forward, about to ascend the porch steps, when the bushes beside it crinkled with noise. A small brown snake slithered from the shadows and crossed in front of them.

"Do not be afraid; it is harmless," Bruin explained.

But Eliza, of course, was naturally unafraid. She gasped with delight at having seen another wondrous part of nature.

"Oh my, and what kind of snake is that?" she asked breathlessly.

She rushed to bend down, peering behind the bushes to catch another glimpse of it.

"It is a racer snake. This kind is only found here and on Sint Eustatius," he answered, lowering himself to her level.

She turned, startled by his close proximity.

"It kills its prey with a venom that causes weakness. Then it swallows them whole."

"Do they bite humans?" she asked, her dark eyes huge.

Bruin shook his head. "They are harmless. Gentle little snakes."

Now Eliza was viewing it more like a potential pet. She peered through the dense greenery surrounding the porch, then felt Bruin pull at her elbow.

"Come, or my grandfather will mistake you for his gardener," he said, losing patience.

They entered the home and were greeted by a stout woman who introduced herself as Mrs. Beaks. The interior of the house was also whitewashed, from the wood panels on the walls to the thick beams that supported the roof. The paint and the natural light from the windows made the polished dark wood floors shine.

But what caught Eliza's attention most was the eclectic array of valuables—gilt mirrors, oil paintings, bronze busts—that were scattered throughout the house. The opulence contrasted with the white simplicity of the structure, and as Eliza studied these objects, she silently wondered how many of them were stolen. It was like wandering through the fabled mermaid's lair, the valuables of men and different cultures all placed haphazardly in every nook and cranny of the house, with no understanding of any of it, besides the simple fact that all of it was expensive.

An older man, who Eliza presumed was Bruin's grandfather, entered the room and exclaimed something in Dutch. He looked at Eliza and greeted her, shaking her hand, and that was one of the last times she heard English spoken. They were led to an elaborate wooden table, outfitted with two dark carved chairs and a series of smaller mahogany chairs that did not match. A crystal chandelier hung from the arched ceiling. She was about to take her seat when another man, much younger than Bruin, joined them. He had a haughty air about him, surveying Bruin as if he was surprised he had returned alive.

"Liza, this is my uncle," Bruin said in a low voice.

He directed her towards him, and the man shifted his arrogant glare towards her. He took her and kissed her cheeks three times, pausing at the end as if he meant to appraise her like the art that hung on their walls.

She stepped away as soon as she was able to, uncomfortable in his presence. They sat down at the table and began a vigorous conversation in Dutch. Its distinct rhythm, harsh, throaty words, and its maddening up and down on every other syllable made her head hurt. At first, she pretended to show interest, pretended that she could at least follow along with obvious sounding words, repeated words even, but she was too fatigued and sun scorched. She watched a tiny ant crawl around the table in dizzying circles before Bruin's uncle slammed his hand down on it. It was a return to society, although the society itself was questionable.

The conversation continued for nearly an hour, and Eliza heard her newly given name repeated multiple times. She would look up at the grandfather, at the uncle, and at Bruin, as if to indicate she was listening, but she knew they understood she could speak no Dutch. Outside the windows partial views of the lush mountain slopes called to her. She wanted to leave this gaudy, outlandish house. Servants came and went, their dark hands placing baskets of bread and plates of fish seasoned with exotic spices Eliza had never tasted on the table. The pleasure of meat, a luxury travelers by sea craved, still evaded her. She barely touched her food, and her hosts did not seem to care.

Bruin finally remembered to include her in their talks. He explained what the grandfather had wanted to tell her. Most Sabans spoke English, and there was indeed an Anglican church next door, but the old islanders were Dutch, and the records of the colony were kept in that language. A Dutch flag, alongside one of the Dutch East

India trading company's flags, flew proudly in the town center. There was no fort on the island.

Eliza suppressed a smile. She could not imagine invaders trekking up that dusty path. There was nothing of value in this place other than what nature provided.

Saba's main crops were indigo, tobacco, sugarcane, and its famed giant cabbages. But Saba served mostly as a provisioning outpost for passing ships. The current *Gezaghebber*, leader of the island, was a man named Thomas Dinzey, whom the family seemed to despise. Bruin's grandfather had designs to become the next governor and had already made an attempt to secure that role by marrying off his daughter, Susan, to the governor's son. The Dinzeys were English, and thus began an entire diatribe against all of England. Eliza was torn between squirming in her seat and appearing to be engrossed in Bruin's quick translation work.

Now something the uncle said made Bruin laugh. He turned eagerly to Eliza, ready to repeat the story. His uncle had caught one of his slaves stealing cassava bread and a goat, and he was commiserating with freed black men down by the banana fields. When he questioned the slave, the slave defended himself with overbearing language, and then he beat him near unconscious with his cane.

Eliza did not laugh. This evidently upset the uncle.

"And why has he brought *you* here?" he asked smugly.

So he did speak English;, he simply chose not to.

"I am here looking for —" she began.

Bruin cut her off.

"I am helping her find a husband," he answered quickly.

"A husband ..." His words stuck out to her. Perhaps it was only a slip of the tongue, the difficulty of switching languages so fast.

There was a bizarre dynamic between this younger uncle and his much older nephew. She could tell they did not get along, much like quarreling brothers. She looked at the grandfather. It was clear he'd had his last son very late, most likely as a replacement once Bruin's father had been killed. This is what probably drove Bruin's insatiable greed. His uncle would inherit everything first, and then *his* two sons. Apparently, they were also ship captains and were currently out at sea.

She still did not understand what this family did for a living. Bruin's father had been hung trying to provide for his family, but the Bruins were clearly wealthy. Their taste left much to be desired, but they were still quite rich. Eliza did not have many answers. She wondered how much they knew of Bruin's true profession, or if his lies had crafted a careful story that explained the money he brought them. She doubted that they knew of his criminality, and from their haughtiness, she assumed they only thought of him as a merchant trader, like his cousins.

The uncle's eyes narrowed, and he stared at Eliza, as if she wouldn't have had a seat at the table if it were up to him.

"Ah, I see," he finally said. "We will discuss it later."

"Without her here," Bruin quickly said.

"*Ja.*" And their conversation returned to Dutch.

Eliza's chest burned. These men knew the whereabouts of Charles, and it was clear from their hatred of all things

English that they would only wish him ill. She most likely felt unwelcome because of the favor Bruin was about to ask them. She prayed he could convince them to give her husband up. She would take Charles and leave, never to return to this beautiful place. She would do anything they asked for that.

The old Mrs. Beaks suddenly spoke up, engaging Eliza in conversation.

"You must be pleased to be in Hiram's company again, Lady Hastings," she said, peering through wire-rimmed spectacles.

Eliza did not know how she knew of her maiden name or why she felt she could use it. Bruin must have told them about it. She looked nervously at him now, absorbed in a vigorous debate over something with his grandfather. What lies was he telling them? Perhaps it was better if they did not know her true name? Perhaps it was better if she hardly spoke. It was hard to trust someone when everything in her rallied against him. She nodded, pretending to be more demure and polite than she truly was.

"I must say, I think it is an act of folly. It is all pre-destined. The Negroes deserve their lot, and so do the British. You know the British did that to your father, Hiram," the uncle said in English in a condescending tone.

"*Nu niet oom! Niet nu!*" Bruin spat. "Not now, Uncle. I said not now!"

But his uncle did not care. The situation only amused him further. He turned to Eliza, his eyes scheming some plot. He swirled his wine.

"It has always been my observation that flowers are

prettiest right before they start to fade," he said, indicating her.

Eliza colored, unsure whether he intended to compliment her or insult her.

"My family feels strongly about the British. Especially after what they did to Sint Eustatius back in 1781," Bruin said quietly. "You see, the fates of Statia and Saba have always been linked."

"What occurred in '81?" she asked.

The uncle slammed his glass down on the table, enraged that she did not know. She jumped in her chair.

"Of course, you do not know," he sneered. "Half of the weapons the Americans used in their rebellion came through Statia. They helped with their mail bound for Europe; they helped them defeat the British. Your king and his Admiral Rodney wanted it destroyed. They attacked the Jews and exiled them to St. Kitts. They gave them one day to upend their lives, and wreaked irrevocable damage. They stole their possessions; they vandalized their very graves. Now that the Jewish merchants have left, we are in dire straits. *You* destroyed our economy; you reduced us to a state of general beggary! Do not let the trappings of this house fool you."

His words were pointed and fashioned in a personal attack. Eliza had never heard of what happened on St. Eustatius. It angered her to be spoken to like that.

"I know not of what you speak. My king's actions do not make mine. I am only a woman," she retorted.

The uncle shook his head, casting a disparaging look at the grandfather. Mrs. Beaks clasped her hands and looked down.

"It is in your cursed blood. Now that there is no war in America, there is no trade. We have no livelihoods, yet you English will attack us with claims of piracy."

The uncle clearly sought vengeance and took that desire out on her. She thought him mad.

"Did you know we Dutch loan money to America? We could help finance a second war against England with your lost colonies," he said, continuing his rampage of words.

"That is all you can do. The Dutch could never surpass British naval prowess, and you know it. That is why you hate a man like Admiral Rodney. You fear him," she said, glaring at him.

He was infuriated that she even dared to speak back to him. Veins pulsed at the sides of his temples. The grandfather whispered something to him in an attempt to soothe him.

"You are nothing but a *trut* that does not know when to silence your tongue," he said.

"What did you call me?" Eliza asked.

"A fool, a fool, he called you a fool," Bruin said, waving the tension away with his hand. But Eliza could tell he was nervous and that he was lying. The uncle shot up from his chair and stalked out of the room. All was silent, except for the plants swaying in the strong breeze outside.

Eliza's anger quickly simmered down to quiet panic. She had enraged a man who held Charles' fate in his hands. He already hated the British, and now she had made it worse. A door slammed on the other side of the house. The grandfather laughed, apparently pleased with his son's impassioned temperament.

"I should have given your father my name, Hiram. Edward is a good, strong name. Not Jacob. Your grandmother was foolish to name him that. It made him weak," he said as he sighed. "The men in this family normally live long, natural lives. Your Uncle Edward is promising, though. He will make an excellent *Gezaghebber*," he said. He cleared his throat and quickly added, "After me, of course. God's will be done."

Bruin clenched his fists under the table by Eliza's knee and bit his lip. She was slowly starting to see why Bruin was the way he was. She could see why he avoided this pristine hilltop and took risks on the open sea. The longer she stayed at that table, the more it all made sense.

"And you brought the money?" the grandfather asked, as if his previous cutting words had left no mark at all.

"*Ja, opa. Ik heb zoveel meegenomen als ik kon dragen,*" he said in a disgusted tone. "Yes, Grandfather. I brought as much as I could carry."

"*Ik hoop dat het genoeg is,*" the grandfather replied. "I hope it is enough."

It was disturbing to see a fierce man like Captain Bruin be reduced in such a way, as if his only function was to provide this fragmented family with money while they sat in their pristine home and complained about the British and other so-called enemies. Eliza was still shaken by what had occurred at the table. She feared she had ruined any chance at recovering Charles. Bruin took a deep exhale and turned to her.

"Come, let Mrs. Beaks show you your room for the

night. I have important business to discuss with my grandfather," he said, placing a hand on her arm.

Eliza curtsied. "Thank you for your hospitality, Mr. Bruin," she said, her voice strained. She truly wanted to say nothing at all, but knew it was better to be polite to the patriarch of the family.

The grandfather looked at her strangely, as if he had forgotten English. Mrs. Beaks understood her assignment and stood up, shifting slowly to the hallway. Eliza was unsure of her relation to the family, whether she was an aunt or some matronly guardian of the property who ensured the premises still retained a feminine touch. The house desperately needed it.

Bruin walked Eliza to the doorway. He looked at her like he sought support from her, some encouragement to better deal with his family. But she had none to give. She was pale with worry.

He noticed. "It concerns your husband. Let me handle it."

She nodded, tears nearly overcoming her. She was tired, so very tired.

"A *trut* does not mean a fool. I am not stupid," she said in a near whisper.

"No, no, I am afraid it does not. But his words do not make you one," he said.

There was a peculiar emotion in his eyes, one that she could not place. She pitied the man and hoped he could successfully negotiate her husband's release. Surely he was better used to his family's cruel antics, and he knew how to maneuver his way around them.

He bent and kissed her forehead. The tender move surprised her. It was like the absence of the *Fortuyne* stripped away the coarser side of him, and once back in his childhood home, he was vulnerable and made bare again.

She left him, following behind Mrs. Beaks, in a hallway studded with portraiture, who promptly showed her a pleasant white room with a bed. It was pleasingly sparse compared to the rest of the rooms filled with manic decorations, and it offered her something better. The view from the windows and the door that led out to a small porch on the other side of the house quickly distracted her from her worries. A wispy cloud covered the peak of The Mountain again. The evening grew cooler, and the air was pleasant to breathe in.

Further down on another side of the house, she could hear Bruin discussing Charles' release with his grandfather. Their voices were loud, animated, and then unbearably quiet. It did not matter, as she could not understand their Dutch words anyway. She sighed and prayed to God that all would be well tomorrow.

CHAPTER XIII.

The views from her section of the wraparound porch were stunning as the sun slowly rose that morning, coloring everything in the deepest hue of green. The doves had woken her up, their voices loud yet soothing. She sat in a chair, waiting for a hummingbird she had spotted to return to a flowering bush in the garden. It did not seem to be in a hurry to come back, but Eliza would happily sit there all day with a book in hand.

The air was like warm soup against her skin, and the top of The Mountain was covered in mist. She had spent a lot of time thinking last night, tucked between the dark hills framed by humidity and moonshine, suspended between reminding herself to be more careful with what she said to the Bruins and bursting on the edge of excitement for the day to come. But she was also nervous. She did not know what state she would find Charles in when she did see him again. She prayed that his days as a prisoner had not hardened him against her.

Eliza had fallen asleep in her comfortable bed, counting

down the hours behind her closed eyes and waiting for the moment she would be returned to his strong arms, a triumphant reunion in the island sun.

The hummingbird did not make a second appearance, but now she noticed a beautifully spotted gecko perched on an elephant ear leaf. It curiously did not move when she approached, and she managed to cup it in her hands. It had a tan body marked with large black spots, almost like a jungle cat. For a breathless second it stayed, tilting its head sideways as if to study her in turn.

"What do you have there?" she heard Bruin's voice. "Ah, that is an anole. It is a beautiful creature."

His eyes seemed to want to say "like you." She turned her face away, and the gecko leapt from her hand and returned to the plants.

"What a shame," he said as he watched it disappear from sight.

But Eliza was honored to have even held it for that long. It had seemed such an intelligent creature.

"Beautiful creatures are not meant to be confined," she said quietly. Then she turned to him. "What news?"

Bruin looked down at the ground and then back at her, his eyes filled with excitement.

"I have been successful. My grandfather has agreed to it. Now it would seem all that is left is securing you a husband," he said, with an air of calm and confidence.

Eliza could feel herself filling up with unshakeable hope.

"Then let us go to him. Take me to him!" she said. Then she tempered her emotions and clasped his hands. "Thank you, Hiram. Thank you," she said in a softer tone.

Free from the distractions of the ship and the rigors of command, Bruin seemed a different man. His company was tolerable again, like when they had watched the orange lightning side by side on one of their very first evenings together, although she did not quite understand his eagerness. They would soon part, and this harrowing chapter of her life would come to an abrupt end.

But perhaps he was merely self-satisfied with how he had handled the negotiations. He had his eye on his royal pardon and his gold. She thought of Pleasant Hall and how he had demanded it as payment for his assistance. She feared Charles would be upset. She herself found the reward excessive, but she would say anything to get her husband back. Charles' return had come at a steep cost, but there was still time to sort out the details. Charles was the most important aspect of this entire deal.

Bruin led Eliza out of the house, and she said her goodbyes to the old Mrs. Beaks. The grandfather and his uncle were nowhere to be found, and she was grateful. They walked down the quiet lane back to the pack mules, and Bruin helped her get on one.

"There are certain rules we must adhere to. You cannot see the spot where we are going. Their rules, not mine," Bruin said, his voice nervous. He produced a red sash, and she nodded, compliant and willing to do anything to retrieve her husband. He tied the cloth around her eyes, and she was immediately disoriented. Bruin tied her mule to his, and they began their slow, wobbling journey further up The Mountain.

If Eliza thought the ride up from Ladder Bay to The Bottom was uncomfortable yesterday, it was even more so now. Her legs cramped, as though fearing that if she shifted her body in the slightest, she would lose her balance and fall down some unseen ravine. She gripped the mule's reins and worried that if she pulled too hard, the animal, in its stubbornness, might try to toss her from its back.

The ride was silent for a while, and then she heard Bruin speak.

"There have been the same five families on this island since it was settled over a hundred fifty years ago," his voice smooth. "Can you picture yourself ever living here?"

The mule's shoulders bumped into her, and she almost tilted too far to the side.

"I can certainly see a different type of life now that I did not see before," she answered.

In truth, she could see nothing but the glowing red light of the sun that crossed into the fabric of her blindfold. She assumed this was his meager attempt at fostering conversation on the long, hot ride up to their intended destination. For a while, it was only the snorts of her mule and the wind as it steadily increased, but then they finally stopped. The suspense was excruciating. She heard his footsteps approach, and he guided her off the animal. She clutched at whatever she could grab, and blushed when she realized that he held her in a half embrace. The blindfold came off, and their close proximity was revealed. Behind her, the red sash drifted away in the wind.

She stumbled away from him and then stopped, entranced by one of the most spellbinding views she had ever beheld. They stood on the edge of a huge drop, a sea of waving grass that sloped downward and to the left, straight to a small rocky beach with light blue, glowing water, fringed with white surf, mixing with black pebbles. Beside it stood a smaller mound, a more compact cousin of the infamous Mountain. Bushes of pink oleanders with their spiky leaves waved in the breeze, dotted with cloudless sulphur yellow butterflies that bobbed up and down, as if the wind could not tamper with their delicate flights.

And if that wasn't enough to steal Eliza's breath away, out in the distance, in front of a soft, flat blue horizon, stood neighboring mountainous islands, looming so large and vast that she felt as though she could grasp them if she only stretched her hand out far enough. She had never seen anything like it before. This expansive sea and the slow, drifting clouds that left discernible shadows above the waves were so perfect they did not look real. This sea did not resemble the same violent force that took men's lives away. Looking down from the summit, high above it all, in the very center of all this savage beauty, Eliza felt as if it were her kingdom, her own paradise bursting from the wilderness.

A kaleidoscope of the yellow butterflies swirled in a dizzying spiral around her and above her. But then she turned, searching for signs of other people. Were they meeting the men who held Charles captive? Why were they up here alone?

"I give you the West Indies in all its glory," Bruin said proudly. "First, there is Statia, then Saint Kitts, and the island of Nevis behind it. And Montserrat in the very back."

Eliza heard his words, but her mind was racing with questions, and this chain of islands before her did not give her the answers she sought. Confusion and horror began to take hold. Something was wrong. Something was terribly wrong.

"But where are the others? Are they coming?" she asked, trying to still her trembling voice.

He did not answer. Now he turned to her, an air of gravity covering his features.

"It would seem a ship is your natural element, and perhaps more … the wife of a captain," he said. "I saw it on the very first day."

His words were unwelcome and unexpected. Eliza froze, then took a step back, but Bruin only followed her movements. *Where is Charles?*

"I have maneuvered tirelessly behind closed doors to reach this point in my life. And on the verge of attaining it all, a rare creature stumbles onto my path, which makes me question everything I know. I had reservations, but no one has ever made me stop and make a consideration like this. That night on the ship, I felt something from you. You were built to sail the seas. With *me*."

He paused to take a deep breath. Eliza wanted his mouth to cease talking; she feared his next words.

"Liza, will you marry me?" he asked, his eyes searching hers.

Her heart dropped, like a stone tumbling down the severe slope before them. His proposal felt like a slap to her face.

"Mar—marry … marry you?" she said stupidly. "I have

a husband."

"Yes, one lost for two months at sea. One that is now presumed dead."

His words were cold and unfeeling.

"But we are searching for him …" she said, her voice breaking, even as it became obvious that Bruin had never truly intended to reunite them.

"Liza! You are merely wasting time. Cease this fruitless search!"

Eliza said nothing, her mouth open in shock. End their search? But they had hardly searched for him!

Bruin had lied to her and tricked her in one of the worst ways imaginable. He took her hand, and she knew he was serious. The yellow butterflies danced up and down the slope, oblivious to her devastation. She pushed him away.

"Where is he? You said you knew where he was taken!"

"All marriages end, Liza."

"That is not my name!" she snapped. "Damn you to hell!"

She recalled what she had heard him say last night.

I am helping her find a husband. Not her true husband. A new one. Now that she thought of it, he had accidentally revealed his true plan a number of times on their journey. It was no gaffe of translation, no awkward speech adjusting to a second language. It was the smallest piece of honesty escaping from his lying tongue.

"Your passion for exploring the world is the perfect match to my navigational skills. I admire your optimism; indeed, only the strong survive a life like this, and you have, Liza. I am in awe of your defiance, that fire within you that contrasts with your startling innocence. You are unlike any other woman I have ever met."

He said this so casually, ignorant of the horror he was causing. She regretted the flush that spread to her cheeks. Despite his charming accent, she knew better than to be swayed by anything that left his mouth. Their relationship had been one of business, arranged as a means to an end and nothing more. Charles' life was at risk, and the fate of the slaves at Pleasant Hall hung in the balance. Too many lives were simply at stake to indulge his delusional fantasy.

She looked at Bruin, only too aware that he was a perfect stranger to her. She had not seen this coming. She felt like she would faint, and the ground beneath her feet seemed to sway.

He latched on to her arm, his face filling with concern. "Is it the height, Liza?"

Her eyes grew huge. He was beyond mad. He was *disturbed*. There was something very wrong with him. She grew afraid of Bruin, a terror that only increased by the minute. She was returned to the place he had cast her down in the dining room when he threatened to kill her, when she had been forced to sign the articles of the ship that very first day, the afternoon on the quarterdeck when he had wiped another man's blood on her … and that night in his cabin where she barely escaped with her virtue intact. She had only managed to stall his intentions. Now the sinister threat had returned with a vengeance. She shook her head, disbelieving it all even as it unfolded further.

"I have more power of serving you than any other person I know," he said, his voice earnest. "This is what I am offering you, if you will only give me a chance."

Eliza was grateful her stomach was empty, because her torment would have made her retch. Her hands were shaking, and she felt only a cold, hollow emptiness. She had been led on for weeks, believing in a happy ending that was not meant to be. She looked into his blue eyes, deep and calculating, surveying her for any hint of agreement. It was this air of calculation that unsettled her about him. Heaven and earth seemed to merge in this spot, but she recognized that this man before her represented neither realm. Bruin was full of a selfish darkness.

The yellow butterflies started flying furiously, as if panicked, flitting fast as if to escape an unseen predator, flying in mad dashed angles. They mimicked her strained, shortened breaths. Her chest grew tight with panic, and she clutched her skin there, trying to steady herself. She could not fall apart in front of this man; she could not let him win.

"I can carry you away to another life ..."

"You already have," she said bitterly.

"I can show you the world. Think of Kapstaad. Just say the word, and I will bring you there as soon as we marry."

Not even the promise of Africa could calm her. Eliza shook her head again.

"As if my happiness could result from voyages and adventure alone. It does not."

"I will bring down the very moon for you if that is what you want," he said, thinking himself clever.

"I want my husband!"

Bruin's face went ashen, but then his resolve fortified.

"You have given me your confidence; I know what a rarity that is."

"I cannot give you what you want," she said, her voice breaking.

His hands held her face.

"Shh … Liza, yes, yes, you can," he whispered, his eyes dark.

She felt his lips on her forehead, then his face as he leaned against her.

"You said so yourself. We must wait. We are here to save each other. Those were your words. Let us enter into a covenant before God, and when I take you tonight, there will be no sin."

He began to sway with her, his movements from joy, hers from a lack of resistance brought on by weakness. It did not matter to him that she was so far removed from happiness. He only thought of what he wanted. Dizziness threatened to consume her again. Bruin was taking her words and twisting them, words that had once offered her escape only promised Hell now.

"You took me away from my son …" she cried, her voice a whimper.

But he had an answer for that too.

"We can have more children of our own. We can start today."

She broke away from him, reeling in shock.

"My grandfather has given us his blessing. My uncle does not favor you, and it was no easy task. But my grandfather finally granted permission," he said, swelling with pride.

Is that what they had discussed last night at length? She was a fool to think any of it had to do with finalizing arrangements for Charles' safe return.

"We can get married in the church next to his house. You saw it. It is Anglican, it is your faith. Do you not see? I cannot lose what is mine. Neither you nor the gold coins you have will ever fall from my grasp. That is the very reason you took them in the first place. God has brought us together, Liza."

God? None of this was the work of God. What kind of deity did this man believe in?

"God? You dare to speak of God? You are stealing another man's wife!"

But he had a smug answer for that too. "It has been done before."

"You are a liar, a profound liar!" she hissed.

Bruin watched her, unaffected by her vitriol, seemingly devoid of any moral capacity.

"Consider the march of age, the eventual loss of your beauty. I urge you to seize this opportunity. You only have me left!"

"You brought me to this cursed island under false pretenses!" she exclaimed, struggling to control the steadiness of her voice. "I cast aside my feelings for something more important than myself. I overcame my concerns in pursuit of something greater. And yet you stand here, asking for my hand and know nothing of me. I am like Charles. *He* is my other half."

"And you can do it again," he said, encouraging her to end her emotional tirade. "Why do you fight this? All he ever caused was pain."

"No," she growled. "It's not true."

"Think, Liza! You are not a stupid woman. Your husband is dead. You are free to marry. He is no longer your concern."

She bit her lip as angry tears ran down her flushed cheeks. "No, you are wrong!"

He took her hand, pulling her towards him.

"What other future do you see? If not this?"

"One without you in it," she said, relieving herself of him.

"He offered you nothing. Nassau is nothing, Liza. Nothing but mosquitoes and bush."

"I trust that Providence will restore him to me," she said firmly.

Bruin's patience finally wore thin, and he grew angry.

"Whatever might befall him is the will of God; spare no more thought to him. You must think of your future."

She shook her head, willing to argue with him until the very end.

"My future lies with him; indeed, it is tied to him!"

"*Godverdomme!* He is gone, Liza. Stop this!" Bruin shouted. "Charles is dead. I captured him. It was me! I took him under the orders of Lord Dunmore, and I sold him to *El Maldito*, the Accursed. I sent him to a place where he can never be recovered. *El Maldito* is of the true shadow world. No one even knows his real name."

"Why?" she asked with trembling lips.

"The men he keeps prisoner are never seen alive again. Your hope is a weakness. He is never coming back."

Eliza dropped to her knees, looking up at him with a tear-stained face, eyes full of hurt and betrayal. She began to repeat her mantra, the one that kept her sane in times like this. Charles was not dead. She thought of her most recent dream; now it represented her last remaining shred of wounded hope.

"My boy is alive," Jane says, her eyes wide and sparkling, green like the moving leaves that surround them.

But Charles was lost in a watery underworld. She was no closer to finding him. Her job now seemed infinitely impossible. The immensity of her hopelessness threatened to swallow her whole.

"You have lied to me," she said, her voice faint. "You served him into the hands of his captors, and now you ask for my hand …"

She closed her eyes to steel herself. She could feel her control slipping away.

"I am sorry, Liza. Forgive me. But it is already done. I regret it. I —"

Eliza cut him off mid-sentence. He repulsed her.

"You regret nothing. You express sympathy for my plight, but it is the most cursory kind. For you caused it, and you admit it, unabashedly. How can you lay your sins bare in the sunlight and think you will suffer no consequences for what you have done?" she asked, baffled.

"Liza, please believe me when I say —"

"A wicked administration has ruined my life, and you were a part of it. You have created a rupture, which time can never heal!"

"I believe you have a good chance at securing your

greatest happiness in matrimony," he replied, as if he had not heard a word she had uttered. "Let me help you."

He spoke as if she had won some coveted prize, as if the journey by ship had been a test, and she had passed all of his trials.

"Do you know what you have done? Charles was going to free them …" she whispered. "He was trying to save them," she said, her voice shaking.

"Who? What are you speaking of?"

A cry escaped her lips. "The slaves at Pleasant Hall."

"That is bad for business; you would not maintain your style of living, Liza."

She rose to a shaky stand, leaning forward with a flash of anger. It was a waste of words to tell him what she and Charles had once planned. Especially to a man who only hungered for wealth. She was nothing like him. Charles was nothing like him. She despised Bruin.

"I would not marry you for all the money in the world," she said, hoping her words shattered him.

But Bruin would not take her refusal for a final answer.

"Nothing can ruin us. Not your anger nor your words. You are upset now, and I understand why," his voice was unreasonably calm. "Come, let us go to the church and be wed."

But when he touched her this time, she snapped. She started beating him on his chest, pounding away as hard as her fury allowed. He caught both her wrists, causing Eliza to lose her balance, and she tilted, swerving dangerously near the ragged edge of rocks. His grip tightened painfully, and he pulled her upright, pushing her back to the pathway. She had the sickening impression that Bruin was thoroughly enjoying watching her come undone.

He had only one question for her.

"Will you become mine?" he asked. His eyes held a warning.

She could hear the shrill voice of Eurydice, before she died a second death, ringing in her ears. *"What madness caused you to destroy us both?"*

How did someone trapped in a tragic myth escape their tragedy? Eliza knew the terrible truth: she would never see her family again. She had gambled it all away and left what was most precious to her in this world in this wicked man's hands. It was then that she discovered the Devil did not entice you with brimstone. He deceived with beauty. She looked to Bruin, to that now painfully stunning vista behind him. Eliza wanted to push him down the ravine, to end her troubles once and for all.

As if he could read the dark contents of her mind, he came for her, steering her back into the hard cliff face. He laughed now, unable to hide his satisfaction at her tirade.

"Come, Liza," he said, with a smile, "You have no intentions of being tamed. You are too wild. I recognize it in your eyes. I would not want you to fall to your death."

He pushed her harder into the rock, scraping her back. She winced.

"Freedom now beckons at your door. I can give you *everything* you have ever dreamed of. You should celebrate," he said, his face on top of hers.

"You would only cage my soul," she replied, her voice laced with venom.

He paused for a moment, and she prayed her words had finally broken through his barriers and hurt him.

"I see you will not easily forsake your husband. What a lucky man he once was." She could see she was finally trying him. Bruin was tight-lipped and self-righteous, watching her in wounded silence. "It is a waste, Liza …"

"You have taken leave of your senses. You are bewitched by this attachment, one most unfortunately formed," she said.

He readjusted, pinning her down harder. She was brought back to that night he had attacked her on the ship. Only now there was no escape to be found. He was a desperate man, lost to all reason, and that made him even more dangerous.

"But there is no denying it has formed," he countered. He smiled, that curve of his lips that she had grown to utterly hate.

"You use me ill; you are a vicious and worthless man."

"Perhaps it is from your witchcraft. You have control over me like no other. I would never allow it, but I make allowances for you."

"*You* are deluded by the Devil."

There were more dangers from this man than there ever could be from the wind, the salt, and the sea. The rocky wall dug into her back. She was trapped.

"I thought you were my savior in my darkest hour. How very wrong I was."

Her statement excited him, and he grabbed her face, pulling her into a kiss. She bit him and kneed him between his legs. He released her, cursing, and nursing himself.

"Do not ever touch me again," she panted.

She rushed over to her mule and climbed on his back without Bruin's assistance.

He watched her in stunned silence, unable to accept that her answer had truly been one of refusal. Eliza's heart broke with every lopsided stride of the animal. It scattered into little pieces like the ripped off wings of a butterfly, tumbling and drifting in the wind, wafting away from her.

CHAPTER XIV.

Eliza no longer saw beauty around her—she only saw her rage. She quickly realized that traveling up was much easier than coming down. Her legs burned from clutching the sides of the mule as it brought her lower and lower. The constant forward-down motion made her feel as if she could slip off and tumble headfirst. Its gait was becoming unbearable. More than a few times, the mule's hoof stumbled, and it had to readjust its path.

She cursed when she heard him coming, the sound of his animal growing closer and closer. He was riding his mule faster than was wise.

"Where do you think you are going?" he shouted, his voice too near for comfort.

"I will take passage on another ship. If you think I am remaining with you and your crew, you are mad."

"Liza, this is Saba! There is no boat traffic."

Her mule's ears perked up, and it suddenly stopped with a snort. She prodded it forward, but it would not move an inch. Bruin came up alongside her, and she kicked the mule's sides to no avail.

"There is no boat traffic. What you will find are only men who work for my grandfather. The last he heard was that you were to become my wife," he explained dryly.

Her mule edged away from him, and she realized the animal did not like him. She wondered if he had ever beaten it.

"Then he is grievously mistaken. I don't give a damn what anyone thinks. You have revealed how very little you understand me."

Eliza climbed off the mule's back and started to slide down the curving wall of the path so she would not have to walk all the way to the end and around it. Bruin watched her stubbornness on full display, and Eliza continued her slow, careful drift across broken rocks and dirt. But then she reached the next section of the path, a level below him, and she took off at a brisk pace. She was getting off this damn island no matter what.

She did this a few more times, hearing his laughter echo in the distance, but then she finally made it to the Ladder Bay stairs. She ignored the small man who guarded the customs house and hiked her skirts up, now full of dust and torn from her descent.

At first, she rushed down the stairs, but after the fourth set, her legs tightened up to stiffness and her vision grew blurry. She had to slow down or she would fall. Eliza took a deep breath, her heart raging, the sweat rolling down her face to her chest.

After an unbearable ten minutes, she reached the bottom to the small rocky beach. The *Fortuyne* was still moored off in the distance, and she saw the men on board like ants preparing rigging and adjusting sails. She plopped herself down on a section of the rocks, the pebbles digging into her rear, and she bowed her head over her knees.

She was exhausted in more ways than one. Once she regained control of her breathing, she looked around her. A second party of men was further down the beach, hoisting casks of water and puncheons of wine and rum. She watched them trundle the heavy barrels up the beach—supplies of salt pork, molasses, more hardtack biscuits, and fresh produce—and load it onto a longboat. They then ferried supplies to the *Fortuyne*. The crew on the ship pulled the items up over the gunwales, placing the barrels and crates with care so as to not have too much weight placed near the stern. If it were not for these men, Ladder Bay would be devoid of activity.

She wondered what the purpose of the customs house was. True to what Bruin had said, there was not another ship in sight. She clenched the soiled hem of her dress with frustration. Once again, she was left with no other recourse. She mused about a British naval ship swinging around the edge of the island, past the arches formed by ancient lava, seeing the dark ship, and blowing it skyward with all the men in it. But there was no British naval presence here. She was alone.

"You are a fast walker," she heard his smooth voice say.

Without thinking, she reached down and grabbed a small rock and threw it at his face. It glanced off his temple, and he made a small noise. Blood began to appear by his hairline.

Eliza stood up now, her legs shaky and spent, and she backed away from him. She hoped that had hurt him. She reached down for another rock, but then the metallic zing of a musket ball pierced the air and bounced off a small boulder next to her feet.

She looked up. One of the Dutch sailors had his pistol fixed on her. The men in the longboat had seen her pathetic attack. She was about to run again, although there was no way to go except back up those horrible, curving stairs, when Bruin waved at them, ordering them with a silent command to hold their fire.

He laughed, wiping the blood off of his forehead. "You have good aim."

Eliza did not answer and only glared at him like a trapped animal.

"What do you want me to do?" he asked.

"Bring me to a port!" she blurted, unsure of where she had to go.

She wanted to be away from this island, away from him, away from it all. But she could not return home either. She had no home now. Her home lay with him, with Charles. And she did not know where that was.

"I will take you there myself," he said softly, trying to reassure her. "Only tell me where."

She sighed, looking at the ghost of a naval ship that only existed in her mind. Then she had an idea. There was another source of help. And it was in the one place she had called home for most of her life. England.

"You will set sail for London. We will go to the central Admiralty of the Royal Navy, and you will confess all that you have done, and testify about Lord Dunmore's true character and what has happened here."

She saw a flash of anger darken his features. He did not like being told what to do. Anger simmered in his response.

"Why would I do that?"

"To save your neck from hanging in a noose. I will vouch for your honor and that you delivered me safely to England. And perhaps I can manage a pardon, although the blackness of your soul does not deserve it."

Bruin said nothing, staring at her. Then he walked over to the party who had just returned to shore. After a torturous five minutes of chatter in Dutch, he returned.

"Jan tells me that the men have completed the necessary repairs and procured every article the *Fortuyne* was in need of. The carpenters and sailmakers have also finished their work. It normally takes much longer to set off, but the men are confident with what work they were able to get done. So we can indeed leave today if that is what you want."

She said nothing and marched over to the longboat, refusing all assistance. She understood that, in a way, he was still getting what he wanted. She would be trapped on a ship with him once again, and for a much longer voyage. She convinced herself that it had to be done, and her uncertain fate be left with Providence.

The sailors ferried her and Bruin back to the *Fortuyne*, and for a third time she returned to her wooden prison. There would be no dinners in his cabin, no pleasantries. This final trip had all the potential to become brutal, especially if they encountered any storms crossing the Atlantic. But she had done it once before. She could do it again.

Eliza climbed back aboard, her feet touching the unsteady deck she had sworn she had left behind forever. The usually cantankerous quartermaster lumbered up to her.

"Welcome back, Mrs. Bruin …" he started to say, his voice more cheerful than she had ever heard it.

The look Bruin shot his quartermaster reduced him to silence. He understood what had happened without a word being said. He tried to cover his mistake by talking rapidly.

"The carpenters have caulked the decks in the areas ye pointed out. And we have an adequate supply of food and water."

"So the ship is indeed ready?"

"Aye, Captain," he said, puffing his chest out. Then he added in a lower tone, "Are ye sure ye not wanting to stay longer?"

When Eliza heard that, she turned on her heels and made for her cramped cabin. She hoped it was the same way she had left it. She did not think there were any whores in Saba, although it was a provisioning island. She looked up at The Mountain, cursing its emerald beauty. She had never had her hopes dashed away so cruelly. She could not wait until it drifted far away from her view, never to be seen again.

"Liza, please, wait," Bruin said as he joined her up on the quarterdeck. "May we talk?"

She left her back to him, refusing to look at him. She would be forced to endure his company for a month or more now, however long it took to reach England. That was punishment enough. She could not take a moment more.

"Liza … *Eliza*, please."

He used her name like a lure to coax her back to softness. Now she looked at him. She wanted to strike him, to knock the pride and arrogance right off his features.

"Please …" he said quietly as he got on his knees. He was going to beg her for something. He couldn't be stupid enough to repeat his proposal. She turned red, mortified. Some members of the crew stopped in their tracks, amazed to see their hardened captain turn so submissive before a woman.

"What are your demands? Tell me and I will meet them."

His voice sounded different than she had ever heard. He sounded honest, although she did not trust him. Was the cold reality of her refusal only hitting him now?

"Do not suffer me as an enemy, now that I have turned down your … offer. And do not obstruct my immediate return to England."

"You shall have it."

"I would ask that you take an oath to act as my safe conductor across this sea. My foremost mission has always been to seek the return of my husband, and I will not stop until I have achieved that. I now seek the Admiralty's help. And if you bring me to England, unscathed, I will vouch for your honor and do my utmost to help you receive a royal pardon from the king."

"And you do not wish to return to Nassau? I can have you there in a week."

She looked horrified at the suggestion.

"No, it is no longer safe for me there. I cannot return."

"I will proceed as I have done. I will bring you to London, and I will keep you safe."

His words meant little to her. She wanted to say, "No, keep me safe from yourself," and away from his own scheming hands. She bit her lip and looked out at the water. The sight of him kneeling before her made her uncomfortable. She could not tell if he was sincere, although, understanding what she did know of him, he took a great risk exposing himself in front of all his men. He could be ridiculed, mocked—they might lose respect for him.

"Is that all?" he asked.

The way he said it made her fear that she needed to spell out more immediate demands. *No*, that was not all. He was not to touch her in any way. He was not to seduce or manipulate her. He was not to poison her drinks. He was not to trick her. He was not to kiss her or force himself on her. They were to act as sea captain and passenger. Nothing more.

"Eliza, look how I humiliate myself for you in front of all my men," Bruin said.

She scoffed. "I did not ask you to do so."

"I swear I will bring you to England. Safely. I swear I will make up for all the wrongs I have committed."

"Get up," she snapped, unable to tolerate the sight of him like that any longer.

He slowly rose to a stand, but his eyes were searching for something else. The look faded, and he returned to the business at hand.

"A vote must be taken by the crew. We must agree on the destination, Eliza," he said, his voice pained. "I will ask them now."

Her heart sank. What if the crew refused to take her? Bruin stepped towards the edge of the quarterdeck and addressed his men.

"There has been a change of plans. I now propose to sail to England at the discretion of Lady Sharpe. All those in favor, say, 'Aye.'"

His voice rang out across the ship, broken only by the mewling caws of white sea birds.

Eliza waited for an agonizing minute, fearing the worst. It would be too easy for Bruin to say he had done all he could. If the crew did not want to sail eastward to Europe, Eliza was truly stuck.

The answer wasn't forthcoming. She turned, about to retreat to her cabin, when a loud roar of "Aye!" boomed on the main deck. One small voice dissented, but the rest of the crew had miraculously agreed. She stopped, feeling emotion well up within herself. Her new plan could work; it *would* work.

"*Dum spiro, spero.*" *While I breathe, I hope* ... she thought, satisfied with herself.

Eliza did not see the calculating smile Bruin flashed at his crew as he descended to the main deck.

She leaned against the railing, peering down at the sapphire water below. Somewhere in this dark sea, Charles and her future waited for her. She refused to believe anything else. To question it would mean ... no, she refused to go there. She would focus on her love for him and her fidelity to him alone. For years, she had seen Charles as only an obstacle to happiness, but now she realized he represented it, the elusive fragment that drifted from her fingertips time and again.

Bruin gave orders to run out all canvas. The crew jumped to the halyards. The main sail was hoisted up, and she heard the slack pieces of canvas raised on the other masts with chaos and yelling as the men worked to get the ship back into movement as they adjusted the lines.

"Ready about!" a helmsman commanded.

The crew answered that they were ready and dodged the boom as it turned.

The helmsman then shouted, "Helms a lee!" and the ship slowly turned and came around into the wind, starting her northeast course. The sails rapidly filled, and she moved out of the bay and into the open water as the men continued to modify the angles of the sails. It took over half an hour before the *Fortuyne* cut through the waves with any speed. She was fully loaded with provisions now and carrying a lot more weight, but their new journey had begun.

The way Eliza left the island was much different than the way she had arrived. Yesterday her heart had brimmed, overflowing with a sense of peace and wonder, knowing that her trials were at an end. Now she left Saba, the shock and devastation still palpable on her skin, an unfathomable pain threatening to consume any hope she managed to muster.

How quickly the vast jungle mountain disappeared now, compared to the journey there. It was no fault of the island itself, only the men who claimed it. Corrupted it. Saba was a special place, but it had lost all charm to her now. She stared at the endless straight line of sky, always in awe of how very distant these waters ran. She contemplated how far England seemed to her, how far even Nassau now felt with these dark, foreboding waters. Her home. Could it even be considered that if she was not with him? If she could not retrieve him? *He* was her home.

Where was Charles? The world seemed so immense, and for the first time, she no longer admired it; she regretted it. Its infinity signaled finality. She felt torn and pulled in multiple directions. Her son was on one island, her husband's whereabouts unknown. Only the sea knew, and she wished it could whisper its secrets to her.

As always, she still found some measure of comfort in its depth, its blue vastness, holding hurts deeper than hers. The *Fortuyne* glided serenely over the water, oblivious to the horror she had just endured. But the sea, the sea knew her, and the unspeakable pain she carried deep within her. And now this same ocean would reconnect her with Charles, one way or another. Eliza well understood the risks of a long voyage. There was a possibility she would never see her son or the Bahamas again. She distantly thought about how Philippe's one-year birthday would pass in two days, and she feared it would be the start of many milestones she would be absent for. But her new plan was already set in motion.

Eliza sighed, praying her troubles would disappear like the haze on the horizon.

Two weeks had passed since they had left Saba in all of her strange beauty. Eliza made her way down to the main deck, curious as to why the *Fortuyne* had stopped moving that afternoon. The air was hot and rank, and burned when drawn in through the lungs.

A young girl, no older than sixteen, rushed at her.

"*¡Ayúdeme!* Help me! *¡Oh, gracias a Dios!* Oh, thank God! Help me!" she cried, latching on to Eliza.

Eliza froze in shock, not moving, in complete confusion as to how she had ended up there. A second girl followed behind her, much younger.

"I am Luisa de las Casas, and this is my sister, María. We are nieces of the governor of Havana!"

"Governor's niece? Did I hear that right?" a man laughed, holding a thick rope in his hands. "I told you boys her name wasn't Jane. Now look at the fish we've caught."

The girl named Luisa paled with horror, releasing Eliza.

"You are in league with them?" she asked, her eyes wide.

"No," Eliza said, shaking her head. "I am not with them."

"Then you are a prisoner too?"

Eliza shook her head, unsure of what to say.

"*Ella también es una pirata!*" the girl's sister whispered. "She is a pirate, too!"

All Eliza understood was "*pirata.*"

"I am not a pirate, I am a passenger," she explained.

The girls remained unconvinced.

"Go to hell!" Luisa shouted.

Her vitriol surprised Eliza, and she desperately looked around for any trace of Bruin.

The man holding the rope grabbed Luisa, and another man took her sister. They dragged them over to the mizzenmast and lashed them to it. The girls began to cry and scream.

"Wait, what are you doing?" Eliza asked, following close behind. The scene was spinning around her, too fast and chaotic for her to understand. Where had they come from?

"Captain's orders, Lady Sharpe."

"Is that your name?" Luisa demanded. "I will remember your face and my uncle will see you hanged!"

Eliza backed away, helpless and awkward. She could do nothing to help them.

Finally, she saw Bruin perched on the quarterdeck, a spyglass held to his face. She ran to him.

"Captain, the men are mistreating two girls down below. They have tied them to the mast!" she said, exasperated.

The air was still not moving, and she was covered in sweat. She hoped by using his formal title, she could restore some sense of order to her surroundings.

"Here," Bruin said, with an air of indifference. "Look due south."

She peered through it, searching for something in the distance. Then she saw it. A bright orange light, or a reflection, wavering in the heat. Then she saw a sickly trail of black smoke billowing next to it. It was a ship on fire.

"That was the *Incendio*. We followed it for days before striking. We hoisted the Spanish colors until we drew near, then we flew our black flag and boarded her. No need for a broadside. Perhaps that is why you slept through it," Bruin said, as he took the spyglass back. "The fools inquired if we had any letters. They thought we carried news from their homeland. My men made quick work of it this morning." He studied her reaction with a smile.

Eliza's heart went cold. The *Fortuyne* had attacked a ship and taken these two girls prisoners? Worse, they had stalked the ship for days, unbeknownst to her. And she was an unwilling accomplice to it all.

"Men like us cannot go to the prize courts and sell a ship. We can only set it ablaze or set it adrift. My men were hungry for a prize, and we made out well. Bales of silk and tobacco, lots of it. And those two."

"They claim to be nieces of the governor of Havana. Do you know what you have done?"

Bruin smirked, clearly unbothered by the entire affair.

"Yes, indeed," he said. "And soon Spain will find out, too."

Eliza looked down at the mast where the girls were tied, a crowd of men gathering around them like hungry dogs. She recognized their leers; she had been exposed to the same behavior right before she had jumped from the ship in the Exumas. Only the thinnest thread of control kept the main deck from exploding into unbridled violence.

"It was a lawful capture. The vessel was Spanish. I am on assignment sponsored by the monarch, Liza," he explained. "I am legal under the eyes of the law."

It was ironic that these men used the shield of the king

to protect themselves from the gallows while also damning his name every time they drank. Their sense of morality was twisted, if they harbored any morals at all.

"But they are innocent girls! Why not plunder the ship and leave it?"

"The Spanish did try to fight us. Their mistake," he said darkly.

She watched Bruin grab a rope and loop it, knotting it like a noose. He absentmindedly did this as he talked to her. She feared he wanted to use it on the new prisoners. Every inch of him was comprised of an unspoken casual cruelty.

"What do you think keeps the hopes of these men afloat?" he asked, setting down the noose. "It is the idea of growing immensely rich. And for that to happen, we need to seize more than a handful of coins."

"Do you plan on hanging them?" she asked, her voice wavering.

Bruin looked down at the noose and laughed.

"What, this? No, it is only meant to scare. Fear is a powerful tool."

Eliza backed away from him, disturbed by his mannerisms. She did not want to know what would become of them; she knew no good could come of it. Eliza fled to the safety of her cabin and remained there. She did not want to participate in whatever barbarity the men were planning.

A few hours later, a knock sounded at her door, and she assumed it was the porter boy, John, bringing her dinner.

But it was Bruin who delivered her tray. He seemed on edge. She balked when he appeared at her cabin door.

Something had shifted within him, and instead of his customary calculating look, he gazed at her with cold eyes.

"I have brought you your food. The situation on this ship has changed. I advise you to stay in here. There is a certain order in which we do things, an order you may not understand."

He was right, she did not understand. But his sickening smile told her the decks would not be safe tonight.

Bruin came in her small, dimly lit cabin, placing her food on the table. He turned and faced her, a different air about him.

"Liza, I had a dream with Charles in it last night. His spirit—he forgives me," he said quietly, "Now I only need you to do the same."

His presence in that cramped room made her feel cornered.

"Do not lie to me," she answered, her voice tired of constantly battling with him. "I told you on the path to The Mountain. I refuse."

"You know, it is a curious thing, Liza. Death is not frightening. No," he said, with a scoff. "Solitude is. Being alone. Here and in the next world."

His eyes penetrated hers. She took a step back, but in truth, there was nowhere to go.

"My belief in the future is greater than my fear," she quipped.

"Ah, ever filled with hope," he replied. "It must be so very tiring to maintain. Especially for a man who never gave you his heart. He only removed your dress. There is a difference."

"Do not underestimate my hatred, Bruin. And I would ask you to remember your promise to me."

"Oh, we are still headed towards England, if that concerns you. I would not lie to you," he said.

Even that was a lie. She feared they would continue to pick off ships, always claiming to be still on track for England. A month-long journey could easily extend into half a year.

He pointed towards the table. "I left you a decanter, should you wish for more wine."

"I do not want wine," she snapped.

Bruin grew agitated and was about to leave when he paused. In her mind, she screamed for him to get out.

"Was it a mistake to assume you were not looking for a husband? You have a child and no protector now," he said softly.

When he said that, all she saw was Charles on a very different journey by boat over two years ago.

Charles took her hand in his and pressed his lips to it. "Be reassured, my dear. I am your protector in this world."

"It was a mistake to assume you could ever fill that position."

Bruin's eyes narrowed, and he leaned against the bulwark.

"Tonight, my men and I will drink, and they will be rowdy. And when they lose control, there is no telling what they will grab. There are far more of them than me. It is customary to celebrate after taking down a prize. Besides, it is the least you can do for the crew since they agreed to bring you so far."

All Eliza thought of was the Spanish girls.

"But they are nieces of a governor!"

"Yes, indeed. And women are a convenient remedy. As will you be if you dare set foot in this melee. Now be good and remain in here."

He was about to step out of the room when Eliza accosted him.

"You bastard! What do you plan on doing to them? They are but young girls!"

She wanted to run down to the main deck and untie them. She wanted to protect them. But where could they run to on a ship? Where could one hide when there was nowhere safe?

"There are nights when dark urges take hold of my mind, and tonight is one of them. You can do more with a dead body than you can with a live one, but I would never allow my men to commit such atrocities. Although hearing them beg and plead for their lives, as they will shortly do, is always arousing."

Eliza listened to his words, terrified. He took another step closer.

"But fear not, I will be faithful to you alone," he said, as if this mattered to her. He stroked the side of her face. Her stomach turned. It had not taken long for his dark side to return.

But he would not leave her cabin. He stood inches away from her and toyed with a piece of her hair.

"I admit I have an obsession. There is something about the curl of your hair, this mane of dark locks. It makes me want to ravage you," he whispered.

She recognized the arousal in his voice. It made him speak in a low and dark tone.

A scream sounded from the main deck, and then another. It was clear that both girls were yelling. Bruin broke their forced closeness.

"Oh," he said. "They are starting."

"Starting what?" Eliza asked with a quivering lip.

"The celebration."

Eliza followed him to the door, but he blocked her exit.

"You must stop this!" she cried.

"I am only in the mood for pleasure tonight. What you are in the mood for is of no consequence."

Bruin slammed the door in her face and battened her in the cabin. His laughter drifted away as he left the quarterdeck.

Eliza stared at the door, barred from the outside. She had no way of stopping him from returning. She was afraid he would come back, drunk and enraged with her, finally sick of her refusal to become his. He had already asked her once; he would surely not be so polite the next time. He would simply take what he wanted.

The girls' agonizing cries pierced her soul. Eliza tried covering her ears, but she still heard them. Now the men were cheering. She screamed out of desperation, praying it would stop. She kicked the bulwark with fury. But it did not end. She turned to the wine on her table and took it with shaking hands, gulping it down. She did not want to hear. She did not want to feel. She wanted to quit this place.

But filling herself with drink did not prevent her ears

from hearing their gut-wrenching screams, and the alcohol only amplified her already fraught emotions. The one named Luisa had accused her of being one of them. And since she could do nothing to help them, she was just as guilty as the men who tortured them now.

Her imagination ran wild. A ship could easily turn into a machine made for breaking bodies. Heavy boat hooks and iron bars could be used to beat them, axes and hammers to cause them wounds. Ropes of all sizes swung from every corner of this boat, to whip and strangle them, to stretch their bodies and limbs, to lash them to the shrouds and rigging.

And then there were the men themselves. She knew that fear; she had lived with it. For a man, it was only a few moments of pleasure. For his victim, it was devastation without end. Her thoughts ventured to the darkest parts of herself, the shadows where her deepest pain lingered, too uncomfortable to ever be truly released. She thought of the first two times Charles had slept with her, how mistreated and ashamed she had felt. How he had taken her body away with his, how he had silenced her voice. She could only imagine how sharpened the horror and pain would be as a young girl, wholly unaware of the way men worked, already tense with fear from their capture. How many men did they witness slain who had tried to protect them in vain? And now, how many men would they witness violating every inch of themselves, stealing away pieces and parts they had not even had the time to discover existed?

Eliza began to weep, working herself into such a frenzy

she dry-heaved. They were only girls, only children, and she could not stop it. They blamed her, and she knew she deserved it. A woman was supposed to protect other women. And she had failed. Her affliction was mental, and her misery was more than she could handle.

She rushed at the door again, slamming her body into it. But it did not budge. She took a step back from it, their cries so much louder through the cracks. She emptied the glass decanter, pouring it directly into her mouth. When it was empty, she hurled it at the door, but the barrier was invincible against her rage. The glass burst into small shards all around her feet.

She was only there to save a man who had once wronged her, but the girls' screams tempted her to revoke her forgiveness. She was trapped in hell, threatened by a new kind of monster.

Guilt and reasoning returned to her senses. It was this cursed ship. Charles was nothing like these men. She thought of that night after she had rescued Alastor from a fiery death in the stables. The way she and Charles had done the impossible and mended their relationship, broken piece by piece.

She turned her neck towards him, craving more of the touch that she once feared, and when she finally felt his lips trail there, the unexpected pleasure was nearly unbearable. They moved slowly, savoring every point of connection. They had not met for the first time on that sunny afternoon in Somerset, now more than two years ago. They had become acquainted only tonight on this small, vulnerable island fraught with danger.

"You are caught between two ways of life. Between two

modes of being. I fear I cannot yet trust the man you are be-coming. The wound from before is too deep."

"I love you, Eliza. Please, let me show you."

He stepped back from her, slowly taking her forearm and studying her injured hand.

"You are my soul, my director, my conscience," he said, his eyes connecting with hers.

He pressed his lips against the pale inner skin of her arm, kissing her slowly until he reached the soot-covered fabric near her elbow. The sensation of his warm breath gave her chills, and she converged with him. It seemed inconceivable that the very same man had hurt her so deeply. The heat she felt from his body against hers made her head spin. The man who had once hunted her, served as her enemy, could now be a lover. A true husband in every sense of the word.

And now he was gone. She shed tears for him, for his memory, for the painful loss of a future now threatened. Would they ever be reunited? Would she ever experience bliss in his arms? Would she make it off this ship alive? She feared she would suffer untold indignities at Bruin's hands.

Eliza slid down to the floor, lying on her side and grounding herself, connecting to flat wood and the rocking of the hull. Her mind traveled further back, to a spring morning at Bleinhill Manor.

"Why do men justify killing, Papa? Why do men believe they can conquer nature?" she had asked, closing her book.

Her father's eyes widened with pride.

"I may be biased, but I have no doubt you are the brightest girl in Somerset." He smiled.

When Eliza saw his face, and then her mother's, her

weeping started anew. She saw brighter days in the garden, bursts of color from the flowers calling to her. She had felt her old way of life to be a cage, and even in the safety and peace of her childhood home, thought of nothing but daring adventures and voyages. Now she had had her fill of it; she would do anything to return to innocence and a softer, safer world. Her sadness threatened to overwhelm her. She began to pray; she prayed for the girls below on the main deck; she prayed for her safety; she prayed to be reunited with Charles. Celia's words to Shango that day in the sweltering heat echoed in her mind.

"There is no reason to fear, you will be with me and you will help me in all of my needs … *oba koso* …" Eliza whispered into the gloom.

She drew her knees in tighter and repeated it again and again. In the troubled darkness outside, hot rain hammered down on the wooden decks, drowning all other noises out. She closed her eyes, drifting into a numbing sleep, and heard nothing else.

CHAPTER XV.

Eliza stretched, rolling over to her side as she felt a steady stream of sunlight wash over her. She could hear that sad, mournful whistle that she had heard once before, the very first day she had found herself on the *Fortuyne*. The song was clear and precise, beckoning her to awakening. Then she remembered her cabin did not afford the luxury of full light.

She opened her eyes and, with horror, realized she was in Bruin's bed, in his cabin. She looked at the much larger room, confused as to how she had gotten there. It was daylight again; she had slept through the night.

"The men grew too wild last night. I could not take the risk," Bruin said from over near the table area.

Eliza eyed him uneasily.

"You are not to touch me," she said, her words quavering.

She stood, her mind still racing to catch up, her legs trembling as she eyed him warily.

"You were not in your bed. I found you on the floor where the rats crawl."

"I do not remember. It was a terrible night," she replied.

"And there was broken glass all around you," Bruin said, taking a step closer to her. "Were you trying to hurt yourself, Liza?"

She did not like the look on his face, and she ran out of the cabin into the steaming heat. Looking down from the balcony on the quarterdeck, she saw no trace of the girls. It was like they had never been on board. It was eerily quiet, covering the scene of a heinous crime, a brutal pirate ship masquerading as a peaceful one. A few of the crew looked back up at her, then turned away, ashamed. Her womanly presence reminded them of their sins.

Her stomach dropped with fear, both from the sight of a recently scrubbed deck and from the sensation of Bruin standing right behind her.

"What happened to the girls?" she stammered.

She backed into the hard wooden railing that lined the edge of their deck.

"They used their sweet cunny for what it was worth. The crew all had their share, and they fell overboard," he explained, as dryly as commenting on the weather.

His words were so terrible she could not comprehend them. But one thing was clear: they had been murdered. Eliza's eyes narrowed with fury and disgust.

"You liar, you threw them overboard."

"No, Liza, not me. Some of my men. I would have held on to them longer," he said in a sinister tone. He placed an arm on either side of her, boxing her in.

When she connected with his gaze, she knew she looked into the eyes of a killer. He was nearly twice her age; he had experienced double the years of her lifetime.

And he had used those years to destroy countless lives. It was disturbing in its implications. He was no soldier defending a kingdom like Charles. Bruin killed for pleasure, spilling blood as if it was merely a natural duty of any ship captain. She wondered how many lives he had taken and how many more he would take.

He sighed. "They ended up in a bad way. It is better off that they are gone."

She refused to make eye contact with him, choosing instead to stare at the gold chains underneath his shirt. She felt like she was sinking into a hole. Two young innocent girls had been brutally savaged and tossed overboard to their deaths. Bruin had no reaction, no sense of shame or remorse. What would he do to her?

"It seems the current took them out faster than we thought."

Eliza began to cry, despite her best efforts to hide her emotions. She did not want to stir any sense of twisted amusement within him. She wiped away her tears with shaking hands.

"They could not swim; they probably begged for their lives. Why did you do that?"

Her voice came out as a weak whisper. He shifted his weight.

"One day you will understand the sea. Knowing how to float only prolongs the agony. It is better to submit and sink to the bottom quickly, rather than struggle in vain."

Eliza felt chills run down her spine when he said that. She knew he was speaking in a dark metaphor, trying to impart some sick lesson to her.

"But they were nieces of the governor, you could have ransomed them …" she said, beginning to rationalize a different crime in her mind. Yesterday, she had feared this incident would delay their progress to England, but today it was clear that the men had never viewed their prisoners as anything more than a temporary diversion. Something to break up the monotony of their days at sea.

"I did you a favor. Those girls would have reported you to their uncle. Do you see what power you have on my ship?"

"A favor?" She felt sick to her stomach. "Can you be so terribly unforgiving?"

"You were not harmed," he said, an edge of defense to his voice. "I made sure of that. You should be grateful."

Bruin peered over her shoulder, looking down at his men like he was disgusted only by their weakness, not their bloody hands.

"There are other satisfactions besides pleasure, like ones having to do with power. Other men are ruled by their thoughts or their loyalties. I am ruled by impulse," he remarked, turning back to her.

"You are ruled only by wickedness," she snapped.

But her words pleased him.

"Yes, and unlike other men, I accept it. It brings me no dismay. I always savor the rush."

His lips curved into a smile.

"Not much can be done to govern the urges of my men on long voyages like these. For the gratification of their burning passion, they would entail universal destruction upon the whole world. I do not blame them," he said. He lowered his face to hers, his dirty blonde hair touching her cheek. "Be fortunate it was not directed at you. I would slit their throats if they ever tried. They know better than to touch what is mine."

His hand reached for her chest, and she flinched, unable to back away from him.

"I procured this for you. The older girl was trying to hide it," he said, pulling a necklace out from the top of her dress. "Wear it as a symbol of our friendship, if nothing else."

Eliza tensed up. He must have put it on her when she was asleep. What else had this man done without her knowledge?

Bruin's eyes simmered with a dark pride. He held it, turning the front towards her on its long chain. It was a beautiful gold pendant, crafted with curlicues so fine it looked like lace. It was set with two square emeralds, one nestled in the top portion of the golden scrolls and another smaller one that mirrored it on the bottom. He adjusted it against her skin—a dead girl's treasured necklace, the only proof she had indeed existed.

"It looks better on you, Liza," Bruin said, with a crooked smile. "A real woman."

She felt his hand caress her right breast ever so slightly. In that moment, Eliza had never understood the nature of men better—their callous ruthlessness, their destructive nature. Her stomach tightened, fearing he would not release her.

His maniacal ways were more than a passing madness. He was deranged, brutish, and gratuitously cruel. He was a sinister force pulling at her, again and again. The death of his father had profoundly changed his outlook on life, and despite the presence of the Jesus painting in his cabin, there was only darkness in him, threatening to consume every inch of her. Indeed, Bruin brought nothing but hazard to her life. It was then that she learned there were no monsters at sea, only men. The wind whipped and tugged at her dress.

A commotion broke out from the men dangling high in the shrouds, and Bruin broke away from her, looking upward to decipher their frenzied shouts.

"Sails! Off the starboard quarter!" The wind carried the lookout's voice down from the crow's nest.

Bruin ran back to his cabin and returned with his spyglass. He turned towards the stern, angling the lens so that it captured the water behind them. When he set his sights near the mark the lookout had indicated, he tensed up and cursed.

Eliza looked with her naked eyes and saw a large ship, her sails full and powering across the water. If she did not know any better, she would have assumed it a Fata Morgana, a mere optical illusion. But the sea was not playing tricks with her. It was a ship pursuing them, hot on their trail. She had no doubt it was another Spanish ship, and she knew they wanted retribution. It was the height of arrogance to burn their ship, for by destroying it, he had sent a signal to all other vessels in the area.

Bruin left, dashing down the steps to join his crew. Eliza ripped the necklace away from her with disgust, holding it in the palm of her hand. Bruin wanted to do all he could in his power to implicate her in their terrible crimes, but Eliza would have no part in it. She raised her arm back, ready to fling the damn thing in the sea. Then something stopped her.

Luisa. This had been hers. It felt like casting the girl into the water a second time. A second death, like Eurydice. That myth weighed heavily on her mind. It was like a soothing balm for the tragic events that unfolded around Eliza now. She needed what transpired to make sense, to belong to some kind of order. Because if she admitted how cruelly the girls had been used, how they had been killed without a second thought, and how she was powerless to stop it, it would overwhelm her.

The pendant glinted in the sun; it was strikingly beautiful. Whoever had crafted it had made it with care, and whoever had given it to her surely loved her. Eliza closed her fist around it, fighting back tears. No, she could not be so careless as to toss it over the side. The least she could do was take care of it, and in doing so, preserve some part of the memory of the girl's life. When she reached England, when she actually made landfall in that fantastic future, one without Bruin's sinister presence and with the protection of Charles, she could use this necklace. It was proof of Bruin's crimes and the *Fortuyne's* sins. She carefully put it back around her neck and pressed it to her, feeling some strange, indirect connection to the girl who had been so full of life only yesterday.

The approach of the enemy ship set the men's nerves on edge. Eliza watched them for hours as they cleared the main deck, preparing the *Fortuyne* for inevitable action.

Bruin ordered the men to raise the Dutch ensign. They removed any unnecessary timber that might shatter under fire, while other men started spilling trails of sand in zigzagging serpentines across the hot deck. She assumed it was to prevent fire, but an overheard snippet of conversation from the crew clarified that it was in anticipation of blood. A deck slick with gore was a slippery one.

Eliza observed their change of behavior with increasing anxiety, until the hour of action was upon them. Bruin had made a costly mistake when he attacked that Cuban sloop, and his ship and all those on board were about to reap the grim consequences.

When it could no longer be avoided, the *Fortuyne* shuddered to a stop as the other ship came alongside them within hailing distance, the revered space where two ships met at sea. Eliza ran back to her cabin; she wanted nothing to do with what would unfold. Most of the crew had also disappeared, leaving Bruin alone with only two other men. She heard the captain of the other ship demand to know their vessel's name and their intended destination. He barked questions, expecting immediate answers. Bruin's reply was a lie.

"We look for *piratas!*" the other captain shouted next.

Eliza pressed her ear to her cabin door, straining to hear.

"I told you already, we are Dutch. This is a Guineaman!"

It was a foolish statement to try to use as a deception. The *Fortuyne* was far too clean and free from the usual pungent odors that accompanied slave ships.

A banging noise sounded at Eliza's feet, and she

stooped down to the floor, peering through a gap. The rest of the crew was hiding belowdecks. She could hear them shuffling and breathing in their confined space. They lay in wait, ready for their captain's orders.

The two captains continued their tense conversation, but the wind carried their words away. Eliza slipped out of her cabin and crept into his. His windows would provide ample views. She moved past the bright panes and strained her neck trying to catch a glimpse of the other ship. Men were lined up along their railings, peering down at the *Fortuyne*, surveying it. She backed away, afraid they might see her.

Bumping into his desk, a stack of notebooks toppled over, and she rushed to fix them. She did not need a man like Bruin to assume she was a thief. She feared the repercussions if he caught her alone in there, but something caught her eye just as she closed the last book. On the inside flap, Bruin had written his name in a scrawling script. Only it did not read Hiram Bruin, it read Hiram Beaks.

She stopped, her chest tightening. She immediately understood that Beaks was his true last name. Eliza pictured the elderly Mrs. Beaks back in Saba. They were related. What was he trying to hide by not explaining their connection? He was not a true Bruin. Had he been adopted? Her fingers brushed the hasty signature. Perhaps his mother had never died, her body succumbing to illness. Perhaps she was alive, and she was indeed the polite, older woman who had shown Eliza to her room. How could he have been so cold and callous to the woman? Did he truly possess no love, not even a glimmer of it for his mother?

His past had always been shrouded in mystery, but as she came to terms with how little she truly knew of the man she had spent the last month with, her stomach sank. Who was he? And what was he hiding from her?

She held the book with a quivering grip, flipping through the rest of the pages. Everything was in Dutch, and she could not read it. But there was something thick and square towards the back of the notebook. It was an old gazette, yellowed with age and the creases of a hundred fingerprints.

The front read "The Oxford Gazette—Published by Authority—From Thursday, February 2, To Monday, February 6th, 1775. PYRATE KING DEAD!" The rest was illegible, blotches blurred the lower half, as if something wet had dropped on it. She lowered the square of paper, checking to see if the men were still engaged in their discussions. That was when she saw something more disturbing. She froze, taking a step back. There, carefully laid in the back of the notebook, was a clipping of her dark curls, tenderly wrapped in a silk ribbon. She immediately felt around her hair, and true enough, there was a shorter section near the back of her neck. Eliza pulled the shorn piece forward, looking with horror at the jagged way it had been cut. Likely from one of his many blades.

She had no time for panic. Her instincts to survive drove her frenzied footsteps back towards the windows, and she pushed on the glass frame before realizing it could not be opened. She grabbed a bronze candlestick and slammed it against the window, shattering it, and then cringed, terrified someone had heard. Now the conversation between the captains was loud and clear.

"I ask you again, are there any women aboard your vessel?" The Spanish captain was arrogant and in no mood for games. He wore a resplendent navy jacket, threaded with gold.

Bruin laughed in an attempt to disarm him.

"Women? This is no place for women," he replied.

Eliza grabbed a handful of her skirts and jammed it through the fractured glass, cutting the top of her hand in the process. She leaned out as far as she could manage, waving it like a flag of surrender. The men on the neighboring ship noticed immediately. One sailor ran over to the captain, whispering something in his ear. The captain's face turned grave, and he looked back at Bruin, glaring at him with suspicious scrutiny.

Now their captain said nothing, and he no longer addressed Bruin. He shouted out orders, and grappling hooks flew across the space between the ships, landing hard where they fell.

"Do you intend to board my vessel?" Bruin shouted over the water.

She could hear the nervousness in his voice. Bruin received no answer. She could only imagine the fury in his face, the perceived slight ignoring his queries would cause.

A thunderous boom of a multitude of footsteps sounded down below, and Eliza knew they had been boarded. But then a single pistol shot sounded, and all hell broke loose.

Shouts of "To arms, to arms!" followed, and Eliza heard the rush of the men as they swarmed topside, taking their

Spanish opponents by surprise. "Give no quarter!" Bruin's voice roared above the noise.

A deafening explosion sounded below Eliza, and she watched as a cannonball flew at the main mast of the Spanish ship. It toppled with a great bang, disabling the other ship instantly. Now their position was unfavorable, and their return fire weak. Eliza crouched inside his cabin, trying to avoid incoming fire by the windows. She regretted waving for help; now that the confrontation had turned violent, she was trapped in his quarters. If she tried to move, she would surely be killed by the crossfire. She could not remain on the ship either. She thought of the girl prisoners and what had happened to them. She was powerless against a man like that.

But then the door slammed open, knocking into the wall. She screamed and ducked. It was a Spanish man, his hair dark, his tan face covered in stubble. He was thoroughly armed, but his hazel eyes showed a sort of kindness she had not seen in a long time.

"Luisa?" he asked.

Eliza pointed at herself, questioning their abrupt interaction.

She did not confirm or deny anything; no other words were exchanged. He reached and took her hand, pulling her across the balcony and down the steps into the bloody fray. Small shot whizzed through the air, ripping through sails and ropes, tearing flesh apart. Her ears began to ring from the noise, but her gallant knight continued dragging her through the rattling fray and across the shaking deck slick with blood. He slashed his way through the thrashing bodies of men deep in conflict, carving a path for her to follow.

Not one place on the *Fortuyne* was free of hot blood. She saw Bruin for a brief moment, covered in gore, heard the sound of his knife pummeling into flesh, twisting and ripping into thick organ. He took pleasure in being cruel to anyone. He shouted more orders until his voice was hoarse, and when the melee was too loud, he signaled to his men with hand signals. Eliza was so busy watching him in his natural element that she slipped on the wet deck and staggered to the side when it pitched. But her would-be savior had such a steady grip on her hand, she did not fall.

Bruin's crew had the firepower of a small army and seemed invincible to her. She feared for the Spaniards. The pirates were serious and grim: they knew all the risks, and when the smoke cleared, they would be made either richer or dead. Musket balls whistled past her, fired from the Spanish vessel. Lethal splinters rained down from every angle, and one sliced through the surface of her cheek, while other shards tore her arms like scarlet ribbons. The Spanish fought valiantly, but Bruin's crew drove them back, hitting them hard with the butt ends of their muskets, slicing vulnerable areas where they could. She recoiled at the sight of a man hanging dead, upside-down, his foot tangled in the rigging. Blood dripped from his gaping mouth in long, slow strings. Another one of Bruin's men next to her was struck down, his throat torn out by grapeshot, and he collapsed on the tackles of a large gun by the edge of the boat.

Through the unrelenting fire and the spasms of the

dying, Eliza raced behind the Spaniard. Terror of imminent death drove her to march directly into it. He climbed on top of the railing, urging her to follow suit. It was an enormous risk, but one worth taking. With the clamor of the struggle all around her, she had drifted into another place that left her numb to the dangers pulsating around her. She saw the promise of safety in the man's eyes and stepped forward, hiking her dress up, and joined him. Across the way, a man on the other ship was cleaning his firearms when a sharpshooter from the *Fortuyne* struck him down. He fell overboard.

The sight of his death made her reconsider. She was afraid of crossing the space between their ships; it looked far too vast. She did not want to knock her head, feel the heat of a bullet, or get sucked under the current.

Her guardian sensed her hesitation, and he swung across first, pulling her with an outstretched hand. But then the shot she had feared would land in her, entered his back. He turned at the last second, his noble eyes frightened. He had failed. She could feel it through his grip, the way it tightened and arched. She was suspended, not fully balanced on the *Fortuyne,* falling forward but not yet in the air, when a second pair of dirty hands grabbed her by the waist, and she was pulled backwards.

She landed on top of the Lincolnshire man whom she had read to weeks ago, but she did not view him as her rescuer. She turned on him now, beating his chest and screaming, "Let me go!" Eliza broke away from his understandable confusion, peering over the gunwales, looking for any sign of the man who had almost saved her. She found him lying on his stomach, bobbing like cordwood, plunged into the water below as it churned and foamed with blood. Sharks began to appear in pale silhouettes, curious at first, then violently tugging at unmoving flesh. She recoiled in horror and looked away. The sight and smell of so much blood was offensive to her senses, and she gagged.

She stepped over fallen men and found the Spanish captain on his back, his eyes lifelessly gazing skywards. He had no doubt been the first victim of the skirmish. The clouds of acrid smoke shifted away, and she saw Bruin, his eyes maddened with dark rage, as he advanced on her. Her heart hammered against her chest as she bolted from him, navigating around puddles and ducking to avoid the ricochet of bullets. But it was an unequal contest. She felt his iron grip seize her as he threw her into the opposite gunwales, knocking the breath out of her. Bruin was not like Charles; he did not create order out of chaos, he thrived in it. The death around them only emboldened him. And he knew she had betrayed him.

He grabbed her by the throat, lifting her to a stand with sticky, reddened hands.

"You bitch! Did you signal them?" he demanded with a guttural yell. "Answer me!"

"No," she managed to squeak, coughing for air.

"Do not lie to me!"

Her hands flailed at his, struggling to free herself. He loosened his rough hold but shoved the tip of his knife under her ribs.

"Speak!"

"I am not brave enough to lie to you," she said, her voice breaking.

Behind them, a joyous cry rang out. "Surrender! They surrender!" Pistols once meant for opponents, now fired in the air without particular aim. But Bruin did not see satisfaction in their victory. His free hand left her, clenching into an angered fist. Eliza had tried to escape and had nearly broken free from him. The near loss of his control over her was too close to bear.

"Look what you did! Look what you made me do!" he shouted in her face, spit hitting her scratched cheek. "These men are dead because of you. I have lost good men because of you!"

From the mess on the deck, she could tell they had only lost three men. Most of the damage had been wreaked on the enemy. Their bodies were strewn all over, and more floated in the sea.

"I did not —" she started to say.

He struck her full across her face, sending her flying to the blood-soaked deck. Bruin stepped back, gasping for breath from the exertion of how hard he had hit her.

"I am doing as you asked. I am taking you to England. And you have betrayed me!"

He was in a foul mood, pacing the decks of his ship, observing the cost of this unexpected battle. One of the topsail spars hung cracked, and the rigging was ragged and shredded. He gazed at the fallen men. But the sight that had upset him the most was seeing her try to flee from his coiled grasp. Shooting down the ruffian who had tried to take her was satisfying beyond measure, but her treachery still stung him.

Eliza cowered on the floor, struggling to get to her feet. When he saw her attempt to move, he turned to his men as they watched the spectacle of the once-untouchable woman be brought down to her knees.

"Tie her up!" he shouted. When they did not budge, he ordered it a second time. "*Godverdomme!* Tie her to the mizzenmast! Now!"

Two of the black sailors came forward, willing to do what the others hesitated to. The rest of the crew feared Bruin's capricious moods and the thought of certain retribution should he change his mind. The sailors dragged her over to the last mast on the ship, stretching her arms wide and binding her wrists tight. There would be no wiggling free from her ropes. These men were master knot makers. She was trapped, and she had enraged a dangerous man.

It was a mistake with deadly consequences.

CHAPTER XVI.

Sounds of destruction carried over the rippling water. Eliza was securely bound to the mizzen-mast, but she was still afforded a horrifying view of the damage the pirates were now currently inflicting on the Spanish ship. The engagement had lasted no more than half an hour, but the loss was as visible as the blood that dripped from the fallen ship's gunports. The ship now lay motionless, her main mast leaning at a dangerous angle. Her sails were in pieces, and burning shards of letters floated in the air between the two ships as Bruin's men ransacked it.

The *Neptuno* was ironically the very ship the *Incendio* had mistaken Bruin's ship for, and now the treasured letters from loved ones, and others containing important news from political kingmakers and allies drifted away, lost to sea. She heard the ship's name over and over again as sounds of glass smashing and drunken carousing erupted across the way.

The ship's second-in-command had surrendered on behalf of his crew. He had offered Bruin and his men

25,000 pieces of eight if they would leave peacefully, but there was no need to offer anything of value. Bruin would simply take what he wanted. He was still hungry for blood, and his pistol answered the desperate man for him. Bruin's sharpshooters in the tops had picked one Spaniard off after another, until none remained standing. They took everything of value and assaulted the crew that remained alive, beating and exposing them to other cruelties while Eliza kept her face turned away. She could still hear their pitiful shrieks and smelled new smoke wafting over to her. Bruin and his crew positioned themselves on their main deck, then made busy work of finishing off anyone who remained squirming and moving among the dead.

Memory was a strange concept. Before this attack, Eliza could almost convince herself that the girls' kidnapping had been imagined, that the way they had been discarded was nothing but a vision from a nightmare. The sheer horror and violence simply did not make sense to her. But the gold necklace still laying against her chest and the new atrocities she witnessed now reminded her of the awful truth. This was all very real.

She watched now as one burly carpenter chased down a Spanish sailor all the way to the bowsprit and then cut him down with his adze. She closed her eyes, wincing, then continued her fruitless struggle against the ropes that held her down. Her shoulders already ached with the unnaturalness of the position, and she feared they would be stuck that way. A continuous blaze engulfed the *Neptuno*, and she witnessed what she had missed the last time. Even if she looked away, she could still smell the flames and hear the moans of the dying. And with a twist in her gut, she knew she would also be forced to witness the crew's latest celebration. She was terrified that she would be a key part of it, their next unwilling prisoner. When the wind brought the heat of the fire over to her, she feared without reason that they would burn her alive.

The booty they seized was uninspiring and made the death around her feel even more pointless. The officer's offer of coins proved to be a hopeless ruse, meant only to stall for time. But he had not realized that monsters like Bruin and his men did not operate within reason. Defense of their beloved ship and the sight of blood was sufficient to excite them. Now they transferred their coveted prizes back across the water: more bales of silk and cotton, barrels of tobacco, some spare sails, an anchor cable, half a dozen slaves, and some sea charts. The eclectic decorations she had seen in the Bruin household made more sense to her now.

And Bruin would kill for this? No, he killed for a vicious reason: it fed his violent impulses.

"I am ruled by impulse. It brings me no dismay. I always savor the rush." His lips curved into a smile.

She turned her head, looking for his tall, lanky figure on the ship across the way, but did not see him. He had already returned to the *Fortuyne*, leaving his sobriety behind on the other burning ship. She heard his boots march along the deck before she saw him, his steps staggering despite the relative calmness of the sea.

He stepped back a pace to survey her condition, delighting in the stiffness of her shoulders.

"Liza, Liza, Liza …" he began. "They could have blown us out of the water. I have every right to cut you down and throw your body into that bloody mess below. Or should I put a rope about your neck, and hang you from the yardarm?"

Eliza would not look at him. Bruin grabbed her chin, forcing her to.

"You belong to me now. And you will learn obedience."

The atmosphere had surged from the open adrenaline of battle to something between him and her, more intimate, more hidden in nature.

"You cannot lower me to any fear I have not visited before, no matter how desperately you may try to," Eliza replied with gritted teeth. But she was not a gifted liar like him. She was scared, and she was trapped, but her attempt still roused his ire.

"Apologize. Apologize to me!" he erupted, shouting into her face. "Say you are sorry, *Godverdomme*, or I will throw you overboard with weights tied to your legs. Your pretty ankles will snap the minute you hit the water, and you will sink so slowly, seeing the light on the surface get ever farther from your reach."

She wanted to keep a brave facade, but she couldn't. Her body ached from standing, and all eyes were on them, watching in silence.

"You swore to protect me," she urged.

"Apologize!" he repeated, squeezing her face.

"I am sorry, Hiram," she said quietly, as if her soft voice could elicit some untapped mercy from deep within him. "Please, untie me …"

"You cost me a carpenter and two other men. I gave you everything and get nothing in return!" he said, pushing her shoulders into the wooden mast. "Look at all the men you caused to die! And for what?"

She shook her head, eyes watery with terror and pain.

"Please, Hiram, do not do this. I will do anything," Eliza begged.

He reached out to touch her face again, then pulled back with disgust as if she was no longer worthy of his unwanted attention.

"Say you do not love your husband," he said, his voice low. His troubled eyes narrowed with impatience.

She opened her mouth, but her voice faltered.

"Say you do not love him," he repeated with a growl.

Eliza's face flushed red, keeping her lips clamped shut. He slammed into her body and reached for her left hand, wrenching her gold wedding band off her clenched finger. She cried out in pain. When he had achieved his aim, she watched with horror as he ran towards the edge of the railing and threw it overboard. His disgust with her unflinching loyalty to Charles overpowered even his love for gold. She understood that this moment would be the most perilous yet.

He stormed back over to her.

"There, now you are free to remarry, *Liza Hastings*." He glowered at her.

"A ring does not a marriage make," she hissed.

"No? But one does need a living, breathing husband. And I have already accomplished the deed. Charles is never coming back," he replied. His grin was hideous to her.

She leaned forward and spit at him. He wiped it away with a dark laugh and leaned closer to her.

"I should take you right here, in front of them all," he threatened, parting her legs with his knee.

She looked at the snake in his eyes.

"And then we can all watch your beauty come undone," he whispered in her ear.

She would not respond. When the reaction he sought from her was not forthcoming, he reached down for his boot knife and slammed it into the wood next to her face with a frenzied shout.

He brushed his blood-stained hair away from his eyes, trying to recover himself from his rage. "You will remain here until I say. Let us see if you have learned to sink or if you will still fight the current."

Bruin pulled his knife back out, finally tired from the day. Slaughter and drink had made him weary. It was probably the only thing that saved her from his threats of assault. Bruin wiped the sweat from his brow and stalked away. She released a deep breath she had been holding and bowed her head, her arms burning.

Minutes turned into hours. She did not know it yet, but there were signs unfolding around her that warned of an impending storm. A long, slow sea swell began to rock the ship. In the beginning, the setting sun burned her eyes, the heat from its red glare unbearable, and when the bank of heavy clouds appeared, she was grateful. The first drops of rain began to fall, and she could feel the moisture in the wind. She savored the relief, but then it grew steadily worse. The lash of torrential rain grew in intensity. A fog began to roll in, the thick mist making it impossible to see the front of the boat.

The change of weather intruded quickly, like the press of Bruin's grip on her aching shoulders. The clouds began to churn, and the *Fortuyne* bucked over whitecaps. The winds increased to a high-pitched whine, then into a howl. There was a frantic shouting of orders as the shrouds hummed and ropes snapped with the force of the gale. A command to close-reef the sails and batten the hatches was issued just when the first unexpected wave struck the ship. Cold water rushed up the main deck, sloshed over her, and disappeared again over the side, carrying away a spare sail and a yard. Lifelines fore and aft were established, but the uneasy crew, deep in their superstitions, feared their bloodlust from hours ago had returned to haunt them.

"Let off your fore sails!" the helmsman shouted.

"I can't reach!" a sailor yelled back in the shrieking wind.

"Reef all the canvas! We'll have to ride out the weather!"

The task was accomplished with the manpower of two other men, and they retreated back to safety belowdecks. She knew other sailors remained, tasked with preserving the ship and everyone on board, but the wet and the wind played tricks on her perception. She was alone, bound to a mast that could crack asunder at any moment—by the push of wind, a wild wave, or a streak of lightning. She watched another set of men throw two of the guns overboard to lighten the heavy load of the struggling vessel, and with bated breath, she wondered if she was next.

Thunder clapped from multiple parts of the sky now,

and the ship rolled with a massive swell. The sea was rough, the waves carrying long overhanging crests, the winds reaching well over forty knots. It was nearly impossible to keep her eyes open for long, and she had to turn to take a breath from the force of the gusts barreling down the deck. Cold rain stung her face and chest like pellets. The *Fortuyne* plunged and reared like a mad horse, and Eliza felt herself tossed up at every pitch into the dark and furious clouds. The ship would plummet down another mountain of frothing water, and then fly back up into the heavens. The hull creaked as if it might splinter into pieces, and she prayed the ship would hold. With every downswing, her stomach rose up to her throat, and she finally threw up, disoriented by the wind and rain. Incessant squeaking and clanking, the clatter of lumber, and the maddening creaking of the ship drove her to terror.

She forced her mind to distraction, repeating meaningless things, counting to one hundred, saying her name. *Eliza Hastings, Eliza Sharpe, Liza Hastings* ... she stopped with disgust. He intruded on her even now. He had decided her fate the moment he had chosen her new name.

And who was the man who captained this ship? Hiram Beaks. Her mind roved over what she had discovered in that notebook. He was hiding much more than his true name, and his fascination with her bordered on obsession. He had sought her hand in marriage, and she had refused, and yet she was still trapped in his claws. There was something dark within him that he had tried to bury in his past, something he could not banish that drove his ruthless actions. Now she had been sentenced to a long, slow death. She thought of the slaves at Pleasant Hall and how no one would free them from their misery now.

Beside her, she kept seeing another ship from the corner of her eye. It was not the *Incendio*, nor the *Neptuno*, but some other phantom vessel careening through the waves alongside them, appearing and then vanishing in the rainswept darkness. It was the first slave ship she had ever seen, nameless and forgotten to her memory until now.

"But I do not see any slaves. Where can they possibly store them? Their hold is not very large," she had asked.

Another deceptive man from her past with dishonorable intentions answered.

"Oh, they've managed to figure that out, Lady Sharpe. You can fit an infinite number of bodies in a hold when you lay them flat. It's simply a matter of organization. They are likely headed to Charleston. At their speed, they'll make port in nine days if the winds hold true."

How did they make the bodies all fit? Living men, women, and children reduced to cargo, to great sums of cash. Wooden ships made caskets across the water, for if death did not come belowdecks, it would arrive later, guided by the whip of an overseer's hands.

"Slavers. There are most likely four hundred slaves on there, I wager. If they've had a good haul this run," he had explained.

Four hundred souls. And how many more ships like it sailed the Atlantic, crisscrossing one another, perpetuating the cycle of violence? And she had married into this system, becoming a planter's wife. Lady Sharpe. The proud Conch family, unaffected in their loyalty to the Crown, carving out a living on limestone. She was one of them now. Her finger was bare of her gold wedding band, but she still carried her name. His name, the one thing he had given her that Bruin could not throw into the sea.

The comfort the thought brought was minimal. What did a name signify now? The dead did not need a name. The ocean would never call her by it. The ship buckled, colliding with a huge swell. She screamed, knowing no one could hear her in the roaring wind. Something dark arced through the clouds, and she saw vultures swoop above her, unaffected by the gale, circling the ship that seemed more real than illusion. Messengers of the dead … had they come for her? One spoke to her now, his calm, grounded voice loud in her heart.

"I used to get scared when the storms passed through here, Lady Sharpe. But when I was young, Lord Sharpe would say, 'It's all right, you just frightened. It just happens.' And they always blow away," Josiah said, his eyes distant. "He told me that when I was real young."

He stood looking out at the startlingly blue water.

"Before I came here, my people used to say things about storms like that. And that was some storm, Lady Sharpe. Before I knew better, I thought a man rode the clouds. A great warrior. That's what I remember my mama telling me."

Eliza's interest was piqued.

"You mean from where you came in Africa, Josiah? What do you remember?"

"I don't remember much about her. But I remember that. She told me a man would come down when the lightning struck, and he would come to take away those who weren't right. That was his job. He was a king from the old kingdom,

and he'd come from the sky and carry out justice. That's why folks get scared when the storm comes. If you done wrong, you might see him."

Why had she returned to the ship? Why had she ever given Bruin a chance to destroy her again? But what other recourse did she truly have? She had to leave Saba; she could not return to that strangely bright house, filled to the brim with stolen artifacts, and endure the contempt of his uncle. If that even was his uncle. Perhaps that is why such a strong hatred existed between them.

Eliza could not wait for help to arrive. She had learned long ago that she had to take matters into her own hands or risk losing Charles forever. She thought of the other time she had seen Shango on the shores of Pleasant Hall. It was right before Jean was executed, when Eliza was deep in the throes of a secret affair.

"If you done wrong, you might see him," Josiah's words echoed.

He was dead now too. So many unnatural deaths had happened around her. She had not seen Shango when Celia had taught her to pray to him. Fear was colder than the water that shot over the gunwales, striking her.

"But you may not like the answer you receive. Don't start anything with him that you can't finish," Celia added ominously.

Bruin was certainly no answer—he was a death threat. She had needed his help, and he wanted to take it all.

The ghost ship broke through the waves again. Shango only appeared when she made mistakes. She had returned to the ship, but it was no mere journey from west to east.

She lived in the company of pirates, and she feared she was as guilty as they. People were dead now who would have continued living if Eliza had not set foot on the *Fortuyne*. She could not save those two frightened girls, and she had let a kind stranger fall to his death as he tried to save her from a situation she had chosen. She had chosen this.

"But it wasn't only that, Lady Sharpe. Like I said, he was a great warrior. He protect the people too. And it keeps me going. Maybe he gonna come back one night," Josiah's voice rang out.

The wind had knocked all the remaining sense out of her. Eliza was the victim of a brutal, callous man. Shango was a warrior; he protected those seeking justice, and she had prayed to him. The only person who needed to fear Shango's ancient wrath was Captain Hiram Bruin, the man who had upended her life, who had severely wronged her. She strained against the biting rain and did not see the otherworldly ship any longer. It was all a trick of mist and spray, the desire from her mind for some distraction from the damp and the cold.

Colossal waves drove the ship backwards, but after it surpassed every new watery ridge, it rocketed downwards at a sharp tilt, racing to the bottom of the waves. The ship bucked through the spray, crossing waves that at times seemed impossible to surpass. The water broke over the vessel with great violence, driven by furious currents, as the ship clashed against waves larger than thirty-two feet. The *Fortuyne* jerked like a sick animal, listing unhappily, battered by an onslaught of unremitting waves.

Downpours of numbing rain drenched her, chilling her to the bone and chafing her skin raw from the friction of her wet dress. Blinding lightning forked all around, and the ship continued to dip and spin against the surface of the Atlantic. If Eliza had not been tied up, she would have been washed away over the side. She watched the dizzying dance of the cold water on the deck, swirling to the left, then back again to the right in reeling circles. It only made her queasier, and after another plunge downward, she retched again.

A rogue wave, and then another, like a succession of furious mountains, swelled before the struggling ship, and Eliza recognized death. The *Fortuyne* sounded as if it was cracking and splintering to its breaking point, like her own miserable, dripping body. She screamed until her throat was raw as the ship rose into the dark and starless sky, and the storm bludgeoned the ship into submission.

The remnants of a wave collided with her, and her hearing was dashed away to nothing but a ringing in her ears. She coughed and choked on the briny water, leaning forward, stretching her limbs beyond the limits of her comfort. Her heels ached from the pressure of standing, her back sharpened with cramping, and she dropped her legs, swinging to one side of the mast in a crumpled heap. Her body started to fail, exhaustion and coldness making her lose control. The dampness made her bones ache, and the tautness of the rope burned her sensitive skin, every roll and pitch of the ship painful.

Eliza weakly prayed for a calm, for the mountainous waves to stop, that the ship would make it through. She just needed to make it to England. She repeated this idea again and again, never before feeling so very far from her homeland. Greedy waves began to swallow the ship from one side to the other, and after all she had been through and survived, she now confronted the prospect of a meaningless death. Of drowning in a sea she did not recognize or claim, without ever seeing Charles or Philippe again. She thought of her darling boy and how he did not deserve to be made an orphan. His life would be shaped by unbearable cruelty before it even truly began. Images of her sisters floated before her, and her deceased parents.

She would never return to England; she would never again feel the flat safeness of the ground beneath her feet. Dark thoughts like this flooded her mind, like the rush of seawater that streamed down the hatches.

I will die here. Is this what death looks like?

Bruin, that heartless devil, had left her out here to perish. If she would not become his, she would forfeit her life. Her bindings would not hold; they would wither down threadbare and snap, and she would be washed out to sea. No one would ever find her body.

Which wave would be the one to end her? Dragging her down, further and further, until the burning in her lungs made her unwillingly gasp, swallowing the ocean whole, sinking into darkness? Water poured up on the deck as the ship buckled and flooded. She could not fathom the misery she would be forced to endure as she died. She knew how to fight water, but this was a fight she could not win; indeed, it was one she could only slowly, painfully lose. Eliza knew the ship would eventually founder and destruction would come for them all, starting with her first. Or maybe her agony would be extended, only drowning once the vessel had truly sunk, pinned against her will, sinking down with the ship's shattered hull.

This accursed vessel, captained by a wicked man, would be her downfall. The *Fortuyne* had driven her to her nadir, the lowest point of her life, a place where no hope could be summoned. She had foolishly and willingly returned to the ship, accepting her fate. Now she would reap the bitter consequences. It was an exacting price to pay.

She saw Charles' face flashing before her. She would never see him again. Would he ever even know what had happened to her? How hard she had fought to recover him? Eliza had cheated death on so many occasions. She would not succeed this time. Eliza had fancied herself the female version of Orpheus, descending deep down into a watery underworld to recover a love that she had lost. But now she could only see herself as Eurydice, as a victim without a voice. She was no hero, only a foolish woman, tricked by a man as easily as a naive girl. She had been bitten by a snake, a charming creature that had promised her the world but only delivered betrayal, and died fleeing the unwanted advances of the minor god, Aristaeus. Now she was doomed to be sent down to Hades, imprisoned not by fire but by a sodden grave.

She could not determine if Bruin's presence in her life was more like the unrequited desires of Aristaeus or the snake itself. When she looked at the turbulent, foaming sea before her, she understood. He was her Hades, a being more encompassing than a mere god alone. He occupied a space, a place within her and without her; he was her personal Hell. Eliza's stay in this world would be of the briefest duration. Brilliant like a flame, but when doused by saltwater extinguished, with only a wisp of smoke remaining. The ship would drive her, flying from the roiling surface of the earth, into oblivion. She would have no grave, and no one would mourn over her except for the sea creatures who would clean her bones.

The winds reached a pitch unlike anything she had yet endured. What if a tremendous gust split the foremast, toppling it like the mast of the *Neptuno*, damning the ship to the depths of the bottom? The *Fortuyne* faced an avalanche of water, hurtling down into a chasm of salt and spray. A great crash sounded as the ship tumbled, and with the sudden movement, her left arm twisted as the boat rocked and lurched. A sharp, stabbing pain spread across her arm, unbearable muscle spasms radiating from her shoulder blade down to her elbow, racing up to her neck. Her shoulder had dislocated from the socket, and she cried out, the pain excruciating. Her consciousness shifted into a thin veil, and the mist forced her stinging eyes closed, sending her into unknowingness. When she couldn't hold on any longer, she sank into delirium.

She slipped into a different space, one of cloudless sky and the warming sun. Calloused hands, warm, rough, familiar, held her. Charles stood before her.

"I am your protector in this world," he said, reassuring her with his touch. She had missed the feel of him, and collapsed into his arms, finally free from the cruel ties that had bound her for hours. She had done it. It was all worth every moment of pain.

But it was not Charles. In a flash of ragged lightning,

Bruin's wet face lit up against hers, only she did not see it.

He lashed out at her, crying, "I forgive you! I forgive you!" Now he was willing to say what he dared not repeat when she was awake. He pressed his forehead against hers, ocean water mixing with his deranged tears.

"Do not leave me …" he moaned, leaning against her lifeless body. He clutched her to him, and carried her, her ghostly figure dangling in his grip, across the rolling deck and back into the illusory safety of his cabin, free from the howling wind and the rain.

CHAPTER XVII.

*P*lease God, do not let me burn …

Charles floated in darkness until he felt solid earth below him.

Eliza leaned over him, her dark hair touching his face.

"Eliza, please, I beg you, do not swim in the water. It is too dangerous," he said, his voice raspy.

She smiled and answered, "I am waiting for you. Come back to me."

"I am lost. I am so far away from home."

But he did not impart his panic to her. Her eyes lit up, and she put a hand on his exposed chest.

The warmth of a gentle tide rose up, seeping its way underneath his back.

"Come back to me …" she repeated.

This once indomitable man had grown weak, sprawled out where the turquoise ocean met the white sand. There was a sensation of being dragged further up onto the beach, someone's hands gripping his shoulders, and then he was sliding over the damp sand. He was under severe distress—disoriented, sun-blind, exhausted from the fatigue of swimming, and intolerably hot. He felt the coolness of shade and the clattering of palms overhead. The distant roar of the sea served as a soothing lullaby, and he returned to sleep and haunted memories.

"Sentiment does not suit a true man," his father said. "She was no friend. She was merely a plaything. A toy. And you've outgrown her."

"But she is not like the other slaves. We played together in this very yard as children!" Charles argued.

His father was cold and unfeeling. "One day, when you take my place and you run Pleasant Hall, you will cease this maudlin nonsense. Perhaps then you will appreciate all I have done for you."

Charles looked out the window, watching his brother Elias sitting on the steps of the back porch, hands idly twisting a broken strip of palm leaf. He sometimes felt so alone; his brother had grown distant, and his father was hardly sober.

"I do not understand why you cannot assign her work in the house. Why send her out to the back fields?"

His father walked to his study, and Charles followed him, impatient to achieve his goal. The old Master Sharpe organized some papers, then laughed.

"This is precisely why I have sent her as far from the house as I could manage. Celia is nothing but a slave; you would be wise to remember that. She is that bitch's daughter and will only cause trouble. How you cannot see that is beyond me."

"Perhaps she is sour because her mother is missing," Charles answered, gritting his teeth.

His father's venom was palpable.

"No one is shedding a tear for that witch."

"Her daughter has! Do you hear yourself?"

His father would not answer.

"Where did you put her, Father?" Charles demanded in a low voice. "Where did you put Tabitha's body?"

Now his father's eyes narrowed; he did not like to be challenged.

"That does not concern you."

It was the closest thing to an admission of guilt Charles had ever managed to elicit from him. He looked at his father, increasingly feeling the loss of any familial bond between them. He wished his mother was still alive. She knew how to manage him. She would know what to say and do, but his father had snuffed that life away too. He assumed he was too young to put the pieces together; he never realized where Charles had hid that night, cowering under her nightstand.

His memories played games with him. It was only a pillow fight, some strange game adults played with one another. His mother would open her beautiful green eyes again; she had only allowed his father to assume he had won. But no; it was cruel, calculated murder. Charles had felt the warmth leave from her still body. He had seen the horror on Tabitha's face as his father stormed out of the room. He had to listen to lies about how she had run away. How her yellow fever had returned and claimed her. Lie on top of lie, falsehoods that cancelled the previous ones out. All he understood was that his childhood was over, and that his father was no father at all, but a monster.

"It does not concern me? One day, when I inherit this —"

His father slammed his hand down on the desk.

"If, Charles! If you inherit Pleasant Hall from me. You are not proving your worth."

Then a bold, radical idea took hold of Charles.

"I do not want it," he said, not realizing he had spoken aloud.

"What?"

Charles looked up, drawing his fingers into fists.

"I do not want Pleasant Hall. I refuse to live here. I refuse to perpetuate this cycle of misery!"

"The only thing causing misery is that you are weak like your mother. At least Elias knows his place. You never did."

He never spoke of his mother with kindness. Charles had grown up yearning for her presence, hearing her name slandered again and again. That she was a whore, that she had been seduced by the slaves outside, that she planned on undermining his authority.

The situation only grew worse after her death. His father spoke with excitement of an heiress from the Carolinas who would soon become his wife. Charles and his brother Elias would finally have a mother. But it was not to be; the woman never set foot on the ship that was to carry her to Nassau. Nothing ever changed, and matters only deteriorated. Now Celia no longer spoke with Charles. They had been reduced to a slave and a plantation owner's son. She blamed him for her new position tending the fields. Of course, she assumed Charles had more power than he actually did, but no one had authority over a man like Jeremiah Sharpe. Their fraught friendship was precisely what signaled to the old Master Sharpe that it needed to be destroyed, eradicated like a creeping liana vine.

"I am leaving. I am going to join the army, and I will never set foot on this island again."

His words caused his father no hurt. He had no heart to

break. Charles could not make his problems disappear, but he could leave his problems behind. A battlefield of glory and brotherhood miles away sounded like the only paradise he needed. He yearned to become strong, to become a brave man who could stop his father, unlike the weak and scared boy who had miserably failed to do so.

"Fine. Perhaps they can make a man out of you yet. I will purchase a commission for you. Calvary or infantry?"

"Calvary," Charles said breathlessly.

In a strange twist of fortune, the impenetrable wall that had blocked his happiness for years now offered the very thing that would set him free. His emotions swirled between hurt for the lack of attachment on his father's part and joy for his unexpected generosity.

"You are attached to those damn horses. Very well. I will try to purchase a captaincy or something worthy of the Sharpe name. That way, the fools do not use you for cannon fodder. Now, leave me!"

Another memory presented itself now, one that was tinged with regret.

Charles sat in the Green Turtle, a popular tavern located on Bay Street. He conversed and drank with his new companions in the army, and one old friend, Jean Charles de Longchamp. They were to leave the island tomorrow and set sail for New York to quell the rebellion in the American colonies. They drank in celebration of their new assignment and to honor Charles' latest victory. His instincts for action and his tactical acumen had led to the capture of a pirate ship that had tried to covertly dock in the harbor. The leader of the regiment had been impressed with Charles, and there was already talk of a promotion in the works.

"How is your father's health?" Jean asked, drinking his ale.

"I have not known him sober for over fifteen years now, I wager," Charles answered.

"The drink most likely pickles him. The meanest man I ever knew was a drunk, and he lived to the ripe old age of eighty," another soldier chimed in.

Jean looked troubled. "Are you worried about Pleasant Hall? What if he runs it into the ground while we are gone?"

Jean was always concerned with assets, with wealth. He was a trader's son, and he knew how valuable a property Pleasant Hall was. Charles did not share his interests. Sometimes he felt Jean acted too desperate, too eager to please others, to stamp his mark on society. Charles only cared what his commanders thought.

"Good, let it rot," Charles said, with a bright laugh.

His companions did not see matters the same way he did. Charles' family was easily the wealthiest among them.

"But surely one day you will want a wife, and you will need to impress her family. You need Pleasant Hall," Jean warned.

"I need nothing except my horse and my saber," Charles said dismissively.

One of their friends found the patriotic statement inspiring.

"For King and country!" he cheered.

"We need to remind our American brothers of the same …" Charles uttered in a low voice.

"When we return, I will ask Anna for her hand," another soldier said.

"If she doesn't look at your brother first, George."

"I have no interest in finding a wife," Charles said. "I

want to see the world beyond this island. We are not all as well traveled as you, Jean."

"We can start with America. I hear the ladies in Philadelphia are particularly charming," Jean answered with a sly smile.

But a pounding sounded in Charles' head now—the sharp staccato punctuations of an ear-piercing fife and drum, edging the men on to battle. He remembered the incessant drilling, the constant fear of death, the panting of his horse, all shaping him into who he was to become. The army had hardened his hatred of his father and his overwhelming rage into utility. It made him more resilient than his companions. He was the only man from that table still alive. He alone had survived.

Charles awoke with a start to find a stranger ogling him. She was a woman in her thirties, thin and pale, and she stared at him. She sat in a crude chair with no cushion, the floor beneath her bare feet strewn with sand.

"Are you feeling better?" she asked him.

Charles slowly raised himself up on his elbows. He was situated in a hut composed of odd wooden planks. Looking out the hole that served as a window, he could see that it sat at the edge of the tropical bush, crouched along the waterfront. There were few belongings inside the dwelling, and Charles could tell the woman was poor.

"Where is Chibueze?" Charles asked, as if she would know. "The man with marks on his face. Did he make it?"

His voice was faint; he was still so weak. Her expression remained unmoved, and she shook her head.

"Only you washed up ashore. When I was collecting conch shells for supper, I noticed a large piece of jetsam, and then you lying further down. I feared you were dead."

Charles wondered what had become of Chibueze, if indeed any of the other men had made it out alive. The thought sobered him. He had lived. He should be dead.

The woman got up and walked over to a crib, scooping up her newborn and slowly rocking it.

"Where am I?"

"This island has no name. It is a small cay, but further south of us is British Honduras."

"So we are on the Mosquito Coast," Charles said, calculating a map inside his mind. He had not drifted very far from where the ship had been.

"What is your name?" he asked next, trying to get his bearings.

"I am Sally. Sally Perkins."

"And the babe?"

"Oh," she said with a peculiar smile. "He is Henry, after his father. I am waiting for him to return."

When Charles looked at her, he could not help but draw a comparison to Eliza and Philippe.

"I am Charles Sharpe. I am a Lieutenant Colonel in His Majesty's army," he explained. But when he spoke those words, a change came over her, and she grew agitated.

"It pleases me to find myself in the company of an English woman. I have suffered through quite a trial," he added, trying to compliment her. He was not sure why her temperament had changed so. He also did not want to relay too much information about himself.

Charles adjusted the moth-eaten blanket, feeling suddenly awkward in her presence. In the corner of the room was a dead tarantula, its furry legs upright and curled inward on its upside-down carcass. He wondered why she did not sweep it away.

"Henry is well behaved," Charles said, trying to keep the conversation going.

Now she seemed to settle down and gazed at the child in her arms.

"Yes, he is a quiet boy," she said with love in her eyes. "I revived you with some water and brandy. Would you like more? Or perhaps you would like some food? I have peas and rice. I can go to the beach and catch a fish for you."

At the mention of real food, Charles' mouth watered. She placed the child down, sound asleep, and walked out of the hut. He saw her heading down to the beach, leaving Charles to lie on his back, staring upwards at the palm-thatched ceiling. This house was not much different from a slave dwelling, but it was much brighter and breezier. The sounds of the ocean breaking on the beach were soothing and made him recall Pleasant Hall.

Sally came back an hour later and began preparing his food. "Who is she?" she asked after some time had passed.

Charles looked confused.

"The woman. Eliza. You said her name again and again." Sally stirred the peas and rice in the pot over a fire she had made near the entry.

"Oh, she is my wife," Charles said, happy to talk about the one person he could not stop thinking of. "I am anxious to return to her."

Her spoon stopped, and she clenched the wooden utensil.

"Oh," she said, her voice tense and quiet. "She is fortunate to be wed to such a handsome soldier."

Charles felt his cheeks turn red. He began to wonder when her husband would come back. There was only one bed in the hut, and he questioned where she had slept since he had taken up the pallet bed.

"How long have I been here?" he asked nervously. He feared the husband would think something indecent had occurred.

"Three days and three nights," she said, staring at him again.

Then he realized why her mood so often turned sour.

"Mrs. Perkins, I would like to extend my gratitude. You have saved my life," he said slowly. "I am indebted to you."

The tightness in her shoulders softened, and she walked over to him. Her small hand brushed his arm.

"No need to call me that. You can call me Sally if you please," she said. She looked down at his tattered clothing. "You can take some clothes from my husband. He has no use for them."

Charles swung his weakened legs around to the side of the bed, gazing down at his appearance. He was in desperate need of a new shirt. His breeches had suffered similar damage. Sally turned and dug around in the one chest that stood in the corner. She moved an English Bible off to the side and pulled out a pair of new clothes.

"Here," she said.

But she did not offer him any privacy. Charles began to take his shirt off, distracted by the new look of his body. His solid frame had been eaten away by hunger. His stomach was hollow, and his ribs showed. His muscles remained, but they were meager versions of what they once were. He looked up, surprised to see how invested she was in him.

"Excuse me, if you don't mind," Charles said, pointing to the doorway.

She understood at once and rushed out of the hut. He peeled away his sand-covered breeches, and when he reached for the new pair, her figure by the window turned at the last moment, her eyes widening. She had seen him naked.

Charles adjusted his stance so his back was to her, coughing and clearing his throat. He seriously feared she was trying to implicate him in some unwanted liaison. He did not want to think ill of her or assume she had no virtue, but she was acting very strange. Perhaps she was lonely. This cay, although beautiful and serene, was an isolated place.

She returned before he could signal her.

"His clothes fit me well," Charles said, trying to dispel the awkwardness between them.

"I know," she answered. Her eyes looked hungry.

His attempt to dispel the tension was not working. He pretended to be engaged with the view outside the windows. They had no glass, but the view of the beach was stunning as the sun dipped towards the water.

"Will your husband return soon?" he asked.

She nodded and went back to the crib, holding the baby and singing him a song with her melodious voice.

When night came, he offered the pallet bed back to

her, but she refused. She curled up on the floor with a blanket, resting by the baby's crib. Her back was facing him, and Charles was grateful. He feared waking up to angry shouting and accusations from her husband. He lay on the bed, listening to the shoreline of palm trees rustling in the breeze. He had rested for so long that sleep evaded him now.

He soon found out why Mosquito Coast had received that moniker, as their assault on his skin was relentless. He felt pity for the child; his crib had no netting. Night creatures clicked their metallic noises until the sound of hot rain quietened them down. A delicate floral scent, from unseen plumeria trees, wafted into the hut. Charles thought about Eliza while he lay there. She would love the chance to explore this island. She saw beauty in everything. He looked down at the dead tarantula, still not swept away. She would even be fascinated by that.

Charles laughed silently, then felt tears filling his eyes. His throat grew tight with emotion. He was one step closer to returning home. He feared what awaited him once he reached Nassau, but knowing he could hold her again, pressing her against him, gave him the strength he needed to carry on. He would salvage something from this defeat. Lord Dunmore would pay, and so would his minions.

"I am your opponent," the man said boldly.

Hiram Bruin would die. He no doubt assumed Charles was dead. Bruin's greatest mistake was that he had not killed Charles himself, although that had already been tried. Charles' hand grazed his thigh, the site of his old stab wound. He had survived so much; he only needed to leave this island. He had had many hours of silent thinking to come up with a plan. He would return to the island and try to convince the soldiers at the fort, his men, to rise up and displace Lord Dunmore in a coup. If the island was to be ruled with violence, then only violence could stop it. Perhaps Wylly had been successful with his latest petition. Charles could only hope that a legal solution to the exploits of Nassau's infamous governor was already in the works. But he did not know if the deed had been accomplished, and a piece of paper was useless against brutality.

He sighed. Charles could not return home. Not yet, at least. If this unsanctioned coup failed, he would surely be branded a traitor and be tried for treason. Instead of impressive arguments and legal counsel, maybe Whitehall needed to hear firsthand what had occurred in New Providence. And maybe he was the best example of the wickedness of Lord Dunmore.

His heart sank thinking about making Eliza wait longer for him to return, but how much sweeter a reunion would it be if he carried news of Lord Dunmore's dismissal with him? If he arrived back at Nassau with a small army, ready to quell whatever plans the governor might have in store? England seemed like the only sound strategy. He already had the element of surprise to his advantage, and soon he would have the full might of the Crown backing him as well.

Charles finally drifted to sleep just as the darkness began to fade to light. A curious sound, one he had heard before, stirred him to wakefulness. Then the smell of something burning followed. Charles sat up with panic as the roaring sound grew louder. There was a fire. The woman and her child were gone, as was the chest that had stood in the corner of the hut.

He rushed out of the bed and ran outside. All the palm trees on the western side of the island were engulfed in massive balls of flame. He made his way to the beach, raising a hand to shield his eyes from the sun. How had this happened? Charles scanned the island up and down and saw a longboat resting on the wet sand. Then he spotted something miraculous. It was a large British naval ship, moored a small distance away from the cay. The Union Jack had never looked so strikingly beautiful. He dropped to his knees in gratitude, reeling from the shock.

"You! What are you doing here?" an irritated voice asked.

Charles turned and saw two young British soldiers walk up to him. Had they set the fire?

"I am Lord Charles Sharpe, a Lieutenant Colonel in the 47th regiment," he explained.

Their scornful attitudes lightened to wonder. They snapped to attention. He gestured for them to be at ease.

"Bloody hell! What happened to you?" one soldier asked. "Are you a castaway?"

Charles sighed, the enormity of his story stilling his tongue.

"I was captured by pirates and escaped," he finally said.

Their mouths dropped open.

"That's a turn-up for the books. My God, you're half starved!" the second one exclaimed.

Charles laughed, running his hands through his hair.

"What are you doing here?" he asked, pointing at the ship.

"Common patrol, sir. We are tasked with patrolling these cays, making sure nothing nefarious takes place. Looking for smugglers mostly, sir."

"I see. What are your names?"

"I am William Taylor. And this is Adam Jones, sir," Taylor said.

"Thank God for this," Charles said quietly. "But why set the island ablaze?"

"Oh, we're just trying to chase out Mad Sally," Taylor answered, his eyes huge for dramatic effect.

"Mad Sally?"

"Aye, she's barmy. Surely you've had a run-in with her if you've been stranded on this island, sir?" Jones asked, with a laugh.

Charles turned pale. He gazed at the modest hut, visible at the edge of the palm trees.

"Mrs. Perkins? Yes, of course. She actually pulled me from this beach. She nursed me back to health," he said with a touch of defensiveness.

Taylor and Jones exchanged a puzzled look, then bent over with laughter. When they saw that Charles did not share their amusement, they tightened their faces.

"What bad luck you've had, sir," Taylor said.

"Aye, are you cursed?" Jones asked.

Taylor elbowed him in the ribs. Jones turned red and silent.

"Mad Sally builds herself a homestead wherever she sees fit. She moves from one cay to the next. She's probably in a boat on the far side of this island as we speak. We couldn't find a trace of her," Taylor explained.

"Mrs. Perkins? She was waiting for her husband to return. She has a small child. Why set everything on fire?" Charles asked with scorn in his voice. "That home is all she has!"

The two men looked at each other, only realizing the depth of Charles' ignorance now. Jones began to eye him with suspicion.

Taylor cleared his throat and spoke slowly. "Mrs. Perkins is a widow. Lost her husband and her child to tropical fever years past."

"Aye, I heard she was from Port Royal originally. Couldn't pay off her husband's gambling debts. She ran away to the Mosquito Coast here. We see her sometimes. Once she threw rocks at me, she did," Jones chimed in.

Charles shook his head with irritation.

"We cannot be speaking of the same woman. Mrs. Perkins has a young child named Henry. He's the most docile creature."

The men's eyes grew wide.

"That ain't naught but a coconut husk with some cloth twisted around it. Her baby is dead," Jones said.

Now Charles blanched. He had never heard the baby cry nor make a single noise. He turned back to the hut once again, the creeping waves of fire nearly on top of it now.

"That's all right, sir, you've had quite the ordeal," Taylor said in an attempt to smooth over the tension.

"Aye, that's Mad Sally, that is. Belongs in Bedlam, she

does," Jones added.

Charles was speechless. Now it all made sense. Still, he pitied the poor woman. She probably cursed him as she slipped away, connecting his position as a soldier to the same ones who chased her and left her without peace. When he had mentioned who he was yesterday, that was the first sign that her mood had shifted.

Then something darker gnawed at him. Eliza could easily end up sharing Sally's fate. He had left her with fraught finances. She, too, had a child to raise all by herself now. He needed to return to her. He couldn't waste a second longer.

"Gentlemen, I need you to bring me home," Charles said.

He'd had enough talk about the poor, disturbed woman. He watched the palm trees burn, and a large piece of frond snapped and landed on top of the dry thatch roof, sizzling in the air. Charles watched the blaze, wishing her well in his mind.

"And where would that be, sir?" Taylor asked.

Charles felt the keenest regret in what he was about to say, but knew it had to be done without delay. Eliza would have to stay strong for a little while longer.

"I need to go to London at once. Whitehall needs to know what has been going on in this part of the world," Charles said, standing taller. "Before our empire loses the West Indies to our enemies."

This was a battle without a war, a bloody contest between cruel men and the cruel sea on the Caribbean frontier. A soldier like Charles did not fight such battles spurned on by hatred, although it threatened to consume him as he envisioned his revenge. No, a soldier like him continued the fight because of the precious things he had left behind that he loved. He was separated from his beloved wife and child, his heaven on earth. And he would do anything to protect them, even if the longer wait caused him pain.

CHAPTER XVIII.

The barrister glares at her. Sweat beads on her pale forehead. Eliza blinks rapidly, waiting for his next query.

"And then why did you set foot on the Fortuyne in April of 1794 on the island Saba? For a second voyage? Surely, by now you understood what kind of men sailed underneath the command of Captain Hiram Bruin?"

Someone in the back of the court coughs.

"I needed to get to England. He had a ship."

"And do you recognize this name scrawled here, at the very bottom?" The barrister steps forward, holding a familiar paper.

She peers down at it, knowing full well what he held in his hands.

"That is my name," she says quietly.

"Ah. And are these not pirate articles? The very contract that binds all those sailing under a black flag together in one unified party? Why is your name here?"

Eliza swallows nervously. "He made me sign it," she answers.

The barrister makes a face of mock surprise.

"Who made you sign it? We do not have all day, Lady Sharpe," he snaps.

"Captain Hiram Bruin. I was under duress."

"And does this so-called sea captain stand before you today?"

Eliza scans the room, seeing nothing but a sea of unfamiliar faces. The man she seeks does not stand among them. Bruin is not there. That man always evades justice. Her chest tightens, knowing her answer will not satisfy her interrogator.

"No, I do not see him …"

"And so, who can be blamed for these atrocities? Hmm?"

"I know not of what you speak," Eliza says, her voice quavering.

"You stand here today, accused of the crimes of piracy and the death of two young girls!"

Eliza shakes her head.

"That was not me! I did not do it!" she cries.

She looks up into the crowd again and sees the Spanish girls, watching her with fire burning in their eyes. Luisa and her younger sister, Maria, haunt her from the bench. They sit, drenched with sea water, a puddle massively growing beneath their cold bare feet, their ankles crooked and broken. The dark water creeps closer and closer, filling the wooden floor.

Luisa rises to a stand and opens her mouth, as a small trail of blood spills from her lips. "I will remember your face and my uncle will see you hanged!"

Eliza opened her eyes, gasping for air. A hand pushed her back down again.

"Mind your shoulder, Liza," a voice she hated said.

Hearing Bruin so close to her only startled her even more, but the pain in her left shoulder made her stop. She winced and tried to compose herself, even as she fought the sinking feeling in her gut. Morning sun streamed in through the tall windows. The weather had broken, and she saw slants of sunlight dancing on the rug. She was in his cabin again, in his bed. Her dress was gone, and she wore a dry shift. The heat of shame washed over her. He had stripped her and put on a new shift. She had no stays. He had seen her naked, and she remembered none of it.

She glared at him, dumbfounded with rage.

Bruin sat in a chair, his knees spread wide, watching her with a morbid intensity. Then he realized why her eyes shot daggers at him. He grinned.

"I did not want you to catch your death of cold. Should I have had one of my men take care of your wet clothes instead?" he asked, amused by her fury. "I do not think that wise. Your dress is drying over the galley stove as we speak."

It was evident that he savored his new power over her.

"The situation we find ourselves in is, of course, regrettable. But as we both know, I surely cannot be held accountable for storms." He flashed a grim smile.

She was about to snap something in response, but she realized she had lost her voice. Bruin laughed when he heard the meek rasp come out of her mouth.

"I enjoyed hearing your screams," he said with a twisted gleam in his eyes, "But then you stopped. You have rendered yourself mute."

Eliza felt the walls of his cabin closing in around her, pressing against her. Columns of black obstructed her watery vision, and all that remained was his formidable form, sitting in the center, observing her. She was grateful to be out of the storm, but now she faced an equally terrifying fate. She was reduced to a weakened version of herself, her voice stolen by the wind, her left arm in a sling. And she knew that he enjoyed this new development. Now it would be so much easier to restrain her. The thought of herself lying there while his cunning hands peeled away layers meant to protect her, reducing her to nakedness, unconscious and unable to defend herself, made her sick.

Bruin sighed, standing up and preparing a cup of hot tea for her.

"I think we can both agree that now you have learned your lesson, Liza. I daresay you will never upset me again after this."

Eliza squeezed her eyes shut, willing the scene to disappear. But he was still there, and she was still in his bed.

He came back to her, handing her the teacup. She imagined throwing the hot water into his face, but she was immobilized by fear.

"Your lips were blue last night," he said quietly. His eyes flicked up, holding her gaze captive.

And then his voice shifted, blending into a mix of angst and sadness. Of misplaced admiration. "Your stubborn will … that even I cannot break. Why will you not submit? You refuse, even if it means you could save yourself. You still refuse."

Eliza clutched the cup, watching the water come dangerously close to the edge of the rim as the boat rocked. Her breaths were shallow. She studied the liquid with suspicion.

"Drink the tea, Liza," he said, scolding her like a child.

Eliza forced her voice out.

"No." It was harsh and grating.

Bruin's eyes narrowed.

"I am not leaving until you do," he warned her.

Then you will have to wait all day.

He shifted his position, crossing his legs with his ankle over his knee. "I returned your shoulder to its rightful place. You should keep it in that sling for at least a fortnight."

She had no interest in this conversation. She focused her attention on the sea outside the ship. There were no more white caps on the waves. Then she saw the stack of notebooks on his desk, and the one book that concealed a lock of her hair. Remembering it existed there, hidden beneath the pages, paralyzed her with hopelessness. She had never faced an enemy like this.

But Bruin was still waiting for her to follow his orders.

"I see you require another lesson, Liza," Bruin said as he left the chair. He towered over her and flashed his boot knife at her. She had not even seen him reach for it. It was like an extension of his hand, enabling his domination of her.

"Drink. It."

He would not repeat himself again. Despite her refusal, she felt her defiance wither away to nothing. She was running out of fight. Eliza brought the hot tea to her lips and sipped it. Satisfied with her obedience, Bruin returned to his chair and replaced the knife in his boot.

She drained the cup with disgust, dreading the arrival of the warm fatigue she knew so well by now. But this wave came stronger; a fever flushed her face, like she was burning alive. Then the room softened into a blur.

"We have clear water before us, Liza," she heard him say. "You should be grateful."

His voice was closer now, right above her ear, his body leaning into hers. He had joined her in the bed. She heard the mattress creak with his weight. Her stomach twisted into an uncomfortable knot, her limbs heavy and unmovable, her eyelids weighted down. Bruin's words from another day, farther in the past, now resurfaced in her mind, as she felt him coil against her.

"It kills its prey with a venom that causes weakness. Then it swallows them whole."

She felt his lips press against her neck, and then she lost control. She had tried to kill her pain, she had tried to escape from his grip, but she had failed. Now the ache she felt was worse. She was no longer tied to the mast, an unwilling prisoner. Instead, she was bound to him.

June 17th, 1794—Portsmouth, England

A woman's memory was capable of doing strange things to protect itself, to shield the heart from reliving unpleasant things, to rewrite lived days to a different melody. Time became an abstraction as countless hours blended into one another. Eliza remained powerless to Bruin's threats, to his demands for her to swallow another drink, to the grip of his unwanted touch. In total two months had passed from the time they had left the island of Saba to their arrival in England. The storm was a delay that had driven them terribly off course, and the days aboard the ship had passed like one unending event. It was a long sleepless night that bled into daylight, a patchwork of muddied sounds and sensations, a cruel cycle with no end in sight.

Then one afternoon, Eliza saw the cliffs of the Isle of Wight. Her fingers gripped the railing of the ship until her knuckles turned white, although she no longer had the same strength in her left arm as she once did. She was free of the sling, but it brought little comfort. She was still weighed down by mental chains, invisible links of fear that Bruin had slipped over her struggling shoulders.

The *Fortuyne* sailed through the heaving grey water, and they began to pass the glow of lighthouses that dotted the coastal towns. The boat rode low in the ocean from the weight of the cargo, and Eliza beheld her native land with wonder for the first time in three years. The melancholy croaking of sea birds as they wheeled in the twilight sky distracted her tormented mind.

There was one glaring issue. As the boat drifted into the harbor, Eliza confirmed her suspicions. They were not heading to London. They would dock amongst the tall ships at Portsmouth Harbor, home of the Royal Navy and one of England's most heavily fortified cities. She would soon be returned to English soil, but not to her choice of port. Bruin was clearly plotting something, and Eliza feared what it would mean for her in the coming days. Why would a pirate, an outlaw of the seas, sail straight into the lion's den?

Day after day, she had watched him as he looked out at the ocean, casting a worried gaze out over the darkening waves. The fresh water stored in the casks had grown foul-tasting, covered with a thin veil of green slime, much like her strained relationship with Bruin. The closer they grew to reaching their intended destination, she could almost feel an oppressiveness crushing his spirits, as if he instinctively knew that delivering her back to England would signal the end of their twisted arrangement. When Bruin forced her to drink his concoctions, she was unable to move away from him, to separate herself from his shadow, but she would soon step off this cursed ship and out of his life forever. As the sight of land grew closer, she knew her moment had finally arrived.

Later that evening, the ship docked at North Camber, a wharf where merchant ships unloaded their wares, situated in the same harbor as the Royal Dockyard. The crew was busy with washing the deck and unloading cargo from the hold. A harbor attendant strode up the gangway and onto the quarterdeck, greeting Bruin with a terse formality. Eliza watched in silence, subdued, a shell of her former self.

The stout man began to ask Bruin a series of questions.

"What cargoes do you carry? You must await the arrival of the purser and the customs inspector, who will verify your manifest and the unloading of your goods ..."

Eliza turned back to the dockside, looking wistfully at the brick storehouses that lined the waterfront. She heard Bruin's voice grow irritated with the man's persistent questions.

"My papers are in order, I assure you," he mumbled

in a low voice.

The man sighed. "One can never be too careful, Captain. The French have spies that watch these wharves, and you are a stranger to me. I am only doing my due diligence."

The two men began to quarrel, and they moved inside to Bruin's quarters. Eliza saw a yellow post-chaise pull up alongside the barrels and crates that had already been unloaded. Bruin did not want to linger any longer than usual, and his men had carried on with his orders despite the dock master's instructions. That was clearly the source of the disagreement.

Eliza felt a rush of hope, something she had not experienced in many weeks. She had repeatedly told herself she only needed to make it to England, and now she had. The deed had been accomplished. The gangway was briefly empty of Bruin's crew, and it had never been clearer that it now represented an escape. Without turning back or gathering her belongings, she rushed to the main deck, carefully stepping down the slippery gangway with trembling legs. Heat seared her back as she reached the dockyard, nervously awaiting the shout of her name or an eruption of curses. But nothing happened.

She reached the post-chaise, its bright paint like sunshine encouraging her faith. Before she crawled inside, she addressed the postillion, the rider who sat ready on the left lead horse, with a quick instruction. Bring her to the Admiralty House. Bring her to the Navy headquarters; the ride would not be long. He motioned to step down and open the door for her, but she waved him away, preferring to do it herself. The quicker she was out of sight, the better her chances were.

Once she took her seat, she rapped on the carriage frame, signaling she was ready, and when she felt the slow rolling gait of the carriage begin, she slumped with a sigh of relief. The ship disappeared from view. She was safe. She was free. She closed her eyes, savoring the feeling. It had actually worked.

But she did not realize that death was following her with furious footsteps. Without warning, the coach door flung open, and she heard the postillion shout.

Bruin climbed inside like a crazed man, his pistol still withdrawn, ignoring the horseman's rebukes entirely.

"To Basingstoke!" he yelled back, slamming the door closed.

Eliza screamed, and his smile grew wider. She crammed herself to the edge of the other side of the vehicle. She regretted the intimacy of their new quarters. Bruin was panting from his frantic dash off his ship. He had altered his appearance, wearing his curly, dirty blonde hair tied back with a ribbon. Gone was his black leather jacket; it was now replaced with a long navy fitted coat. It was his attempt at appearing more genteel and less pirate. It did not fool Eliza. His new attire fit him awkwardly, as if his black single-breasted linen waistcoat was suffocating him. There was no doubt he had drastically changed his style to hide from the authorities in town.

He sat stiffly, his reaction to her daring escapade still uncertain. She realized he was preoccupied with a copy of the latest edition of *The Times* laying in front of them. His eyes scanned it in silent horror, like an invisible noose was tightening around his neck. *Officer Returns! Survives Astounding Voyage* … Before she could finish reading what had stopped Bruin in his tracks, he grabbed it off the seat and flung it out the door. Eliza stared where the newspaper had laid, shocked by his manic behavior.

"*Godverdomme* … did you not want to wait for me? That is very rude, Liza," he said, his chest still heaving.

Eliza tried leaning forward and reaching for the coach door. His arm flew out and blocked her, sending her back into the seat.

"We are not going to the Admiralty House," she said breathlessly, her eyes growing moist with trepidation.

"You are a deluded woman, Liza. Do you actually think I brought us here because *you* demanded it? Do you really think I would risk losing the respect of my men and beg for your forgiveness? This was my plan all along. I told my crew before we even docked in Saba. We were to head to England, whether you agreed to become my wife or not. The vote was staged. I knew I would get what I wanted one way or another." He laughed, running a hand through his sweat-dampened hair. "And I knew I could control you by making you believe you had a chance. You and your eternal optimism. It will be your downfall."

"But I was supposed to help you with a pardon; I need to speak to the Navy. I need to find my husband," the words tumbled out of her nervous mouth.

"He is dead, Liza."

His voice was cold and unfeeling. His words tore through her like a knife.

"No," she said with a wavering voice.

She had survived the long, terrible journey by ship. She had overcome impossible odds only to have her last dreams quashed before her. Then her dismay rounded into fury. She thought of the few words she had seen: *Officer Returns! Survives Astounding Voyage,* and Bruin's extreme reaction to an otherwise harmless newspaper. She saw it all so clearly now. It represented the truth he so desperately sought to hide from her. She prayed she was right.

"Charles *is* alive. That is what you read in the paper. Your time is running out. That is why you have changed your plans. That is what precipitated this mad flight ..." she said, her voice growing louder.

His blue eyes narrowed with agitation. His hostility emboldened her into knowing her assertion was right.

"That is why, despite all your efforts, you are afraid now!" she exclaimed.

Livid outrage slowly spread across his face like cracks in wet sand. Bruin's attack on her was swift and savage. He lunged forward, throwing a punch straight at her right eye. She felt the cold metal of his rings against her skin. Eliza reeled in shock, stunned by the escalation in violence. The confirmation was painful and brutal. Her hands started to shake in her lap.

But he was not through with her yet. He grabbed her by the collar of her dress.

"Do you feel that, Liza?" Bruin hissed. "That is how much control you have now. None."

The carriage sped up, and as the town of Portsmouth slid by the windows, she felt the last vestiges of her strength leaving her.

"Can you imagine what life is like when someone has to watch their every word because they are liable to receive a thrashing? Can you imagine what life is like to live with that kind of fear? Because you are going to live it with me now. I am going to show you what it is like to own nothing, not even your own body …"

He grabbed her chin, forcing her to make eye contact with him.

"Some men do not like to mar something so pretty. I do not mind. And now, every time you see your reflection, you will remember to never cross me."

When she looked into his eyes and only saw a hollow blackness looking back at her, a new level of fear unlocked inside her.

"You may think me cruel, but every gentle method has been exhausted. I asked you, Liza. I pleaded with you for your hand, and yet you would not give it. As if I was mere dirt," he said with disgust. He faced her fully. "Tell me, Liza, did you really think I would allow you to have your freedom? This entire venture was wholly your own seeking. You could have changed your story. Now we will handle matters *my* way."

Eliza swallowed nervously. Her sense of stupidity burned her face more than the mark his fist had left behind.

"What do you intend to do with me?"

She was terrified of his answer.

"I do not want a pardon from the king. I want the fortune of an heir," he said.

The carriage rolled over a hole in the road and slanted, but her body was already wracked with tension.

"You see, I know your relatives by marriage to a degree better than even you do," he continued, with a sly smile. "We are heading north to visit a certain widow, Lady Adelaide Sharpe, a dowager who owns Grenewood Hall outside of Basingstoke. We should reach it in two days."

Eliza's expression was mired in confusion. She had never heard of this person.

"I do not know her."

"All the better, for she will not know the difference between fear and fatigue on your face. She will surely want to know about the tragic death of her nephew and adjust her will to include the newest member of her family, her great-nephew, Philippe," Bruin said, stretching his long legs forward. He sighed. "It is not enough to acquire wealth. I seek to own land. Land confers status, even to those with pasts like mine. Wherever the respectable world goes, those belonging to the underworld are never far behind. Everyone knows this, Liza. One only needs influential friends at their disposal, and that can be obtained through wealth and a family name."

He cracked his knuckles. "That boy will be raised the heir to a vast fortune. Far more money than I could ever clear in my industry upon the seas. We all know that land is the true sign of wealth. When I am done, I will own this Hampshire estate *and* the plantation in New Providence. And I will be rich beyond measure."

Now Eliza's lips curved upwards with a smile. She had finally found a weakness within him.

"You cannot take what is to become Philippe's. You do not understand English law."

She felt very satisfied with herself. He was smart but still capable of making crucial mistakes. But Bruin bowed his head with a laugh.

"Oh, yes, I do, dear Liza. Coverture. What is yours is mine. In fact, it is no longer yours the moment we marry," he said with an insidious delight. "Once we leave Grenewood Hall, we will make haste to the border at Scotland and be wed. And I will become the father of Philippe."

She refused to believe what she was hearing.

"He cannot inherit entailed property or the baronetcy. He is a natural child!"

"You and I know that. He is the bastard of the Frenchman. But Charles, that fool, accepted him. So, he is his legal heir. And Philippe will inherit, unless anything should befall him."

The threat was as loud as his spoken words. She would die before she let Bruin harm her child. But Bruin was not finished explaining his wicked plans.

"It is a mercy the boy is young. He will not remember any of this. There is time enough to cultivate his affections. Children are easy to trick. And he will soon grow to love the only father he will ever know."

Eliza's right hand clutched the side of the vehicle, looking for a solid surface to steady herself. Bitter tears rushed to her face. Her misfortune fueled his adrenaline, and his voice was animated.

"The sun is not rising for me or my kind any longer. It is setting. And I will take you down with me," he warned.

He placed his hand over hers, but she did not react. She

was stiff, desperate to control her wild emotions.

Bruin continued. "There is nothing worse than being poor. You are reviled by those above you. But you wanted none of the gilded privileges of the class you come from. You left that all behind. Why?"

He tilted his head to study her, but she kept her face towards the window, watching the city as if this act alone could deliver her from him. Old houses and churches crowded amongst newer brick buildings and shops, streets choking with other carriages like the pervasive coal dust that lingered in the air. She was home again, in the heart of an empire that stretched over vast oceans, built by the sweat and blood of men who conquered seas and death in far-flung reaches. She tried to pretend he wasn't there, but it was an impossible feat. When she felt Bruin was still watching her, she summoned the courage to speak.

She looked at him with a deepening glare. "You are not even fit to serve as a valet to the gentleman you have ruined," she spat.

He tightened his jaw. "Your husband has earned his position in life. As have I. Through blood and dirt. You will do as I say. Do not let the blood be yours. Or that of your son."

Then he produced a single red shoe from the depths of his pocket. He held it out to her frightened eyes. It was Philippe's missing shoe from the night his men had stormed Pleasant Hall. Bruin added no other words, but his gesture said it all.

Eliza knew it was a deception, a cruel trick. He had simply taken the shoe, and Celia had assumed it had been lost. The women had never found the shoe that night. She had lied to him after she had left Cleo's old dwelling.

Then doubts began to take hold of her. What if he really did have Philippe? What if Captain Johnson and Celia had not been successful on their mission? She raced back and forth in her mind, his psychological grip on her more than she could bear. She did not know for certain, and that was enough to make her question everything. She could not remember; he had robbed her memories. She bit her lip and began to pray silently.

"I left behind a small contingent of men at Pleasant Hall. Perhaps you noticed. They have hold of the boy."

She realized there was one man she had not seen on the ship this entire time—the brute who had grabbed Lucy in the hallway when they had shared that awkward meal. And worse, she did not know what transpired after she had fallen asleep. It was a gaping hole in her disturbed recollections.

With an audible intake of breath, she tried to speak in broken, fractured sentences, more unsure of herself the harder she tried.

"You are a monster," Eliza finally managed to say. She hated how helpless he made her feel.

"I am a rogue. You spent enough days by my side and you still did not recognize such traits? I thought your mind was sharp."

She clutched her face with both hands, her breaths quivering.

"You are a deceiver!"

He sneered and barked out a laugh.

"Does this surprise you, Liza?"

"No, no, no, no …" she muttered under her frightened breath.

"You lost your freedom the moment you handed it to me in Nassau."

Eliza was suspended in a space between anger and devastation.

"I never agreed to any of this. I will neither assist you in such a design nor suffer you to put it into execution. Your plan will not work."

"I only make gambles I know I can win."

"You picture yourself the noble outlaw. But there is nothing good in you. You have no allegiance to any country or to any person. You only operate for your own selfish gain."

"I am still better than a common man. I —"

"You are nothing more than a common pirate. And the tree they hang you from will see no marked difference either!" she shouted.

"And you, my dear Liza, are an accessory to an accused pirate. A willing accomplice to this outlaw. You signed our articles, and it bound you to our cause and thus to me. You did not resist me."

"You forced me to!" she cried.

"Did I hold a pistol to that porcelain cheek?" His lips curved.

Eliza thought of the recurring nightmares she had of standing before a merciless barrister. It was clear that she was involved with the crimes of pirates, and she found it more and more difficult to soothe away her worries. People bandied the term "pirate" about, but in truth, it was difficult to try men like Bruin under charges of piracy. The crime was complicated to prove; what happened on the high seas tended to remain there, drifting under the current into oblivion. That is, unless a murder was known to have been committed. And that sin had most certainly occurred.

A trial unfolded in her mind. Charges of conspiracy, aiding, abetting, possession of stolen treasure, swirled in her thoughts, knocking down all her reassurances. Then defiance rose up in her.

"You kidnapped me! I participated in all that transpired under duress, you monster!"

He leaned on her, pushing her against the carriage frame.

"And I will force you to do worse still …" His voice was a threat, like darkness creeping into her skin.

The view outside the post-chaise turned to rolling green hills, and the fewer people she saw, the more vulnerable she felt. She sank deeper into the stark reality that unfolded around her, pushed by the hands of a cold destiny that rolled her forward to a cruel and unwanted fate.

"The authorities will hunt you down like a dog. You have committed crimes against international law and now English law …" she said.

"It is not a crime to steal a child," he replied.

He placed the small red shoe on her lap. She looked at it with dismay, praying that Captain Johnson and Celia had delivered Philippe to safety. She shook her head, pressing herself towards the window and claiming whatever small space she could take apart from him.

"You have no choice, Liza. You are nothing. You have no right to freedom. You are what I say you are. I took your husband away. And I can take your son away, too."

She clutched the shoe in her left hand.

"Is your ambition so restless, so boundless that nothing will satisfy you?" she whispered.

"You have not even thanked me for this post-chaise. You will travel in style to Basingstoke," he said proudly.

Eliza took a long inhale, steeling herself. "I am the daughter of a viscount. Your private coach does not impress me."

"Oh, I know. You cannot rid yourself of all the arrogance of your class. I did it for myself. I am a selfish man."

Eliza's eyes narrowed. "And members of my class do not generally admit criminals knowingly into their society. Your plan is bound to fail."

Her words had no effect on his confidence. A feeling of dread hit her. How long ago did he plan this wicked scheme?

"Nothing can stop me," he said, tilting his head back. "I am feeling godly."

Eliza feared it was the one true thing he had uttered on the jaunting carriage ride.

"You cannot measure gentility by the weight of your purse. You cannot wash away the taint from your character, for you have none," she hissed with contempt. "Do not be so pleased with yourself. Our alliance was never built on trust, only a cheap imitation."

She spoke bravely, but her terror was debilitating. Bruin would be her downfall, one that she could not escape. She vacillated between fear and the shock that her life was changing faster than she could control. Then she thought of a plan.

"I will say you ravished me," she threatened. "Those words can take down any true gentleman."

He regarded her with slight annoyance, knowing what she said was true.

"And is that worth the boy dying?"

She hated him and the words he so carelessly spilled from his mouth.

"What do you want me to say, Hiram? That I love you?" she asked, her voice losing steadiness.

"No, that is not what I seek. Love is not necessary for a marriage. Others will think it suspect, and I cannot have that."

He claimed he did not seek such a protestation of feeling, but his obsession with her was obvious. She feared it was another one of his many lies.

"What has Charles done to warrant this appalling hatred?"

"Nothing. It is simply greed. I want his life."

She shook her head. "You know nothing about his life."

"I know a great deal more about it than you do," he said, his tone menacing.

His presence was overpowering, as if all the air in the stuffy carriage had been sucked out, smothering her. Her bearings spiraled into disarray, and she found it harder to breathe. She grew dizzy, and she did not know if she was adjusting to the new jerking motions of the vehicle or if it was because her life was decidedly no longer her own.

Bruin peered out his window, watching the English countryside pass by. He was a decade older than Charles, but his added years had only sharpened his savagery.

"How can you lie so? Is it as natural as breathing is to me?" Her voice came out small.

Bruin faced her, looking her up and down. He almost seemed to pity her.

"You would lie to me about the color of fire, about the hue of the very sky," she said with wet, dull eyes.

"It is true. I tell lies until I tire even myself."

Eliza gripped her skirts. She wanted to remind him that she would not submit. She was stronger than he assumed.

"I can handle pain for far longer than you can imagine," she declared boldly.

Bruin looked amused by her statement. "Oh, I know. I have studied you for a very long time. That is why I chose you for this life. You will learn to enjoy it."

Then he pressed his hot body against her, his lips against her ear.

"Your endurance will be your undoing …"

Bruin lingered for a moment, studying the way the emerald necklace bobbed up and down with her shallow breaths. Her chest tightened with panic; there was no way out of her predicament. She did not know how she would make it out alive, and others would no doubt suffer as he carried his plans to fruition. His prideful ambition and his ruthless vengeance marked him as a perversion of a gentleman. Bruin was an agent of destruction, and he had chosen her world to burn.

CHAPTER XIX.

It took Eliza a few moments to recognize that people were staring at the darkening bruise on her right eye and not at the man who stood beside her. To their eyes, Hiram Bruin appeared as any normal traveling gentleman. She had nearly forgotten the savage attack; she found that his words always cut her deeper. She watched Bruin adjust his pocket watch to the time of the public clock in the courtyard of the Golden Cross Inn, then they stepped inside its shadowy interior.

Her nostrils were immediately assaulted by the stench of coal and air made sour by spilt alcohol. It was a rancid den, and a true lady would only ever venture inside if she had no choice. It wasn't safe for a woman to be surrounded by men drowning in drink, but Eliza viewed it as an improvement from sharing a carriage with a monster. The hard wooden bench she sat against and the rustic table between them offered the much-needed distance she sought from him. There had been a time when her younger, more naive self was desperate to see what happened in inns late at night. She thought of her first night alone with Charles with a heavy heart, before they had boarded their ship to Nassau. That seemed like ancient history now, an event more rooted in myth. Still, when she saw a flash of a red officer's jacket, her eyes grew wide. She knew it wasn't Charles, but the mere sight of the uniform brought her a small dose of comfort.

Eliza was the only woman present, except for the inn-keeper's wife. She kept her place behind the bar, refilling tankards of ale and keeping the men's egos fed with her steadfast attention to their bawdy jokes. Eliza sipped her own drink, her stomach turning as the warm ale sank down her gut, but she savored the way it soothed her nerves in the loud, crowded room. Pieces of conversation wafted past her ears: fears of food shortages, of the terror of inevitable French invasion. Other men complained about the state of the Irish. Not much had changed in England, and the Caribbean seemed a world away from the one these complaining men occupied, as they leaned back and smoked from their creamware pipes.

Bruin sat across from her, watching her every move, the wavering candlelight shifting the angles of his hungry, narrow face, his eyes darting side to side like a rat's. Eliza preferred to study the jagged cracks in the wooden table or the rotating back of the officer's red jacket from where he stood at the front of the inn. Bruin had ordered food for both of them, but her plate remained untouched. She could tell he was itching to speak to her; the tension crackled in the air between them like the hiss of the logs in the grate as the flames consumed them.

"Since we are to be married, Liza, you should know …

all of me," he began, his words slow. "I want you to know my secrets. There is no pleasure to be had when you keep everything to yourself. Some men are motivated by titles, others by pleasure, but I am not."

"You are ruled by wicked impulse," she said, her tone clearly indicating that she was unimpressed by him.

He had spoken such sentiment before. It was nothing new to her. She took another swig of her drink.

"And my impulse is ruled by revenge," Bruin said.

She didn't like the dark sparkle in his eyes when she looked up.

"Everyone has something they seek to protect or destroy. And on this night, it seems appropriate that I confess this. I only seek to destroy." The excitement deepened in his voice. "And I have marked your husband for such a downfall. I will not quit at this late hour. I have nearly accomplished the goal."

Bruin captured her hand on the table, and he squeezed it. The dimly lit room seemed to tilt as she dreaded the arrival of his next words.

"Your husband took someone very dear to me, and I will not stop until everything he loves is destroyed. That island has a history, Liza."

"We have left the Bahama islands. We are not even in the West Indies, but still, you talk of nothing else. It tires me."

"Nassau is indeed the only reason we sit here tonight, Liza."

"Do not call me that," she groaned.

"What I am about to speak of did not start the moment

you stepped shoreside. You are only a new addition to what has unfolded. It makes me pity you, for you surely had no idea what you walked into when you left the harbor that day. When you agreed to marry your husband." He spoke slower, his deep voice lower. "My father was Captain Jacob Beaks. He did his best to bring wealth to us, to keep us fed. But he was arrested one day by a young, intrepid British captain. Captain Charles Sharpe." His hold on her tightened to an uncomfortable pressure, as if he intended to punish her for associating with the villain in his life. She tried to pull her arm back. "The British hung him for piracy and murder. My father died because of Charles."

But Eliza took satisfaction in his confession.

"Then he was a pirate like you. I am glad you have clarified the matter."

"He was a captain from Saba; he committed no crimes. It was lawful trade."

"And the charge of murder?" she hissed. "I believe nothing that leaves your lips."

He released her with a sickening smile.

"Oh, my Liza, after all this time, you still hesitate to trust me? Who else in this world do you have now?" He folded his hands on the table, sitting up straighter. "You fail to recognize that you do still trust me. Even if only by the finest sliver."

"You speak errant nonsense." She lifted the tankard to her mouth, wishing the alcohol would dull her senses. She had no other comfort.

Bruin's lips turned upwards into a grin.

"You surprise me. After all this time, you still accept a

drink from me. I thought by now you would surely know better." Bruin leaned back in his chair, confident of his hold over her. "Of course, this required a stronger dose. I fear after all that time on the ship, you have gained a tolerance for it. It works even better in ale, although most women will not go near it. This tincture is too detectable in wine. But when you are thirsty, you will always accept the poison."

The look on his face disgusted her. She knew what he meant by it, but his meaning did not materialize until she recognized the feelings she now braced against. The slow and steady blurring of the room, the way her heart raced, banging against her sluggish limbs. She thought she saw a mouse in the corner, but when she looked again, it was only a shadow. Unwanted details stood out to her—the severe crack in the wooden table that made her stomach ache even more, the pungent scent of smoke from the fireplace that made her queasy, the awful pitch of raucous laughter and slurred voices around her, and the calculating pair of eyes that watched her with depraved amusement from across the table.

Bruin was openly speaking of their sinful arrangement. He was bragging of the insidious ways he had overpowered her. It was murky and obscure, like her memories. But one evening stood out from the rest; from this night she remembered the events with crystalline clarity. She wondered if he had used his tricks then, but she doubted it. She had a feeling he had chosen not to, as if the way he toyed with her was part of a grand experiment. She knew he was driven by compulsions unknown to most men, and because of this, Bruin was the director of her innermost nightmares.

"Charles does not need to know. Parting your legs will be my greatest secret."

She had escaped his advances that night. But Eliza thought of the way she had been kidnapped and brought aboard the *Fortuyne*, the fingerprint bruises pressed deep into her thighs, the very first time she had awoken in his bed, how she had distinctly recalled his body aligned with hers after the storm as she sank deeper into a feverish haze. These fragments implied a terrible truth. She did not want to speak it into existence; she did not want the words to cross the rank air. She felt sick.

"The Frenchman and I made a wager on how easily he could bed you. He bet on one ball, and then another before he lost patience. I gave him a solution. I told him what to slip into your drink. He sent the footman over to you, and I sent you a note."

It took her a minute to register what Bruin was gloating over now. Then she recalled her second ball at Lord Dunmore's house—her final dance, the one right after she had learnt of the death of her parents. Her first Christmas alone and away from home, and the only love she had at that point recognized in her life. How very lost she had felt that night, how many drinks she had downed, how she had only focused on seeing Jean. She had wanted another colorful conversation in some secluded room. But he and Bruin had evidently planned on taking so much more.

The truth was ugly, and she recognized it as one of the few times Bruin was not lying to her. It twisted her gut;

she was afraid of what else he wanted to reveal tonight.

"Butterflies …" she whispered, her voice unsteady. Then anger flared up in her. It was easy to tarnish a dead man's name; Jean was not here to defend himself. "You lie. Lord Dunmore poisoned my drink with it."

"That fool learned it from me. He learned a great deal from me. As did Jean."

Her face and chest flushed red, and she looked away, struggling to compose herself.

"Do not feel ashamed. You would not have your precious son, now would you? Your liaison proved very useful to my designs. It nearly ended your marriage."

Her mind raced to recall any spoken words she could retrieve from the haze of her memories.

"Why?"

Jean looked down at the floor.

"As a means of seducing you," he replied through gritted teeth.

"I must tell my husband. Yes, I should leave. I need to leave!"

Jean blocked the door.

"He will not understand. I have seen this happen before."

"How do you know of this? You speak with such certainty."

"Men at court in London are no different from the false kings that inhabit this island, Eliza."

"Stay with me," she implored.

"I cannot. I will not impugn your honor."

"You wandered upstairs, looking for the butterflies. Jean knew that would lure you to us. I watched you from the end of the hallway. But then he turned coward. He was afraid of Charles and his wrath. He locked you alone in that room."

"Why are you telling me this?" she whispered.

"To prove how very far I am willing to go in order to destroy Charles. To show you how long I have toiled at my endeavors. I was surprised to hear that he had returned to the island, even more so with a bride. Everyone knows that the way to the heart of a man is through his wife."

His words touched every inch of her, wrapping their way around the deepest parts of her, exposing her weaknesses, leaving no part of herself a mystery to him. But he was not done relaying his motives to her.

"I am tired of secrets. It weighs on my back. I was faced with a question. I heard that Pleasant Hall was abandoned. But I could not decide whether to break his neck or poison his drink. I wanted to take the house. I walked over to him, rotting in his chair, his eyes cloudy with whiskey." He paused momentarily, waiting for her to realize he spoke of Charles' father.

"We had a decent conversation before it set in. I complained to him, I told him that I could not stand the way you people spent your money. I told him I would have women in here, scores of them. But that mattered little to someone like him. No woman would lie with him now. I told him he squandered it all. I nearly pitied him when he realized what I had done. I made him tell me where he hid his valuables. I then learned about the gold he had buried out by the beach. Death can be a strangely intimate affair. He confessed many things to me."

Eliza shook her head, refusing to comprehend his words.

"The old Master Sharpe drank himself to death."

Bruin leaned forward.

"And I handed him the bottle, Liza. How I savored that night. I knew I had scored a point against Charles, but I did not realize it would serve as the impetus for his return."

Bruin sighed and downed his drink, then called for more ale. "I knew no one would miss that old drunk. But I severely underestimated the sense of duty Charles possessed. On one hand, I felt bitter defeat creeping in. Nothing would change. I had not made Charles pay for his sins. But then I saw you in the parlor at the governor's mansion. I found another angle."

Eliza's eyes grew wide. Bruin had always acted very familiar with the rooms of Pleasant Hall. He had always strode about the place as if he owned it. Now she knew he considered it his.

"All that remains now is the house. And you … his woman. I tried bankrupting him at cards, but he is too disciplined to lose his fortune by gambling it away, although he is doing a fine job destroying that estate and draining its wealth by freeing his slaves. He made quite a few men very angry. I found villagers willing to torch the stables. I almost took care of two problems. But then you ran into the fire, trying to save that stupid animal. You have cheated death many times, Liza. You impress me."

Eliza's face paled, and she tried to flee. But he stopped her.

"Where do you think you are going?" He laughed and drew his chair closer to hers, boxing her in between himself and the hard wooden bench. Her hands clenched her dress, her heart beating rapidly.

"I gave you something stronger tonight. I cannot afford to have you run off into the countryside. There is a storm." He drew his face closer to her, carefully studying her pupils. "There we go. It should begin working shortly."

She looked to the man next to her, as if he could aid her in her plight. His face was pockmarked from surviving smallpox, and the glance from his disfigured face belayed no sympathy. Eliza was in a crowded room, but she was alone, isolated with this villain.

"My lover, Anna Snyde, was the wife of my captain. I gladly slit his throat for her. I escaped justice, but happiness was not to be ours. I could never bring her the wealth she needed. She wanted to control my every move. She gave me a child, but I could not stand his snivelly cries, his constant need. He was nothing like me. I forced her to throw our son into the canal, to drown with the mud and the eels."

His words made Eliza remember the callousness of another sentence Bruin had once said.

"I cannot stand the sound of a baby crying. Make him stop."

"He was a living reminder of our sins. He did not deserve parents like us." Bruin looked down, as if some shred of humanity had crept into his consciousness. Then his features hardened again. "And when she saw the blackness of my heart, she threw herself in. Some people think I joined them in death, and I let them believe I had taken my life, too. I stole the ship of Captain Snyde and made his crew my own. I changed my name, and then I returned to the West Indies.

"But the man I sought to kill, Charles, had left to fight the rebellion in America. The war kept us on separate paths. I even tried following him to Gibraltar, but my attempts were unsuccessful. I received my first letter of marque from the governor there. Still, I retained my hopes. I knew he hated New Providence; I knew he would never return. The house would be mine. I only had to get rid of his drunkard father. But then his duties abroad ended, and he came back with you. I would have calculated differently had I known that."

She had heard him utter those words before, nearly two years ago, the very first time she remembered encountering him, inside Pleasant Hall.

"Those fools think I threw myself into the canal, that I too drowned in the silt at the bottom. But I am a creature of it. I changed my name to *bruin*, brown, like the mud. I thrive in it," he said, delighting in the terror he saw in her face. "I made the name of my father my greatest secret. I should have been on that ship with him. I should have fought beside him in his final battle, but I was too busy following my own selfish desires. My father did not deserve an undignified end like that. He did not deserve to die alone."

His voice trembled with pain. The room grew more distorted the longer he spoke, and Eliza knew she was running out of time. She fought to stay alert, but it was a losing fight. The light and shadows shifted and flashed around her.

Bruin was staring at her. "Now you know all of me. Do you understand who I am now?"

He placed a hand on her knee, and her instincts of flight activated. She could not bear another second of his presence. When the back of the red-coated officer turned towards the door, she saw her only opportunity of escape about to leave. She ducked underneath the table, bypassing Bruin, and ran. She rushed across the flagstones riddled with spilt wine and half-chewed food. Fear increased her speed as she bumped wildly into other patrons, not stopping no matter how loudly they cursed her. Eliza reached her intended target and grabbed him by the arm, surprising the young man with the unexpected encounter.

"Please, officer, my husband is a Lieutenant Colonel in His Majesty's 47th Regiment, in the West Indies. I am looking for him. His name is Charles Sharpe. I am his wife, Eliza Sharpe. I have been kidnapped; I need to contact him. I must reach him or the authorities, please, sir, I beg of you; can you aid me? Please, I …"

But her brave speech was cut to a halt the minute she felt Bruin's pincher-like grip enclose around her. He seized her so violently she would have lost her balance were it not for his cruel hold.

"Excuse my sister, sir. She suffers from hysteria," Bruin lied. He moved in closer to the confused soldier. "Her husband is deceased, and she suffers most terribly from it. Please accept my apologies."

The officer cast a scrutinizing look, and she saw a look of repulsion cross his features. It was unsuccessful. Her bold risk would not pay off, and she knew she would be punished for even trying. She had finally mustered up the courage to escape, and she had miserably failed. She looked up at him, continuing to beg with the tears that came to her eyes, and then watched him leave. He had not said a word, but she had recognized the cold judgment on his face. The ground floor of the inn dissolved into a blur of noise and moving shapes, guided only by the force of Bruin steering her back into her seat.

Her chest heaved from her efforts. Bruin was not a man driven by reason but by the madness of revenge. After he shoved her back down the bench, he sat beside her, and she felt a new pressure in her side. Eliza looked down and saw his knife.

"Attempt something foolish like that again and you will pay for it," he growled in her ear.

"I am not afraid of death. Not anymore," she panted.

"But you are afraid of *me*. You know I can carve up your pretty little figure piece by piece. I do not need to kill you. At least not yet."

The pain ceased as suddenly as it had first started. She fought the urge to close her eyes, shifting her tense legs. Her mad dash had taken up the remnants of her strength, and now she was rapidly fading.

Someone stood before their table, peering down at them like they were a misbehaving unit, complicit in their indecent display.

"Good God, man. Control her. Why ever did you take her out of the house?"

Eliza's ears burned.

"Forgive the recent scene, sir. My wife has lost the baby, and she is unwell."

Bruin's capacity for lying never ceased to amaze her.

He was brazen, willing to change the details of their situation without warning. Understanding washed over the stranger. He nodded. "But one cannot tell the heart to forget," he countered.

"We tried bringing her to the seaside," Bruin explained.

The man smiled a toothless grin.

"Aye, me neighbor's wife suffered likewise. They put her up in one of those hospitals, say she's cured now. Either that or mute. I'd consider that a blessing in and of itself."

The men shared a comradely chuckle. Bruin bid him a good night. Eliza turned away, humiliated in more ways than one.

"It is so easy to fool people. It nearly steals the enjoyment out of the art. But not entirely. I will still enjoy this. Very much. You have fight left in you, but not for long."

She closed her eyes in an effort to stop the room from spinning. Eliza heard him laugh.

"You live and die by my rules alone now. It simply was not meant to be, dear Liza. That is the way life works."

She was fighting a wave, a dizzy, yet familiar contrast of sensations between a pull and push, a heightening and softening, a heady, confused rush of pressure. It was like a chasm had opened up beneath her, and she was suspended before it, waiting for a final blow to send her into blackness. Bruin took her hand, studying the scar in her palm that she had received after she had rescued Alastor from the stables fire. Part of her feared he had truly poisoned her, but another part of her feared what he planned on using her for tonight. He was a master of deception, whether it was the way he hid the vials he poured into her drinks or the knife that he concealed in his boot.

"You think you know about death. You do not know anything about death. You only think death is powerful because you do not know a thing about it," he whispered into her ear. She felt his cheek against hers; the lack of space between them made his words even more menacing. "Killing people is easier than breathing. It is easier than blowing out this candle, Liza. A flame one moment, nothing but smoke bleeding into air the next. There are a lot of men in here who can snap your neck like a twig. Death does not impress me. Breaking your defiant will, reducing you to nothing, *that* is what fascinates me …"

She opened her eyes. The room remained the same. It was as if no one saw her captor or the pallid fear in her face.

She swallowed, finding her voice; some new spark of fight ignited in her.

"You of all people should fear it. For you are going straight to Hell."

Bruin grabbed her chin, forcing her to face him. He kissed her then, his tongue colliding with hers.

"And I am taking you down with me," he breathed into her mouth.

Eliza started to shake, chills wracking her body.

"Shhh … be still," he whispered.

He bent her hair to his lips, pressing her with his false, hollow affection.

"Let us not speak of damnation. Not tonight. We both know that under the eyes of God I did no wrong. Murder is only wrong when you kill the innocent," he said, still holding her face. "You are lying to me, Liza. You are happy to be free of that man. His father was a monster, not unlike him. You never have to fear him again."

Tears crowded her eyes, and she hated that Bruin would likely interpret them as confirmation that she agreed with him. Bruin signaled for the porter to return to the table. She distantly wondered what he wanted to order now and questioned how long this evening could drag out. Bruin did not eat much food, and their drinks had already been replaced multiple times. Finally, a sweaty and overwhelmed porter shuffled over.

She was free of Bruin's proximity, and she leaned to the other side, struggling to hold on to her wakefulness.

"No rotten cattle, please," she heard Bruin's voice say.

Time dragged on at an uncomfortable pace, and Eliza felt the heaviness of sleep come over her. Then she heard a set of feminine voices.

"Ah, the oldest and most necessary evil of the world," Bruin laughed.

Eliza opened her eyes and saw two prostitutes crowding the table, their eyes dark with lack of sleep, their cheeks overly reddened with rouge. Then she was moving, away from the table, away from the loud room, up narrow and creaking stairs. She passed defaced portraits and stepped by overturned chamber pots in the hallway. Then they were in a room, the sheets on the bed already tousled. The maid had not had the time to change them for the next guest. Eliza hesitated to continue walking into the room when she saw that. But she was pushed into a chair, and the door was closed and locked behind her.

The women lavished praise on him, and the sounds of

their lips smacking against each other, with their perfectly timed and manufactured shrieks of delight nauseated Eliza.

"You make my cock stand …" Bruin said, squeezing the backside of the younger whore.

Small hands pulled at Eliza, pushing her onto the bed, but she was too far gone to protest.

"You have been too long at sea now, Captain. We will show you a good time," one of the women said.

Eliza felt hands pulling and tugging at her, but when her skirts were lifted, suddenly the noise in the room stopped. All she could hear was the pounding of her pulse in her ears, mixing with her long and shallow breaths.

"I'm not touching her. She's on her bleeding days. You'll need to pay more coin than that, sir!" one of them protested.

A scuffle ensued, and an argument broke out. There was the sound of a slap across unguarded skin and a scream, and then the women rushed out, leaving her alone and defenseless with her tormentor. It took her entire willpower to shift to her side, as if facing the wall could afford her protection. When time passed and she was no longer touched, she thought in the haze of her delirium that she had been spared. The wall's smooth surface was soothing to her, and she focused on it, allowing her fixation to disconnect her from reality.

But the return of his voice disturbed her. "They wanted double, and I refused to pay, so you are untouched. You are indeed lucky," he said, as he lay down beside her.

A rush of abject terror coursed from her stiffened body

to his eager limbs, as he lined himself along the trembling shape of hers. She could still feel his excitement from the prospects that had almost unfolded, firm against her lower back.

"I would have never done this to you if you had only agreed," Bruin said, his breath in her ear. "You are having a hard time keeping your eyes open. It is uncanny how strong sensations can be when we close our eyes. How much we can feel in the darkness …"

His hands cupped her breasts, pulling her in closer to him, wrapping his leg over hers.

"To feel you shake like this … the fruit is always sweeter when it is forbidden, Liza," he moaned, his breaths ragged. "Let me possess you."

She tried to scream, but no noise would come out. And then he stopped, with a violent pulse that shook her entire frame.

"I am not a good man. I have done many reprehensible things," he said, as a change came over his voice. Bruin pressed his face into hers, embracing her intensely, his movements bordering on the verge of taking her but restraining himself. Eliza prayed for it to stop. His hold over her was so tight, it made breathing even more difficult. She was immobile in his grip, beyond exhausted, and trapped. He inhaled sharply, an intake of breath that sounded more like a pained cry.

"You have saved us again. Thank you," he said, his voice shaking. He hugged her to him. "Tomorrow is a new day for us. A new start. You have suffered enough at the hands of the colonel. That is why he drove you to the Frenchman.

But I am here now, and I will never let you go, Liza."

His twisted sense of faith and sin had reigned in his darker urges. Bruin buttoned his breeches and returned to her, wrapping a hand around her torso and another up around her throat. Horror made her breaths shudder out of her body as a single tear ran down the curve of her cheek, wetting his hand.

"They say you should not covet the wife of another man. But you belong to no one now, I made sure of that. All that is left is me, and I cannot covet my own," he said, as he played with a lock of her hair. "But I will wait until we exchange our vows."

He was silent for a few moments longer, and she almost surrendered to sleep, unable to fight it any longer.

"Thank you for reminding me to rise higher than my temptations. Than what my carnal flesh desires. God has truly saved you for me."

His wet breath brushed across her neck. She wanted to rage against every terrible word that he said. Her spirit wanted to destroy him, but her body had been weakened beyond redemption. Tonight, she would sleep in his arms, entrapped in his hold, even though the thought turned her stomach. His sickening words devastated her; she knew she was ruined, filthy like the bed he held her down against.

Thunder rumbled overhead, and a few drunken jeers cheered at the disturbance downstairs. Death was waiting for Eliza, pursuing her in a chase that had begun all those months ago on the porch, when she had missed her mark. She should have hit him that night; his life should have ended in a rush of blood and force. Instead, he had taken her power away from her, breaking her down slowly until now, at the very end of her tolerance, she prayed for release, for the sudden peace that would come when he finally ended her.

CHAPTER XX.

Charles gazed at his reflection in the gilt mirror. The first time he had seen the way his appearance had changed had shocked him. He had not recognized himself. His cheekbones were more prominent, and he could not mask the fact that he had lost weight. His newly measured regimentals molded his body perfectly, but he could not shake the feeling that he had lost half the man he once was. Not knowing Eliza's fate had that effect on him. He was missing his other half, and no amount of time spent amongst society could restore true normalcy to him. Not until he held her in his arms again.

Yesterday, he had received the crushing news that Eliza was not waiting for him back at Pleasant Hall in the Bahamas. She had been taken against her will, kidnapped by the very man he now hunted. Her life was in danger, held captive by the same fiend who had once captured him. A pale sliver of sunlight broke through the heavy clouds, lighting specks of dust that floated in the quiet hallway. He prayed he would receive the answers he so desperately needed. He could waste no time.

A liveried servant strode up to him. "His Lordship will see you now," he intoned.

The servant led him through a massive carved wooden door, into an office study lined with leather-bound books and maps. Lord Malmesbury, a top diplomat and trusted advisor of William Pitt, the Prime Minister, sat at his massive desk. He seemed excited to meet with him.

"At ease, Colonel Sharpe, no need for such formalities between us," Lord Malmesbury said.

It was a symptom of etiquette, and nothing more. Charles could never truly be at ease until he rescued Eliza. He reluctantly sat in a leather chair, anxious for the news he was about to hear.

"And how did you find your journey to London?" the diplomat inquired.

"The winds were unpredictable and the water was rough, but we made good time. I confess I am not built for life aboard a ship."

Lord Malmesbury made a face of disbelief, not able to conceive how a man from the islands could not tolerate a seafaring life.

"And I hear congratulations are in order for your recent promotion, Colonel. I cannot think of a man who better deserves it, especially after the trials you've endured. How did your audience with His Majesty go yesterday?"

"Very well, I should think. It came as an honor and a surprise to me. His Majesty showed great interest in my story. He presented me with a very fine gold chain, and his spirits were delighted. His pleasantness of mood is no doubt owed to Admiral Lord Howe's recent victory over the French. The court is abuzz with it."

His recent promotion, a goal he had worked to attain all his life, as well as his private audience with the king himself, would have normally overjoyed Charles. But he found it all hollow and meaningless. Nothing mattered until he received confirmation that Eliza was safe. Every minute spent in London was another wasted as far as he was concerned, and the man before him could help end his stay at court and send him on his way. He doubted Lord Malmesbury understood the pivotal role he was about to play. With his insistence, the future of the Bahamas could change forever.

Unfortunately, he was more taken with Charles' most recent adventure.

"But you are a key figure in the story of British competence, as well. You remind us all of the possibilities of inner strength. My God, what you have survived … it is remarkable," Lord Malmesbury said with wide eyes. "Have any publishers approached you for your story? I confess I am highly interested in it, myself. I know a gentleman in the business. He would pay you a great deal for the rights."

Charles suppressed an internal groan. He had repeated his ordeal ad nauseam for so many courtiers. He was on edge and had no tolerance left any longer. He was there on urgent business. He wanted an update on Lord Dunmore's recall from the governorship of the Bahamas. His superiors in the military had suggested he meet with Lord Malmesbury because he had access to information that others were simply not privy to. In particular, he held extensive knowledge about Dutch affairs, and he had been tasked with sourcing information about Hiram Bruin. After what Charles had learned yesterday, nothing else mattered. He sought to obtain all the information he possibly could on the despicable pirate.

The diplomat continued, counting coins in his mind. "You should really consider authoring a pamphlet. I haven't seen such excitement like this since Lieutenant Bligh returned after surviving that mutiny. If you find the task too daunting, I could help you publish an account of your ventures. They are a sensation. We could commission plates of artwork and charge three shillings a piece!"

Charles exhaled and shifted his weight, not bothering to hide his displeasure.

"And the story of how you reunited with your young son only yesterday, here in London ... it is remarkable. That a slave, with no moral compass to guide him, would rescue the boy from the devilish grip of pirates and have the fortitude to bring him to the safety of England ..."

Indeed, the joy of seeing Philippe alive and well was shattered when Captain Johnson had conveyed the rest of his disastrous news. Charles had never suffered from such an intense crash of emotions. He had foolishly assumed that most of his problems had been taken care of, only to learn something that utterly broke his heart. But he did not want to share that information with this man. He stuck to the topic at hand.

"Captain Johnson is no slave. He is a free man. He was part of the Ethiopian Regiment during the rebellion in the American colonies, my lord. He has saved my life on a prior occasion."

"I can confess nothing but wonder at the whole sordid tale. My neighbor owns a plantation in Barbados. I doubt he would be able to cultivate such faith in his slaves as to entrust the very safety of his own offspring in their hands. What an exceptional being that man is."

The difference between a free man and an enslaved one was not registering with the diplomat.

"Yes, Captain Johnson is a remarkable man. I have recommended his promotion to the position of Major. He is owed nothing less," Charles said tersely.

"Ah, the bonds of fraternity. What a gift one can harvest from the dark times of war. One might say the obstacles you faced were insurmountable, but yet here you are," Lord Malmesbury said with pride in his voice.

His flattery fell flat for Charles. He sighed.

"I am anxious to discuss other matters. Lord Dunmore's recall and what information you were able to obtain on Hiram Bruin for a start."

He looked at Lord Malmesbury and feared he had spoken too rashly. But he also knew that diplomats could oftentimes talk the ear off anyone who was willing to listen. His recent days had taught him the value of not wasting time. Lord Malmesbury's beady eyes surveyed Charles for a moment, then his face regained a more serious disposition. The man clearly wanted to be regaled with tales of pirates and brutality on the high seas, not be bogged down with administrative work.

"Yes, yes of course," the diplomat said, gathering a stack of papers. "I have good and bad news in that regard. I will start with the good."

Charles readjusted himself in his seat, positioning himself at the very edge of it.

"This situation with the Earl of Dunmore is a rather tricky proposition. He certainly has no friends in Westminster, especially after the fiasco in the former Virginia Colony. But he does have a trusted ally in the figure of Mr. Henry Dundas, a man many informally regard around here as 'The Uncrowned King of Scotland.' He wields a great deal of power. The prime minister is loath to get rid of him."

"Lord Dunmore views himself as an island king. I see they operate in a similar manner."

"Indeed. However, Dundas is due to leave his office as Home Secretary next month, with the Duke of Portland to take over his tenure. The Duke of Portland and the Earl of Dunmore have had a longstanding feud; it is no mere disagreement in politics. I believe he will be more sympathetic to the colony's petitions. And then there is the issue of Lord Dunmore's foolish progeny."

"Progeny, my lord?" Charles asked.

Lord Malmesbury raised his eyebrows in question. "Of course, you are not informed of all the scandals at court. At the end of last year, Lord Dunmore's daughter, Lady Augusta Murray, married Prince Augustus, in secret and without the consent of the king. It caused quite an uproar. Their annulment should be finalized any week now. It would seem the greed of that family knows no bounds. It may prove the key to Lord Dunmore's undoing. And with the Duke of Portland's new appointment, I believe we are in good hands."

"What else do you expect from the Whigs?" Charles scoffed.

"That faction is certainly fragmenting. The war with France has changed things here at home. Lord Grenville, the Foreign Secretary, accomplished much in his outline of Lord Dunmore's crimes. He has quite the nose for sniffing out corruption. We have been able to use the evidence he and his men gathered back in 1791, before the troubles with France erupted."

Charles knew he spoke of Jean, who had secretly worked for Lord Grenville before he was executed. Affairs on the small island of New Providence had a way of trickling across the waters of the empire.

The diplomat smiled slyly at him. "I think you would suffer no other governor but yourself, Charles. I can recognize the ambition in you."

The thought disgusted Charles. He only wanted to salvage the pieces of his own life. He chased after peace, not power. He pictured Eliza strolling along the beach, the glint of the sun making the waves sparkle. He yearned to return to that. He needed to save her.

"You confuse ambition for obligation, my lord. It is every man's obligation to destroy the tyrants in his life, and those who would profit from their abuse."

"But surely you know as well as I that you could become a king there. Do you not seek the position?"

"No, I am hardly fit for it. In station and in heart. I only seek to return to my home and the love of my wife and son."

Charles did not want to disclose Eliza's fate to this stranger. He feared he would lose all sense of self-control. He kept it close to his chest, eagerly waiting for the man to finish telling him what he had found out.

"But surely that would be a waste of your talents. A man with your acumen and strategic mind, your knowledge of the islands, your penchant for military thinking. Do you realize how rare it is to find a man of your caliber, native to the West Indies? You even have the support of your people, the Conchs! I have seen their letters myself."

"I am only interested in the recall of Lord Dunmore."

"There is an extraordinary opportunity here. I would highly recommend you to His Majesty. You could sail back to Nassau with the order in your hands. It is not Lord Dunmore's cause you have been called to defend but your country's."

"Indeed, I uphold nothing but my country's honor and the downfall of those who would squander it."

Lord Malmesbury sensed he had made no progress with his political aspirations. Some men could not be persuaded with appointments to office. The colonel clearly belonged to that rare set of men.

"That is precisely what we try to cultivate in young men's minds. Your father did a remarkable job with you."

"Indeed, he taught me my greatest lessons," Charles responded with dark irony.

Lord Malmesbury started going off on a tangent about how unbearable the weather was and how this summer portended to be the hottest on record. He did not seem to care that Charles, habituated in the tropics, found little to be impressed with. Charles decided to cut him off and return to the topic at hand. He had run out of patience and did not care how upset he sounded.

"And the warrants for Joseph Jennings and Hiram Bruin? Have you prepared those?"

"The Jennings fellow, yes, that was no great matter. I have it prepared and ready to go. But I have nothing in regards to this Hiram Bruin."

"Nothing, sir? What do you mean?"

"I mean, I cannot find anything on the man. He is like a ghost. There is no record of him, and I cannot make a warrant for a man that does not exist."

Anger flared up in Charles. The pressure of his desperation was too much; he was on the verge of disclosing his secret. But he held back, retaining his composure.

"Nonsense. The man received a pardon from Lord Dunmore himself. He is a privateer with a dubious past. Surely, there is a record of the royal pardon. Some would posit that he is Lord Dunmore's right-hand man."

Lord Malmesbury shook his head and sighed.

"I could not find a single record. It would appear that the pardon was not real, if he indeed ever received one. I have even inquired with acquaintances of mine from when I worked as an envoy in the Hague. They are no strangers to matters of Dutch politics, and the name Bruin holds no significance to them."

Charles' face turned red with fury. The diplomat quickly finished speaking.

"But I did find something of interest. Do you recall a man named Jacob Beaks? A sea captain?"

"The name does not signify."

"I would think it should. He was your first arrest when you were, I believe, nineteen years old. He was a pirate, captain of a ship that hailed from St. Eustatius back in early 1775."

"Yes, I recall the incident, although I do not much recall the man. The West Indies is teeming with pirates. They are, for the most part, unremarkable."

"I believe you are very familiar with his son," Lord Malmesbury suggested.

"His son? I had a few brief moments of interaction with him when I captured him. I do not recall any relation being present. What does this have to do with the topic at hand?"

Charles stamped his boot and leaned forward, not caring if he intimidated the diplomat.

"His son is Hiram Beaks. And we have deduced that this is indeed the very same Hiram Bruin that you seek."

Horror washed over Charles as he finally realized the depths of their complicated association. There was a history between them, one he had never fully realized.

"This captain, Hiram Beaks, is a wanted man. He has been an outlaw for over three decades. I can tell you that he is already wanted for crimes of piracy, kidnapping, murder, and robbery on the high seas. His father hailed from the island of Saba, and St. Eustatius, a neighboring island, employed his services.

"It is very common for the islanders there to undertake joint enterprises. They have a close partnership. The pirates of these islands steal ships and divide the spoils between the two colonies. Transshipping and laundering prize ships are the only industries Saba knows. Their carpenters repaint and rename any captured vessels, and then they sell the disguised ships to the island of St. Thomas and sometimes St. Bartholomew. The governors of Saba and Statia receive no wages, only what plunder their pirates can bring them. It is a crooked affair."

"I oftentimes gambled with him, but Captain Bruin never shared his confidences with me. I only knew that he was a privateer with an official letter of marque from the king. Although, learning that I did not even know his true name, makes me doubt the little knowledge I do understand of him," Charles replied. "He is a mystery to me now."

His mind raced back to the many conversations he had shared with him over cards, the intensity of his calculating glances only registering now. Bruin had planned this for years, patiently waiting for the right opportunity to strike. It was more than a mere grudge—it was vengeance fueled by blood lust. Bruin had ingratiated himself with the corrupt governor not in order to save his own hide, but to encourage the enmity between Charles and Lord Dunmore, in order to help take him down.

How had the man sat there, ball after ball, casually engaging in meaningless conversations with Charles, the very man who had captured his father and sent him to the gallows? When his father's ship had docked in Nassau harbor to sell its looted goods, Charles had never applied much thought to it. Jacob Beaks had been a criminal; he had broken laws, laws Charles was bound to uphold. The only significance the event had held for him was confirmation that he was indeed useful and necessary to the army. But after all these years, a shadow had latched itself on to him, and now it threatened to take more than just his life.

As he listened to Lord Malmesbury, it became clear that his capture in Nassau was not a singular event. Bruin was like a spider, weaving a complicated web that had taken years to construct. The depths of his powers of deception chilled Charles. Bruin was no ordinary criminal. He was cunning, and he was overwhelmingly patient. And now he had taken his wife. Where else would his need for revenge take him?

Lord Malmesbury shuffled a stack of papers and applied spectacles to the bridge of his nose.

"My confidents in the Hague reported that he has been on the run since 1764, after he murdered his employer, a certain Captain Snyde of Amsterdam. He kidnapped his widow, who was later found drowned in a canal. A weight had been tied to her ankles. There were reports that a baby was also drowned, but my leads on that are less conclusive. He then stole Snyde's ship and his crew and went by various false names, including Breakes and variations of his given name."

Lord Malmesbury reordered the pages in front of him. "There are some gruesome accounts regarding the ingenious ways he murdered the entire crew of a Chilean vessel called the *Acapulco* in order to plunder its cargo of gold bars. I do not recommend reading them. You would lose your appetite." Lord Malmesbury cleared his throat, pausing before he continued. He looked at Charles square in the eye.

"And worse, there are other documented instances of what he did to a convent off the coast of Minorca, in Spain. He harbors a particular hatred for Catholics, it would seem. They stole all the valuables from the premises, including some fine oil paintings. When the subsequent ravage of the nuns was about to occur, he took it upon himself to officiate in a grand matrimony ceremony, so the souls of his crew would remain clear from damnation. They then dragged the women on board with them, and they were never seen again."

Charles listened to every word, his hatred for the man only increasing by the second. He gritted his teeth. The depths of his crimes sickened him.

"Surely, you have prepared an arrest warrant for Hiram *Beaks* then?"

"Yes, but it is no simple matter. I received word that he has recently attacked two Spanish merchantmen. He has now taken two young girls hostage, but he made a dreadful mistake with that Cuban sloop. They were the nieces of the governor of Havana. Spanish authorities are on high alert for him. We believe the girls to be murdered. They are still at this moment searching for the young ladies … but if his past conduct is any indicator of his behavior, I would deem it a lost cause."

Charles looked down, fearing the worst for the two girls. But he was truly terrified about Eliza's prospects. Was she still with him? Had she already been killed?

"His cruelty and barbarity know no bounds, it would seem," he said quietly.

He bit his lower lip and looked out the window, using all of his strength to keep from crying. He felt helpless. The Atlantic Ocean was too large a body of water. Bruin could hide for years and escape from any justice.

Lord Malmesbury sensed something was deeply upsetting Charles, but he continued, his voice wary.

"There is something else you should know. A ship with counterfeit papers recently made berth at Portsmouth Harbor, and the captain fled before he could be questioned further. When customs agents inspected the ship's cargo, it was clear that the goods were stolen. And Spanish in origin."

"Portsmouth? When did this occur?"

So Bruin was in England now. Charles' plans began to readjust in his mind. He gripped the arms of the chair, feeling a fresh stirring of hope.

"Two days ago. And what's more, an officer in Medstead reported a strange encounter. A woman of Spanish descent accosted him, pleading for help. A man claiming to be her brother quickly regained control of her, only it was clear to the officer that the two held no familial bonds. She had a deep scar on the palm of her hand. He reported it to his superiors, who then reported it to us. There have been escalating incidents of gypsies reported in the area, and he did not like the attitude of this man. He was clearly foreign and not English."

"Perhaps it was indeed Bruin with one of the missing kidnapped girls? It would seem one has survived."

Charles indeed prayed that someone had survived Bruin's captivity. It meant that Eliza still had a fighting chance as well. Bruin had left a bloody trail in his ship's wake, and he hoped that the blood was not his wife's.

"I do not think so. She was older, in her twenties. The officer mentioned that she claimed to be called Elizabeth, although after a night of carousing, the details of her full name are unclear. We cannot figure out what this man is plotting. What would draw a pirate from the sea?"

Charles turned pale. He immediately knew that he spoke of Eliza. He could see how she could easily be mistaken for having Spanish heritage. The wheels began to turn in his head, coupled with the new information he had just received. A plan formed in his mind.

He stood up with a gasp.

"What is it?" Lord Malmesbury demanded.

"He has my wife, my lord," Charles said slowly, the words devastating to his own ears.

"Isn't she back in Nassau? Thousands of miles away?"

"I was told by Captain Johnson only yesterday that Bruin, I mean ... Beaks ... had indeed stolen her from the house. I have told no one else. That description is of my wife; I can have no doubt. Down to the very scar in the palm of her hand."

Lord Malmesbury looked unconvinced, but he did not care. Charles knew in his heart that the other soldier had encountered Eliza. She was indeed alive, but only if he moved quickly.

"Good God," the diplomat said quietly. "But why would he abandon his ship and travel inland?" he asked, confusion furrowing his brow.

But Charles had an answer for that query too. It rocked

him to his core, and despite his urge to act, his heart still sank.

"He seeks a greater treasure. And I believe I know what he is after. My aunt has a seat in Hampshire, outside of Basingstoke. She is an old dowager widow who lives alone. I believe—I must, I must go …"

Charles turned to leave, nearly knocking his chair down. He retreated to a dark interior place he had prepared for himself on the prison ship long ago. It had helped him survive the harrowing past weeks. He readied himself to brace for the worst. His wife's precious life was in a monster's hands, and he would not stop until that monster was slain, damned warrant issued or not.

Lord Malmesbury also rose to a stand. "To heavens! That is a two-day journey by horse, in this heat—"

"It is no heat to me. I was the fastest horseman in the Legion; only give me the steed and I can make it," Charles said, standing solidly, his shoulders pulled back tight.

Lord Malmesbury fumbled to ring the bell for his servant. The liveried servant rushed back into the room, cognizant that something terrible had occurred.

"A horse, the fastest one we have, at the ready. Now! Run if you have to!" the diplomat ordered.

"Thank you, I am indebted to you," Charles said in a low tone.

The servant took off running down the hall, with Charles following behind him.

Lord Malmesbury slowly sat back down, his hands outstretched in delighted shock. It had all happened so quickly. He was thrilled by the prospect of playing a role in the colonel's latest adventure. Surely he could tell the tabloids what had occurred. This was now his story.

But there was more he needed to do. He had to tell his superiors to formally issue the warrant for Hiram Beaks' arrest, now that his identity had indeed been confirmed. He could notify the local regiment at Basingstoke to be prepared to assist in the pirate's capture. He believed the garrison for Hampshire was located in Winchester, but he would need to check. He had important letters to write, important letters that could save lives.

Lord Malmesbury wondered if his missives or the gallant man on horseback would reach Basingstoke first. He heard the echo of hooves out in the courtyard now. Lord Malmesbury rushed to the window, giddy with adrenaline.

"My horse, yes, yes, I gave the man one of my horses. And how he galloped out the gate to save his bride! Godspeed, Colonel Sharpe!" he said, as he watched Charles disappear.

But then the full realization of what the colonel's mad dash meant settled over him. He looked back at his desk, strewn with reports of Hiram Beaks' terrible misdeeds. His hands grazed over the bloody exploits, one more horrible than the next. This was not some fantastic play in the Theatre Royal on Drury Lane. It was real, and the man Charles chased after was not fit to walk free amongst society. He was deranged, violent, and showed little mercy for women.

He felt a tinge of shame and regret that he had so easily been excited at someone else's misfortune. No matter how fast Charles pushed that poor animal, he doubted he could recover her. Lady Sharpe would become the latest victim of the Dutch pirate. And that was a headline he did not want to see.

CHAPTER XXI.

The yellow post-chaise carried them through the rolling green velvet hills of Hampshire, over the flowing chalk streams, and deeper into the English countryside with every passing hour. It drove through a sleepy village with its carts of produce for sale and a lone herder with his flock of sheep. Eliza's ears perked up with the sound of a familiar noise. She heard the rhythmic march of a drumbeat and the sharp pitch of a fife, and she spotted a red-coated regiment gathering into formation. She raised her fingers to the window, immediately thinking of Charles. She had never chased after regimentals like her sisters, but now she understood the allure just the same. The soldiers represented order and protection; they kept watch over the thatch-roofed town. The music stirred some deep emotion in her and sharpened the pain she felt over Charles' absence. She had never reacted in such a way to the sight, but now that she had suffered a loss like this, her heart ached.

Bruin studied her with scrutiny.

"I hate this place. It is filthy, and yet you English think

you are better than me," Bruin scoffed, settling further back into the seat as they passed the regiment. "You should see the beauty of the Dutch countryside."

"What would you know of it? You come from Saba."

"Yes. We could have had a pleasant life together under The Mountain. But you are too difficult to satisfy."

Bruin planned on evading capture, oblivious to the destruction he had caused to bring them to this point. Eliza's thoughts wandered back to the two Spanish girls.

"You think too highly of yourself. There are thousands of ships in the sea. Do you really think your actions have gone unnoticed, not once, but twice now? Word will eventually reach the governor of Havana. The authorities in Portsmouth will surely suspect something."

"A false name and a bag of gold can do wonders, Liza," he replied, his lips curved upwards. "I would know."

They rolled past a stone church where small children played a silly game between the tilted tombstones. Those days of innocence seemed so far gone now.

"Why have you wandered so far from God? It would have been better to suffer than to have sinned as you have done," she said, her eyes focused on the scene outside, her mind drawn away from that current day.

"Beloved, never avenge yourselves, but leave it to the wrath of God," Bruin answered, his gaze running over her. "For it is written, 'Vengeance is mine, I will repay,' …" He began to play with a strand of her hair, twirling it between his tanned fingers. "I have not wandered as you have, Liza," he said slowly. "I am His wrath."

Eliza's breath shortened. Something was missing deep

within Bruin. His cruelty offered one unexpected benefit: for once, she did not have to fear the presence of highwaymen. She looked down at his two loaded pistols. He also carried an unknown number of hidden blades. For the first time in her recollection, she prayed for some violent intervention.

All that was delivered was an unexpected bump in the road. It sent her colliding into him.

Bruin grinned at their newfound proximity. "I always enjoy watching bruises turn. It is like a flower opening. Will it continue to be more violet, or will it go straight to yellow? This one is doing nicely. I think they refine the beauty of a woman."

His fingertips grazed the mark he had left on her. Eliza turned away, leaning towards the window and the pastoral distractions it offered. She began to count the wildflowers, painfully aware that he was still staring at her. She entertained wild delusions of rushing outside the rumbling carriage and bounding through the meadows, sure that if given the chance, she could escape him. But then the hilt of his pistol rubbed against her hip, bringing her fantasy to a sudden end.

The road curved and entered a tree-lined avenue, and soon a great, red-bricked edifice loomed on the horizon. There was a classical portico with Grecian columns in the front, and the sides were surrounded by a wall of venerable elms. A spacious pastureland dotted with horses sat off to the side; this was indeed Sharpe property. Bruin leaned forward with anxious excitement, surveying the property as if his name was already on the deed.

A new fear tightened in her throat. Soon this drama would not simply exist in the crowded, humid space of the carriage. They would involve a third person, an innocent bystander, and Eliza was powerless to stop it.

"You are to remain silent and only speak if the elder Lady Sharpe addresses you. If you try to warn her of my designs or if you try to run, I will kill her. I do not think you want to be responsible for the death of an old woman." Bruin began to preen himself, adjusting his jacket and his hair.

"Why don't you just kill me and be done with it all?" Eliza muttered, not caring if such a statement angered him.

She knew the reason why. Bruin needed her alive so he could perfect his story. Philippe was the latest link in the Sharpe inheritance, and since the boy was not here, Eliza would serve as the closest tangible reminder. But there was something more unsettling behind his machinations—Bruin's fascination with her. His unflinching preoccupation bordering on unstoppable fixation. The way he sought to control every aspect of her was feral, and the more defiance she showed, the tighter his hold became over her.

"I await the day I'll see your decaying body swinging along the banks of the Thames. You deserve nothing less than to be gibbeted in the water until your bones break apart," she said, feeling emboldened as the post-chaise drew up to the entrance of the grand house.

Her despicable words had little effect on him. He was on the verge of seizing the greatest prize in his life, more so than any rotten ship or glittering jewel. He took her hand and kissed it.

"Come now, Liza, the life of your son will depend upon your performance. Do not forget it," Bruin said with malice and a smirk.

"To heavens that something like this could occur, under the nose of the Royal Navy no less!" Lady Adelaide Sharpe barked out.

Eliza's trance ended with the interruption of her shrill voice, and she was at once brought back to the dinner table where they had gathered an hour after their arrival. It was a lavish mahogany piece with carved lion's feet, laid out with hand-painted yellow and white china, dripping with freshly polished silver. But Eliza saw little that impressed her. Her new opulent surroundings only made her feel sad.

The old woman continued. "You are fortunate the ruffians did not break your nose, Lady Sharpe. I always say that a woman's appearance is her crowning glory. What a terrible ordeal."

"Indeed, I feared her life was in danger had not my men and I interrupted the scene," Bruin said. "Through great lengths and even greater effort, I have delivered her to you. The tropics present more than one kind of danger."

He had altered his voice into a softer, slower version of its usual self. It disturbed Eliza, but the poor woman had no other conceptions of him. She watched the candle closest to her drip, burning down as her dread increased. A genteel gold clock gonged for the hour with a diminutive chime. Eliza looked down at her beef escarlot with disgust. Her hunger evaded her.

"We owe you and your crew a great deal, Captain Browne," Lady Adelaide Sharpe said.

It felt strange to return to England, even more so now that Eliza was firmly lodged in the kind of setting she was most familiar with: an aristocratic house. Built in the early 1500's and refashioned into a mansion suitable for living in the 18th century, Grenewood Hall still retained much of its Gothic airs. She learned that the Tudor estate was comprised of five hundred and forty-seven acres of land, a rich meadow suitable for grazing the thoroughbreds kept on the property, and a vast woodland. A handful of tenant farmers operated to the north and west of the house.

As Bruin and she had entered through the portico, they had stepped into a grand entrance hall with plasterwork like icing, and turquoise runners on the dark wooden stairs. The structure was old but had been furnished with the utmost care and latest stylings. There were innumerable, nameless rooms, with high ceilings and hand-painted chinoiserie wallpaper imported from the Orient. Every space Eliza passed shimmered with crystal glass, touches of gold and silver, and massive gilt furniture studded with striped cushions. The house was a study between antiquity and comfort, and now Bruin sought to fool the dowager widow who occupied it. His scheming eyes eagerly took in his surroundings, deducing every *objet d'arte's* worth with furtive glances.

"As I have already mentioned, I believe the best course of action is to prepare new paperwork, a remainder which ensures that this estate will go to your grandnephew, little Philippe, on maturity, with a provision that the young Lady Sharpe will serve as a regent should that time arrive sooner."

"I would have liked to meet my grandnephew," the elder Lady Sharpe said, her small voice saddened.

She looked up at Eliza with a melancholy smile. Eliza did as Bruin bid her and hardly said a word. She did not care to follow his instructions for her own sake, but for the poor woman who seemed so excited to greet a new member into her family.

"Yes, but his constitution is so frail after his troubles, we feared a second journey," Bruin replied in his new voice. "Lady Sharpe wants nothing but to go back to the child. She is a natural mother. I encouraged her to stop here first. We must tend to legal affairs and ensure the security of the future of the boy. Life is very precarious, but this is the world we find ourselves in."

"Many people do not tend to think of such matters until it is too late. I confess I did not even know I had a new heir. I do love children; I have lost all of mine to sickness."

Bruin pretended to be distressed by her words. He bowed his head.

"It is a familiar story to my ears. I have worked with great houses before. I so hate to see estates like this slip into decay. The history that is present in these walls … it deserves to be tended to. It reminds me of a certain house I know in Amsterdam."

His eyes cast a look up at a massive oil painting that hung on the blue damask wall, the gold-leaf frame that held it valuable in and of itself.

"You must seek a reward for your heroic efforts, Captain Browne," the old woman said. "And for your crew. You could have been injured!"

"My honor is to witness her here, breathing at this table. That is reward enough," he reassured her.

It took all of Eliza's willpower to not roll her eyes as she listened to the fraud who sat next to her. She looked at the old woman, trying to impart some silent warning to her, wishing that they had never crossed paths.

"At least you are sensible, Eliza. I see you have not donned this new, hideous fashion. I speak of the new muslin dresses, of course. I hardly know the point of wearing something so revealing. I saw the Lady Hatfield the other day, and she looked a picture out of ancient Greece. Like she was wearing only a chemise and nothing more!"

Eliza looked down at the pineapple dessert the servant had just placed before her. She was starting to hate pineapple. In her experience, nothing good ever came from eating it: she thought of when she had first landed in Nassau and learned of Charles' former opinions on slavery, or when she had drunk a small cup of its juice and then succumbed to yellow fever. No, nothing good ever happened from eating that fruit. The elderly Lady Sharpe seemed quite pleased with herself; it was produce from her hot house, and she acted as if the Caribbean treat was also exotic to Eliza.

She sighed. It was clear the woman understood nothing about the Bahamas. Charles' aunt continued complaining about the latest whims of fashion.

"You could see the girl's garters, the fabric was so sheer! I wager the stable boys appreciate this trend if no one else does," she continued. "This is not ancient times!"

Eliza smiled, still saying nothing. She poked at her fruit, playing with it on the plate. A servant approached her side again and left her a dainty crystal glass of cherry brandy. This she took, fully confident Bruin had not tainted it, and downed it. Then she remembered herself. She needed to act more demure in front of her newly acquainted relative. She needed to demonstrate propriety, even if such decency had long left her.

Bruin started a discourse on Eliza's many sensible charms as a highborn woman, making extra emphasis on her virtue that these pretend ruffians nearly stole. Bruin was no savior; he had accomplished the feat himself.

"But it is strange you are not wearing black mourning for Charles," the old woman interjected.

Eliza was not prepared for her pointed remarks. The combination of her surprise and the brandy that burned down her gut hit her like a rogue wave. She was so very tired of hoping and praying that Charles was still alive, somewhere out there in the vast world. Hearing his aunt's cold remark only reminded her of the impossibility of it all. That newspaper in the carriage, with the possibility that its half-read headline had contained, the very one that had haunted Bruin, seemed less convincing now in the face of such overpowering worries.

"I was only able to flee with the clothing on my back," she spurted out, her voice breaking.

She felt tears run down her cheeks, and she looked off to the side, studying the intricate swirls of the woven carpet.

"My dear girl!" the old woman exclaimed. She signaled to a liveried servant who stood sentry along the back wall, and he pulled her chair out for her. Before Eliza could stop her, she shuffled over, pressing her wrinkled, leathery hand on top of her own. This only made Eliza cry more. It was with the most unfortunate timing that the weight of her terrible fate crushed her now, pulverizing the last remnants of her restraint to dust.

She gasped for a breath. "I do not even have my wedding band," she continued.

The old woman looked horrified at the scandal that had occurred.

"The loss of a husband like my nephew is not easily borne," the elder Lady Sharpe counseled.

Eliza shook her head. But when she looked up again, the monster in the room was watching her, in awe of her dramatic performance. Now a burning hatred for him consumed her. It was all going to plan. This is exactly what he had wanted from both of them; Eliza was to play the traumatized victim, while the aunt was to bestow her tender sympathies on her. She wanted to shout out that he was the true enemy, that this was indeed all his own wicked doing. Eliza broke away from his gaze before those words could leave her mouth. She feared for the old woman's safety; she was vulnerable, and she was overwhelmingly kind. Bruin could destroy her without a second thought. Her liver-spot-covered hands still held her, and then she touched the emerald-studded pendant at her neck.

"What a lovely piece this is," she said, trying to compliment a sobbing Eliza.

"Thank you," she replied in a low whisper.

She dared not explain its provenance.

"When these Sharpe men depart this world, they tend to leave great holes behind. I would know," the elder Lady Sharpe said softly. "They say grieving grows easier with time, but that is a lie. Jones, another brandy for her, at once!"

She left her side, returning to her seat with her jagged steps. Eliza tried to steady her breaths. She did not want to belong to the club of widowhood. She did not want to grieve for her husband. Not here, not like this. She focused on Philippe, on remaining strong for her boy. There was something disarming about sharing another woman's presence, a sensation she had not felt for a long time. She would need to ensure her guard was up, or she feared her tears would not stop flowing the next time.

"Perhaps I was too harsh on the boy when he was growing up, but I wanted so much more for him than that miserable rock of an island," the elderly matriarch said.

"Nassau is a beautiful place, Lady Sharpe," Eliza countered, finding it as natural to defend her beloved island as breathing.

The aunt smiled. "Ah, I am glad he found a companion like you to match him. My wish for him was to go into politics or to take a home post, not act as some traveling mercenary. But he wanted to see the world." She sighed, her eyes wistful and filled with the past.

Eliza's tears started afresh. She remembered a conversation she had shared with Charles, one of the very first they had ever exchanged. She was back on the iron bench at Bleinhill Manor, giddy from chasing the Polyphemus moth.

"I, myself, have no inclination to marry. But it begs curiosity …. What would a lady like yourself have a mind to pursue?" Charles had asked her.

She blushed, confused by his sudden interest in her. Perhaps he found her lack of ostentation amusing.

"I'd like to study more. And read. As well as travel."

"To the Continent?"

"The world."

How perfectly similar they had once been, and what a precious match to lose. She had squandered it, without ever fully realizing its potential, and now it was too late. The second glass of cherry brandy seemed to mock her. It was empty, like her heart.

"I am sorry. I upset you again," Charles' aunt said.

"It is a brutal world filled with brutal men, Lady Sharpe. I would know," Bruin said to the dowager widow. The look of false compassion he displayed towards Eliza sickened her. "Heaven itself shed a tear when he breathed his last. The men of the island implored him to take the governorship, if you can believe it."

Bruin continued to regale the aunt with Charles' exploits, blending fiction with fact in a way that was nearly undetectable and so signature to his manner of speaking, with its rhythmic ups and downs. Eliza studied the sterling silver cutlery that remained on the table. On the handle of the knife, she saw an engraved "S" inside a shield, a family crest. *Sharpe.* She had no wedding band, nor proof of their union, but Charles had given her his last name. With the boldness of drink, and when she knew no one was looking, she swiped the knife from the table and shoved it inside her dress pocket. Its heaviness was a comfort to her; it felt like it belonged in her possession. The weight pulled the fabric of her dress down, but it reassured her.

"Your nephew may be dead, but his son still lives … this is the best you can do for his future," Bruin was saying to the elder Lady Sharpe. He was focused on nothing but convincing the dowager to prepare those papers as soon as possible. "I think you can understand that."

There was more to Bruin's design against Charles; it was against the entire name of Sharpe. Eliza's ears burned, and she began to doubt whether or not the servants had noticed her theft. The spot where the knife had once stood looked glaringly empty now.

Eliza stood up, excusing herself for the night, her cheeks still damp from crying. No one questioned her, and a servant brought her past a long gallery encased in glass windows, up the elaborate staircase, and to her private bedchamber. When the door closed behind her, she locked it and slumped against its frame, exhaling a tense breath she had kept inside for far too long. She had assumed her heart had hardened, as if it had corroded from the same salt water she had crossed to reach these shores, but the truth was that her wound was still very raw. There was a gaping hole in her, and the time she spent in his family's home only exacerbated it. These hallowed walls and the stories of his aunt displayed a side of her husband that she had never known, but it was all too late. And a night of miserable solitude was just beginning. She knew sleep would not come because her mind could not will it. The prospects of tomorrow haunted her.

The slosh of her bath water echoed in the room. It was past midnight, and the great house had settled into a quiet so impenetrable it unnerved her. Eliza was used to noises: the rocking of a ship's hull, the creak of wood, the rumble of carriage wheels on a bumpy road. Her room, although decorated handsomely, unsettled her. It was too large and empty, its shadows unfamiliar to her despite the many lighted candles that flickered and bent in the draft.

She hugged her knees to her chest under the water. A tall looking-glass faced the porcelain tub, a luxury she had not experienced since she had left Bleinhill Manor three years ago, and a dozen wide towels crowded a small cabinet. A multitude of colorful glass bottles stood on a curved table, offering everything a discerning lady could possibly need. Eliza wondered how often the elder Lady Sharpe entertained guests; it seemed no expense had been spared to ensure her comfort during her unexpected stay. A cheerful fire burned behind a polished steel grate; the early summer nights in Hampshire were still chilly. But despite the luxuries that surrounded her, she fought against a surge of darkness. It all meant nothing to her.

Bruin would deceive this gentle old woman, and then he would abscond with Eliza, dragging her over the Scottish border. They would elope, and then everything that had once belonged to the name of Sharpe would become his. Charles' life had never been enough; Bruin would take it all. He had acted like a perfect gentleman tonight, with his formal address and the careful distance he had maintained. For once, the word "Liza" had not left his lips, and he had not touched her, even when she had broken down in tears. It was all a delicately crafted deception. Bruin was a master of lies.

Eliza looked at her reflection, her right eye darkened with a bruise. But she was puzzled when she noticed inflamed welts trailing along her neck. The marks led down to her shoulder, and with horror, she realized what they signified, that at some point his teeth had sucked her skin. She did not recall the act, and a broken cry escaped her lips. She began to scrub her skin, tearing at her flesh with her nails. Eliza could still feel him on her; his past touch made her feel dirty, like a lingering filth the rose-scented bath water could not soothe away. She studied the rest of her arms, noticing for the first time the thin white scars from the splinters that had cut her when the *Fortuyne* had fought the Spanish ship.

Her body was no longer her own; it was no wonder her mind struggled so hard to fight his smooth voice in her head. The way she had felt last night infested her; his lingering fingerprints, both darkened and unseen, seeped deeply into her pores like an unwanted invasion that laced throughout her blood. Eliza still felt trapped even though she was finally alone; this juxtaposition rocked her body, and she began to sob. She had taken a bath because she was so tired she could not sleep, and she had wanted to wash away the mud and exhaustion of her forced journey. But then she realized that she could not wash away what tortured her the most.

She could not break free from the prison he had constructed over her mind. She could not stop the panic that bubbled up her chest, only understanding once she had secured this precious solitude how she could truly feel the effect his blackness had on her. It was loud, jarring, like the buzz of the silence in her empty room. It was like he was taking over her again. She was broken and defeated, and only in the uncomfortable stillness of night could she finally acknowledge it.

This was no way to live. Eliza tried to reassure herself, to force herself to make peace with the things she could not change, but she could not soothe the memory of the crippling, dark nights she had endured at his hands. Her present was uncertain, but a single image of the future had fueled her this entire time. Without Charles, she knew she had no future to cling to. Pangs of regret stabbed her. She spent her days at the side of a selfish man, and it was clearly rubbing off on her. She still had a child to protect, to live for. Then a certain numbness settled over her, and the tears dried up.

"Dum spiro, spero." While I breathe, I hope …

She forced her breaths to grow steady, elongated, controlled. She lay on her back, feeling the reassuring brush of the lukewarm water rise and fall on her chest. And when she had regained a shallow peace over the raging torrent of her emotions, she climbed out of the tub, toweling herself dry.

Without warning, the cruel silence was broken by a low, pitched whistle, a wavering song, precise like the sound of a bird at dawn, clear and decisive in the horror it brought to her. She stumbled to the edge of the wall, peering fully into her once-empty room.

"Why are you crying?" Bruin's voice said, closer than she assumed. He leaned against the paneling that separated the two areas of the room. "You do not have to perform for the old crone now."

She went to scream, still trying to calculate how he had entered her locked room. She saw the servant's doorway ajar, and she cursed herself for not blocking it off with a chair. His hand flew to her lips, muffling her cry. She dropped the soaked towel, her eyes watering with terror.

"Shh … Liza," he said, walking her backward towards the tub and the standing looking glass. "You sit on the edge of having a fortune. Should we take a turn about the house and pick out your true room? This one is fair, but not the grandest, I can assure you. I took a tour just now."

He dug in his pocket, looking for something, and she feared she would see the glint of his knife. Instead, she saw the glimmer of a huge diamond that dangled from a necklace. Bruin turned her so that she faced the mirror, her back to his front. He draped his stolen treasure over her naked body, watching it catch the candlelight as he swung it over one hardened breast to the other. She looked away; she did not want to gaze at her reflection next to him. She clenched her legs, trying to cover what he had already seen.

"I took this for you," he said, admiring his handiwork. He paraded her body like it was a prize itself.

"Where did you get that?" she asked, through gritted teeth.

For someone whose life depended on this plan working to fruition, he was relentlessly brazen. She could only pray that his pride would lead him to make a mistake. It would only take one to bring him down.

"The store room. The butler foolishly left it quite unattended," Bruin clicked his tongue. "I could kill everyone in this house as they sleep tonight, and they would be none the wiser. But I prefer to steal the legal way."

He fumbled with the necklace until he secured it over her. Then he took her and began to sway with her from side to side.

"I missed you, Liza," he said, as he pressed his face into the side of her damp hair. "If I can get to you when you are most vulnerable, in your bath, I can get to you anywhere. So do not try to run …"

Eliza swallowed, trying to pull away from him.

"Where else can I go?" she answered with bitterness.

"And if you do betray me, you will never see your boy again," he said, his hot breath in her ear. His clutch on her tightened. "I have been thinking. After all that has transpired, I do not need Philippe alive. He is only in the way. *Our* way."

Her eyes narrowed, knowing he took delight in toying with her. "You are scarred by your past. But you cannot undo it, no matter how many lives you destroy now."

The grin left his lips, and he stopped moving her in his silent dance.

"Do not pretend to feel any loyalty to the Sharpe name. Liza Hastings. It is as foreign to you as it is to me."

She crossed her arms over her breasts, trying to block what she could from his view.

"You have proceeded to such great lengths for what? Destruction of a family?"

"Revenge, dear Liza," he answered.

He pulled her arms down, pinning them to her sides, studying the curves of her body. Her stomach twisted with a flutter of discomfort, her chest turning red.

"Am I to be the villain inside your story?" he whispered, his eyes roaming over her.

"That is up to you," she said, in a near-quiet whisper. "This is indecent."

Bruin laughed, his hands running over the swell of her hips.

"Oh no," he began. "You and I are going to be happy. Very happy, indeed."

His tone was ominous. Eliza realized her resistance would be stretched until she finally broke in his savage hands. He took pleasure in the way she trembled and waited for her to speak.

"I don't believe you possess either the honor or the patience to wait until we cross the border."

She gripped the edge of the table, and the little glass bottles clanked against each other. Bruin came to her again, pulling her to him.

"How little you regard me. There is no need to be impatient for something I have already had in Nassau," he whispered menacingly, each word uttered slowly and wrapped in disaster. "Why do you think I have not touched you since?"

Eliza's hand flew out as she tried to slap him, but he caught her wrist and bent it, lowering her down to the floor in pain. Now he towered over her.

"You do not realize that I have already had you? You are smarter than that, surely. My dear, foolish Liza. I came into your room that first night, when you were sound asleep. I could have let my men each have a turn with you, but some spoils I like to keep for myself. I enjoyed watching you lie there, oblivious to it all."

"You lie," she hissed. It was all she could think to say. The truth was too terrible to bear. She thought she could wound his ego and added, "I felt nothing."

He knelt down to her level. "I think you enjoyed it. There is that possibility, you know. Your muscles were not tense." Bruin leaned so close to her, their faces nearly touched. "When I was inside you, I felt nothing but a warm suppleness from you. And I took my time."

Eliza felt the very floor crack open as if it could swallow her whole, as if she was falling through it. She recognized the symptoms of a fainting spell, but she did not lose consciousness. Not this time. She was still trapped, leaning against the hard porcelain of the tub, with no way to escape him. What he confessed stunned her, but the implications for what he had not said terrified her more. She recalled every single time she had woken up in his bed, not recalling how she had ended up there. And to think that her torment had started that very first night, in the safety of her bedchamber.

The significance of the red stain in her inner skirts only dawned on her now, and she was grateful for its confirmation. One part of her still remained free from the taint of him. She whimpered, covering her face with her hands. An image of another abused woman flashed before her.

Jane squeezes her hands. A breeze passes between them, and something trembles next to Eliza's face. A butterfly is stuck in a spider's web. But distance separates the women now, and she is far from her. "He is a thief," her voice echoes. The spider attacks the trapped butterfly, but it continues to struggle in vain.

This was her darkest hour with him yet. He took Eliza's legs and spread them, crawling even closer to her.

"It is hard to believe this body already bore a child," he said, his eyes wandering to her most sensitive parts. "It has left you without a mark." His touch descended lower, and she tried to fight his hand away. "I have pity for the men in your past. How can anyone have you and not lose themselves?"

"Please, Hiram," she begged.

She could think of nothing else to say. It was the wrong choice of words; they only excited him.

A hand shot out, squeezing her throat tight.

"One more day, Liza, and it will be a sin no longer," he replied with a smile.

Eliza closed her eyes, refusing to sink down in the pull of his leer. An excruciating series of minutes passed, and she knew he would not wait. There would be no merciful gap in her memory, no delay driven by his ever-shifting morals. She would descend even lower that night, to a new level of hell.

"I sometimes consider how I would take your life," she heard him say. "I would wring this elegant neck, perhaps as I am deep inside you. The thought of your last breath pooling around my wrist thrills me."

His hand shook, wobbling over the limits of his control, as he struggled against some silent battle. She would leave this world in a puddle on the cold marble floor. Eliza said nothing, trying to keep her terror at bay. Surrendering to him seemed the safest option, the only way out. If she fought him, she knew his grip would only tighten. She was tired, and she had run out of struggle, out of clever excuses, out of ways to stop his relentless assaults.

But then his hold on her softened, and she heard him walk away. She slowly opened her eyes.

"You did not try to stop me, Liza," he said, disappointment coloring his tone. He chided her like she was a recalcitrant child. He was irritated, senseless, without reason, and that made him more of a threat than before. He stood on the precipice of becoming a new man, and tonight, on the eve of seizing even more power than he had ever dreamed, the lure of such domination had gone to his head.

She managed to reach a shaking stand and ran past him and towards the door, her fingers about to ring the bell for the servant. She did not care about her nakedness any longer. He stood next to the bed, his long form a shadow in the shifting light. But she could still discern his awful smile.

"Ah, ah, ah … do not ring that bell. You seem to have forgotten about your son," he warned, as he stepped closer to her.

"Do you really conceive such power by causing me misery?" she demanded.

"Nothing brings me greater pleasure," he said, as he crossed the space of the room.

Then he paused, listening carefully for something.

"I will leave you now. But I implore you to simply remember this: remember how Charles treated you. Let that banish any doubts from your mind, dear Liza."

Eliza stood stunned, unsure as to why he slipped back through the servant's stairway. Then light footsteps sounded outside her door.

"Is anything amiss, Lady Sharpe?" a young girl's voice asked.

The servant's door closed without a noise. He was gone.

"Yes, yes, I stumbled before," she spoke through the main door.

"Do you require anything, Lady Sharpe?"

Eliza hesitated. She needed to be saved from the man who had just left.

"No, thank you. Good evening," she said, her voice tense.

Her hands raced to undo the necklace. Eliza waited for the girl's footsteps to recede, and then she took a chair, blocking the entryway Bruin had used. She was aware of a great divide in her life now; there was a marker that stood before Bruin *and* after him. And she feared what this next chapter would look like. She crawled onto the bed, wrapping herself in the sheets, choking on her sobs, the restored silence raging in her ears.

CHAPTER XXII.

With a twisted knot of dread and anxiety, Eliza knew that when she returned to the dining room that next day, her entire life would shift into a new, terrible direction. The cream-colored paneling and the blue damask wall hangings did little to improve her mood. If anything, the formality of the room and her surroundings of gilt moldings and cornices only suffocated her. The sun was out today, but it shone with a different light, a different embrace; one that hardly touched.

They took their seats, with Bruin and Eliza on one side of the large mahogany table, and the elder Lady Sharpe on the other, with her back to the fire. She held a series of legal papers, her wrinkled hands quivering.

"I do not want to waste another moment away from your young son, Lady Sharpe," the old woman said.

Eliza smiled, but it was contrived. Bruin would serve as her advocate, and he took the opportunity to leave his seat and stand behind Charles' aunt. Eliza's chest tightened with fear. What if he did not need her to actually sign the papers? What if he chose to whip out his blade and slit the thin skin of her throat right there?

Words she had spoken in her youth circled back to her now.

"Why do men justify killing, Papa? Why do men believe they can conquer nature?" she had asked, closing her book.

She began to pray that he would leave the old woman unscathed. Bruin lurked behind her, like the predator he was, scanning the contents of the papers her attorney had drawn up earlier that morning. The widow's dower would be transferred to an heir of her choice. The aunt nervously looked behind her, disturbed by his unwanted proximity. Eliza had to look away.

She distracted herself with a large globe encased in a handsome rosewood stand. Eliza studied the display, one much like the kind she had gazed at with her father over the years. The Bahama Islands seemed so distant from the shores of England, they were hardly noticeable in the expanse of blue on the western side of the Atlantic. On the freshly polished table, lumps of sugar in colorful bowls stood proudly as part of the tea service, coveted products of trade from the West Indies. Steam curled off the dark tea in her teacup. She was diminutively aware that she had come full circle in life, and now she felt even more that she did not fit in the storied halls of Grenewood Hall or on any tame English lawn. She had become foreign, like the crystallized sugar, another form forced from her old body, and the sensation screamed loud and raw in her ears. The damage Bruin had inflicted on her had created another woman out of her, and she could never return to the shape of the girl she once was.

"Sign it, Lady Sharpe," Bruin's voice said, interrupting her reverie, bordering on the edge of a thinly veiled threat.

No, England was nothing like the Caribbean. The weight of paradise, everything it promised with dazzling vibrance, and all that it had failed to deliver, pressed on her. She inhaled sharply. But she did not have a quill, and she could not sign her name underneath the old Lady Sharpe's. She was glad for the interruption; it signaled that the entire affair was wrong. It should never have occurred. Bruin clenched his jaw, impatient with the delay. She savored the fact that the universe had made a small score against his mechanizations.

"Tarry a moment, dear, I have run out of ink," the elder Lady Sharpe said. She motioned for Bruin to pull back her chair, and she shuffled slowly out of the painfully quiet room.

Eliza dared not meet his eyes. She fiddled with her knuckles under the shadows of the table. Bruin sighed and took his seat next to her. No, England was nothing like the Bahamas. But her problems had followed her here.

For the space of ten minutes, they sat in tense silence. A pair of hand-carved lions stared down at her from the wall, as if their wooden frames could barely constrain the wildness rippling beneath their bodies and unmoving eyes. An older version of herself would have loved to explore every inch of this house, to uncover its ghosts, to see what its grand library contained. But none of that mattered now; death had a way of dulling things that had once brought her joy.

Bruin cursed, shifting in his seat. "She is taking too long."

Eliza did not listen. Pockets of sun streamed through the window, then grew shaded by massive clouds. The gloom was broken with a change in the winds, and a warm brilliance swept across the empty room. And then from the corner of her eye, she saw a sudden flash of red. And another. Red, like an officer's jacket, the uniform of a soldier, filtered past the windows of the long gallery across the way, visible through the windows of the room she sat in. She knew without a doubt that it was the regiment from the village. It was a cardinal red, like blood, like Shango, like justice. Her heart pounded with a new sense of hope.

But Bruin's mood grew darker. "The old crone is lying! Her servant would fetch it for her!"

He attempted to leave his chair. She needed to distract him.

"Wait!" she said, grabbing hold of his leg, much like she had done when they had sat in Pleasant Hall. Desperation drove her to touch him. "You are so close, Hiram. Do not spoil this moment, for it is nearly ours ..." she whispered to him, her voice a seduction, fastening him to that chair.

She could tell he did not quite trust the change that had overcome her. She looked down and, with a nervous swallow, continued her act.

"I did hate Charles. But I also hated you. You did not confide in me. But now you have, Hiram. It is not wrong to avenge your father."

But she was not convincing him.

"No, no, this is all wrong. We need to leave. She suspects

my intentions," he replied. For the first time, she detected an edge of panic in his voice.

But she could not let him leave. She anticipated the door to fly open at any moment. She leaned closer to him, holding the side of his face with her free hand.

"Stay the course," Eliza said, reading the emotion in his eyes. "This is the day you waited for. I had a dream last night … it is you." She paused, her eyes huge and moist. But it was really her fear; the intrusion she prayed for was taking far too long. Her own words terrified her. "We will start a family, and you will have a title. It is true, I did not try to stop you last night. Because I want you, Hiram. All you have to do is take it from me …"

And then she gave it her all, taking him into her shuddering kiss, willing him to remain where he was. She felt him sink into her touch, loosening up, and he kissed her back, his grip deepening on the back of her neck. The eagerness of his desire alarmed her, and she feared he would lose all restraint and take her there on the spot.

The heavy door finally flew open, hitting the wall from the force. She wiped the wetness from her lips and looked up, screaming when she saw the soldier.

It was Charles. Lord Sharpe had returned.

The colonel stood there, sweating, panting, taking up all the energy in the room. His green eyes blazed when he saw her.

He was a seamless blend of toughness and refinement, driven by his love for her and his fear that he was too late. He was everything Bruin could never be. He had ridden as hard as he could for a day and a half, past the muddy cobblestone roads, through unending fields to get to her. He had only stopped to change horses, pitying how hard he had driven the poor beasts. Charles had somehow survived an unspeakable ordeal, and now that he was nearly at the end of his long mission, nothing could stop him.

Bruin spoke first. "You have come back from the dead …"

He did not give his statement the pleasure of a response.

"Thank you, Captain, for the care you have shown my wife," Charles said, speaking only to create a moment to collect himself. He turned and slid the lock of the door into place. One of them would not leave that room alive.

The sound of his voice set her heart ablaze. Eliza could tell that her husband had lost weight; he looked haggard, his cheekbones protruding from his exertions, but she recognized that familiar fire in his hawkish gaze. And then he saw all of her, as she turned to face him fully in her seat. The bruise on her face told him what she could not say.

Shock crossed his features, and he was slow to regain himself. He saw nothing now but the mark by her eye. His face darkened with rage.

"What are your terms?" he growled at Bruin.

Eliza knew that Charles truly saw what was unfolding in that room; he was not a stupid man. Beads of sweat began to form on Bruin's temples. Charles had expected to see the pirate, yet he seemed profoundly affected by Bruin's presence just the same, his lanky body occupying the unfortunate space between him and Eliza. Charles' gaze lingered on her bruised face. She looked away. She was accustomed to the nature of his oppressiveness when he entered a room, but this sensation was something altogether much different. It was electrifying. The tension between them all grew unbearable.

"You have won. Take her. I admit I have wanted nothing more than to kill you, but I grow weary. We three have had quite the journey, have we not?" Bruin's voice was smooth, overly confident.

He was stalling. He depended on trickery. Charles could once have overpowered him with his brute physicality, but this had been greatly reduced, and he could tell the man was worn out from his ride. Bruin would not lose; he had come too close and fought too hard to only be stopped now.

"All I seek is my freedom and a pardon. Surely, you can understand that having regained yours, Charles," Bruin continued, with a scheming smile.

"It is only because of your greed that I was a prisoner."

"We must talk. Be reasonable. Take a seat," Bruin said, polished like the table beside them.

"Very well, no weapons. We shall talk as gentlemen do," Charles said, his words a direct command.

This made Bruin laugh. "No pistols? As you wish."

Charles removed his weapons, placing them on the side table next to him. Bruin followed suit, laying his two pistols on the table. But Charles was trembling and white with anger. He locked eyes on her again, as if he could read the keenest anguish on her battered features. She could tell unspoken emotion was surging through him, but one remained above all—fury.

Eliza was Charles' one weakness; Bruin had calculated

perfectly. Charles played right into Bruin's hands. He was distracted by Eliza's presence in the room, and she wanted to disappear. He did not understand the nature of Hiram Bruin the same way that she had been forced to over the grueling months.

Bruin sighed, adjusting his calculations as he watched Charles lose his focus. Bruin savored this. He wanted Charles' attention directed to the wrong place, just as much as he wanted his blade inside him. "I am not here for mere words. I want to take it all. Everything you have. Just as you have from me," he finally said.

Charles' eyes flicked back to Bruin as the man stood up, patting his knee. It was as if he was trying to reassure himself of something as he walked, advancing closer to the source of years of pent-up rage he had expertly hidden for so long. Despite what had been uttered before, it was clear that Bruin would not let her go. So far, the man had deftly concealed his aggression, but he seized his opportunity, bending down to snatch his hidden boot knife.

"And I will not stop until you are dead!" Bruin seethed, jumping at Charles.

The ferocity of the lunge shocked Eliza—it was so quick, with a snarl that emanated from deep within his gut. She knew what a knife could do in his hands. Charles was wider and more muscular than Bruin, but a blade was a great equalizer, especially in a skilled assassin's hands. Charles shouted in alarm and tried to trap the hand that held the knife in an effort to stop the attack. The two men strained in a clenched position, in close quarter range—a collision of indomitable wills.

They knocked down the chairs, stumbling, nearly losing their balance. Bruin managed to pummel Charles into the door, and he swung the dagger free of Charles' grip and brought it down on him. Eliza screamed when she saw blood on the blade. Charles kneed Bruin, and the two engaged in a wrestling match. The fight was clearly more of a struggle than Bruin was used to, but he was fueled by so much hate in his movements, relentless in his big, open swings. He would make Charles pay for what he had done, and he was fast with his attacks, hoping to overwhelm him into submission.

But Charles had a response for every strike, despite the injury he had already received. He tried to isolate the knife, to get behind the driving arm, and duck from every slash that came at him. Bruin shouted in his face, trying to weaken the stubborn wrist that blocked him from cutting his target. In the contest, he managed to nick his cheek, but Bruin sought bigger damage than that. He wanted to end him.

Eliza watched from her chair as the control slipped away from her life. Everything was determined by these two men; her fate lay on the edge of a quivering blade. Her helplessness threatened to overwhelm her. Then she felt the weight of the Sharpe family crest knife heavy in her pocket, reminded of its presence. In her turmoil last night, she had not remembered to take it from her dress. She felt the coolness of the metal against her quivering fingers, and she pulled it out, staring at it in her hands. She looked up at the roaring fireplace, not even turning as the men's groans escalated, and she heard the clatter of porcelain smash into the hardwood floor.

"What are the prayers?" Eliza asked, nervously staring at the decorated fireplace of Pleasant Hall.

"You can say Oba koso … Baba Shango … Omo Shango …" Celia said, her tone more reverent now.

"That is all? Surely there must be more words."

Both women kneeled before the fireplace, and Eliza began to feel awkward next to her new teacher.

"Shango does not want you to pray to him like a god. He wants to show you your power. To remind you what you are capable of."

The weight of all her mistakes nestled comfortably into a new and sudden awareness that they did not constitute mistakes at all. They all represented fragments of herself, lessons she had not asked for but needed to overcome. She would not be who she is today: a mother, a wife. She had said "yes" to one man for a reason, and that reason stood starkly before her now in the midst of all the chaos and violence, blinding like the beam of sunlight that bore down into the room from the long glazed windows.

And then a warmer voice, the one that belonged to Cleo, the one person who had always comforted her with solid answers to Eliza's toughest mysteries, beckoned next. She was returned to the hot porch, covered in sunlight from more peaceful days, reading her book, when Cleo had spoken her last words to Eliza.

"It is good to be underestimated, Miss Ellie. Remember that. It is an opportunity. The truth will always come out."

The cries of the men's struggle escalated, bouncing off the damask walls. She turned, her terror increasing as she watched the last remains of Charles' willpower fade, even as he continued to try to push Bruin off of him. Charles was losing his edge in the fight, and the men continued to clash, each fighting for supremacy. Bruin was a madman, completely losing himself to his lust for blood. She feared he could not be stopped in time.

His hold over her tightened, even though he did not see her, did not touch her. He was too bent on destroying her husband. A jumble of recent memories crowded her mind, and she squeezed the knife in her lap.

"What will it take to bring you to submission? I performed an astonishing act of restraint. I could have had you the very first night in my cabin." He kneeled over her, taking his leather jacket off and tossing it to the floor. His shirt came off next.

"I am aware, it only excites me more. Charles does not need to know. Parting your legs will be my greatest secret."

Eliza would not look at him. Bruin grabbed her chin, forcing her to.

"You belong to me now. And you will learn obedience."

"Can you imagine what life is like to live with that kind of fear? Because you are going to live it with me now. I am going to show you what it is like to own nothing, not even your own body ..."

And then his words from last night surfaced.

"But I implore you to simply remember this: remember how Charles treated you. Let that banish any doubts from your mind, dear Liza."

How Charles had treated her ... she thought of how he had saved Philippe from the foundling hospital and agreed to raise another man's child as his own. How he had decided to free his slaves, despite the anger it raised in the other colonists. The way she had watched him break down on the beach when Cleo had died. How, despite surviving hell, he stood in that room now, still trying to protect her, to save her from a monster.

Memories flitted by her: the sounds of their wedding organ in the church, the way his strong hands felt in hers, the sunsets from the porch, the coolness of the glowing sea, the dizzying sway of palm trees. How viciously they had once argued, how fiercely she had kissed Charles in the wavering candlelight after she had saved Alastor from the fire, how her footsteps had chased the mysterious brown moth that had led her to him. The way his glass-green eyes had shone as they walked on the beach with Philippe, a family found in strife, beauty salvaged from turmoil. And now it was slipping away from her with every determined stroke from Bruin's knife.

She heard Charles' voice like an echo.

"I will wait for you, Eliza. I was too eager to love you, but I now know that one day spent with you in friendship is greater than I deserve."

"The only way this ends is if one of us dies," she muttered to herself, watching the wavering candle flame.

Charles cried out now; Bruin must have cut him again. Witnessing Charles fight so hard and shout in pain changed something in her, even if she was terrified from where she sat.

Eliza had tried to forget, to seal herself up like a stone—like the hard limestone rock that had cut the soles of her feet by the Black Reef on the edge of the island. Her mind continued to race, searching for an escape, a reason to explain it all away, to sink into comfortable oblivion. Hot waves of anger ran through her, waves that started from her core and strained her breaths as her lips trembled with a pang of nausea. Her quivering hand unknowingly clasped the gold necklace at her neck. She wanted to cry, but no tears would come.

She knew if she did nothing that Charles would die. And there could be no future without him. She refused to go backward; it was not in her nature. Another sound came from Charles, a pained whimper, as he grappled against the frenzied attacker. Eliza suffered through the uncontrollable urge to act, despite knowing full well that she, as a woman, could do nothing. She fought the urge to spring from her seat until the moment she was finally freed.

She looked up from her new position, her hand cramping from the amount of force she had used to drive the dinner knife into Bruin's back. Eliza let out an exasperated sigh; her determination to stop Bruin raged within her. She alone would have to defend herself from the violence of men. She refused to be the victim of their schemes for one day longer, and this was how she chose to set herself free. Violence would become a vehicle to her agency; never again would her voice be silenced, her importance downgraded because of the curves of her body.

She refused to let Bruin destroy this family, *her* family. She had taken that surge of feeling, the sour taste of fear, and grasped it as tightly as the knife she now held, angled in her clenched hand. How liberating it felt to conquer trepidation, to champion what once ruled her.

Eliza had plunged the blade in deep, penetrating the navy jacket, and she looked at it with curiosity and disgust, still not fully cognizant of what she had done. Bruin swung his knife behind him with instinct, slashing her forearm. She cried and stumbled backward, clutching her dripping arm. Then he turned to look at her with a look of surprise that mingled with silent horror, realizing the attack had not come from his opponent. But she had given Charles an opening, the single chance he so desperately needed. He powered up, driving Bruin back with a decisive kick. He fell to the ground with a yelp, Eliza's knife still sticking out of him. Charles lunged over him now, kicking him again in the ribs. He squatted and ripped the knife out of his hand.

Charles forced him to a shaking stand, his arm wrapped around his throat in a chokehold, his own knife now directed at his torso, a reversal turned against him.

Bruin's eyes narrowed, baffled by what she had done. "You have betrayed me … Liza," he managed to cough. He could not comprehend that the one thing that had stopped his endless attack was her; the force that had driven into his unsuspecting back had come from her hands.

"You understand this," she said, her voice trembling. "You understand nothing else."

She panted, taking another step away. Her face paled as she watched the destruction she had wrought. A small trickle of blood was gathering in the corner of his lips.

Tears gathered in her eyes as she watched his slow, drawn-out death.

"I nearly forgot. You have a curious mind." His left hand wrapped around her lower back, and he squeezed. "If you puncture a man here, the kidneys, he cannot live long. Only one strike …"

She felt sick to her stomach, flooded with unreasonable guilt and shame. She pressed her shaking hands to her sides, adrenaline she was unfamiliar with coursing through her. She wondered if the same sensations riddled her husband. And then he drove the knife into Bruin's side with a brutal wrath.

"You have chosen the wrong family to destroy," Charles fumed, clutching him tighter as he spasmed with pain. He twisted the blade, extending the misery. "I want you to hear every word before I send you to Hell. Every member of your crew has either been arrested or pressed into the Navy. Your beloved ship has been confiscated. And you will die here, in this room, at my hands. Tell me, was it worth it?"

Bruin's reddened lips curved upwards in a smug smile, and he gurgled out a demented laugh.

"Look at my wife!" Charles demanded. "I want you to watch her as you die. Do you see the relief on her face? I want her to see you reduced to nothing."

Bruin's hands fumbled at Charles' hold, unwilling to capitulate.

"May God have mercy on your soul," her husband said with finality. He pulled the knife out and slashed across Bruin's neck, a stream of blood spilling over his white shirt.

Charles dropped him in disgust and threw the weapon to the side. He lurched towards the door, flipping the lock open, and doubled over with exhaustion. Eliza watched

Bruin die in muted astonishment. There was blood every-where, and the scent of it made her queasy. She wanted to see him take his last breath, to take whatever measure of closure she could. He had stolen so much from her; this was the greatest victory she could take back. It was the start of her peace slowly restored to her, piece by broken piece. He could no longer hurt her or hurt anyone else, for that matter.

His lifeless eyes gazed upwards at the blue damask-covered walls. The pressure was gone; it had left the room, and along with it the constant fear that had haunted her for months. She released the tension she had stored in her shoulders and exhaled, her burden dissolving in the pool of blood on the carpet. But when she glanced up at Charles and saw the look he gave her, how hungry he was for her, a silent desperation that threatened to consume him, she nodded, not bothering to fight the new onslaught of tears that gathered in her eyes.

She ran to him, to her future, to her freedom. Her life was not over; it was starting over. Charles caught her in his strong arms, pressing her upwards to him, slathering the back of her dress with blood.

"I love you," she said, her voice quaking.

He squeezed her tighter, and the room disappeared. It was only the two of them, like a column of adoration, confident in the feat of their collective victory. She took his face in, a face she had feared she would never look upon again. Eliza saw new lines by the corners of his eyes, but he was the same man she had remembered. And he was hers. She looked down at his new uniform, torn and slashed.

"Did he get you? You are bleeding!" she panicked. Bruin's attack had been so fast, and she saw blood blooming underneath the fabric of Charles' jacket.

Charles shook his head, incredulous at the spectacle of death that had nearly conquered him.

"I have been cut, but it is nothing," he said, trying to reassure her. "Your arm is bleeding …"

Eliza looked at the rivulet of blood that ran down to her wrist. It burned, but she would gladly receive it again. It was a small price to pay. But her mind was on other matters.

"He forced me to go along with his plan. He threatened to kill your aunt, he threatened to kill Philippe, he —"The terror would not leave her.

"I have him, I have him, Eliza. He is in London with Captain Johnson and Celia," Charles explained.

Eliza sank to her knees with relief, bursting into tears. Her child was safe. Her plan had worked. God had protected Philippe. Charles raised her, scooping her up. They had finished off Bruin together, and they had survived together. She collapsed into him, understanding that the ordeal was truly over. The truth overwhelmed her.

Now they held a silent conversation, and though words were wanting, their shared meaning was understood between them. Tears and broken laughs, utter disbelief, overpowering joy—it was the language of love, shaped by fire and fiercely fought for. Her cries sprang from longing and relief, but they also grew from her other emotions, ones too complicated to name.

The door opened again, and a handful of soldiers filed

in with confusion, unsure if the threat had truly been neutralized. Charles kissed her then, in front of all of them, the starving man that he was. Because in truth, no amount of rest, food, or drink could truly satisfy him until she was safely back in his arms. And from the way she clung to him, her breaths shaky and disturbed, he knew she felt the same. The distance and trauma between them had remedied something that peace simply could not. The scoundrel was dead, and the rest of their lives would start today, renewed in their commitment to one another.

They remained in their embrace, and then she saw the elder Lady Sharpe appear in the doorway, observing the destruction that had been wrought.

"Don't let her see!" she cautioned Charles, sure that the sight would terrify her.

Charles did not react, and the old woman stepped inside the fray. She went first to the papers on the table, chucking them into the fire with distaste. Then she made her way to Bruin's body, where Charles and Eliza stood, still holding on to one another.

"Take it all away. You've ruined my rug, Charles! We brought that from Constantinople in '70!"

A young soldier began to drag Bruin's corpse by the foot, hesitant to offend the matriarch any further.

"No, no, no, roll that filth up in it. It's all rubbish now," the old Lady Sharpe barked. She turned to a pale Eliza. "I am sorry, my dear. A letter from London arrived the same day you did. Precipitous timing, really. But I had to ensure you weren't privy to Charles' designs. I knew you were sincere when you cried at the dinner table. Captain

Browne ..." she said with repulsion.

If the elder Lady Sharpe hadn't been trained with decades of decorum, Eliza was sure she would have taken aim and spit at the man. She had transformed from a scared and confused elderly lady to a conniving matron of the Sharpe family.

Her small, frail hands gripped Eliza now with an iron grip.

"I knew something was wrong. My nephew would never marry a mouse of a woman. I am happy to meet you, although I regret the reason for such an introduction. I sent Harriet to check in on you last night. I tried to give you separate quarters, far from each other. Lord knows that is the one thing this old house can be useful for."

Eliza said nothing, utterly astonished by her demeanor.

The elderly woman looked down at his fallen form, not unsettled by the gore. His blood was like a blackness pooling on the woven rug, staining it with his unshakeable greed.

"I cannot leave my dower to an heir. It is a life estate, a temporary interest. It expires on my death. Selfish fool," the aunt said, with venom in her voice.

Charles released Eliza and began to give the soldiers orders. "Take him away. Write to General Hill and tell him that the threat is no more. Thank him for the use of his men."

A soldier stood to attention. "Yes, right away, Colonel Sharpe."

Several men gathered around the fallen pirate.

"Wait, check his person. He is a wanton thief. Search

him," Charles commanded.

The two soldiers who began to search Bruin quickly uncovered a handful of jewelry and a loose gemstone.

The old lady's eyes grew wide. "That jewel is not mine. Is that a Burmese ruby?"

The elder Lady Sharpe quickly joined the search, holding the gemstone with awe. Eliza stifled a laugh. She did not care for treasures like that. She looked up at Charles with pride in her eyes. She was proud to stand beside him, proud to call him her husband. She buried her face in his red woolen jacket and thanked God for their deliverance. It was long overdue.

CHAPTER XXIII.

Charles had taken the time to update Eliza on all that had occurred. Bruin had indeed left men behind to guard Pleasant Hall after he had stolen her in the night and taken her to his ship. But Captain Johnson had patiently waited for three days before he dispatched them, singlehandedly, showering them with musket balls from the thick bush that surrounded the house. His only regret was that he had not been able to stop Bruin, and he feared for his mistress' life in the hands of such a wicked pirate.

He was like a patient ghost that guarded the estate, until additional help arrived in the form of William Wylly, who had finally returned to the island and responded to Eliza's old queries with alarm. He arrived in the yard with a handful of his own armed slaves and the legal protection garnered from years of practicing as a seasoned attorney. When the threat of the creditors had been eliminated and Wylly had offered to protect Pleasant Hall in his stead, Captain Johnson set off to England with Celia and the baby, according to Eliza's wishes.

The house was secure, and all its grounds, and most importantly, Wylly ensured that none of the property or its remaining slaves were taken. Lucy, although frightened by the entire tragedy that had unfolded, was remarkably safe and untouched by the vile men who had once taken over the house. Wylly furnished Captain Johnson with an address of George Chalmer, a close friend in London, the chief clerk of the Privy Council for matters related to trade, and when the strange couple arrived in London over a month later, he promptly directed them to a group known as the Sons of Africa, headed by a freed slave named Mr. Equiano, residing on 10 Union Street in Westminster. Eliza had not needed to give them her sisters' addresses, and they were successful in delivering the Sharpe child to safety. The Sons of Africa quickly gave the couple the resources they needed to begin anew, and when Celia set foot in England, she, too, was finally granted freedom from a lifetime of bondage. She used her new opportunity of a second life to marry Captain Johnson, whose courage and steadfastness during the entire ordeal only increased her attraction to him.

In the interim, Captain Johnson was approached and interviewed by many officials in Whitehall who heard of Lord Dunmore's vile and corrupted ways firsthand. The captain had witnessed it all, from his flight in Virginia during the rebellion to the ways his incompetence and greed had ruined New Providence years later. There was heightened interest in what he revealed, especially after the scandal Lady Augusta Murray had caused from her secret marriage to one of the king's sons. It seemed as if his daughter had managed to bungle his political career that all his years of villainy could not.

Lord Dunmore's recall was initiated and inevitable, especially now that a new ally in the form of the Duke of Portland had arrived on the scene. The House of Assembly in Nassau finally reconvened and was set to hold new elections later that year for the first time in a decade. Wylly had his sights set on becoming chief justice, and there was much support for so great a needed change on the islands. Lord Dunmore might continue to try to pursue them, but time was ticking firmly against him.

And then Charles had arrived in London, shocking the entire court with his feat of survival from the hands of pirates. The country was of a naval inclination, eyes turned to exploits on the sea as the threat of French ships impinged ever closer, and the story of his persistence in the face of such persecution only inspired those who encountered him. Newspapers featured his updates, from his first days returned to English soil, to the honor of his audience with the king, and the country was abuzz with the newly promoted colonel's bravery. People spoke of nothing but Admiral Lord Howe, who had secured England's first naval victory at the Battle of Ushant earlier that month, and the inspiring tale of Colonel Lord Charles Sharpe, who had conquered such devastating odds in pursuit of rescuing his beloved family.

When Captain Johnson had presented his son to him, thriving and healthy despite the harrowing journey, many ladies of the court had declared that they had never seen so heartwarming a reunion. Philippe was now over a year old, and he squirmed with delight when he saw Charles for the first time in months. All that was left was for the boy's mother to hold him, her darling child whom she had fought so hard to save from Hiram Bruin's plans. And like the message she had seen in a butterfly-covered dream from Jane, the spirit of Charles' mother, Eliza understood that a mother's love was unconquerable.

Now, Charles sat on an iron bench, facing the blooms that burst up in front of the yew hedge of the walled garden in his aunt's estate. Eliza passed by rows of fruit and vegetables, dotted in between with clusters of wildflowers, as she followed the pebble-lined path to join him. A centuries-old brick-domed building stood guard, containing the property's secrets within its walls. Bright red poppies, blue towers of larkspur, and cheerful corn marigolds swayed in the gentle breeze, in rhythm with the droning buzz of industrious bees. The elder Lady Sharpe was particularly proud of the dahlias her gardener cultivated in August, but they would be long gone by then.

Eliza sat next to him on the bench, the light flowing fabric of her new dress pooling at her sides. The neighbor, Lady Hatfield, had wanted to partake in all of the excitement and had generously gifted Eliza a new set of dresses, in the latest cut and fashion. Eliza felt strange without the restriction of her trusted stays. The fitted bodice stopped just below her bust, and a loosely fitted skirt skimmed the rest of her body. The new scarlet line that ran down her forearm was on full display, but she was in no position to protest. She understood how charitable the young woman was, although the elder Lady Sharpe made her opinions known on the sheerness of the dress. Eliza was never one to chase after the latest trends in fashion, and she was certainly not going to begin caring now. Charles raised an eyebrow at her new appearance.

Eliza sighed. "Everything is changing. We approach a new century," she said quietly.

"I think it suits you," he said, in a voice that made her blush.

She rubbed her fingers on the delicate fabric. "Your aunt finds it displeasing."

A turtle dove cooed in the hedge, hoping to attract its mate. When Eliza met Charles' eyes, she was reminded of another afternoon, an older summer, on a different bench. He seemed to be of the same mind.

"I must confess, it is curious to see *this* creature on this side of the Atlantic," Charles said, with a smile. He leaned on her, dissolving the space between them.

Charles spoke of no alluring strange creature with wings, but of his wife, recently restored to him. He was transfixed with rapt attention.

"I'll have you know I was born and raised in Somerset, sir," she replied, fixing her skirt.

"Your hands are pale." He took her hand and clasped it with his. "We must remedy that at once and return you to the Bahamian sun."

She missed their home, but above all, she missed her only child. She yearned to hold Philippe again. The boy, still in London, was the final piece of her life that needed to be restored to her. But she was troubled. They could return to Nassau, but she could not return as the same woman she had once been. She feared explaining what had happened these last few months to Philippe once he was older. But there was still time to figure out the many difficult things she would one day share with him.

"My hands are sullied now. I have helped kill a man."

Charles looked at her with his intense gaze, startling to her still, even after all this time.

"I see no such stain," he replied, pressing her hand to his lips.

She closed her eyes and exhaled. She loved him sufficiently enough to die for him. Now, sitting on that cold bench, she knew she was capable of killing for him as well. Longing for love and survival had driven her against moral instincts, and she had done the unthinkable.

"Why do men justify killing, Papa? Why do men believe they can conquer nature?" she had asked once.

Only now she understood; she appreciated the honor of serving the king, of defending those one held most dear. A weapon in the hands of a villain destroyed; a weapon in the hands of a good person protected. There would never be a day without evil men, but there would always be a balance, a cycle like the seasons found in nature. From the barren cold death of winter, a sprout of new green life always followed.

Eliza studied the great, crooked tree off to the side. It was over six hundred years old, and she wondered at what it must have witnessed throughout the years. In the distance past it, two swans hovered over the glassy water of the pond. One would never know the violence that had erupted in this storied house.

The secluded garden was the perfect place to pause and breathe. She needed to slow down; the events of the last few days unsettled her, as if she had broken free from the nightmare, but its smoky tendrils still lingered, gripping the edges of her consciousness. It all seemed surreal; she could not have fathomed this outcome when she had first arrived. Trauma was so familiar to her now that she could not fully trust happiness, but the man who sat beside her challenged her to try. Every unanswered prayer, every detour, every delay—it had all played a role, and she could clearly see that now. There were no setbacks, only divinely supervised redirections. When she had lost control of every aspect of her life, at her very lowest, when even her consciousness had been robbed from her, there was still a directing force, delivering her child to safety, guiding Charles to her. And together, united at last, they were unstoppable.

Her story did not end with a flash of Bruin's knife; it was only beginning, and she could feel again. She looked down at their entwined hands. Charles was cool and intrepid among dangers, patient and firm in other situations where others would have run. Other men would have given up, fallen prey to selfish desires, but here he remained, by her side, holding her with his steady and reassuring grip. She herself was bruised, but not destroyed, and she faced the future knowing she was stronger than before. She looked at tomorrow not as an obstacle, but a challenge, and she wanted no other man to walk beside her.

Now they could return to Nassau, and they would finish what they had started. Charles could manumit the enslaved workers at Pleasant Hall. The Spanish Kingdom had placed a great reward on Bruin's head, a sum bigger than anything Lord Dunmore had ever promised him, and money was no longer an obstacle. It would be a long and slow process, but the couple was confident that between Charles' determination and Wylly's legal oversight, the feat could finally be accomplished.

Charles laughed suddenly. "You know, you were like *eke*."

Eliza looked at him questioningly.

"*Eke?*"

"When I was a prisoner on that ship, I met a warrior from Africa. *Eke* is a sacred serpent. I was told I needed to be like *eke*. To lie in wait. To not let them see me. And then strike. That's precisely what you did yesterday."

Charles had told her of his adventures, of his descent into the underworld. It was nothing short of a miracle that he had survived, although the same could be said for her. She, too, had been an unwilling prisoner on a ship, although she had suffered no shackles. Her fate had driven her from one danger to the next. She had chosen to descend to a place most women of her age would retreat from; with sheer will and determination, she had ventured into the abyss of criminals and lived to tell the tale.

She thought of Orpheus and Eurydice, and she wondered who she represented in the myth. Perhaps it did not matter, as she had made the myth her own. She had done what Orpheus could not; she had recovered her lover from the bowels of Hell. Eliza had overcome a descent into darkness, of impossible longing, and unbearable loss.

But she had come out the other side. She had discovered the resilience needed to move on, to continue living, and self-awareness settled over her like the warmth from the pale English sunshine. Charles made her see how the world *could* be.

"I saw a snake in Saba. I should have known that family was cursed. That no good would come from it," she replied.

Charles raised an eyebrow. "I think it was a warning. Something sent for good measure."

"So now you believe in signs? You surprise me."

She was mostly teasing him. She knew that he also saw unexplainable things, especially in the house that sat on top of the beach. She wondered what they would see when they returned.

"Our relationship is fraught with them. Wouldn't you say?"

They watched a pair of yellow butterflies descend to the poppies, paler and tamer cousins of the ones found in the Caribbean, then circle away. She thought of the strange dream she experienced before the *Fortuyne* had dropped anchor at Saba, and of the giant moth nestled on the porch that she had found after she and Celia had prayed to Shango.

"I knew you were alive. No one believed me," she said, in a near whisper. "I could feel it."

He squeezed her hand, as if to reassure her he was indeed real. Then he changed his tone.

"You know, Eliza, you are supposed to run from a knife, not to it," he said now, with a sliver of amusement in his tone.

"You should remind yourself, Charles. You did the very same."

"Indeed, it would appear we were made for one another," he joked.

Eliza closed her eyes, soaking in what little warmth she could from the weak sunlight. A breeze stirred her skirts and her hair, and the birdsong soothed her weary bones.

"What I have endured did not break me," Charles said. "And now my heart is lighter to see that it did not break us."

She thought of last night, and the way she had clung to him in a new bed, in another one of the nameless rooms of the old mansion. She had let him see all of her, every mark, every bruise, every scar. And she knew that when he saw what she had suffered, it only made him love her even more. The touch of his body had beckoned her to forget, to erase everything she had endured. It did not avail her to find fault with what had passed between them before; he was in front of her now, and she refused to let him go. The promise she found within his eyes, the way he looked at her, was sufficient enough to suppress her fears that they could never reconcile their differences. Their torturous time spent apart had dashed them away. He no longer wore a mask; he displayed his vulnerability openly, and the way he had looked at her when he had kissed her weakened her into a softness she thought she could never feel again.

"You have taken me over four thousand miles, only to end up where we began," she said, studying his profile. "I once yearned to return here, but now it is unthinkable."

Her nerves got the better of her. She had forgotten

his usual silence and how he only spoke when he had something meaningful to say.

"I fear you think I am mad now," she said quietly.

"You are the same woman as before, Eliza."

"No," she said, shaking her head. "I am greatly changed. I fear I am no longer the woman you left. I am brutal now and cold-hearted."

Charles turned towards her, understanding written in his gaze.

"It only enhances your beauty, my dear," he said as he carefully stroked her face. "He is at fault, not you. Never you."

"I am not the same," she protested, her voice breaking.

"I saw it in you all along. From the very first day I met you. The world needs your fire."

She looked up at him, still not convinced, and he leaned towards her, his lips brushing hers in a gentle kiss. She crumbled underneath him, surrendering, craving more. She nearly slipped off the bench, but he steadied her. Charles was enchanted with her, as if she was not a mere woman, but some fantastical part of the garden that he had the privilege to sit next to. His lips curved upward, a smile mixed with admiration; his loyalty and dedication to her were unshakeable.

Eliza realized that she was not here on this earth to endure relationships that felt like a cage. She was here to feel love that felt like the heat of the tropics dancing across her skin. To live next to a man who made her remember what it was like to breathe again. To see flowers unravel, the dance of butterflies in flight, the glow of his green eyes beaming with love. Charles was her home, a refuge for her body and for her soul. The new world was here, on the dawn of another century, and it belonged to them. The brilliant white clouds appeared closer, as if she could reach out and grasp them, at his side. No other man had ever loved her like he did, and no man ever would.

"I will take this pain from you, Eliza," his breath had whispered by her cheek, as they lay underneath the billowing sheets last night. "And I will be with you until the end. You are the only good I have ever done, and if I cannot spend my life with you, I do not want anyone."

They had lain there, naked in their embrace, wreathed in an intimacy not borne by the movements of their bodies but in the way they exposed themselves with their words, with their glances. She was still not ready for him in that way, and he did not ask. They held each other, chests rising and sinking with slowed breaths, finding bliss enough in body warmth. Eliza believed in the tides to come; she could feel the splintered fragments of herself finally return, settling into her being. Charles alone held the door open to happiness, and she was choosing to walk through it. Their attachment was so strong that no circumstance in life could dissolve it. Life was precarious and unstable, and offered no promises except the present day. And it was a glorious one when she sat next to him on that bench.

Love: she had found him again. But she knew that he could still be lost. She held his hand now, consciously, aware that this could be the last moment she felt the radiance of him. But the truth was sharper. She would lose him again: through disease or age—she prayed from a quickened breath in his sleep, and not the violence they had already endured.

An old idea that once brought her discomfort resurfaced. *All marriages eventually end.* Even though it would break her heart, even though this loss would be the greatest she would ever endure, it was worth it. What they shared on this bench, in this English garden, was irreplaceable. And she would do her utmost to stand by him until that end, until one of them finally left this world and moved on to the next. They were bound to each other, and death could not break it.

She recalled a conversation with Cleo from a long time ago.

"I never agreed to any of this. I only …"

"Agreed to marriage. To a union with him. We may not like what we're given, but we are given what we need."

"I am tired of riddles! I cannot comprehend this. What do the bones say?"

"Longevity, but there is a split, a fracture, the bones grow around it, grow stronger."

"What can that possibly mean? A division? Do I leave him?"

"I cannot stop you. It just may take longer for you to accomplish what you are supposed to. Your place is here."

Her place was next to him. This world was cruel; it was dark; it was strange. The brilliance of a beautiful paradise could cover the looming darkness of threatening shadows. But when she looked at Charles, she saw a man who was capable of withstanding life's trials. A partner who was strong enough to survive, and as she recently learned, as strong as herself. Fairy tales were never real, but this, whatever this was, was quite real. And it was hers. Theirs. It was a journey together. She would take all the risks to be with him. To stay with him and accomplish everything they dreamt of. This life was harsh, but every moment with him was a step closer to peace. To heaven. And now she was ready for whatever might come. Ready to unravel, to heal, and then rise up with him again.

There was much work to be done back at Pleasant Hall, but the turquoise waves beckoned her. She was ready. She yearned to sail into Nassau Harbor beside him, the ramparts of Fort Charlotte keeping watch over the town, the orange orb of the sun sinking low towards the flat horizon. The final chapter was theirs to write, and it started now. Time to rest could be found on the ship that would carry them to New Providence island, back to Pleasant Hall.

"A man that first day said Nassau was an Eden. A strange one. Do you remember?" she asked.

"We have to make it one worthy of such a name." Charles sighed, but she could see the excitement washing over his chiseled features.

She stood up, pulling on him.

"Let us make it our own. Take me home," Eliza said, her eyes sparkling.

THE END.

Author's Note

I wanted to take my readers full circle, and so we have started and ended this sweeping tale on an iron bench, nestled somewhere in an English garden, a refuge of peace in the often violent and conflicted world of the late 18th century. Even though Eliza's tale frequently took a brutal and heavy turn, it was essential to me to still carry a thread of hope and give these characters a chance at peace and resolution. Coincidentally, the image of Eliza and Charles sitting together on a bench was one of the very first scenes I envisioned of them a number of years ago, and it felt like the perfect way to end their Caribbean Gothic story. I hope you feel the same.

Each book in the *Strange Eden* series makes a particular statement: book one sets the stage with a beautiful paradise masking a brutal, ugly truth that lurks beneath the tropical wilderness, making it a decidedly *Strange Eden*; one man has claimed power on New Providence, but another is destined for it in *The Island King*, shifting perspectives of who is the villain and who is the hero in the story; and finally, *Color of Fire* begs the question of whether Eliza, our flawed heroine surrounded by desperate circumstances, can trust the one man who seeks to destroy everything she holds dear. The entire series wrestles with challenging the patriarchal society and dynamics of power in Regency England, one that sought to rob women and enslaved people of agency. I am always looking to challenge preconceived notions and perceptions, and I hope you have enjoyed reading and learning about the Bahamas and the British Empire in the 1700s.

In book one, *Strange Eden*, we understand almost none of Charles Sharpe's viewpoint, but I purposely opened up with his perspective in *The Island King*. It was only fitting to have *Color of Fire* split between Eliza's and Charles' dual points of view as we follow along on their harrowing journey to find one another and reunite. In my historical trilogy, I wanted to present a story that was constantly evolving, one that shed more layers of truth page by page, that was nuanced, and raised the stakes even higher, book by book. I wanted readers to have drastically different opinions of my characters as they moved between each novel, with Charles' redemption arc in particular shaking old conceptions. Readers also come to realize that Lord Dunmore, the haughty governor of the Bahama islands, is not the true villain, just as in life the real enemy is most often the one you do not see coming. Above all, I wanted to write a series that had the potential to become re-readable and take on fresh meaning within its pages.

In the conclusion to my series, I really wanted to high-light what it felt like to live on the edge of empire, to transport readers into a dark, violent world that oftentimes feels hopeless. By the start of the third book, the outcome appears particularly dim. Jean, a Crown official sent to the island to investigate the corruption, is already dead, killed in part for his brazen disregard for the powers that be, and even though Charles and Eliza finally reconcile, they are surrounded by the same vipers and are ultimately torn apart by these very forces. *Color of Fire* is a story about revenge, the depth of secrets, the underworld of piracy, the cost of freedom, psychological torment, and feminine rage, with an echo of warning from the myth of Orpheus and Eurydice.

The title on the surface is about Eliza's justified inability to trust a word that leaves Captain Hiram Bruin's lips: "'You would lie to me about the color of fire, about the hue of the very sky,' she said with wet, dull eyes." But it also brings up a statement made earlier in the series, in *Strange Eden*, by Cleo, the otherworldly Obeah practitioner, "The fire you are born with is the color I can see. All people have their own color inside, and it hangs around their shoulders. I can read what every color is, and I know what each one stands for." The *Color of Fire* explores the shifting nature of perception, truth, and empathy, as well as the unknowingness of who is trustworthy and who is not. It also examines the stark cruelty of particular life challenges, where we are sometimes presented with no good options, only less awful ones.

The concept of the *Strange Eden* series has been with me for a number of years. I first conceived the idea for Eliza and Charles on a trip to an abandoned plantation on St. Kitt's in early 2009. Then I sharpened my interest in Caribbean history by studying it for my undergraduate degree at New York University. Some of the scenes in *Color of Fire* in particular have been with me since the beginning, back in 2017 when I first started writing this series as a fun way to decompress from the stress of wedding planning. In total, I have spent over eight years traveling and extensively researching the topics I cover in the series.

My travels have taken me on over ten research trips to the islands of the Bahamas, especially to New Providence, and to exotic Saba, a beautiful gem I had the privilege of visiting back in 2023. I have also visited England and traveled to Amsterdam, as well as Cape Town in South Africa. The *Vasa* ship in Stockholm, Sweden, was also an invaluable learning resource for me when discussing the nautical world of tall ships. If you are ever in the Baltics, I highly recommend visiting this one-of-a-kind museum. I wanted readers to simply feel like they were on a ship and not get bogged down by foreign nautical terminology. I hope I have accomplished that.

This book is the darkest in the series, and it is easily the most disturbing work I have penned to date. I wanted to immerse readers in an unbroken thread of tension, of pure desperation, grief, and suffering. That pressure peaks during the final fight scene between Hiram Bruin and Charles, a fight that has been brewing in the shadows for years. The vision I had for this book was like a clock face that marches on, one where every sweep of the dial hand makes the situation only grimmer and harder to turn away from. Eliza's grief in losing Charles at the start of the novel is amplified by the increasing despair she feels in realizing that the institution of slavery in the English colonies means human bodies are counted as financial assets. And despite Charles' secret plan to manumit the slaves he has unwantedly inherited from his drunkard, cruel father, his enemies' greed and that of the island creditors allow for no cursory sympathy. Bills must be paid, and the faces of the enslaved are translated into currency and little else. When

Eliza turns to Hiram Bruin for aid, the king of the pirate underworld, it is a choice made from utter hopelessness.

English people of the Regency period were obsessed with the ancient world and classical myths, and it only felt fitting to pair the myth of Orpheus and Eurydice with Eliza's descent into her own version of a Caribbean Hell. I wanted to showcase her character arc from a place of trauma to strength, to have her evolve as an unlikely survivor of all that she endures. Like Orpheus, Eliza is intruding into yet another world, a male dominated space, one where thieves hold the reins of power and men trade human lives for the luster of gold. She is blind to how terrible her situation truly is until it is too late. She, like Orpheus, is trying to recover someone she has lost while also holding on to her sense of self. This tragically occurs after enduring the loss of a familiar world where she had finally felt she had attained some measure of order and conquered chaos following the loss of her first lover, Jean, and the overdue reconciliation with her husband, Charles, in the previous two books. The violent absence of Charles from her life is especially harrowing because he was the one man who had made her see how the world could be; their shared story transformed an irredeemable situation into a brighter possibility of hope. Now she is forced to reframe the underworld into a glimmer of salvation, but as the novel unfolds, it is clear that such idealism is doomed to fail. That is, until she decides to choose her own destiny and not have the men around her dictate her circumstances, and to ultimately save the man she once viewed as an enemy.

Captain Hiram Bruin, i.e., Hiram Beaks (sometimes spelled Breakes) is a real historical figure steeped in a different kind of myth, making him a perfect character for me to explore. My apologies for sticking with his crafted alias (Bruin) for three books straight, but I felt that was a necessary part of his character identity. Little is known of him, except that he was unusually tall for the time period and regarded as handsome. He was also ruthlessly violent and strangely obsessed with religious ideals in a career path that seems at odds with such notions. The tales of his escapades with Anna Snyde (who is also referred to with various spellings of her married name in different historical accounts) and the subsequent murder of her husband, Beaks' first captain and one-time mentor, are true, as well as his exploits with the capture of the *Acapulco* ship and the kidnapping of nuns from a cloister in Minorca and his exceptional cruelty towards people of the Catholic faith.

His home island of Saba (pronounced like SAY-bah), part of the Dutch West Indies, is a stunning island, and I was so grateful to have the opportunity to visit it. If you have never seen images of its extraordinary beauty, I encourage you to look it up. It was actually used as the backdrop for the original *King Kong* film in 1933, and it is truly awe-inspiring. The views of its southern island neighbors of St. Eustatius, St. Kitts & Nevis, and Montserrat are likewise jaw-dropping to behold. When I saw this view in person, I knew it would be the perfect backdrop for a tense and heartrending proposal from the scheming Bruin. I love to contrast tropical beauty with darkness, and I thoroughly enjoyed writing that particular scene.

Historically, the Beaks were one of the founding families to settle this Dutch colony, and his younger uncle lived well into the mid-nineteenth century as its leader. It is a Caribbean community frozen in time, idyllic and unique among islands.

Hiram Bruin is one of the most disturbing villains I have written, and the scene with Eliza and him on the porch at Pleasant Hall was one of the very first scenes I ever wrote for the series. Interestingly enough, Hiram Beaks is credited for coining the now-famous pirate catch-phrase "Dead men tell no tales…" and I couldn't resist including it in the book. I thoroughly enjoyed filling in the blank portions of his mysterious background. While historians claim he killed himself by throwing himself into a canal in Amsterdam, I posit this: why would a wanted man *want* to be found? One could argue that he slipped back into myth itself, or, as I have done, that he reinvent-ed himself with a new name and chose another English colony to operate his shadowy dealings from. He was granted a British privateer's commission from the gov-ernor of Gibraltar, and as a privateer, he could operate in and around English colonies with impunity.

Lord Dunmore, in particular, was known to have made alliances with many questionable men and outright crim-inals. As for his historical role, he was recalled as gover-nor of Nassau in 1796, and the reasons for this are still unclear. I have no doubt that the scandal of his daughter, Lady Augusta Murray, and her illegitimate attempt to marry into the royal family, the various investigations of his notorious corruption led by Lord Grenville's men, and the complaints from islanders like William Wylly and the House of Assembly, played a heavy hand in his subsequent removal from the island.

This brings me to the topic of pirates. By now, you know I love to expose lesser-known elements of history. The line between private and privateer (a private individual or a ship licensed by the government to legally plunder and attack other ships) was blurred, and the infamous privateer's license was oftentimes not worth the paper it was printed on. There is a trend in modern society to regard pirates as noble outlaws, akin to Robin Hood figures of the sea. And while there were undoubtedly many elements to question and protest in the late 18th century, pirates were far from the rebellious heroes they are often portrayed to be. First and foremost, they were roving bands of violent men and outright criminals, and while there were some exceptions to the rule, they were few and far between.

Some common myths that I tried to dispel were that pirate ships were floating bastions of democracy, ones where, for example, enslaved men could find their freedom. While it is true that many Black pirates existed, very few of these sailors were regarded as equal partners by their white counterparts. As David Cordingly points out in *Under the Black Flag: The Romance and Reality of Life Among Pirates*, that these Black pirates "did not carry weapons is an indication of their status as servants to the rest of the company" and that "pirates shared the same prejudices as other white men in the Western world." Another fable I tried to disprove was that pirates always seized other ships for dazzling amounts of treasure, glittering piles of gold, silver, and gemstones, when in fact most pirate hauls amounted to little else than basic trading commodities like barrels of tobacco, bales of silk and cotton, spare ship parts, or carpenter's tools. When Eliza sees what prizes Bruin and his men were able to take from the *Neptuno*, it sickens her to witness such senseless death. I did not want to romanticize any aspect of piracy in *Color of Fire*. By the late 18th century, the Golden Age of Piracy was long over, and the few remaining pirates who roamed the seas were ruthless and violent. Piracy was a desperate operation in the period between major wars among the European powers, as privateers made little money during peacetime. However, they would not have to wait long until the West was completely embroiled in the Napoleonic Wars that erupted a few years after the close of my series. But that is a tale for another time.

If you ever have the chance to visit Nassau, Bahamas, I highly encourage you to check out Fort Charlotte, which still towers over the town today, the historic streets of Nassau, including Christ Church Cathedral, dating from 1670, as well as the ruins of William Wylly's plantation site at Clifton Heritage National Park. There you can walk in the footsteps of Eliza and Charles. While the island has modernized and is usually booming with cruise ship visitors, its colonial past is still accessible to the curious reader today. For those of you who would enjoy exploring the aquatic world like Eliza, I highly recommend a stop at the Exumas and the famous Thunderball Grotto, which inspired Bruin's treasure cave. The Bahama islands offer so much more than a brief cruise stop, and I have always savored my travels among them, whether it be on Eleuthera, the Berry Islands, its countless cays, or Harbour Island (which has many features named after Lord Dunmore to this day). For further reading, check out my bibliography. I've personally read and recommend all the books and articles mentioned, and I've added several new items to the list since the last book. While the *Strange Eden* series has reached its close, this is not the end. It is only the beginning. Thank you for being so supportive. I hope you will join me for another foray into the humid, dense airs of the past in the not-so-distant future.

As always, the past is a very different place, and it may not always be palatable. But it serves as an invaluable lesson to us all. Thank you for taking the journey with me. I am grateful and honored by your company.

ACKNOWLEDGMENTS

The *Strange Eden* series was my debut venture into the world of publishing, and I cannot thank you enough, dear reader. Thank you all for the incredible support you have shown my books. Because of you, my books have both hit #1 bestseller status for Historical Caribbean & Latin American fiction on Amazon, not once, but multiple times. I have so enjoyed all the messages, reviews, and excitement you have shown, and I am especially honored when readers who don't normally read historical fiction, or haven't read it in quite some time, pick up one of my books. I am not backed by any traditional publishing house, and I handle all the aspects of book publishing and marketing on my own, so your support means the absolute world to me. Thank you, thank you, thank you! I am so grateful that you are here.

I dedicated this novel to my husband, who has shown me the most steadfast and undying love and support for the historical world I recreated. Hearing and seeing your reactions, especially for this last book, has kept me going and encouraged me to keep writing. Thank you for being my rock and for all the Maccies and drops I could ask for. Thank you for your incredible insight, especially regarding character arcs and archetypes, and for believing in this project from the very beginning. Your nerdy love for the world of comic books and anime is the perfect blend for my history geek self. I love you so much, and I am so excited for our future. My favorite part of writing is getting your feedback and all the many conversations we have about the past. Thank you for reaffirming my belief in happy endings.

A huge thank you to my mother, for the countless ways you have always supported me and my art from day one. "Thank you" is not a strong enough word for everything that you do for me. I am grateful for your wise Scorpio ways and all the lessons you have taught me. Thank you for your opinions on stories, whether they are in book form or film format. It helps sharpen my storytelling skills. Thank you for taking care of so many things so that I could focus on writing. Thank you for helping pack up all the book mail for readers around the globe and for keeping me company in the post office line. These books wouldn't exist if it wasn't for you. You are my Bunnay.

As always, I would like to thank God, my Circle, and all of my ancestors. I would also like to thank Elizabeth Daisy Williams, a very special person and my best friend. One of the greatest outcomes of taking the risk and hitting publish on these books has been our friendship. It still feels so surreal that these books helped bring us together across the Atlantic. Thank you to Kevin Chapman: I am so honored that the process of reading my books has rekindled your love of reading in general, and your excitement about the series is such awesome encouragement. Here's to many more years of friendship! And thank you once again to Norimasa Suzuki for helping me heal and for all our conversations about geopolitics and history.

I am extremely blessed to have two amazingly talented editors who worked with me for the duration of this series: Cath Lauria and Barbara Bowen. Cath, thank you for saving this series at the beginning when I presented you with a jumbled mess and you confirmed that it had to become a series. Thank you for your direction and guidance every step of the way over the years! Barbara, thank you so much for always being ahead of schedule and focusing on details like no other. You always leave me confident that my work is in its best shape after your perusal. The two of you make editing enjoyable, which is something not many authors can say.

Thank you to all the many artists I have had the pleasure of commissioning work from. A special thank you to Lindsey Carr for your beautiful 18th-century-style illustrations that are featured at the start and end of the book. You understood my vision so clearly and quickly, and I absolutely love how their character portraits turned out. I would also like to thank Karina Giada, who created a beautiful watercolor portrait of Eliza. She listened to what I envisioned for the scene and captured it so well that I used it as inspiration for when I started writing months later. It was such a fascinating process to have another artist bring to life something that only previously resided in my head. I am incredibly grateful for Nakita Gonzalez, who captured the most amazing photos for my author headshot at virtually the last minute. You took a nightmare situation and made it into a beautiful moment. And finally, a huge thank you to Lark Sloan, who also came to the rescue close to my deadline and crafted the most perfect maps for my series and the *Fortuyne's* journey across the sea. If you want to see even more fantastic character art commissioned for this series, follow me on Instagram at @ginagiordanobooks.

Thank you to the Bahamian people for their generous hospitality and beautiful, vibrant culture. It was my absolute honor to have my first published works feature your stunning islands, and the Bahamas will always have a very special place in my heart. A huge thanks to Perry Claire for providing rides for all of my ten-plus research trips and for pointing out all the bush medicine on the side of the road along the way. I would also like to give a shoutout to Michelle Dawn, who has created a very special community of support on Bookstagram. Marketing this series would have been immeasurably difficult without the community of book lovers, both readers and authors combined, that you have gathered under your wing. Thank you also to the staff at the Earl Gregg Swem Library of The College of William & Mary in Williamsburg, Virginia, for providing me with access to Lord Dunmore's personal letters, including his infamous recall letter from the Duke of Portland in 1796, to enhance my research.

Last, but not least, I would like to thank my assistants, Goonie, Tippy Bouvier, and Teddy Roosevelt. Goonie, you understand book marketing like no one else. Thank you for messing up all my notes and sitting on them when I really needed to see what was around me. I also enjoyed it when you stole my seat and didn't care about my deadlines. Your distractions kept me sane. But in all seriousness, thank you for helping run my social media on days I didn't feel like doing it. Tippy, please stop stressing out about everything. You're a cat. Teddy, thank you for honoring me by allowing me to pet you. I truly enjoyed writing this next to you.

Bibliography

Adkins, Lesley, and Roy Adkins. *Jane Austen's England: Daily Life in the Georgian and Regency Periods*. New York: Penguin Books, 2013.

Alexander, Caroline. *The Bounty: The True Story of the Mutiny on the Bounty*. New York: Penguin Books, 2014.

Aron, Paul. *Founding Feuds: The Rivalries, Clashes, and Conflicts That Forged a Nation*. Naperville: Sourcebooks, Inc., 2016.

Benezet, Anthony. *Some Historical Account of Guinea, Its Situation, Produce, and the General Disposition of Its Inhabitants with an Inquiry into the Rise and Progress of the Slave Trade, Its Nature, and Lamentable Effects*. Project Gutenberg eBook, 2004. https://www.gutenberg.org/ebooks/search/?query=11489.

Bethell, Arnold Talbot. *The Early Settlers of the Bahamas and Colonists of North America*. Third ed. Westminister, MD: Heritage, 2008.

Block, Sharon. *Rape and Sexual Power in Early America*. Chapel Hill: The University of North Carolina Press, 2006.

Burstein, Andrew. *Jefferson's Secrets: Death and Desire at Monticello*. New York, NY: Basic Books, 2006.

Byrne, Paula. *Belle: The Slave Daughter and the Lord Chief Justice*. New York: Harper Perennial, 2014.

Carpentier, Alejo, and Adrian Nathan West. *Explosion in a Cathedral*. London: Penguin Classics, 2024.

Carpentier, Alejo. *The Kingdom of This World: A Novel*. 1949. Reprint. New York: Farrar, Straus and Giroux, 2006.

Cavendish, Georgiana. *The Sylph*. Edited by Jonathan Gross. Evanston, Illinois: Northwestern University Press, 2007.

Chambers, Douglas B. "Runaway Slaves in the Bahama Islands, 1784–1819," February 2014, 1–97.

Cordingly, David. *Pirate Hunter of the Caribbean: The Adventurous Life of Captain Woodes Rogers*. Random House Trade, 2012.

Cordingly, David. *Under the Black Flag: The Romance and the Reality of Life Among the Pirates*. New York: Random House Trade Paperbacks, 2006.

Davis, Graeme, ed. *Colonial Horrors: Sleepy Hollow and Beyond*. New York: Pegasus Books Ltd, 2017.

Dawson, Terence. *Orpheus and Eurydice in Myth, History, and Analytical Psychology: Loss, Longing, and Self-awareness*. Abingdon, Oxon: Routledge, 2025.

Deren, Maya. *Divine Horsemen: The Living Gods of Haiti*. New York: McPherson & Company, 1953.

Equiano, Olaudah. *The Interesting Narrative and Other Writings*. 1789. Reprint. New York: Penguin Books, 2003.

Flavell, Julie. *The Howe Dynasty: The Untold Story of a Military Family and the Women Behind Britain's Wars for America*. New York, NY: Liveright Publishing Corporation, a division of W.W. Norton & Company, Inc., 2021.

Geanacopoulos, Daphne Palmer. *The Pirate's Wife: The Remarkable True Story of Sarah Kidd*. Toronto, Ontario: Hanover Square Press, 2022.

Gosse, Philip, and Nils-Erik Lindström. *The Pirates' Who's Who: Giving Particulars of the Lives & Deaths of the Pirates & Buccaneers*. Twin Engine Productions, 2022.

Grann, David. *The Wager: A Tale of Shipwreck, Mutiny, and Murder*. New York: Doubleday, 2023.

Handley, Sasha. *Visions of an Unseen World: Ghost Beliefs and Ghost Stories in Eighteenth-Century England*. New York: Routledge, 2015.

Heyer, Georgette. *April Lady*. 1957. Reprint. Naperville: Sourcebooks Casablanca, 2011.

Hochschild, Adam. *Bury the Chains: Prophets and Rebels in the Fight to Free an Empire's Slaves*. Boston: Mariner Books, 2006.

Hoock, Holger. *Scars of Independence: America's Violent Birth*. New York: Crown, 2017.

Howard, Martin R. *Death before Glory! The British Soldier in the West Indies in the French Revolutionary and Napoleonic Wars 1793–1815*. Barnsley: Pen and Sword Military, 2015.

Jackson, Christopher C. "Preservation and the Future of the Bahamian Past: A Case Study of San Salvador Island's Historic Resources" (master's thesis, University of Georgia, 2018).

James, Erica Moriah. *The Awakening Landscape: The Nassau*

Watercolours of Gaspard Le Marchant Tupper. National Art Gallery of the Bahamas, 2004.

Jasanoff, Maya. *Liberty's Exiles: American Loyalists in the Revolutionary War*. New York: Vintage Books, 2012.

Kemble, Frances Anne. *Journal of a Residence on a Georgian Plantation in 1838–1839*. Edited by John A. Scott. Athens: University of Georgia Press, 1984.

Knight, John. *War at Saber Point: Banastre Tarleton and the British Legion*. Yardley: Westholme Publishing, 2020.

Leshikar-Denton, Margaret E. *Cayman's 1794 Wreck of the Ten Sail: Peace, War, and Peril in the Caribbean*. Tuscaloosa: The University of Alabama Press, 2020.

Levy, Andrew. *The First Emancipator: Slavery, Religion, and the Quiet Revolution of Robert Carter*. New York: Random House, 2005.

Mackenzie, Henry. *The Man of Feeling*. Oxford: Oxford University Press, 2009.

Mortimer, Ian. *The Time Traveler's Guide to Regency Britain: A Handbook for Visitors to 1789–1830*. New York, NY: Pegasus Books, 2023.

Nedervelt, Ross Michael. "A Tumultuous Upheaval and Transformation: The Impact of the American Revolution on the Bahama Islands" (master's thesis, University of New Hampshire, 2012).

O'Shaughnessy, Andrew Jackson. *The Men Who Lost America: British Leadership, the American Revolution, and the Fate of the Empire*. New Haven: Yale University Press, 2013.

Peakman, Julie. *Lascivious Bodies: A Sexual History of the Eighteenth Century*. London: Atlantic Books, 2004.

Peters, Thelma. "The American Loyalists in the Bahama Islands: Who They Were," Florida Historical Society 40, no. 3 (January 1962): 226–40. https://www.jstor.org/stable/30139824.

Radburn, Nicholas. "Keeping 'the Wheel in Motion': Trans-Atlantic Credit Terms, Slave Prices, and the Geography of Slavery in the British Americas, 1755–1807." The Journal of Economic History 75, no. 3 (September 2015). https://www.cambridge.org/core/journals/journal-of-economic-history/article/abs/keeping-the-wheel-in-motion-transatlantic-credit-terms-slave-prices-and-the-geography-of-slavery-in-the-british-americas-17551807/0E22287ECE02D4CB1DCF906BF60A5E01.

Reddie, Richard S. *Abolition! The Struggle to Abolish Slavery in the British Colonies*. Oxford, England: Lion, 2007.

Richardson, Samuel. *Pamela*. Oxford: Oxford University Press, 2008.

Ronald, D.A.B. *The Life of John André*. Havertown: Casemate Publishers, 2019.

Rubenhold, Hallie. *The Covent Garden Ladies*. London: Black Swan, 2020.

Saunders, Gail. *Bahamian Loyalists and Their Slaves*. Nassau,

Bahamas: Media Enterprises Ltd., 2011.

Saunders, Gail. *Slavery in the Bahamas: 1648–1838*. Nassau, Bahamas: Media Enterprises Ltd., 2015.

Schiff, Stacy. *The Revolutionary: Samuel Adams*. Little Brown & Co, 2023.

Schoepf, Johann David. *Travels in the Confederation [1783–1784]*. Translated by Alfred J. Morrison. Baltimore: The Lord Baltimore Press, 1911.

Schwartz, Marie Jenkins. *Ties That Bound: Founding First Ladies and Slaves*. Chicago: The University of Chicago Press, 2017.

Shirley, Paul Daniel. "Migration, Freedom and Enslavement in the Revolutionary Atlantic: The Bahamas, 1783–c. 1800" (PhD thesis, UCL, 2011).

Sides, Hampton. *The Wide Wide Sea: Imperial Ambition, First Contact and the Fateful Final Voyage of Captain James Cook*. New York: Random House Large Print, 2024.

Tanner, Lynette Ater, ed. *Chained to the Land: Voices from Cotton & Cane Plantations*. Winston-Salem: John F. Blair, 2014.

Vanhorn, Kellie Michelle. "Eighteenth-Century Colonial American Merchant Ship Construction" (master's thesis, Texas A&M University, 2004).

Washington, George. *George Washington's Barbados Diary: 1751–52*. Edited by Alicia K. Anderson and Lynn A. Price. Charlottesville: University of Virginia Press, 2018.

Weingast, Barry R. "Adam Smith's Theory of the Persistence of Slavery and Its Abolition in Western Europe," *ResearchGate* (Stanford University, July 2015): 1–28. https://doi.org/10.13140/RG.2.1.1354.9924.

Winters, Lisa Ze. *The Mulatta Concubine: Terror, Intimacy, Freedom, and Desire in the Black Transatlantic*. Athens: The University of Georgia Press, 2018.

Wolfram, Sybil. "Divorce in England 1700–1857," *Oxford Journal of Legal Studies* 5, no. 2 (1985): 155–86. https://www.jstor.org/stable/764190.

Worsley, Lucy. *If Walls Could Talk: An Intimate History of the Home*. New York: Bloomsbury USA, 2011.

Wright, J. Leitch. "Lord Dunmore's Loyalist Asylum in the Floridas." *Florida Historical Quarterly*, 6, 49, no. 4 (1970). https://stars.library.ucf.edu/fhq/vol49/iss4/6.

About the Author

Gina Giordano always had an insatiable curiosity and a penchant for history. Born in New York City, she is a writer, artist, and a conjurer of the past. She holds a Bachelor of Arts degree in history and a master's degree in historical fiction from New York University and has traveled to sixty-seven countries across the globe. When she is not climbing ancient ruins or exploring forgotten palaces, she enjoys swimming with sharks in remote pristine waters. Her debut novel, *Strange Eden*, was longlisted for the 2023 Bath Novel Award. *Strange Eden* and *The Island King* have both topped the bestseller chart for Historical Caribbean & Latin American Fiction on Amazon multiple times, and she is grateful for the support of readers like you.

You can find Gina on Instagram under the handle **@ginagiordanobooks.** Her website is **www.ginagiordanobooks.com.**

If you enjoyed reading this book, please consider leaving a review on either Goodreads or Amazon. Positive reviews are extremely crucial for independent authors, and help readers like you discover us.

Lord Charles Sharpe